POWER OF A WOMAN

Memoirs of a turbulent life:
Eleanor of Aquitaine

Robert Fripp

Shillingstone Press

Power of a Woman
Memoirs of a turbulent life:
Eleanor of Aquitaine
Robert Fripp

Shillingstone Press
78 Sullivan Street
Toronto, ON, Canada
M5T 1C1

Cover Illustration of Eleanor of Aquitaine: © Duncan Long
Cover Design: Lorena Beccari
Interior Design: Lorena Beccari

Readers can find a full timeline of Eleanor's life at RobertFripp.ca.

First print edition, November 2006: ISBN 0-9780621-4-0
Some online bookstores offer eBook editions under
ISBN 0-9780621-0-8

Made in Canada

Cover illustration of Eleanor of Aquitaine

Artist Duncan Long interpreted Eleanor's features from a bust in the Metropolitan Museum, at The Cloisters, in New York, where her head is twinned with that of her second husband, the future King Henry II of England. Eleanor left no confirmed likeness, but Henry's features resemble known images of him. The sculpture in The Cloisters once decorated a capital in the Church of Notre Dame du Bourg, Le Langon, in Eleanor's province of *Bas-Poitou* (Lower Poitou). She may have been born nearby, in Nieul-sur-l'Autise. An unknown mason probably carved the twinned heads in 1152, within weeks of their marriage. Eleanor was thirty. A contemporary writer described her blue eyes and fair hair. Duncan has transformed cold stone to warm flesh. In his portrait, Eleanor remains thirty to this day. Eleanor of Aquitaine, portrait © Duncan Long 2006.

Dedication

Power of a Woman. Memoirs of a turbulent life: Eleanor of Aquitaine is dedicated to Carol, Will, Eric, Satwant Gill and to parents, grandparents and relatives who struggled harder and died younger. The late Claude Marks sparked the vision for *Power of a Woman*, signing a copy of his book, *Pilgrims, Heretics, and Lovers* (Macmillan, 1975) to Robert and Carol.

Contents

Part 3. A Woman Alone

Power of a Woman
Memoirs of a Turbulent Life: Eleanor of Aquitaine

Introduction

Eleanor of Aquitaine, that toughest, most resilient of women, dictates her memoirs to a young secretary, Aline. They begin "around Ash Wednesday" (19 February 1203, Julian calendar). Eleanor has retired in her eighty-first year, either to her capital city, Poitiers, or to the abbey she cherished, at Fontevrault.

The former queen, first of France, then England, was wife to two kings, the monkish Louis VII of France, and the hot-tempered, law-giving warrior Henry II of England. With Louis, Eleanor went on Crusade and gave birth to two daughters. With Henry, she rebuilt England, governed their growing Angevin empire and gave birth to too many sons. Leaving Henry, she returned to Poitiers where her Court of Ladies promoted the cause of women. Her subsequent role in fomenting her sons' rebellions against their father is debated, although Henry II himself had no doubts: he exiled Eleanor to England until he died. She was 67 when she became regent of England for her crusader son, Richard the Lionheart; 71, when she raised a ruinous burden of taxes to pay Richard's ransom, at the same time crushing support for a coup by her younger son, John. She was 78 when she crossed the Pyrenees in mid-winter to fetch her granddaughter, Blanca (Blanche of Castile), as a bride for the heir to France.

Through John, Eleanor became the mother of England's Plantagenet dynasty and an ancestor to many royal houses. Her hard, intransigent presence set a precedent that would make it easier for women to accede to the English throne. (The Salic Law barred female succession in Europe.)

A few facts about Eleanor's secretary slip into her text as Aline struggles to keep up with the flow of her mistress's words. Born around 1188, Aline was raised in Normandy. Unusually, she could write; and, after her service to Eleanor, she was destined to marry an Anglo-Norman landowner and live out her days in England.

The poetry of the troubadours, the first of whom was Eleanor's grandfather, makes clear that her name was pronounced Aleänor (Allay-anor). That is how *Power of a Woman* spells it.

Robert Fripp
Toronto, 2006

Power of a Woman

†††

Part I, Fated for France

I. The Royal Road from Aquitaine
1122-1137

Aline, Aline, write faster, child! The ebbing measure of my life must soon be spent. While God still gives me breath I would breathe words before eternal silence clasps me in its fold.

I should have started this long ago. No matter. Life was for living; bloodless recall is better suited to old age. That must be why it pleases our Lord to preserve my wizened carcass: he goads me in my dotage to recount my road-soiled journey through the wiles and wayward byways of mankind.

So write, Aline! I shall ramble from time to time, as old age will have it. Nevertheless, you shall be my inky voice, my steed upon the road of time. Take down my words, the only lasting currency of passing flesh. Until this account is written you will be my shadow in the sunshine and the wraith beside me when we walk in shade. And when I stop to catch my breath, make sure you dip your quill.

I was sired by Guilhem the Tenth, duke of Aquitaine and count of Poitou,[1] in 1122, the fourteenth year of King Louis the Fat; out of Anor, the daughter by a previous marriage of my grandfather's second wife, the former countess of Châtellerault. In one respect things were then as they are now: the fate that a noble family feared worse than disgrace was the division of its estates. That was why my grandfather, who was called the Troubadour,[2] put his son and heir by his first wife to his stepdaughter by the second. Both were of one family—but not of one blood!

Thus I was born, to duty before privilege, for such is the house of Aquitaine. Not a week went by but my nurses would instruct me, and later my ladies and my tutors, that the word *droit* entails duties before it bestows rights.

And so it was. From spring until past harvest time we were on the road, we females as cumbrous decorations, while my father the duke's court moved from town to castle, castle to town, dispensing justice, collecting taxes, issuing warnings and warring rebellious vassals.

I see a vision still, of men-at-arms beyond the dark stone mullions of a window, flashes off bright helmets graven in my head as they ride off to inflict prudence on some Gascon vassal, a lord made over-proud by the fastness of his fortress hedged about by deep ravines. How old was I the day I scaled my father's mounting block and begged to be swept up in the sparkling embrace of his chain-girt arms? How cold he felt. Even in the heat of summer his iron arms were colder than the stones I had just climbed. And yet he was just—a man of justice and of learning and, though the remoteness imposed by high office served to conceal emotion, he was a man who loved.

Thus we traveled, from the Loire to the Pyrenees; from the Massif—nay, from Auvergne—to the piney barrens of Les Landes, where trees dissipate the summer heat and stifle sound. A great baron's court puts more miles behind its feet in the traveling season than a tinker. There were days when Pétronille and I looked down from our upholstered cart and envied the roadside waif his hut. It was his stationary place we craved, not his station.

Ah, Time, you thief in the storehouse of memory! The many bends along the highroad of my life conceal the vistas between this fleeting moment of pure being and ancient recollections coursing like deerhounds through my brains. In a life of fourscore years and more, who can look so far back? So many rivers crossed; too many days. The very richness of experience crowds and clouds the brains. Whole years are banished. Other memories have stamped themselves into my mind as if they were illuminations, painted for posterity upon the wind-whipped pages of a book: now seen, now gone again. Memory can be a stranger in its own house. Or do I mean estranged from its own house? I struggle to recall the crucial things, while trivia come clothed in gilt and shining colors and the fashions of the day.

Do all one's memories speak truth? Some must be wishes masked as recollections, borne as fact upon the current of old time. The loneliness of age bestows one singular advantage: no mortal body from my generation lives to contradict what I shall say.

So write me truly, child! Whether they be false or fact the memories I dictate shall, piercing like an arrow through the mirages of time, one day attain the stature of old truth.

Of my mother I have scant recall. She died when I was eight. My brother, too. Mother was a dainty soul: a woman of her day, they said. She had no reason to connive beyond the limits of her circle: such business was for men. There was an afternoon we sat among the weeds beyond the jousting yard at, I think, Poitiers, and she crowned us both with daisy chains.

Long ago I stopped pretending I truly knew her. But I have invented her, and after such a span of time, is there a difference? Which swish of silk was she? Which waft of lavender as ladies came and, laughing, touched my cheek as I sat, holding court, lounging at the table that was Nana's massive breast? "Aleänor, this is Lady So-and-so." "Aleänor, this is the Countess of the Loire." "Aleänor, this lady is Anor, your mother."

Shall I meet her when I close my eyes at last? No, Aline, don't speak. You are not God to know.

That was my first world. I was fifteen years old when my second world fell apart. I don't recall whence came the news: surely from Galicia, but maybe it was Paris. I received a party of knights and emissaries in my hall at Bordeaux. God, how they stank from riding thirteen hour days in summer heat. Sixty-six years later I still smell them; and my mind's eye can still recite the devices on their tabards, rust-dark as they were, for in the party's haste to bring us news they had sweated through their chain-mail days on end. But even at the time their faces were blank walls, for I was numb. I remember a long, still moment of poise—a woman of my birth betrays no hint of fear or sorrow—while I cast a stern mask of thanks-for-duty-done upon the gathered faces of still sterner messengers. I bid Old Ferat bring them drink and meat; of courtesy I gave redundant orders in their hearing for their comfort and the stabling of horses; then I withdrew, too much in haste, to the womb of my chamber and a flood of tears and anger that I knew must never stop. God, how I mourned him, savagely, as a woman rips the flesh of a treacherous lover. Thirty-eight years old. How dare my father die, at wars with half his vassal-lords, every man of them nibbling at Aquitaine and tearing at Poitou. For days I starved myself, rent garments, bedding, veils.

Father died on Good Friday during a pilgrimage to Compostela. God grant his great soul peace. It has always seemed incredible to me that news of his death was such a sensitive weapon of state that the secret was preserved for better than a month, his retinue sworn to silence.

Then the madness of the greater world, the male world, beat down the doors again. Rumors anew: an army was spurring towards us through the burning days, from Paris. King Louis lusted for us. That we knew. Father had been a less than scrupulous vassal to his king.

Who or what brought me around, I know not. Wet-eyed women everywhere, more in fear for the future than in sorrow for Father. My ladies, washerwomen, maids, tutors, all leveled in an alliance of gender against an iron, bearded world. My bed became the throne for misery and mutual support. Perhaps that was when I decided I prefer the company and courts of women.

When I was calmer, statecraft I had learned in lessons long before was dusted off, explained again. Our lands were greater and richer than those of France. Our Duchy was as great as the Angevin empire and its lands in Normandy, not counting its overseas province, England. Our lands were such a prize that, if either the King of France or the Count of Anjou should master us, the victor would thereby put the pincers on the other. We were a land of inestimable wealth commanded by a weeping girl, a tethered chicken inviting foxes.

That crafty, well-guided devil King Louis learned of Father's passing soon enough. I would in time gain great respect for his advisors. But during those first alarms we knew only that my father the duke was dead, and that rumors of an army outran the French king's cavalry from Paris.

In that same week there came a moment like no other in my life, before or since. The household had been in mourning some three days, maybe four. I stood on the walls, watching the dying sun cast burning amber lights upon the rippled face of the Garonne. My tears were spent, my body racked by hunger, ravaged by exhaustion, shivering with sleeplessness and fear. I never suffered vertigo, but suddenly I was clutching at stone and gasping for breath. Russet ripples of the river turned to fire, enveloped me, and yet I found that I could neither cry nor call, though I was being sucked away. My hands began to shake, my teeth to clench and chatter till I thought that I would surely bite my tongue. I have often wondered how long that parlous state of unbeing lasted. I have lain with men—nay, kings—as virgin and as wife and never known a morsel to compare with that unbidden hour.

Don't blush, Aline, your turn will come, and disappointment follow.

In that instant all my senses drained away, all feeling, too, and with it all my doubts and frailty. How strange to stand there, grasping the parapet, smitten by the thought that I was afflicted by the falling sickness, thinking I might lose my grip and tumble down. And yet I felt no fear, for in that moment God, for surely it was He, instructed me that He would give me strength for ever. Before the sun had fully set I roused myself to courage the troops. That was the first time I commanded men: it was far from being the last.

They say hunger and sleepless nights conspire to cause that sort of inward light. Fathers of the Church—nay, John the Baptist and Christ himself—have wrested wisdom and visions from fasting in a wilderness. Perhaps my experience on the parapet was of that nature, the product of an inward wilderness born from days of mortal hunger and mental strain: it was as close as I have come to a damascene moment of epiphany. It has been a useful instrument. Thank God it left me with the life-long mettle to prevail.

Where was I? Ah yes, prevail. When calmer heads prevailed it became clear that King Louis' embassy intended not to bury me, but to marry me. After that evening on the parapet I was certain to my very bones that I was born to rule. I would have achieved the rank of queen without the whim of a pig!

You smile behind your hand, Aline. Have you not heard the tale?

Louis the Fat's elder son and heir was Philip. Philip had been born to grace; Philip had been bred to rule. By all accounts Philip was wise in learning, skilled in diplomacy, accomplished in arms, in the etiquette of courtly ways and at ease when conversing with women. He was riding one day, escorted, of course, when a sow waddled out of the Seine and thrust her muddy carcass under his horse. What use were splendid knights in all their trappings, set against a pig? That was the end of Philip.

And that was the making of me.

Never fear mighty men, child. They are dumb beasts. It's accidents make history.

In those days the rules of noblesse were stricter than they are today. Younger sons of noble houses were not allowed to marry, lest they and their heirs made claims against their families' estates. Primogeniture was everything. So King Louis' second son, Young Louis, had been packed off at a tender age to the monastery at Notre Dame. Life on his knees, prayers ten times a day, mindless discipline attained through exhaustion imposed by the rule of bells, a diet of guilt and penance for sins he had neither the imagination nor opportunity to commit, and a thorough disgust for the agents of sin, we women. Mark me, he seldom saw one, saving likenesses of the Blessed Mary. Naturally he had a special disgust for women's *parts*. That was young Louis' lot, my Louis, until he was twelve.

Then Philip was killed at the hest of a pig, and Louis was hauled away from his missals and expected to unlearn the habit of humility, to be readied for his father's throne.

Louis-the-Son's limitations were explained to me almost from the hour when Louis-the-Father's force encamped, in splendor, on the far bank of the Garonne. The king himself, sick unto death, had sent as emissaries to my maiden corpus the five hundred richest, most puissant barons and knights in his lands. All this to woo me, and my duchy, into the iron embrace of France. It was the coming of these magnificent men whom we, in Bordeaux, had feared as a raiding army.

Out of consideration for our fears, few among those mighty lords ventured at first to cross the river. They thought that *en masse* they might overwhelm me. Louis' ambassadors were assured in their power, if not their language. To our ears they spoke a garbled tongue, unlike our *langue d'oc*. But this is a detail. That first day, no less than Thibault of Champagne and the king's own cousin Raoul craved audience. Always present, and always leading while seeming to follow, was Abbé Suger, all-hearing, all-seeing, his senses keen to every nuance. Suger had been the coursing-hound and shadow of King Louis' life and reign, his wisest counselor, his truest friend. Such was the importance of this embassy to my humble self, I later discovered, that King Louis had ordered Suger to attend me at Bordeaux although both men must have known that the abbot would never see the dying king again.

I learned from Suger that my father, on his deathbed, had appealed to Louis the Fat to take me under his protection and to put me to marriage wisely. Extraordinary. Father's life was a chaos of unplanned feuds and muddled action. Not till he lay dying did he formulate a plan.

Ah, Suger. How can I express that man, Aline? How does a celibate monk put marriage to a maiden, explain her prospects, joys and duties in her husband's world, and speak of children and the getting of them, hinting all the while at what befalls a woman in her marriage bed? Somehow Suger accomplished all these tasks in my own hall, guiding me imperceptibly away from the battle-freighted glory of the barons.

Those iron men of France found me self-possessed. Yes, I can say that, for so I had been reared. I understood the arts of song and dance, the eloquence of argument and logic, and I could parse a ballad in Latin or French as well as any man, including Grandfather. I had traveled the world throughout, such a world as my forebears knew. I had seen much, visited much, and had all manner of experience to choose from. I had much to compare, and what is judgment if not a juggling of comparisons?

These mighty men came from Paris expecting to meet a trembling maiden. They found instead a fifteen-year-old duchess whose moment of epiphany had strengthened her resolve beyond all men.

Listen to me carefully, Aline, for I can teach you much about the feral state of men, the "better" sex, as legalists and prelates would have us human souls believe.

A knight who holds a weapon ties his hands. He must either strike or be encumbered by his load. Thus he loses his own freedom to be free. A woman may command with empty hands for she is free to use such weapons as she will. Let her choose words, for darts wound faster than a sword. Let her choose frailty, for limpid mud mires heavy cavalry. Let her choose the sheen of silk, for silk attracts as iron repels. Let her choose allure, for thereby she can sap resistance. Let her seem foolish, for men accede to women's seeming folly. Let her be subtle, for subtlety will always out-maneuver strength. Women are as water wearing rock.

Suger knew something of my power for he, too, stored his weapons in his head. We were a match, Suger and I. The others could but wonder as I entertained at meat. I was the female infant sitting at the head of the board in her father's and her grandfather's place, cushioned to see above the viands, upholding with gay laugher all the sunlight and the breezes of our western lands against the gloomy glory that was France.

A moment more, Aline, then you can rest.

Let me speak of Young Louis. Poor sweet Louis, you were two years older than I, but your cloistered life had ill prepared you for a future free of walls. Two weeks we jousted in each other's company, waiting to be wed. Two weeks we rode and talked together, exploring all the ancient wonders of Bordeaux. Did you desire me, Louis? No, you dared not. Despite your tranquil front you feared that hell's flames waited in a woman's arms. You feared my body as a harbinger of mortal sin. You feared the freedom of my spirit as if it were the poisoned apple plucked at Eden, a fruit from which you dared not bite. You had been freed from the cloister five years before you met me, but you were never free of guilt. No, never, so long as I knew you. How those clerics flayed your naked brains.

As for me, I was born to be allianced with a noble house, and there were few more noble than my own. Was it to be Anjou, or France? My frail person was a weapon of more power than all the iron armies in the land. Ten thousand men-at-arms caparisoned for war counted for less than my consent.

To smile at you, Louis, was but to smile at destiny. Why else had God caused me, a female, to be the eldest issue of a duke? Why else had God seen fit to call my brother Guilhem Aigret home to Paradise? Had my father lived he would have done what I did of my own free will. He would have wed me to you, Louis, thereby alliancing Poitou and Aquitaine to France, though Father would have hedged the marriage contract with many more constraints. I had traveled, Louis. I had seen a portion of the world and wondered at the mysteries of peoples, arts and poetry. I saw your life and future crown as a step forward in my own subject people's onward march.

A rchbishop Geoffroi of Loroux married us on a Sunday, one of the hottest days of the year. Mass, and marriage in the cathedral of

St. André. A sumptuous wedding breakfast was rather spoiled—Louis was easily shocked—because when we appeared in the arch of the royal portal the crowd began shouting "plen-ty, plen-ty" as if I were a sow to farrow offspring by the litter. In that respect I failed him. As we walked among the crowd the chanting pounded out a rhythm which I, in my virginity, did not identify. Louis, how you despaired the lewdness of our ordinary folk.

We rose in haste from breakfast, and all but fled Bordeaux. The French numbered but five hundred, plus their households, and we feared our rebel vassals in the chaos of the times. Word had it that those who so conspicuously missed our wedding might still greet us, with an ambush on the road. What richer prizes could they ransom than their duchess with her husband, the heir to France, and all the leading nobles of that land?

Our French escort awaited us below the Larmont hills across the blessed Garonne. I think we put sixty miles behind us on the road to Saintes before our captains felt secure.

It was at Taillebourg that Louis and I, shall we say, discovered each other. For him to love me in that way was a betrayal of everything the monks had stuffed into his baby head. In my innocence I had to instruct him, and what did I know? When he at last plucked up sufficient courage to explore my female parts it was as if he were defiling Stations of the Cross.

Courage, Aline, we'll soon be done!

Louis spent more hours upon his knees that night than in our nuptial bed. Never mind. Despite the heat and prayers the thing got done. It was then that my mind connected with the chanting of the crowd. No wonder the ancients versified their poetry of love in long-short feet. A man at labors in a bed moves not unlike the pulse of running meter.

And now I tire. Pull that screen across the sun and leave me. Go rest your hand, Aline. I need to sleep.

2. Oh Paris, would that you were Poitiers!
1137-1141

Good morning, Aline. I had a dream last night, the most vivid I have summoned in twenty years. Does that sound strange to you? Perhaps the effort of dragging forth the past by day will set its mark upon my nights as well.

I cannot tell if you stammer and blush because you are overly impressed by my rank, by the angel of fair fortune who guards my life, or by the press of years that weigh on me in age. To tell the truth, there are days I marvel at my life myself. I wonder at the smile of God that guided me so far along the way.

Some weeks ago I was watching when two women discovered a leaf which, long before, had been used to mark a place between the sheets of an ancient book. It had lain there for decades before they found it, loyal to the place of a time-lost reader, stiff in age and parched by the astringent march of years.

A sear leaf. There, I liken my frame to a leaf! I should have retorted: that leaf still gives expression to the color and the richness of the sapful spring that raised it from the earth. Look at these blotched, clawed hands! Hands that wore the signet of two Duchies and the *alliances*[3] of two kings.

Even so, the best of histories weighs heavily. Sometimes I fear to travel to the past lest melancholy overwhelm me. Dark humor is a malady of age, child. You will have to help transport me to my past and bring me safely home again.

Perhaps I have started dictating my book to satisfy an ulterior motive. When age imprisons one in unaccustomed solitude, only conversation with one's nearest and dearest confirms the truth of one's past worlds. That is why old women chatter so. Confirmation of their life's reality depends on it.

Enough of sentiment! Where were we? Ah, yes. On the road...

Louis and I made our entry to Poitiers with more decorum than we left Bordeaux. How could we not! We lodged in the tower which Grandfather, the Troubadour, commissioned for my grandmother, the former countess of Châtellerault. To my people's delight, Louis donned the coronet of the counts of Poitou. I should have said this yesterday: it first graced his temples on the morning of our wedding in Bordeaux.

We tarried two weeks in Poitiers, impatient to receive the tardy tribute of certain vassals who disdained to give my lord the homage that was now his due. This delay seemed not to trouble Louis at the time, and I soon forgot the affront altogether. It was later, when Louis returned to Poitou at the head of an army, when I realized how the insult simmered in his brain. Two months later some of my Poitevin vassals rose in revolt, whereon my monkish king became a butcher, chopping off their hands himself.

Don't distress yourself, Aline. Life can be unkind. Besides, those men were unlettered. Not one of them could put his hand to such useful toil as you. I do believe you have as pretty a script in French as my former secretary, Peter of Blois, though Peter—petulant old goat—has much finer Latin than you.

Throughout our life together, aspects of Louis' inner mind eluded me. I was his wife, not his confessor. Looking back, I think he wreaked his fury on Poitou because, while we lingered in Poitiers, his father could linger no longer in Paris. Word reached us while we tarried in Grandfather's tower: the King was dead. Long live my lord and husband, Louis the Seventh, King of the Franks. Barring the messengers, who knelt before they spoke, I was the first to kneel at Louis' feet and with full feeling say, "God save the king".

It transpired that Louis the Fat had endured the heat of July in great suffering, hoping to see his son and Abbé Suger again. And, I'm sure, he wanted to meet the new daughter-in-law whose presence spoke to the success of his long-held policy, the increase of France. But his dying hopes were not to be. There came the moment when he ordered his servants to place him on a bed of ashes, where he stretched out his arms in the shape of a cross, and died.

How life gathers speed, a charger spurred by circumstance. Overnight, the child of a duke became a duchess in her own right. Weeks later I left Bordeaux as wife to the heir to France. I would shortly enter Paris as its queen.

I thank God that I came to Paris for the first time in summer. Had we entered the Île de la Cité beneath gray skies I swear I would have wept for home-sickness and loss. The city that I entered as its mistress was a grim, depressing place. The enchanted worlds of my birthright and of Father's ducal progresses seemed a lifetime ago. But youth is resilient, and at fifteen years of age I was queen of a dank labyrinth, the citadel that had long been the capital of the Franks. Besides, I have endured worse in the sixty-six years that have borne my life along since that unhappy day. I had yet to clap eyes on London. More of that anon.

I do not mean to dwell on the failings of Louis' palace. No doubt in time of siege I would have been glad to poke my way around a stone-bowelled, smoke-blackened fortress with embrasures for windows, dark as the pit of hell. The glory of the Capets was a towering mole-mound starved for light. It had been built three centuries before as an unsinkable ship, a bulwark against Viking sea-raiders, with tightly-winding stairs and narrow passages constructed for defence.

It was there, on that island in the Seine which was Louis' first and only real world, that we jousted in earnest, in joy and in heartbreak, for too many years.

I spoke of Poitiers. If only its leading citizens had shown restraint during the first discontents imposed by our alliance! Louis' campaign in Poitou strained our marriage from the start. Within months, some Poitevins were declaring Poitiers a commune free from rule by my "foreign" king. In hindsight I feel that Poitiers felt a ripple from the splash affecting many Lombard towns: wealthy citizens were making queer demands for "municipal liberties." How I wept, beseeching and scolding Louis privately. But he would not be ruled by me. The dust of our passage to Paris had barely settled when he took an army back along the road to Poitiers and fired my people with a hatred for the Capets and for France.

Louis had no skill in rhetoric or reason. As a monk he obeyed; as a king he was obeyed. As a monk he submitted; as a king, he made others submit. Between those two opposing temples his brain conceived no middle way. Louis' actions were of one camp or the other. Had this revolt occurred in any other city he surely would have led his troops with Christian moderation. But my Poitevins' foolish insurrection was a blow against his bride, and thus his pride. He took it as a slight to the *alliances* with which we pledged each other's troth.

Our Lord spare my city! for Louis did not. The mild monk would not be ruled by God, by argument or by his queen. His vision was too narrow, the contradictions of his life too sharp. Had I been allowed to show myself and reason with my people, no blood would have been shed. But I was not allowed to go: Louis would be king!

It was only after my tearful entreaties that Abbé Suger put aside his great labor—he was rebuilding the abbey of St. Denis—to post like a common messenger in urgent haste to Poitiers. People said God sent Suger in response to the cries and prayers assailing heaven from Poitou. But even Suger had to wrestle night and day with Louis' demons before he finally prevailed. Within months of our marriage it was clear to me, and to the world, that Louis' tutors had instructed him in everything except those qualities he needed most: the skills to exercise the royal power in moderation.

Speaking of the royal power, the bell calls us to offices. Too late for prime; it must be sext. Leave me, Aline, and bid my secretary attend me afterwards. Guy Diva and I have a pressing matter to discuss.

When Louis returned to Paris he buried himself in Notre Dame's cloister again: he was always more an oblate than a king. By the lights of the Church he was the perfect postulant, the novice meek in dress and attitude who would one day take his vows, except that he was the king and therefore, of dynastic necessity, a husband. During those first, unhappy months in Paris I formed the impression that the tower-grotto of the Capets sustained our household on Friday fasts each day of the week, with privations, hair shirts, and a diet which the meanest Poitevin scullion would have scorned. The royal compound at one end of the Island merged with the offices of the Church at the other. Between these temporal and spiritual extremities, there was little to ease the palate or lighten the mind.

I was not alone in grieving our translation to Paris. There was the matter of language. Furthermore, my followers, who were accustomed to freedoms of the mind, a well-stocked board, entertainments and space discovered in dismay that every day which dawned in Louis' flesh-abasing citadel was Lent.

The Franks, of course, took us for hot-blooded southerners and spoiled wastrels. We were appetites in search of satisfaction who lacked for discipline and clamored for minstrels and to satisfy desires. My mother-in-law, Adela of Maurienne, withdrew to her chateau in Champagne. I think her retreat had less to do with frictions between her unworldly Capetians and my boisterous, worldly household than with a widow's desire to define her own place. Oh Aline, would that I had been so fortunate: I would have bolted in a moment, back to Poitiers.

And yet, as a tree disadvantaged for light gropes toward the sun, we found our ways ahead by seeking solace in what was, indeed, an extraordinary culture of learning. In that respect, Paris refused to disappoint. Many an evening I stepped from the solar to the tower heights to eavesdrop on students' voices: they were older than me, drunk on argued subtleties of thought as well as wine. Paris was mother and father to learned men of many lands. Even the unschooled English came to learn. Grammar, rhetoric, logic; geometry, arithmetic, astronomy, music; learned doctors offered the full gamut of the *trivium* and the *quadrivium* as well as medicine and law. We soon discovered that competing doctors of theology claimed Paris as their home.

I see you have to cut another quill. We'll stop awhile.

You are very pretty, Aline. Did you know that? Of course you do. Long dark hair and that delicate nose. Braids behind the ears, free-falling in front. Why do you wear your hair the old-fashioned way? Forgive me, I stand corrected. As you say, it's still the style in Normandy. And contrasting pale cheeks. You look as I once did, but your hair is darker. You're a true beauty, Aline.

There you go, blushing again. If you can't accept a compliment from an old woman without turning the color of raw beef, how will you cope with the eyes and the verses of suitors with lust in their loins?

You're too thin-skinned: your father guarded you too well. But by the time you're done with me you'll be as thick-skinned as a washer-woman's hands that steeped for a lifetime in lye. You'll be the better for it, too. And lucky. A woman's lot is better than it was when I was young. Mark you, the need for change was in the air. Our early years in Paris coincided with a sort of spring emerging from a winter of the mind. People were claiming freedom to find personal paths to faith, through reason, rather than taking doctors' homilies as truth.

But the eternal message of the Church when I was young was simple: faith without reason; faith needs no reason. Blind faith, and obedience: to ancient rote; to learned fathers of the Church who lived and died before King Charlemagne. What did those ancient savants know about the press of modern times?

How old-fashioned I must sound to you, Aline. I hope I can convey how the ferment that coincided with my youth was as a tonic to the women of my household during those first, dreary years.

Our entertainments were limited. Still, it's a poor loaf that wants for leaven. We flocked to the debates—some of us, I fear, to preen before the eyes of men. Much of it was silliness. The doctors' learned treatises called up such fluff as would not raise the eyebrow of a nun, let alone the hackles of the Church. Does a bird fly by the grace of wings or by the agency of air? Is a pig led to market by a rope or by the man who holds the other end? Good harmless Aristotle, but a vehicle for fun.

Am I distracting you, Aline? No? Good. Old women have to talk. It brings the past alive.

Early summers were the best time. Our feet bruised the chamomile lawn beneath the cedar trees, while trailing sleeves and skirts stirred up the smell from the broken leaves. An odor not unlike citrons. A smell of the south, of warm, dry earth. How that little piece of ground, em-battled on both sides by the rushing river, conjured thoughts of home.

Those days, even the most timid among my women were emboldened. We hosted sermons and debates in the royal garden on the Île. How we all looked forward to the fray! There was a Breton preacher, Peter Abelard, who had no fear of God, still less of the Church. He was a favorite, goading doctors of divinity as if they were oxen. His debating skills struck so many doctors dumb that they might as well have been. There really is no intelligent rebuttal to the injunction: "Think!"

Women of every rank loved Abelard. He afforded us such naughty pleasure, mocking the doctrine of obedience, attacking priests as blinkered beasts who drew a plowshare back and forth, year in, year out, along a single furrow. No wonder the riches of each fertile field of faith are never reaped, he would say—he meant each Christian soul—for how can soil be reaped that was neither plowed nor sown? The untilled field that is each human mind must come to faith assisted by the light of reason.

The Church condemned his teachings, twice, the first time before I was born. Rather than give a bishop the pleasure of burning his book he did it himself, and then rewrote it. I had been in Paris four years before the stiff-necked Abbé Bernard silenced Abelard the second time.

Peter's message was: question blind faith, for it is blind. And question that which you obey. That was why we women were so fond of him. Not just for his audacity. In those days women were wombs: wombs to put to marriage; wombs to breed; wombs to command; wombs who would meekly obey. A man served two masters, his lord and the Church. A woman served three, for she obeyed her man before the other two. Abelard raised at least the hope of a free mind. How bold he made us feel. What vicarious joy!

I think that's all I can recall today. This old womb has had her say.

3. Trouble at Bourges; fire and the sword assail Champagne
1141-1144

I had been queen four years when we got into trouble at Bourges. The see fell vacant, so Louis named his chancellor to fill the bishop's chair. Bourges is convenient to Poitou, and Louis, despite the hours he spent on his knees, was not averse to convenience. The town is well placed to host the royal court. My vassals could reach Bourges as easily as Louis'. So we appointed a trusted minister as bishop to serve our needs.

This sparked trouble. The impertinent clerics of Bourges elected their own nominee, who chanced to be in Rome, in the lap of the pope. Louis raised his hand against him, naturally; and stopped him entering the see. So the impostor, Pierre de la Châtre, decamped to Champagne and sent a wounded letter to the pope.

Are you keeping up, Aline? Good. You're a hard worker, child. Writing is almost as useful as embroidering. More women should learn their letters.

The pope, of course—they're all as thick as thieves—sided with the priests and ordered his fellow back to Bourges to reclaim our see. Even then the situation might have been saved, except that the pope sent a letter to Louis' ministers, chiding the king for playing the "foolish schoolboy." Imagine penning such mischief to the court of the king of France. Such arrogance! The upshot was that Louis swore a mighty oath on the holiest relics, vowing that this Pierre would never enter Bourges as bishop. Pope Innocent responded by excommunicating us, and our household with us. There the matter seethed, a matter of profound unease.

You can imagine how deeply this wounded the Capets. Louis—he was twenty-one—had spent his life abasing himself to the whims of the Church. For what!

Still, we had no time to reflect. It was then that my sister's marriage tore our world apart.

❦ ❦ **I**f but a fourth part you might bear..." How does it go? How does it go? Pardon an old woman's fog. I need the words; I need to fetch those words to carry on.

The Countess of Die. Yes. It was her poem. She wrote it some years ago. It can't have been graven too freshly in time; I would have forgotten. The long-past is fresh; it's the past year I can't remember. She's a wonderful *trobairitz*.[4] The first time I heard her verse it stuck in my head with those two awful years. It sounds better in our native *langue d'oc*. I'm wandering, Aline, but take down what you can:

> "If but a fourth part you might bear,
> Friend, of the pain that tortures me,
> Then you would see my suffering..."[5]

Now I'm tired. No, no, we'll go on! I don't want this sorry tale to burden tomorrow as well as today. As briefly as I can:

Louis was still sorely distressed by the Bourges affair when my sister, Pétronille, came of marriageable age. The late king's cousin wanted her. Raoul of Vermandois was ancient, a bull ready for beef, but politics is politics: I saw the benefit of an alliance with his lands in the north-east and the Vexin, which forms a natural line of defence between France and Normandy. A match between Pétronille and Raoul would move Paris to the center of a grand alliance. So I fought to bring it about.

Louis was already beset by anxiety over the Church's reaction to Bourges. Denied the comforts of his Church he was desperate for support. I gave it, of course, with all my love. For the next three years I became his confessor. Looking back, I know I exacted a price, for Pétronille's sake and ours, as I thought. But it trapped us in the end.

Perhaps I over-reached. Raoul was already married, to the niece of Louis' strongest vassal, Thibault of Champagne. Still, due diligence revealed—royal courts are full of hair-splitters—a trace of consanguinity between Raoul and his wife. It took a good deal of persuasion, but I finally found three bishops who agreed to annul Raoul's marriage and marry him to Pétronille. Whereupon Raoul's estranged wife threw herself and her children on the charity of her uncle, the great Thibault. Well, the cowardly schoolboy is always the first to cling to the master's cloak. Which he did. Thibault of Champagne invoked the help of that noisome abbot, Bernard of Clairvaux. Bernard in turn appealed to his bosom friend with whom he had traveled to Rome ten years before, the pope.

Before a season could pass, Innocent II rained anathema upon us all: smiting the bishops who had sundered Raoul's marriage; annulling Pétronille's marriage to Raoul; and forcing Raoul to take his first wife back on pain of excommunication and, what was worse, forfeit of certain lands.

Naturally, Louis held Thibault of Champagne to blame for this surfeit of ills. As if that were not enough, Thibault was also sheltering the pope's pretender to the bishopric at Bourges.

Louis had never been exposed to enough of life's contradictions to forge a middle way. No one had taught him how to argue toward compromise; or better, collaboration. All was black, or white. So he took personal command of an army and laid waste to Champagne. The outcome was inevitable. At Vitry-en-Perthois the townsfolk sheltered in the church and Louis' soldiers burned it down on top of them. Some said a thousand people burned to death, others that the dead numbered a thousand and more. But who can count beyond a thousand? Such a number is beyond reckoning. This took place in front of Louis' eyes. It was more than three score years ago, but they still call the place Vitry-le-Brûlé.

For a year and more I nursed Louis back from his lowest ebb. Poor tortured soul, no peace at all. The Church, of course, had cast him out.

As for my sister, poor Pétronille was in despair. She was a maiden again but no virgin. I advised comfrey, of course. It tightens the passage. Old wives have prescribed suppositories of comfrey since the First Crusade, a hundred years ago. Husbands don't like to return from Palestine to suspect their wives of taking other men. Ho, Aline! You gawp with your mouth wide open, but you don't even blush today. We make progress. It's true, child, quite true. The hymen grows back. Not that *you* will ever need to resort to such naughty subterfuge.

W as I dozing? Yes? Such dismal years, the fourth and fifth of Louis' reign. They trouble me. I try to forget. But each event is a stitch in the tapestry. You are clever to write so well.

Everyone came to Paris to celebrate the re-consecration of St. Denis. We took advantage of the occasion to quiet the ripples from Bourges and the war in Champagne. Not that these were really laid to rest till after our Crusade. But how could any beating heart, no matter its age, forget that awe-inspiring day!

Suger had spent years rebuilding the royal church on the Île, the abbey of St. Denis. Would that he had expended his monies and his labor on the royal apartments! No matter; it ill behooves me to cavil. On the feast of Saint Barnabas in the seventh year of our reign, the priests translated the relics of St. Denis with all due pomp from the crypt to Suger's abbey. The abbey of St. Denis was in truth born again. Like fresh snow, its new dressed stone blinded the eyes. The edifice loomed up like a giant wall of chalk. Dazzling withal, dazzling without and dazzling within! Its colored windows changed a glorious day to still more wondrous rainbows.

Everybody in that press of people fought for breath. The event brought five archbishops, thirteen bishops and most of the barons of France. You cannot imagine the scene. Butchers stole the very air from bishops, bishops from counts, counts from fishwives, fishwives from nuns. Hawkers trampled on dukes' feet, dukes on students', students on market boys'. Was ever such a pilgrimage! Ourselves were several times stopped, unmoving, captives to the crowd, becalmed in a tempest of shouted greetings, blessings, reaching hands, foul breath and pleas for alms. Louis himself pressed back the throng. How wonderful, and yet how wondrous strange. Men and women fought to place themselves where sunbeams touched them after passing through the stained glass images of Jesus, Mary and the saints. To look around was to watch as faces were transformed by being lifted to the colored lights, each mouth agape with awe, each heart touched by the holy spirit, each transfigured countenance a faith reclaimed.

It was at this gathering that Abbé Bernard confronted me. Such a grim ascetic, that man! He had trained himself during a long life in the cloister to ignore beauty—nay, to transcend the material world. For him, this world of impure being distracted from pure, spiritual truth. I mentioned that the abbé once accompanied his friend Innocent II to Rome. People said that he traveled through the Alps without once casting eyes upon the waters of the lakes or upwards at the snow-capped peaks. To Bernard, such things were distractions; all sensations were temptations, base appetites to be eschewed; and all flesh was but straw to stoke the fire of the spirit. Bernard directed his feet through faith, aided by ecstatic visions. Years before, he had taken the sensualist Abbé Suger to task. I was an infant when he began chastising the Benedictines of Cluny for backsliding in the matter of gaudy display:

> "The church clothes the stones of her walls in gold while her people go naked. The church feeds the eyes of the rich from the purse of her poor. Those who seek sensation find amusement; those most in need find only emptiness."[6]

Had Bernard prevailed, Suger never would have restored St. Denis to its present splendor.

It was at this, to him distasteful, gathering that Bernard sought me out. He became in time a formidable foe. He was no fool. My forefathers had scant respect for clergy; my father least of all. But, as the biggest badger shuns the slightest ferret, even Father was wary of Bernard. Father had made the mistake of backing the wrong pope and expelling the bishop of Poitiers, so the Church had excommunicated him, and Poitou with him. It soon became clear that excommunication would not so much as jangle Father's chain-mail, so Bernard intervened. I was three at the time. One Sunday, at Parthenay-le-Vieux, the abbé ran out of the church waving the pyx in Father's face. We never learned what magic Bernard conjured, but Father, a giant among men, fell senseless to the ground.

I'm wandering, Aline. You must hold me to my text.

Briefly, during the festivities at St. Denis, Bernard suggested I use my influence on Louis to bring him to contrition for the misery he had wrought in Champagne; and for the other matter, Bourges. In exchange he, Bernard, was prepared to offer spiritual guidance, to extricate us from the woes distressing the Capetian throne.

I should not mark Bernard down unduly. Did he not tip the scale with the powerful prayers of Clairvaux when I was still without child after six years a wife? We named our firstborn Marie in thanks. The first child a female! Did the bells ring that day in joy or disappointment? Well, even a female child proves that a wife is not barren. And Marie in later years was a wonderful joy to me and a marriage-pawn for the Capets.

Have you noticed, Aline? Men are so cynical. The very *Paternoster* credits them with the act of conception, as if a woman's womb is but *their* vehicle in which *their* child is brought to term. But let a woman fail to give birth or give birth to a girl, then she is to blame. I am weary beyond measure of homilies on Christ's origins: "conceived of the holy ghost, borne of Mary the maid."

Remember what I said about men, child. Never fight them on their terms, or they will win. Bernard bested Peter Abelard by denying him the chance to address the griefs those churchmen brought against him. This grim monk would not silence me so easily.

By the time Bernard confronted me, the Church had begun to demand meekness in women. It is only since I was a girl that statues of the Blessed Mary have been carved with their eyes cast down. Why should not a woman hold her head erect? I looked the abbé in the eye—which meant I had to look down anyway!—and put my sister's case again, and he, wise in his cloistered way, broke off our interview. Mark me, men like Bernard see nothing more than devils in a woman's smile. To such as he a woman is a creature lower than a beast. And a woman with spirit is beyond repair!

Now I've told you: be armed and use your knowledge to advantage. Ride men, or they will ride you. Depend on it, unless it serves their purposes, men give no weight to anything a woman says.

It's getting dark, Aline. We work late today. See how the sunlight moves around the wall, striking columns one by one. Some are bright, some dark. Eventually darkness overtakes them all. I count the offices by those pillars. They are as constant as a sundial.

Constant, that's the word I was looking for. Constant—as men can never be.

What right had they to ask Louis to be constant to the Church? Constant! To obey every whim they foisted on him? Those priests, who kept an infant king upon his knees and made him what he was.

My family reared ten generations of Guilhems, all fiery men: the first was a comrade-in-arms of Charlemagne. From the moment I could reach my father's stirrup I was bred to the history and taste of power. But the Capets raised Louis to impotence. Accept. Obey. Accept. Obey. Accept… His inner man was mild as a palfrey, mild as a statue of the Virgin in these timid, fearful times. When at last in pure frustration he was forced to kick against the Church's endless pricks he had no rein to guide him. No rein but me.

4. CRUSADE
1144-1147

Let's walk awhile, Aline. I love to walk on the path beside the wall after rain. Nana used to call rain the tears of God. Heaven knows the Almighty has reasons to weep. Come! Put pen to paper later. This will give you a chance to embroider your stitches into my words.

Where were we? Ah yes, our troubles in Bourges and Champagne. Well, we were young! That was why Louis strayed so far into *desmesure*, by which I imply over-reaction in a just cause. Not only at Bourges and in Champagne, but during the first season of our marriage when he avenged his grievance against Poitou. How else to explain the litany of woes that befell us in those foolish years?

And all for nothing. I should have known better. Suger did. So did Bernard. But Louis had so few yardsticks pegged in the soil of experience that he lacked for measurements to range his actions by.

That is how it came to pass that we embarked on Crusade as an act of atonement. Though I must say, in its early days I thought of the holy cause as an adventure and a release from tedium. I hadn't married a king to be a nun.

Louis, of course, was the perfect pilgrim. But the Franks would not send an army overseas unless the Germans came too, requiring Abbé Bernard to win over the German-speaking peoples before their emperor would consent. It took a year of persuasion, but in the end Emperor Conrad marched with one hundred thousand, to whom we added almost as many Poitevins and Franks. The larger part of the rabble would see neither hearth nor home again. The lives lost during our actions against Champagne were but a drop in the palm of a hand compared to the bucket of souls tossed in ditches on our Crusade.

No matter. Perhaps the time was right for another great blood-letting. Better minds than mine thought so. Abbé Bernard himself was stirred to preach the way of the Cross to nobles, ruffians and gallows-fodder within a week's ride of Paris.

Louis and his counselors did not share my zeal for a woman's participation, even if that woman happened to be his queen. But the point was not negotiable: Aquitaine and Poitou were better placed than his Franks to arm and fund our great adventure. Besides, the cause of Crusade was in no small part a family matter—my family, not Louis'.

It was late winter in our eighth year when news arrived from the kingdom of Jerusalem: between Christmas and Epiphany a Muslim horde had stormed Edessa, east of Antioch, carrying off Christian merchants and their families to ransom or sell as slaves. Edessa was home to the biblical Medes into recent memory. No longer! The city's fall threatened Jerusalem. It also exposed the town of Antioch and its caravan routes to special peril.

Raymond of Toulouse, prince of Antioch, was my uncle, a younger son of the Troubadour, cut loose with neither prospects nor money; who proceeded to conquer a world and make it his own. I recalled him as a handsome devil, though it was years since I had seen him, either in

Bordeaux or Poitiers. But Raymond had no eyes for a little girl eight years his junior. Of course, the splendid knight of my childish love was nothing but a tatterdemalion squire, twenty years old, with neither harness for his back nor pence for his purse. Soon after that, he managed to connect the links in a long chain of hazards to win himself the fief of Antioch.

It was Raymond who wrote us concerning the fall of Edessa: his friend, the bishop of Djebail, carried his letter. It was Raymond who needed us; and it was the Raymond of my shining if faulty memory who—dare I say it?—drew me and countless thousands forth along that fateful road.

Boredom and absolution. I had no time for the one and much need of the other. And now that my marriage linked Poitou to the Capets, Raymond's call for Christian help gave me the chance to salve both at a stroke.

Are you shocked by my candor, Aline? A little, I think. I have not corrupted you enough to give you the composure of an inquisitor. Not yet. To be blunt, I have spent a long lifetime confessing my every sin to God. Why should I not confide in some small measure to posterity?

At first, Crusade was but a little mustard seed. How fast it grew! I preached it in our language to my vassals in the duchy lands, assisted in some measure by the troubadour, Marcabru. Marcabru was very loyal. He had mourned my father's passing: "Now that the Poitevin has gone / I am, like Arthur, all forlorn." Now he "preached" the cause of Crusade with his "Song of the Bathhouse." Oh Marcabru, fond oaf that you were! He compared the purifying act of Crusade to scrubbing off dirt.

> "God bids the bold and humble too
> Be tested in his washing place."

You've heard it? Of course. They're still singing it sixty years on. The Poitevins sang it on our Crusade; it marched its way to Palestine with Richard, too.

Bawdy songs were not the instrument Bernard would have chosen to attract recruits, but God turns his hand to strange tools. Bernard intended us to be well-attended on the road. He exhorted the faithful everywhere, from the Low Countries through Burgundy, from the Rhineland to Poitou. So many men took the Cross, he later told the pope, that villages were left with one old man for every seven women. What cared Bernard for the miseries of flesh, for death on the road, for the husband-less, help-less women left behind?

"His calls to arms, his preachings, all
Have plung'd my heart in bitter woe."

That's how Marcabru put it. But Bernard's only care was disembodied souls!

Our provinces seethed like a myriad bee skeps swarming in May, the occupants ransacking fodder and food as they fled, buzzing with excitement and wasting their substance far away. Not that there was much to waste: famine had stalked the land for five years past. For many, Crusade would bring a less tedious death than hunger.

At the end of Lent in our ninth year, Bernard preached to a host beyond number at Vezeley. Louis and I prostrated ourselves at the abbé's feet, we took the Cross, and thus our people supported their king, sheep behind their shepherd, ready for Crusade. We marched the following year, after Bernard won the Germans to our cause.

I have pondered this point: if Louis and I were crazed in the matter of Champagne, then the world was assuredly mad in the matter of this massive toil of souls towards Jerusalem. As I said, Bernard's Crusade would cost many more lives abroad than anything our troops had done at home.

Certainly we were crazed when we set out, women no less than men. Three hundred noble ladies took the Cross with me and made their way to Jerusalem. I mustered a female battalion whose mission was to tend the wounded, although methinks we expended more passion in our year-long preparation than upon the road.

What a precious summer: from the city of Metz to the Bosporus in the span of three months. We were more disciplined than the army of Grandfather's day. For one thing, we managed to cross the Rhine without a mass slaughter of Jews.[7] Not that our passage was easy. The might of Emperor Conrad's army marched ahead, a vast German stomach gnawing meats and forage every step along the way. Where our paths crossed, mile after mile resembled a barn laid waste by rats. We followed in the Germans' wasted trail and left behind a further wasteland of our own.

But I have sweeter memories than those. That summer I felt as if I were traveling with Father again, riding with Pétronille in our cushioned cart. Our army was divided: the men from my lands in the vanguard with the women; Louis and his Franks in the rear. He was the perfect shepherd, mustering the laggards in his flock through the German lands and over the Magyar plain. As for me, I was surrounded by rebellious young billy-goats from Aquitaine, younger sons turned out on Crusade with their grandfathers' arms and chain-mail. I must say, as poor as those young men were, I coveted their freedom. I discovered many consolations on that road.

We have walked a long way, Aline. We're back where we started from. I shall sit here awhile. Do you know, I learned to speak my native language again that summer. I learned to listen and sing and jest again in our precious *langue d'oc*. Ah, bliss. It is often better to travel than to arrive.

How strange we found the Greeks. I think they feared us, for the people kept themselves at a distance as if the long, winding dragon of our army might transform to a chimera from an old Homeric myth. Or perhaps, looking down from their strong hilltops, they saw the serpent of our progress as a monstrous basilisk. We thought them a superstitious people. They may be Christians of a sort, but methinks Christ has not yet put to death their pantheon of pagan gods.

How wonderful their land, though; how sweet the fragrance of their hills. So like the broken country of Dordogne, or the Ardèche. The steep, white rock walls glared at us like second suns until the reflected light of heaven hurt our eyes. And yet—how to express this?—the light in that land emits a quality of contrast and purity I never met since nor before. It speaks of the sacred. Every natural crag and terrace nurtured a wild herbarium. Afternoons gave birth to breezes stirring aromas from a dry heath dotted with fragrant junipers, evergreen oaks and the sour tang of boxwood. I hold that summer in the nostrils of my mind. Alas, we passed through Greece too late in the year to smell the thyme.

Ah me, if war were a Grecian summer, I would shun peace.

Our splendid anabasis was, unfortunately, a short interlude. We spurred across Thrace to the Bosporus and there, basking in glory beyond imagination to those who have not seen it, lay Constantinople's walls and towers. What splendors in our eyes, what nagging devils in our brains, for the awe that now assailed our senses was such stuff as our pious western priests inveigh against.

The sensation of a Paradise on earth, of wonder, of a world apart, was overwhelming. Apart from this unease we confronted a more prosaic matter: that of the Germans. We had agreed that Conrad's force would wait for us. But men, mules, sumpter horses, wagons, even their rats and their whores, were gone. Conrad and his Germans had crossed the Bosporus, straining their leash to move on. This made us anxious, for we did not wholly trust the Greeks. Their emperor, Manuel, had some-how contrived a truce with the Turks just before we arrived, a thing more strange than frost in July. Now we mistrusted the Germans as well. Emperors Conrad and Manuel were brothers-in-law. What game was afoot?

Apprehension grew as we approached Constantinople, despite the fact that Emperor Manuel's emissaries had escorted us since we crossed the Danube, weeks before. Our collective mistrust sparked talk of war and siege in the leaders' council. Nor were we the first crusaders to fear the rulers of this jeweled city set at the confluence between two worlds. Earlier soldiers of the Cross, including Grandfather, considered storming Constantinople in order to eliminate the risk of treason. Not to mention the prize it would make! Nor was mistrust on our side alone. Emperor Manuel claimed the Fief of Antioch as his vassal state, but not so much as the hint of a fee did he get from its prince, my uncle Raymond.

My spies told me that Louis' chronicler, Odo of Deuil, had nothing good to say about the Greeks, or about me, for that matter. Leaving aside his opinion of me, he nevertheless voiced our peoples' verdict on the Greeks: "They lightly swore whatever they thought would please us, but they neither kept faith with us nor maintained respect for themselves." We approached this people with caution.

Our fears abated somewhat when Louis and Manuel gave each other the kiss of peace, and events went forward from there in fellowship and harmony. The emperor shone with silks, gold and brilliants, a magnificence enhanced by a retinue almost as splendid as he. When Manuel made his first appearance it was as if he stepped from a particolored window in Suger's St. Denis. What we could not outshine we won over by contrast. Louis' simple pilgrim's gown of coarse gray wool embarrassed many of our murmurers, but it spoke to our Franks' and Poitevins' honest intent.

Constantinople! Never have I seen a human dwelling to compare with your delights. Manuel put the Palace of the Blaquernae at our disposal. A line from St. John's Gospel tugged my ear as we trod the tiled floors in those vast and spacious halls: "In my father's house are many mansions." I wonder still: is heaven like that? To this day I recollect pavilions of exquisite beauty, halls letting onto gardens, gardens letting onto paths between commodious apartments. Orchards, bushes, shrubs and lawns of chamomile: all groomed as if by ladies' tailors. Everywhere, inside and out, a presence of air; of tiles, of precious stones, of inlaid work, of art pressed into some service unknown to us which heightened our sense of well-being. Here was space employed in the service of beauty; beauty employed to enhance the commodious use of space. As we walked in the gardens and arched apartments I felt life's burdens slip away. I experienced that liberation of the soul which has sometimes raised my spirits in Poitiers, often in Bordeaux and, God be thanked, here, at Fontevrault. During that month in Constantinople I pondered: surely, the mission of the Church is to bring the faithful into such a state as I enjoyed. I seldom felt such spiritual ease in the priestly world of Paris. Constantinople enjoys Christianity without guilt, splendor without shame, joy in life without reproach. Where, then, does its fault reside?

Nowhere in our lands, neither before nor since, have I encountered such a gulf of "place" twixt majesty and common folk. Great nobles took their seats only after the emperor gave them the nod. Attendants came at beck, bowed, served and went, silently, like ghosts. Servants beyond number stooped and swept to vanish every crumb and nutshell. I compared the fetid rushes on the floors of our great halls with the spotless tiles in the chambers given over to our comfort. Our ladies walked the floors in slippers of squirrel fur, never hazarding their soles on oyster shells or grease or bones.

It came as no surprise that Louis' scribbler, Odo, described a different city. He found good in nothing, To him it was "squalid and fetid," with "many places harmed by permanent darkness" where crimes "which love the darkness are committed" and "not punished by law." Suffice to say, one finds what one's mind elects.

But these are trivia. The sun has passed the window now, and I am cold. My shawl, I think, Aline.

5. AMBUSH, FLOOD, AMBUSH AGAIN
1147-1148

We tarried too long among those splendors. Time came to move on. In fact, that time was long past: we had not departed our native lands until the feast day of the Frankish patron, Saint Denis. Now we crossed the Bosporus in sudden haste, driving into winter, cemented again into an army bound for war.

We had passed the lake at Nicaea when knights from Emperor Conrad's army, much bloodied and battle-torn, rode into our camp. The highland wastes of Anatolia had reduced the Germans to extremes of thirst and hunger, their steeds pawing at the very earth for forage. These were roads better suited to the camels of caravan trains.

In their extremity the army of Germans stopped while their commanders, sick at heart, argued whether to turn back or go on. While his force was in this weakened state, Turkish cavalry on fresh, speedy mounts ambushed Conrad's army, pouring forth from gullies in the mountains like devils from the mouths of hell. The Turks struck like lightning, routing the rabble of foot-soldiers, hunting, killing or enslaving some, leaving others to starve and die. Conrad's cavalry fared little better. Knights had put off their helmets and hauberks, which trailed behind in the baggage wains. Arrows, darts and sling-shots cut down men-at-arms in swathes. The Turks harried the Germans as hounds tear a stag.

Shouting, beseeching and weeping, the emperor's nephew, Barbarossa, begged us hurry to Conrad's aid. Which we did. Louis made haste to press forward, sending out scourers meanwhile to bring in such stragglers as they could find.

Somewhere in this miserable land my grandfather, Guilhem the Troubadour, had met the same fate on his Crusade. He arrived with a force of seventy thousand and escaped with his horse and his limbs. It was that experience, I don't doubt, which renewed his lust for women and life. Returning home from that debacle he made off with my grandmother and sired my mother, Anor. While we struggled through Anatolia I fought the notion that, if Grandfather sired Mother in response to one Crusade, *my* life might be held in mortgage against the next.

Crusade! What loves, lives and *livres* lost.

When we came upon the Germans, Conrad was for turning back. He had lost much of his force, and all his treasure. At a stroke, the mighty emperor had no more riches than a squire. Some of the German barons turned their faces to Constantinople, and thence to home. But we persuaded Conrad and his remaining force to throw in their lot with the Franks. We quickly turned south and west, coasting the blue Aegean shore. How glorious the views across bright water to those steep-walled isles. How beautiful the westering sun as each day drowned beneath the sea. How powerful the clash twixt hope and fear which hung upon our prayers and perils day by day.

Thus we marched until Christmas, although the holy day that year gave no cause for joy. On Christmas Eve we camped twixt coast and mountains in a pleasant, verdant strand where horses grazed such forage as the land provided at that rump end of the year. It was a place where the army could rest to celebrate our Savior's birth. A little stream cut through the meadow, gurgling from the mountains to the sea. It was such a scene as one expects to find in Paradise. Waking on Christmas morning, we heard divine service.

But then the heavens opened in displeasure. Our tents and pavilions, set in that meadow by their hundreds like brightly colored flowers, were overwhelmed by winds that carried some away. Then came rain. There must have been a steady downpour in the mountains to the east, for suddenly the little stream became a rushing torrent, disgorging a mighty wall of water from the highlands. Animals tethered near the river bank drowned at once. Others were swept away, their tethers with them. Men, tents, horses, arms, all were carried off. Baggage wains that had been stationed by the stream now floated off like boats. I saw men, beasts and engines borne away by water flowing faster than a horse can run, then dashed on rocks or swept far out to sea.

Those Germans who had traveled with us to this point had already suffered greatly at the hands of the Turks. Now they decided that our venture was ill-starred. They turned their faces back to Constantinople, taking with them for their journey such treasure as we could ill afford to give.

We were now in great travail, marching along an exposed shore in winter, lashed by gales, pushed every which way by winds. Our mood was grim. Sometimes it seemed that the courage of Louis' pilgrim soul alone held us to our holy purpose and our sacred vows. The priestly members of Louis' company—Oh Lord, they were legion!—toiled with prayers and sought to cleanse the conscience of each one of us. This was a test, some said, a test we must endure. This was an omen, said others, from which we should learn, and turn back.

We endured until winter gales drove us inland, away from the coast. We followed an established road along the north bank of a river which drove straight through a gorge in the mountains. We were moving due east, so that the morning sun rose in the notch between the mountains bordering the valley. One day we were checked by a brief excitement. A party of fanatic Turks attacked us: our men killed some without loss to ourselves; the others soon rode off. Thus we pressed on, arriving after several days at the shell of a city called Laodicea.

This place was useless to us. The town survived on exhausted glory from ancient times. Its people, surrounded by Turks, would offer us nothing in trade. Priests reminded us that these Laodiceans had been rebuked as early as the days of Domitian's persecution: "Because thou sayest, I am rich, and increased with goods, and have need of nothing; and knowest not that thou art wretched and miserable..."[8] So we heeded the word of Jesus and shook the dust of Laodicea off our feet, knowing that this evil city would suffer worse than Sodom and Gomorrah on the final day. But this was small consolation. Our own final day seemed closer to hand than the Laodiceans'. Our plight was desperate.

Our numbers now were somewhat depleted—not an ill in itself, for we were fewer mouths to feed—we had no guides, and we were locked in the mountain fastnesses of Phrygia. We had suffered the hazards of the coast and the ills of the hills, giving us a choice between two devils we knew all too well. Louis' council elected to return us to the coast. So the army turned south-east from Laodicea, through byways and passes so tortuous that even mounted knights passed with difficulty. The baggage wains perforce fell behind, taxing the courage and strength of horses and men alike. These were among the most virtuous days of Louis' life. He was tireless, exhorting stragglers, couraging teamsters and even their teams, stamping his own resolve upon all who saw him. *In extremis*, Louis was a wonder to behold.

But there is more to come. Set down your pen, Aline. Before this matter mends it gets much worse. I have no stomach to relate more miseries today.

Good morning, Aline. You discover me upon my knees. For the first time, is it not? An improving trait in an old queen, don't you think? It shows she can still kneel before a presence greater than her own.

That was a jest, child. Don't look so shocked. I have taken to praying more often of late. It passes the hours. Besides, when one is approaching one's Maker...

No matter. Help me up! You arrive in time to adjust the veil on my barbette.[9] I have lost too much flesh in my face. God's mercy! my cheeks are as thin as a squirrel's at the turning of spring: this thing flaps under my chin. Still, it holds up my hair.

I fear matins and lauds slip past their time to merge into prime these days. You know how lauds ends, of course, with the last three psalms. Some of us old women have taken to interpreting "let them glorify him upon their beds" too literally. We learn to sleep through bells, content that the "merry nightingale rings out all night the never ceasing lauds of God." Bird song is surely more pleasing to our Maker than cracked voices destroying His sleep.

Such naughty excuses! I cannot compare with Louis. He was as punctual with his offices—or do I mean punctilious—as a watchman on his rounds. Let the wind but whisper through the cloister bell of Notre Dame and he was on his knees in dead of night. And the Franks wondered why I gave him but two daughters!

So, to work! Let us put this monstrous day behind us. No, Aline, I don't mean today. I refer to a terrible night and a day in the Phrygian hills.

Are you ready? More ready than I for this sorry tale.

We had shaken off the dust of that terrible town. Where was it? I forget. The trails to the south and east were difficult for anything less footsure than a mule, and we were marching through those passes with an army. The barons took turns day by day to lead the vanguard. On this day it chanced that my high vassal, Geoffroi de Rançon, was commanding the van. He did not have sole command, thank God: that was what saved his life the next day. The king's uncle, the count of Maurienne, was also to blame. And some fault stuck to me. But we'll come to that.

De Rançon and Maurienne had orders to set up camp for the night on a bleak, windswept highland plateau. The place had been scouted and the decision agreed some miles farther back. But when we in the vanguard reached it, scouts discovered a verdant valley just beyond, out of the wind, with plenty of pasture and water for horses. Of course I acquiesced in the decision to move forward to the new location. Why would I not? But after the events of that night, the Franks made sure to spread the rumor that I ordered de Rançon to move off the plateau, into the valley.

As soon as we dropped off the plateau the van lost contact with the main army, which was held to a crawl by the baggage train on that appalling road. The moment we lost contact—did they plan it this way, or was it a fortune of war?—Turkish cavalry spurred out of gullies on both sides and attacked Louis' Franks and the baggage wains. They repeated exactly the tactic they used to put Conrad to rout—and Grandfather, forty-eight years before. We in the well-armed van were aware of nothing. We set up camp and waited for the army to arrive. We waited in vain.

Meanwhile, the Franks were fighting for their lives on the other side of the plateau we had just vacated. Many men-at-arms had put off their chain-mail to help heave baggage wains up that steep trail. War horses were roped to wagons, and knights were straining side by side with wagoners when the Turks attacked. Arrows and stones did their worst.

The horses panicked, pulling wagons by the dozen into the gully bordering the track. Scores of men fell with them to their deaths. In that terrain the army could do nothing but form defensive clusters and beat off the Turks' attacks. Louis, at the rear, became the center of a group where the press was so thick that his bodyguards forced him into a tree. It was nightfall that saved us. Perhaps the Turks had reckoned that our army would reach that point earlier in the day. And no doubt the enemy was looking for the regalia of a king. They mistook Louis, in plain gray wool, for a pilgrim or a monk.

It was after midnight when stragglers and wounded finally reached our tranquil camp. Among the first was our chronicler, Odo. One by one they told the same tale. All Geoffroi could do—with no useful moon—was to set up a defensive perimeter and ready our force for the morning. Just after daybreak a monk brought Louis, barely conscious, into our camp on a horse he found grazing among the dead.

How many did we lose? Men of all stations, in the hundreds; horses by the dozen; wagons of treasure, arms and armor. Still, Fortune did not serve us the same false hand she dealt the Germans. The difficult lie of the land limited the scope of the Turks' attack, and nightfall evened the odds.

After a semblance of order was restored, the Franks convened a court martial and voted to hang Geoffroi despite his inexperience: he was just seventeen. They would have done so, except that Louis' uncle, de Maurienne, had acquiesced in the decision to move our camp ahead. They were jointly responsible for losing contact with the army.

I freely confess that I shared in the guilt. Someone suggested that we had moved from the plateau to enhance the comfort of the women. Well, in that gathering of angry men in bloody garments, each of them armed with hatreds and loss, what could one say?

In years to come, I looked back at that terrible day and saw in it the start of the end between Louis and me. There is no reproach as telling as silence. How many words and tears did I waste upon embittered stillness? In all my life I have never been made so acutely aware of "a woman's place." Wherever that place may be, it was not there; it was not then. No one had dared to say it before, but after that day the role of my "Amazons" was made crystal clear: we were burdens to carry, burdens to fight for, burdens to feed. We were not men.

It was in this temper—with Franks and Poitevins at daggers-drawn, and my women humiliated beyond measure—that the army buried its dead and made a difficult passage to a squalid port on the coast of Phrygia. This town, Adalia,[10] did our army a singular service: its Greek inhabitants proved so disagreeable that the army's unity was partially restored by a common loathing for the people and their place.

To conclude this misery: we took ship from Adalia at ruinous cost, making landfall at the port that lies a two hour ride from Antioch. To our eternal shame we left seven thousand foot-soldiers at Adalia, a city bounded by an inner and an outer wall. Greeks inside the town would neither admit our men nor barter with them. Turks outside the outer wall waited to kill them. We had left two nobles with orders to lead the infantry overland to Antioch—a forty day march for fit troops—but the men were not fit. Their leaders abandoned the attempt, and then abandoned the men.

Trapped between the walls in a no-man's land twixt Greek and Turk, several thousands of our soldiers died of hunger or plague. In time, those who survived the plague forged an alliance with the Moslem Turks—the lesser of two evils in that sewer—against the Christian Greeks. The rabble of France, whom Bernard had recruited to take the Cross, now joined forces with the infidel.

Ah, there goes the merciful bell. Rescued from this burden of humiliation by a summons to prayer. It's time for tierce, Aline. One of the *horae parvae* to be sure, but today I shall observe the merciful small hours, and pray.

6. ANTIOCH, OF PRECIOUS MEMORY
SPRING, 1148

We thrashed around in the belly of that miserable ship like Jonah in his whale for better than two weeks. No, closer to three—the captain blamed contrary winds—and this for a journey which they said took forty days by land.

I was close to weeping with relief when we made port below the city of Antioch. If a host of angry Frankish eyes had not been watching for my every slip I would have kissed the ground and wet it with my tears. When my foot touched solid earth I became as light-headed as if I were alighting at Bordeaux. Lord, such easement of the heart, such weight and pressure lifted from the soul. Raymond came himself to meet us, riding from Antioch at the first sight of our sails, bringing with him choir upon choir to serenade us with both sacred music and profane. So uplifting were those voices after what we had been through, they could have passed for angels.

How we embraced! With relief on my part. But I tell you frankly, if Raymond had not been my uncle, I had taken him for a lover. There,

I've said what I kept in my brains these fifty-six years, though whisperers long ago had their way with me. Not even in my furies, when I sought for darts to hurl at Louis' ears, did I admit my lust. Fearless in battle, they said, and why not? Raymond was built like a bull. He sat a war horse like a centaur, as if he were its flesh. To clap eyes on the man was to savor his gift for command. Had he but commanded me!

Write it down, girl. Write it down. The world allows the old a certain grace.

I had not seen him for perhaps ten years, since I was twelve or thirteen. When I met him again at Antioch—his own vast and wealthy city to command—he reminded me of my father as I knew him in his final years. They were much of an age by then. Yes, Raymond was a Guilhem. Whether he was more like Father, or Grandfather, I couldn't say, but he was worthy of our mighty line.

Raymond had won himself an empire in the sun while I wasted to a pallor on that prison-galley of an island in the Seine. When he met us at the dock it was as if a decade dropped away. What with the splendid welcome he gave us, the procession and the other wonders attendant on our arrival, it was some time before I noticed: during the weeks we had tossed in the entrails of that ship, spring had arrived. Where we had expected a desert, the slopes were newly green, studded with red and blue flowers with velvet black eyes. Even the processional with which the people greeted us—the banners, the choirs, the men-at-arms in panoply of every hue—even these did not compare with the scenery in what Raymond described as the best time of year. Once or twice on that ride from the port to the city I bethought me of what we had escaped. It took time to shiver those fears away.

The road from the port of St. Simeon follows a river valley into the hills to Antioch. One does not see the town clearly from this approach. Only after we had climbed through its streets and markets, where the commerce of the world lay open to our eyes, did we turn to look back at the wonders of that place. Oh Antioch, that "great and dearest city" to which Constantine summoned fathers of the early Church, eight hundred years before. To this day, Aline, there is no citizen of that proud place—Muslim, Christian nor Jew—but knows that the Council of Antioch was a greater event than that at Nicaea.[11]

Looking down on Antioch, Louis and I saw churches mix with minarets, gardens and houses flowing down the mount along a maze of streets, stitching together market colonnades and counting houses, a mix of rich and poor, Christian and Muslim, the life of the place cascading in waves to the tower-studded, all-embracing city wall. To the west lay the very corner of the sea, blue in its deceptive calm, with the mountains of that terrible land beyond.

We would soon discover that Antioch in our time was as it had been through recorded memory, a meeting place for caravans from the south and east, exotic worlds of which we knew little in our homelands on the western ocean. I watched camel-trains leave the city to go north and west to Constantinople along the route we might have taken, and I shuddered at the thought. I remember thinking: whatever lies between Antioch and Constantinople is surely the speediest path to hell.

Aline, forgive me! I gave you no greeting today. Raymond and Antioch so possessed me that I started reporting that glorious day before you had a chance to charge your quill. Hah, now you're thinking that the old woman has trained herself to bark when her mistress, Youth, comes near! No. Age alone does not make me self-obsessed. It is the loneliness. One gets a sense, not of a continuous past slipping smoothly away, but of vanished and vanishing presents. Then, of course, one is also waiting for one's personal present to vanish into whatever purgatory death may hide. Each time I hear the bell I wonder: will these ears live long enough to hear it toll again? If it rings for sext, will I hear it toll for none, then vespers, compline, matins, lauds? Which one will be my final earthly office? What is a month or a minute to this old flesh? Its moment is as protean as the final, lingering glow in an ember ere its orange life snuffs out and rises in a sudden wisp of smoke. So suddenly an end. It's that which drives the urgent mind to empty out its treasury of memory ere it quits.

You would have desired Raymond, Aline. He was power and glory without pretension. A real man.

I t was Raymond whose appeal had brought us to Antioch, Raymond whose cause had already been the indifferent instrument of many a crusader's violent and lonely end. The western lands had rallied to the holy purpose which, in distant Paris, we had taken to be the repair of Edessa.

But we now found that Joscelin, Count of Edessa, had failed to pay his garrison before abandoning the city to take his ease in a fertile river valley to the east. Joscelin was a kinsman to the Capets, thank the Lord. My people were already subject to the biting scorn of Franks and Flemings in the army, but now my Poitevins had cause to point their fingers, too. Joscelin had abandoned his office to the mercies of the Muslims, surrendering Edessa without a blow. This brought the heathen horde to the very frontiers of Antioch.

Small wonder Raymond sought the succor of Crusade. More than two years had passed since Joscelin abandoned Edessa to its fate. Raymond, a brilliant strategist—he played the *jeu de dames* and also chess—had worked through the political implications of several military strategies in great detail. But he needed our troops and support.

His first tactic was therefore to win over Louis, and to shower the Frankish barons with entertainments, presents and the most exotic foods.

We waited some weeks at Antioch, enjoying all that Raymond and his leading families could provide. We were compelled to wait because in those first weeks we still believed—mercifully—that our seven thousand troops would join us, marching from Adalia. We were sure they were on the coast road, ably led by the count of Flanders and Archimbault de Bourbon.

Then, like a thunderclap, the news arrived: what remained of our infantry had gone over to the Turks. It chanced that most of those men had been recruited by Bernard from the middens and sewers of Flanders and France. In the days that followed, Louis led his barons through the darkest councils of his life.

Our chamber faced east, across the tended gardens of the river valley. But it was to the second, smaller window that Louis was drawn. It gave on a view to the south. He would pace the room and then stop, his eyes fixed upon that notch in the hills though which caravans arrive from Alexandria, and from Jerusalem. Raymond had made the mistake—it turned out—of pointing to that fateful gap while we stood on the terrace beneath our chamber. It was just before we entered our apartment on that first, bone-weary day. Jerusalem. Jerusalem. Had the holy city called its name through a ram's horn it could not have drawn Louis' mind more wonderfully than did that distant notch in foreign hills.

He joined me in our chamber the evening after we heard about his infantry. I recall his silence then. After the attack in Phrygia, Louis' silence of reproach had been directed against me. Now he directed it against himself. He himself had chosen a lesson for vespers that evening: "Oh God, the heathen are come into thine inheritance; thy holy temple have they defiled... We are become a reproach to our neighbors, a scorn and a derision to them that are round about us."[12]

We stood in the gathering dusk, holding hands like lovers until the light went from the window to the south. Then Louis turned to that window, where it framed the darkness of new night, and knelt on the floor, his hands clutching, as if in supplication, at the stonework of the sill. I held him while he wept. Perhaps we were never as close as in that sorry hour. Oh Louis, how was it that we were always most in love when you were most tormented? In truth, you were the perfect penitent. Had you ever learned to be your own man, our lives and fates would have been different.

It shocked him, Aline, to ride through Antioch and watch Muslims live their faith as if it had equal claim to the mind and ear of God. They prayed without a shred of shame. He had been raised—I speak of Louis—to find abomination in the least departure from the narrow, monkish way. We were here to drive these people from Palestine, not to return their *salaams* in the market place.

For me, Antioch was home-coming. Constantinople opened my mind to earthly wonders I had never seen, but Antioch compounded wonder with a warmth I had not felt since childhood. In Bordeaux we traded freely with the Moors. They were welcomed for their courtesy and knowledge of the world beyond the confines of our lands. We even made provision for their faith as the price of their trade. I recall their sails in the Garonne. Dark ochre, some of them the color of dry blood. How sad to view the chances that our world affords through the narrow-meshed sieve of monkish fears.

I lived in two worlds at Antioch. By day I would walk or ride with Raymond: we spoke the *langue d'oc*, a light and playful tongue in which he unburdened his soul and his plan to relieve Edessa.

Antioch / the *langue d'oc*. Ah, I am a *trobairitz* once more. Your company does me good, child. I can feel light-hearted again.

When Raymond tired of Louis' councilors I became his sounding board and his messenger to Louis. Raymond would ask: Aleänor, why does he burden himself with those drear souls? I replied: they are his world, the only world he knows. Then we would walk and laugh for hours, lamenting the state of things in our own tongue.

One of my favorite companions—nay, friends, if a queen be permitted friends—on our journey was my vassal, Jaufre Rudel, lord of Blaye, a day's ride from Bordeaux on the Gironde. Jaufre sang us from Paris to Antioch. "Life is short but art endures," he used to say, making that the title of a song. Alas, Jaufre died in Palestine. He fit perfectly in Raymond's court. He taught them to sing his *chansons*. One day Raymond sang me Jaufre's ballad of "faraway love."[13] It goes: "Beloved in a far-off land, / For you my heart is full of woe..." Then: "God has not willed that there be seen / More beauteous Christian here below / Nor Jewess nor fair Saracen." You can imagine how the tongues and pens of Louis' weasels treated our encounter that day.

After the warm and sunny hours with Raymond and the *langue d'oc* I would return to Louis and hear the Franks' pious intentions for Jerusalem expressed in the *langue d'oïl*. The relief of Edessa, so well articulated by Raymond—so sensible—had no place in Frankish plans. And Jerusalem, safe for the time in Christian hands, had no need of a place in Raymond's. My uncle and my husband were of two worlds, and far apart.

There was always risk of a breach between Louis and me. Raymond and his people shared a common background with my Provençeaux. Since the night attack in Phrygia my people had been itching to rebut the scorn the Franks heaped on us. And here we were in a cosmopolitan city, where my lord and king allowed his brains to be chained by a coterie of bishops, by his official note-taker, Odo of Deuil, and by his eunuch, Thierry Galeran. Their gathered folly burned my ears. Louis' entourage, of course, found nothing but fault with me.

Matters came to a head after we learned the fate of the Frankish infantry. My Poitevins were not altogether displeased to have this subtle vengeance on the Franks, who had been openly contemptuous of us since events in Anatolia.

We had been living on Raymond's largesse for more than a month when he demanded a grand council to settle military strategy. One had but to look at a chart to approve the wisdom of his plan: Edessa lies east of Antioch, a check to the Muslim world. To reclaim the city would once more place a bulwark between the heathen and Jerusalem. Raymond made his points to council as persuasively as if he drew on divine guidance. But the Franks would not hear of it. Louis stood up—no match for Raymond in eloquence—and defended his pious intention to lead his army south, to Jerusalem. His mind was not upon matters military, but upon his pilgrim's vow to kneel at holy shrines. Jerusalem was the mote in his eye, the mire in his brains, the obsession of his holy counselors.

Hah! Aline, you should have seen what happened next. Raymond lost his temper such as only a man of my lineage could. Here, once more, stood my father or my grandsire, venting his ire upon wrong-headed bishops and maladroit popes. He raged to the council, he shouted, he screamed, he roared. Somewhere in that torrent of words he asked, correctly, why a king would struggle for eight months to shepherd an army through hazardous lands if his soul's sole motive was to place the oriflamme of France upon an altar at Jerusalem. One ship might serve that task. What need for an army? Was it but a monstrous bodyguard, an escort for a timid king? Did Louis shrink to spill his blood in a truly holy cause?

Such a child, my Louis. Such a fool beyond a fool. He was driven by churchmen who knew nothing of command, understood less, and claimed the special love of Christ to prod better men to their deaths and the ruin of their estates.

After that meeting, the Franks could no longer rest in Raymond's palaces. His fury made the need for rapid egress all too plain.

I too was overcome by rage. I had endured the hardships of the march, seen men lost by their dozens, by their hundreds, and watched my treasure slip away. All waste and death. I wanted no more part of

Frankish folly. The eunuch, Thierry Galeran, was not merely a jailer to Louis' mind; he was his treasurer. And now my monies, my treasure, the sweat of my lands that I had poured into the cause of Louis' Crusade, were denied to me, his queen.

I sniffed the air of Antioch, the freedoms of its mind, its wealth, its ease of heart, and I demanded release. I have hurled hot temper in the face of kings many, many times. But never to the extent that I lost the balance of my humors on that day!

But first I had to force an audience—an audience with my own husband, mark me!—where I demanded a divorce: a divorce from his bed; from his life; from consanguineous marriage; from the House of Capet; from his dynasty; and, most of all, from his miserable priests. I would return to my duchy and my provinces and serve my people as their duchess in right of my line. No more would Capets squander my people's substance, my inheritance. If my king determined to yield his mind to others, then he would yield my wealth to me. Louis might march his swollen bodyguard of Franks to Jerusalem: I and my force would remain in the city, and perhaps in the service, of Raymond of Antioch.

I challenged them: *auferte malum ex vobis.*[14] Nay, I fear I sneered at them. But I no sooner hurled that charge—written into the Templars' rules by Bernard, of course—than I regretted it. Fools they might be, but I should not have mocked those men their faith.

Too much excitement for today. I have to stop. I told you before, Aline: my consent was worth an army, and certainly such an army as Louis', much of which had abandoned Christ for the Turk.

I said what I had to say, then I withdrew. It was enough.

Not until that moment, though, did it occur to those dullards that their foolish policy might cost Louis his queen and the profit of her lands.

After I withdrew, Louis and his councilors had reason to fear. Would he lose half his army, his queen and better than half his treasure in these distant parts? How long they argued their response, I know not. Suffice to say, they sent their minions for me after dark, seized me in my chamber, rushed me to my cart and bound me. Bound me, his queen, with strips of wool and cords! Then, with drapes pulled down and no *adieu* to the kinsman who had nourished us, Louis led his army in full flight from Antioch, making us cowards in the night.

Oh such shame. I blush to think it, still!

Fetch Sister Hortensia! *Vite, vite*, Aline. My heart bursts in my chest. Beg her hither, child. Tincture of valerian root. Too early in the year to take a draught. She knows. Don't waste time staring. Go!

7. JERUSALEM, A PAUSE IN TIME
1148-1149

And that is how we came to Jerusalem. Yes, thank you, I am in better health today.

No, I mustn't start there. Not yet. I want to say something to you: do you see my mistake, Aline? I made the error of challenging a man's world on men's terms and expecting to fight like a woman. But the threat I threw at Louis was too deep. Had I thought it through I would have told my captains my intentions *first*—their resentment had been on the boil since the Franks first threatened to hang de Rançon and then expelled him from Crusade. I should have ordered them to march my men out of the army and thrown myself on the mercy of Raymond before Louis' councilors could act. They never did anything fast: they were divines.

I think we might have worked out some sort of rapprochement. As it was I was bundled into my cart and traveled some hours as a prisoner, gagged, lest my screams alert my Poitevins. I was livid beyond measure. Raymond's rant before the Franks fell short of mine.

But all to no avail. Ah well. As they say in Palestine: the dogs keep barking, but the caravan moves on. Cry as I might, there was no turning back. I never saw Raymond again.

The army paused for rest two hours after dawn. Louis' haste to be gone from Antioch before the muezzin's call to morning prayers meant that we were well along the road. It was then, in the privacy of my cart, that Louis and I had a partial, tearful reconciliation.

Of course, the matter never healed. Never. Not fully.

And, short of a battle between our troops, I would never have loosed sufficient funds from Louis' coffers to buy my forces independence from his Franks—though much of his treasure was mine! And without funds I could assert no independence. No. It was better to play the woman, weep, fall on Louis' chest and await a better opportunity to sever myself from his fate. Besides, I still honored the man. He had the right to my service and devotion.

But why am I telling you this? She should not teach who cannot learn, and this was not the last time I was locked up by a husband.

As it turned out, reconciliation was an urgent matter from the Franks' point of view. While we fretted in my cart, the vanguard reported the dust of a company approaching from Jerusalem. By the time Louis and I had kissed and wiped tears, the emissaries were upon us, led by Fulk, Patriarch of Jerusalem, and escorted by a company of Knights Templar.

Rumors continued to fly about our breach, but the emissaries had no reason to doubt that they found us of one mind.

And that, as I was saying, was how we came into Jerusalem. They came to greet us at the Jaffa Gate, from the highest to the least. We intended to walk the final mile in full humility, but the patriarch bade us ride, that people might take heart and courage from the sight of a mounted host. Young King Baldwin III met us with palms in hand;

his mother, Queen Melisende; and the Emperor Conrad, who had given us up for lost in the Turkish lands. He had wintered in comfort at Constantinople, taking ship in the spring.

I should say that Queen Melisende enjoyed the reputation of being a forceful woman—dangerous, some said—but that is a tag attaching to women of power. Melisende's story was not unlike mine. Suffice to say, I dealt with her carefully. Long before we arrived she had forced the men to accept her presence in the council of state. Melisende became my ears and eyes in Jerusalem.

The press of humanity come to greet us resembled a restless meadow of flowers of every hue, thrust through with palm fronds waved aloft, as if they were saplings thrusting through the throng. Lord, lord, it was as if we were assisting to re-dedicate St. Denis again. Hands reached to touch us, palm fronds rose to stroke our cheeks and men and women kissed the chain-clad feet of passing knights.

Tears, tears all around. Few guessed that many of mine were shed in rage.

The journey from Antioch—mercifully without further incident—had tired us. But Louis—the whole company concurring with good will—would neither rest nor eat until he should have prayed at the Church of the Holy Sepulchre, which was even then being restored by order of Melisende. Thither we went, on foot, in full processional, with palms in hand, as if it were Palm Sunday. There, amid tears and joy and masons' tools—some fainted, with such force did the Holy Spirit come among us—Louis offered the oriflamme of the Franks as a token of Christian humility to the living essence that was Christ.

Now the Spirit threw us down again. Many in our party, myself among them, cast ourselves prostrate upon the floor. What passion lifts our heart? What passion casts our body down upon cold stones? Assuredly a force must grip the heart no whit less firmly than the brains.

You will find this as you grow to age, Aline: one's eternal soul takes and mingles aspects of our mortal span in order to best provision us against the dark. I have always thought that our eternal life must borrow leaven from the peaks and troughs of our too-transient days.

Thus we toured as many holy shrines as we might encompass on that day. At last we retired, weary to the very marrow, but at peace to the inmost soul. The patriarch had readied an apartment in the Tower of David for us.

How to sum Jerusalem? A victory for my spirit; mortification to my flesh. And, for once in my life, almost a year of peace, God-given peace. I found there something of the towering presence of the Holy Ghost.

Forgive me, child. I stray. But such is the very point and purpose of Jerusalem: a pilgrim's mind is bent to higher things.

I spoke of mortification. Where Antioch was a comfortable outpost of Poitou, governed by my kin, the Latin Kingdom of Jerusalem was of Louis' part. The language was the sober *langue d'oil*, the tone was earnest, and discussion unrolled in great solemnity. I wanted no part of the leaders' councils—nor was I welcome—where the mood dripped with the priestly drear that oppressed me all those years in Paris.

But works of the spirit were rapidly set aside. We had spent only one night in Jerusalem before the lords convened a great council to decide policy. More bishops, more priests: churchmen added the fog of incense to the politics of war.

One thing was certain: Edessa might rot for ever in the Muslim yoke. To my eternal anger my uncle Raymond was but a tick beneath a saddle to these overarching men. His strategy, to take Edessa, was interpreted as no more than selfish interest. In part it was, but all of Christendom would have been the victor.

I should explain my opposition to the mischief of strategy that then ensued. Among my Amazons was Sybilla of Anjou, countess of

Flanders—and sister to my future father-in-law, Count Geoffrey of Anjou. Years before, she had been betrothed to the heir to England, who drowned... Oh dear, here I go again, straying into genealogy.

Sybilla met her half-brother, the young King Baldwin III of Jerusalem, for the first time when we reached his city. The father of these two, the late King Fulk of Jerusalem, had formerly been Count of Anjou, where he sired Sybilla on his first wife. But he gave up his Angevin estates in mid-life, leaving them in perfect order, and traveled to Palestine. He came to Jerusalem at the invitation of its king, Baldwin II, to marry Baldwin's daughter, Melisende. Baldwin II's choice of an heir was adroit, for Fulk became the sword and anchor of the Christian kingdom's welfare in Palestine. Fulk's knightly qualities made him the most puissant Christian leader to confront the Muslim scourge. It was generally agreed that his premature death had encouraged the Muslim attack on Edessa. Had he not died in our seventh year, the misfortunes besetting the Christian cause in Palestine would have been averted.

I stray from my point. Sybilla accompanied her lord, Thierry, and their sons Henry and Theodoric, on our Crusade. (Thierry, I should add, was one of those who forsook the seven thousand at Adalia. He had higher ambitions.) The count and countess took the Cross *en famille* to obtain prizes for their sons in Palestine, as befitting grandsons of the late and great King Fulk.

As a ship is driven by wind, so our council of war was driven in sundry ways by the private interests of these and other mighty lords. The Patriarch of Jerusalem and his bishops might steer the council, but they could not, would not steer against the many privy winds. In the end they decided a course of action which benefited no one party more than others. In so doing they neglected to serve their master, Jesus Christ.

A plague on all their plans! When they decided at last to war against Damascus, I could hardly restrain a yawn.

Damascus! The fools. Great lords, base fools. Now even Jerusalem is gone. Gone to Saladin these sixteen years ago. Those men—Louis among them—planted grains of sand instead of seeds! Had they clawed back the frontier at Edessa... Ah, who knows, Aline, who knows?

Of our assault on Damascus, I have little to say except that the waste of life and opportunity assails my breastwork still. Forgive me, I don't mean to sound frivolous. I should not make light of it, but otherwise it hurts.

Had we tasted victory in any measure, I would have taken lasting pride from our Crusade. By all accounts Louis distinguished himself in the thick of battle—and a wife's anxiety is in no way diminished by the knowledge that her husband hazards his life in a tarnished cause. The three kings' attack on Damascus was clouded by the same misplaced counsels that fouled their strategy. A devil's imp was sapping Christendom, of that I have no doubt.

We learned that the attack pressed forward with every hope of success until some foreign opinion ran like a plague through the several commands. This pernicious whisper instructed a change of plan, a drive from another quarter, causing the army to break off attack when it seemed but a blade's length from victory. In consequence the Damascenes—who were unprepared for war—beat us back, leaving every one in our armies demoralized.

Diligent inquiries failed to find the "first mouth" which had done us such hurt. Since we fought in a righteous cause this quirk of the collective mind was soon ascribed to malice by an agent of the devil. How could it have been otherwise? No human agency could so speedily infest so many brains.

Thus ended our Crusade. Emperor Conrad retired forthwith; Louis assigned command of our remaining force to his brother, the Count of Dreux. And so the great part of our Franks and my Poitevins and Provençeaux departed for our lands.

As for me, I had leisure to tour the holy places. Leisure! What a foolish word. Leisure of the body, to be sure, but my soul burned with hurts and despairs beyond measure. What should have been a joy haunted my days as a never-abating taste of wormwood and of gall. From Tancred's Tower to the Mount of Olives; from the Church of Saint Peter to that of Mary Magdalene: Lord help me, but I could not look upon the holy places after the failure at Damascus without a deep, abiding sense of shame. I saw those precious places, but I did not perceive; I saw, but I did not look. I struggled for the year and more we spent in Palestine to remedy my hurt. Not the failure of one attack, but the failure of our mission, the compromise, the flaws. We were beaten before we faced Damascus' walls.

And Louis. How he struggled to make sense of it. He traveled to Antioch, leaving me behind, to seek belated counsel from Raymond and his captains. And to give the kiss of peace and make amends for the sorry manner of our midnight leaving. Months too late! What did wise opinion matter when our army was disbanded, dispatched and put to sea?

Three years of effort; twice three years of revenues; and all for naught.

We tried, Louis and I, to pull personal salvation from the flames. We reasoned that, at the very least, our mutual torments should, like bitter medicine, help heal our rift. He loved me. He loved me dearly, far beyond his marriage vows. I knew and felt his passion for me; we had been wed ten years. He loved me, not as my lord, but as a man, and with all my folly and my willfulness. Yes, Aline, I confess I have long had that reputation.

In a way I can't or shan't describe I loved him, too. I had watched him wrestle with the toils of our army, day after day, persuading hungry, weary men forward through bitter Phrygia. He urged men on by voice alone, with the presence of a sergeant, the love of a shepherd, the valor of a lion. Louis walked at the rear when he could ride; he wore no garment warmer than his men's; he trod as rough-shod as the meanest vagabond on freezing, stony ground while his fur-lined cloak and boots rode free of pain, with the baggage.

Louis, you were the best of pilgrims and the best of sergeants. If only you had not delegated your duties as a general to prideful barons and thin-faced clerks.

We spent long hours together in Jerusalem. He took me to the Sea of Galilee, to the place where the three kings had camped in May before marching on Damascus. Through my own eyes I saw what Christ had seen: the ring of greenness in the desert, the boats, the nets, the fishers, the leaden-gray water. We camped in that place, and we wept.

Meanwhile Suger was writing to Louis: he wrote long, sometimes frantic letters, begging Louis to return to Paris. Our erstwhile allies in the field had returned to their fiefs and their warlike ways. Feuds once more prevailed. Restless barons were urging the count of Dreux to seize his brother's throne and rule in Louis' place. France was again besieged by subtle enemies and debts of war. The aged abbé's untiring diplomacy bought time against these ills, but Suger alone could not withstand them all. Meanwhile Louis and I were seeking a *rapprochement* which, in the end, we could not find. However, despite the urgent letters and alarums we stayed in Jerusalem to celebrate Easter the following year. Had we stayed longer, we would have witnessed the rededication of Melisende's restored Church of the Holy Sepulchre. The occasion marked fifty years of Christian conquest—fifty years since Grandfather's Crusade.

There were times between Christmas and Easter when it seemed that Louis and I were reconciled. Those precious weeks spelled a tranquil time. Indeed, something precious did emerge from that tranquility.

For only the second time in eleven years I found myself with child. Alix, of course. Dear Alix.

Enough! I have choked my lifetime through on the fishbone of that Crusade.

Here, help me to the chapel. I shall speak to Brother Lord Roger: it is timely that my confessor recites the holy offices today. No, no, your arm, Aline. Not that infernal stick. See how the shadow moves. When it touches the next column the bell will toll for none. I feel a need to kneel and pray.

8. In peril on the sea
1149

Our peaceful circle of a year in the holy city came to an end when we took leave of Jerusalem after Easter. The Knights Templar who had escorted us from Antioch the previous year wore the white tabards granted them by Pope Honorius II. Those tabards had been the Templars' mark and pledge of chastity since I was a girl. By the time we followed their black and white standard to Acre, Pope Eugenius had given their order the right to add the red cross, seal and badge of martyrdom. I have held few men in reverence, but in the company of Templars my voice is stilled: I am in awe. Few among them die a natural death. It is said of them: "They ask not the numbers of the foe but only where they may be found."

At Acre we embarked on two ships and sailed into the evening sun. Louis and his household traveled in one vessel, my women and I in the other; our baggage was stowed in both. Louis had long since learned to keep his starveling zealots away from me. That, and the cramped discomfort of those hulls, made for better domestic accommodation.

Of love for each other we had agreed a truce. To spend weeks tossing in a wooden sepulchre with Louis' household would have undone it.

Thus we passed several uneventful days, our two ships showing lanterns on their bow- and stern-castles to keep sight of each other at night.

We had just passed the peninsula of Malea in the Peloponnesus when a ship approached from the opposite direction flying the colors of King Roger of Sicily. Roger being an ally of the Capets, Louis hailed the vessel and went aboard in search of news. Roger's ship, I discovered later, was carrying men-at-arms to war against our erstwhile host, Emperor Manuel. The three vessels were by now in the channel that runs between the tip of Malea and the island of Kithira. Our two ships stood off, some distance upwind of Roger's, where Louis was hearing word of our lands.

Suddenly, several unidentified galleys appeared around the tip of Malea. Running with a following wind, they overtook us where we lay with booms down, stopped in the water. We became fearful, suspecting them for pirates. Too late, our captains hoisted sail. The strange vessels were almost upon us before we saw that they bore the colors of Emperor Manuel, come to war with Roger. Pirate ships or Manuel's, it made no difference. Sniffing easy riches, Manuel's Greeks put boarding parties on my ship and Louis', seizing us as prizes.

You can imagine our terrors: several vessels bristling with Greeks, unblinking lest they take their eyes off women. Beware of Greeks indeed! And the stench from a galley upwind is a fearsome thing. Louis, some distance down-wind in Roger's vessel, evaded capture because the captain had the presence of mind to run up the flag of some fief allied to Greece. Roger's men-at-arms concealed themselves beneath the gunwale, clutching weapons.

Now began a chase such as I could not conceive had I not been the prey, or perhaps the prize. I have been pursued on horseback, yes, but only this once in a naval encounter. Manuel's ships turned about to make off with us. But now the wind stood in their face, so the Greeks had to ply their oars. Their boarding parties put the crews of our two ships to the oars as well, threatening our men with knives and swords, beating them with the flats of blades. Even members of the boarding parties took turns rowing.

Then, to our relief, more Sicilian ships came up with Roger's and, urged ahead by Louis, the Sicilian fleet gained on us slowly, hour after hour, stroke after puny stroke. Manuel's vessels could easily have pulled away—they were war galleys—but they were loath to surrender rich prizes: all those noblemen for ransom; noble ladies for ransom, or worse; and the royal baggage in our two slow-moving *galea.*

Eventually the oarsmen in the Greek war galleys stopped rowing until our ships came up with them. Then the Greeks took off their boarding parties and pulled away at speed. Imagine my relief when the Sicilian fleet came abreast, restoring Louis to his ship.

This, it turned out, was the lesser of our perils, for hardly had this man-made hazard been averted when nature put our vessels in worse jeopardy. Within the hour a storm pushed our ships apart, never to keep company again. A tempest drove my vessel day after day, the captain fearing to shelter in the lee of the Peloponnesus by reason of Manuel's galleys. So he put out to sea. More to the point, he was forced out to sea. He offered an excuse about unusually strong *meltemi* winds that blow off Greece in summer—the very winds that blew those galleys towards us. This meant, the captain said, that he could not navigate without his landmarks: on the other hand, we would ride out the storm with less risk from wind and wave.

Of the next harrowing month I recall mercifully little except perpetual misery in constant motion, as if a steed of the deep trotted every which way at once. Among the women, those who were not violently sick took turns to sing and pray, so that God might mind our fragile lives upon his dire seas. Everyone thought that we would surely die in our leaking, heaving casket. On top of which, I soon discovered I had better cause than most to be sea-sick. I missed my monthly flux. It was during the thirty days that we tossed and rolled from the Peloponnesus to the coast of Africa and thence to a landfall in Sicily, that I discovered I was pregnant.

Sweet Alix. How glorious to be conceived in Jerusalem. But you might have manifest your little life at a much more favorable time!

9. Rescued from the sea; from Louis, no escape
1149-1150

You look pensive today, child. Or perhaps I mean dreamy. I notice a careful accident leaves your all-too-attractive hair astray; from which I deduce that you would like to be the focus of someone's attention. Hah, I can still make you blush!

You are not trying to arouse an old woman, I take it, so I assume he's a man. Don't tuck it in on my account, Aline. Let it hang. We should enlist more beauty here. Who is he? May I know?

Ah, the prospective suitor came to visit! Is he an Englishman? Oh, a Norman with estates in England. I'm much relieved. I didn't think your excellent father would play such a trick as to marry you to an Angle, no matter how well-born. Your family is Norman, of course. From Eskelling Parfura. There, I remember the name of your manor.

I trust your intended had a fair crossing; the Channel can be wicked. He came into Barfleur, of course. The port is greatly improved, thanks to our Angevin links this past fifty years. It's just a year short of that since Henry and I were crowned.

We had me landing, if I recall, although at the time it felt more as if I had been coughed up by the sea. Even the Channel was never as bad as the month I spent in that ship.

In the end our captain managed to find Palermo, in Sicily. King Roger, bless his memory, posted the news of my arrival to Louis, and *vice versa*. Louis was washed ashore in Calabria, expelled from the sea in what he was wearing, with not a penny to his name. Much of his baggage went overboard to lighten his ship in a storm. It was weeks before I could join him, morning-sickness having taken up where *mal de mer* left off. The last thing I wanted was another sea crossing.

I recall a clerk in Louis' retinue trying to console us by telling us that Cape Malea was renowned for its storms. We, apparently, shared the fate of King Menelaus returning from his own crusade—the Trojan war. A storm chased him from Cape Malea to Egypt while his fleet was dashed on the shores of Crete. I was not consoled.

Louis and I were reunited three weeks after I landed at Palermo. He would hardly touch me lest he damage the child. He had waited twelve years for a son. Poor Marie, born to disappoint the Franks; and then there was Alix. Oh well.

We argued despite our expected child. Louis was the spirit of loving forgiveness. But I, in my Poitevin fury, felt I had done nothing requiring forgiveness. The fault lay not in me. Nor did it lie with Louis, but rather with the priestly spies who held the keys to his ears. I gave him due warning. Not for the first time I told him I would seek divorce.

Shortly after landing in Sicily I learned that Raymond of Antioch was dead, killed in battle against the infidel, his head carried off for a caliph's trophy. Such an expressive, strong, wonderful man. This tragedy left me more alone and dejected than ever. Taking courage from the three kings' debacle at Damascus the year before, our enemies had marched on Antioch. Oh, the folly of heeding the policies of prelates! Would that I had had the opportunity to mourn my beloved uncle. Raymond the youth and Raymond the man have never strayed far from my thoughts since that day. But I could not mourn him openly without giving comfort to my enemies and Louis' whisperers.

You can guess how I came to loathe Louis all over again for rejecting sage councils, only to favor the interests of barons and priests. But life carries on. We were no sooner reunited than we paid our respects to King Roger, who was holding summer court in the mountains at Potenza. We were doubly in his debt: his ships had saved us from the Greeks; and he was more than generous when we were both cast ashore in his lands.

From Potenza we rode north to Tusculum, where I made my anguished and thwarted appeal to the pope.

But enough hard matter for today! Let's talk about your hopes and dreams, Aline.

I placed no trust in Emperor Conrad from the start—not since he insisted on marching his army ahead of ours, then abandoning us in Anatolia, only to run away and hibernate in Constantinople. And he used our coin for his passage. Had we not paid for Conrad's retreat, our funds might have bought passage for our rabble to escape the Turks at Adalia. My first impression of Conrad was correct. He no sooner returned from Palestine then he took up his war against the pope. The man was unworthy of the title holy Roman emperor.

For a number of reasons—Conrad, and a certain Arnold of Brescia, among them—we found Pope Eugenius exiled to a hall in Tusculum.[15] Louis and I must have looked as sick as we felt, exhausted and battered. Eugenius was very gracious: the weight of his burdens was not less than ours.

Louis reported our sorry military tale to the pope while offering suggestions for improvement. More than forty years later, my son Richard adopted Louis' first suggestion: he left the rabble at home. That sort of foot-soldier is nothing but a hungry stomach, ill armed, ill armored, quite untrained. A lice-ridden liability. For the cost of feeding the peasantry all the way to Palestine one can send men-at-arms with their horses and forage by sea.

Then I stated my business, the matter of divorce. Oh Louis, looking back, how could I have done that to you? We sat before the pope as man and wife while I asked him to annul our marriage! Pregnant with your second child, too. Well, I was never anything but bold; and wounded afresh by the grievous news of Raymond's death.

I felt I had nothing to lose. I was twenty-seven. Life was passing fast. The only future I foresaw with Louis was a waste of my mortal span in his miserable palace, my every smile and laugh pricked down as seditious by his acolytes. Not that much laugher remained. Over the years my favorite companions—the ones who made life bearable—had renounced our court and gone home.

Don't misunderstand me: I loved Louis as my wedded lord. But his years in the cloister broke his spirit too early, too often. Although I learned to respect his courage on Crusade, our trials confirmed what I already knew: that he would never change. He was condemned to live by the seal that his earlier masters impressed in his brains.

So I threw my best arguments to Pope Eugenius and he—no doubt more impressed by the swelling in my belly than the syllogisms in my head—threw them back again.

Years before, when I came first to Paris, I busied myself in the culture of learning, hoping other aspects of life would somehow rise, like the tide, to keep it company. I could argue syllogisms like a master. You know the sort of thing: Everything that is animal has substance. Mankind has an animal nature. Therefore that which is human has substance. Those three-phrased arguments were very modish in those days. It amounted to playing Grecian logic with words instead of lines drawn in sand. The art of syllogism has long since fallen from favor. The old schoolmen are frowned on nowadays.

But syllogism was all the rage then. In Paris. But not at Tusculum. I was able to show the pope that our marriage was more consanguineous than others for which Bernard had sought and been granted papal annulments. But all my homework went for naught. Bernard or Suger had reached Eugenius before me. Fifteen months had elapsed since my outburst in Antioch. Louis' allies had used that time to fortify the Church against my argument.

Eugenius was very kind. He said I need not worry—yes, worry!—about close degrees of kinship. Our union was divinely ordained. After all our disasters, were we not sitting in his presence together? Had I not conceived in the Holy City? Both spouses had dynastic duties to perform—mine was even then kicking in the womb—and we need worry no more about annulment. Whatever stood in the way of married happiness was henceforth banished by papal dispensation. Then he referred me—I am sure this was Bernard's doing—to a chapter in Ecclesiastes treating of disillusionment. What I found there was: "more bitter than death is the woman whose heart is snares and nets, and whose hands bind him who is good." My standing with the curia vis-à-vis Louis' could not have been made more plain.

In sum, I got short shrift and little satisfaction from the pope. As if to emphasize his point, he had a large and sumptuous bed prepared for us.

Louis was always torn: between Church and state; between holy and secular ties; between duties and rights; and between his role as a soldier and his divinely-appointed mission as a Christian king. During our years together he was the very model of the schoolman's ass: irresolute, tugged by contending forces every which way.

Now another pair of forces struggled in his head. Ever since my outburst at Antioch he had been of two minds. His love for me was wonderfully deep and perfectly genuine, even if it stemmed more from a spirit of Christian charity than from a protective, yearning man. Even as I asked for an annulment he held my hand. On the other hand he sometimes erupted in fury at my attempts to loose myself from his chain. Oh yes, I know what he wrote to Suger from Jerusalem; thoughts he did not entrust even to the discreet Odo. (In fact, in the interest of conjugal peace, Odo did not long remain with Louis after we reached Jerusalem.)

Mentioning Louis' scribe jogs my memory. Take this down, Aline: we met a young Englishman at Tusculum, the pope's secretary, John of Salisbury. The year before I married Louis, this John was studying in Paris with Thomas Becket and the trouble-maker Arnold of Brescia. I have no doubt John of Salisbury was influenced by Peter Abelard: he heard Peter preach at Sainte-Genevieve. As did Arnold, for that matter. Now *there* was a rabble-rouser; an advocate of communes without kings and a Church with neither wealth nor property. He was a great thorn in our host's side. In fact it was Arnold who was responsible for the exile of Pope Eugenius to Tusculum. He had set up a *res publica*, a commune, in Rome. The very idea! But now I stray...

In time, John of Salisbury became a great scholar in the classics. After meeting him at Tusculum, I encountered him five years later, at Henry's court in London. By then he was serving Becket—they were lifelong friends. We'll come to that. Years later he witnessed Becket's murder in Canterbury Cathedral, a sorry tale that we will have to touch upon. There have been many crossings on the paths of John of Salisbury's life and mine.

I pull aside like an old mare, Aline, departing the track to forage in easier pasture. The longer a life, the more byways it wanders, and the more those byways turn back on each other and cross. You must make me answer the rein.

If Pope Eugenius had granted an annulment I would have saved Louis three more years of my irascible company. But it was not to be.

We bade Eugenius farewell, removed for one night to the abbey at Monte Cassino, and thence to a hero's welcome in Rome. How little the

Romans knew! And what wickedness Conrad's troops had wrought on their city. Ruins everywhere. Would that their leader had exercised his murderous zeal against Damascus!

Thence north, through the Jura to Auxerre and a meeting with the long-suffering Suger—and a new round of whispering behind my back.

Do you know, after two years and a half on Crusade, I was almost happy to dismount at the old olive tree and climb those wear-worn steps to the Merovingian palace in Paris.

I tell you a riddle, Aline. As we journeyed to Paris the world got colder in three ways. In the first place, we ended our separate trials by sea in the southern-most part of the land and moved north from there. Secondly, we landed in July, met the pope in August, and the season chilled thereafter until we came to Paris in November. In the third place—and I don't know to what extent my mood was influenced by the tempers of land and air—the closer to Paris we came, the colder my mood became. That impulse came to me as a couplet, and as a couplet it has stayed. I think we were south of Dijon when it entered my head.

The closer our approach to the prison-island in the Seine the more our journey took on the complexion of Louis' homecoming and my return to a cell. How would the Franks react to our maladroit ventures overseas? I had not been alone in my lapses of judgment. Of that I was sure. Willful, maybe; scapegoat for our misadventures, never!

There was another factor to consider. Would the kicking mystery in my womb emerge as a girl, or cause bells to ring forth for a boy? The child had been spared through the full assault and battery of a storm-tossed month at sea. Did that mean the Almighty had a special purpose for our child? Those days of travel gave me too much time to think. They preceded the inevitable return to the wretched *ménage* I had come to detest in the decade before.

Dear Alix! Such a joy to me; such a curse upon her mother for the Franks. She was born in the dead of that worst of all winters when not a bird survived the frost and rivers froze as hard as summer roads. After her birth I was plunged in such melancholy as—I truly believe—I have not endured before or since. And my life has known a full queen's escort of disasters.

There seemed no release. In Paris, even the culture of learning had died. Bernard had long since poisoned the wells from which inquiring minds might drink.

10. Fond thoughts on Fontevrault

Enough of misery! Escape is looming larger in our tale, but I do not choose to fasten on my final years with Louis in the time we have today. Let us seek release in the pleasures of the afternoon. I want to speak of Fontevrault.

In the time of my grandmothers, worthies of the Church spilled earnest ink and heated breath upon this question: do women possess immortal souls? The men who asked that question held that women were but passive vessels for the nurture of their husbands' seed. Think on it, Aline. The very proposition begs a second question: do women give birth to soul-less snakes or to the souls of men? All men are born of women: so, how is it that a beast-like thing, having no soul, gives birth to kings? Pah! I myself have carried God's anointed. Jesus was of woman born. Even a Church whose one good eye looks kindly upon males concedes the truth of that! So how can it be that women have less claim to souls, or claim to lesser souls?

Fontevrault was founded by a man. But he was a man of vision, a man who dared to find his vision far above the book-bound scribbling of woman-loathing priests. He was a strange man, Robert d'Arbrissel. He came from Brittany, a land of Celts whose ancient tales expound on Brithick legends. They tell of magical and healing powers possessed by women of flesh and faerie in the days of the great King Arthur. Celts are not jealous of female arts: rather they revere them.

But the priests of our day know only that the Celts' great wizard Merlin was, like Samson and like Adam, done down by a woman's guile. Or so they say.

It is, I think, no coincidence that both d'Arbrissel and Abelard were Bretons. Something in the mind of male Celts endows Woman with her full measure of humanity.

D'Arbrissel preached a dangerous sedition: poverty, humility and the Christian way. Our bishops forgot those lessons long ago. Worse, he taught that women interpret the maze of the human mind better than do men. Let no man put you down, Aline; least of all a husband. It is women's souls, no less than our bodies, which harbor and nurture the souls of men.

My father was born in the year that Raymond of Toulouse and his crusaders took Jerusalem. That same year, d'Arbrissel brought his followers, women and men, to this place, to Fontevrault. They say it was named for a bandit, Evrault. How tranquil it is now. A hundred years ago this was wild country, claimed by all and settled by none, because our humble abbey marks the borders of Anjou, Touraine and Poitou.

To settle in no-man's-land was a sound strategic move. There could be no better structure than an abbey of poor penitents to mark the boundaries of three conflicting fiefs. Poverty does not attract invasion. D'Arbrissel piled up his first stones with the support of Fulk the Contrary,

Count of Anjou—whose daughter Ermengarde was Grandfather's first
wife. The support the barons gave to Fontevrault was a wise investment
in establishing a peaceful border.

I visited Fontevrault shortly after I married Henry. The abbess at the
time was his aunt, Matilda, who had once been betrothed to Henry I's
only son, Prince William Atheling. He was lost at sea before I was born,
when the *White Ship* went down.[16] Matilda herself died the year we took
the throne of England, I recall.

How strange is fate: the doomed master of that ship, Thomas fitz
Stephen, came nigh to losing us the throne of England. And yet his father, Stephen fitz Airard, was master of the *Mora,* which carried William
to conquest at Hastings three generations before.

I tire, Aline. I tire. No, child, we'll carry on. I have a few words yet.

So many widows here at Fontevrault: so many women put away.
Ermengarde, Grandfather's first wife, was among the first ladies of noble birth to end her days within these walls. And then Phillipia, his
second wife.

Just four years ago my own dear daughter fled here, betrayed by her
men-at-arms. Poor Joanna! In death her body gave birth to a son who
lived sufficient time to be baptized. Would that he had lived! I have
nurtured children all my days. For a moment I held my grandson in my
arms. God, how I mourned.

We must move on! Too many such stories haunt these walls.

After we were estranged, Henry proposed that I come to Fontevrault
as abbess. Abbess! He sought to steal my lands, my towns, my titles—
countess, duchess, queen—in exchange for an empire which spanned
but the wall of this cloister. Abbess!

I do not mean to mock. By the rule of this house, even the community of lay brothers is governed by the abbess. Who better to run
this family of women and men than a widowed woman who has lived
and suffered with her family in the world? Such was the teaching of our

founder, d'Arbrissel. A wise judgment, too, as history shows. Our order has grown rapidly under women's stewardship. D'Arbrissel's choice for our first leader, Hersende, was a widow from Burgundy; her successor, Pétronille de Chemillé, had also been a wife. She served as abbess for almost fifty years. How well she understood the parable of the talents: how great we have grown.

Scorned and cast off by men. Cherished by Fontevrault. So it has been for a century here.

11. Annulled: Fifteen years and one marriage 1151-1152

You know, Aline, I cannot help but feel melancholy when we take this path between the kitchen and the abbey wall. So narrow. All those chimneys. I never troubled to count; they say they number twenty-one. When they all belch smoke at once it looks like the fires of hell. Laundry-women are always complaining. The kitcheners call it Eleanor's tower. When I gave money to build a kitchen I had no idea I would end my days here, blacked by my own smoke. It was later endowed by my Joanna. Fontevrault grows by pieces and bits. Look at it, all those chimneys, like a soot-black turnip sprouting eyes.

We spoke of Alix, born in that dreadful winter. I suppose that it is part of the Almighty's balance that when He gives one life, He takes another. A year after Alix' birth, God saw fit to take Abbé Suger to rest in his bosom. A full year apart, and yet I have always thought of their conjunction as two ends of one balance. Such a humble man. And yet such power! Suger knit the warring factions of one government together through two reigns. And that included my faction, which was not

inconsiderable. It is a measure of his moral force and gift for concilia-
tion that our marriage lasted as long as it did, and that it did not long
outlast Suger.[17]

But the ages will not remember Suger for that: he will be remembered for the new church of St. Denis. Never *his* new church. Quite
properly he scolded me for saying that. His crews were starting work
when I came to Paris as queen. Dust, the shriek of hoists and stone
chips everywhere. It took them seven years from the west end to the
choir. When they had finished it looked as if an ancient, black and rotted caterpillar hatched as a gorgeous moth. How different it looks. No
one had seen a church quite like it. All those curious pointed windows.
They are being copied everywhere.

On a personal level, Suger was a powerful mediator between Louis and
me. I would to God he had been there to lay his hands on us at Antioch.

By the time we returned from Jerusalem he was exhausted. He met
us at Auxerre after my failed entreaty to the pope. I suspect our journey
back to Paris that November took some months off his life.

Dear Suger. It was you who proposed marriage to me on behalf of
Louis—or, as a matter of protocol, were you acting for his father? Never
mind. You did it so well. Would that I had wed Suger! No, no, don't
write that down. It's a joke, Aline. You are a serious girl! Suger had been
at Notre Dame since he was nine. And yet he spoke so fluently of love
and marriage—and of marital strife.

His death marked us all. Without his unstinting counsel the rift between Louis and me inevitably grew. It came to be a weeping ulcer: it
would not heal. No amount of lotion, potion or poultice could restore
a middle way.

And then I gave birth to a girl—another girl—after thirteen years
of marriage. Alix' birth, and the death of Suger—the combination was
fatal to our marriage. By that time it was better that the final split should
come sooner than late.

Suger died at the hind end of winter. He lingered, as old people will, until first buds attest the renewal of life in the spring. If I live another year, Aline, shall I see spring? Tush, child, no need to remonstrate. I'm but an old dame fussing.

In the heat of the following summer, Count Geoffrey of Anjou came to Paris to do homage to Louis. People called him Planta-genest, because it was his whimsy to wear a sprig of broom in his hat. Geoffrey came belatedly, at Louis' tactful insistence, but he did come. And he brought his son Henry, duke of Normandy.

The Capets knew where we stood with these two. Listen to me, saying "we"! I have made and unmade so many alliances I lose the thread. Geoffrey was the son of Count Fulk of Anjou by the first marriage. Fulk, you recall, left Anjou in mid-life to marry Melisende and rule Jerusalem.

My own father had had wars enough with the counts of Anjou to give me a clear vision of Geoffrey and his politics. His son Henry was a different matter, and not as handsome as his father. Henry had a straightforward title to the duchy of Normandy but—this was the talk at court—he was a pretender on his mother's side to the throne of England.

The two of them arrived at court with a prisoner, a high official of the Franks who had slighted Geoffrey in some way. What a remarkable affront to Louis! The very thought!—hauling Louis' seneschal under guard to Louis' court.

Of course Abbé Bernard saw fit to chastise Geoffrey for his conduct. To which the latter retorted with blasphemy, which won him my respect. Whispers spread—and this was disturbing in the light of events—that the abbé promptly predicted for Geoffrey an early death. Then someone remembered that Bernard had examined Geoffrey's first-born, Henry, when he was but an infant eighteen years before, and pronounced an evil end for him as well: "From the devil he came; to the devil he shall return." Of course that nasty gobbet of old slander found new life while the Angevins lodged at our court. Such a sour prejudice to pronounce upon an infant, especially from so lofty a perch as Bernard's. Certainly uncalled for. We may take it that our sainted abbé had small liking for the Angevins.

Nevertheless, this was the pair, father and son, whom we entertained at Paris.

The Franks have unleashed scurrilous rumors, hounding me for years with the suggestion that I, a wife, encouraged Geoffrey's attentions and succumbed to his advances. Malice has me bedding both the father and the son; it stops just short of maligning the Holy Ghost! Mark me, Aline, Fontevrault is full of women whose husbands have found younger, richer, fairer fare to grace their boards and beds. But let a woman only glance at beauty in a man and she is termed a whore.

No, it was no fault of mine if Geoffrey heard the buzz—surely the talk of every hall and hearth, highborn and low—that Louis and I were often at daggers' drawn. Foul-breathed rumor has me saying: "I thought to have married a king but find I have wed a monk." I rather think the whisperers have inked my voice upon a notion that was plain to every eye.

Both of the Angevins found me attractive, of that there was no doubt. I was but twenty-nine, still beautiful. Past first bloom perhaps, a touch of mottle on the rose, but not without the subtle charms a man may find enticing in a woman of, shall we say, experience. I ask myself: did I entice? And I answer: would a king wish anything less in his queen than grace? Did I dress to catch men's eyes? Would a king wish his queen to appear dowdy? Of course I was careful to uphold, even to set, the fashions of the day.

I laughed and joked with our guests. Would a king wish his queen to be sullen with them? Would he wish her to deny them her brightest conversation, the very latest news? Is it not a husband's privilege to take pleasure in others' envy of his lady's charms?

When I wore oil of violets I took care my husband sniffed it first: no matter that Louis preferred the whiff of incense.

How is it, Aline, that violet flowers have no scent in autumn? And those that grow in spring, though scented, award the nose one whiff, just one, and then benumb the sense of smell. That is how men sniff women. Oh yes. In the spring of her womanhood they seek to conquer and move on. In her autumn, all allure is gone.

So, may a young queen not act her age when she is young? And if not, when? Must wrinkles plough her face before she can express the spring and summer of her beauty? Must she wait for winter in order to act her youth as well as age? There is no sin in a touch of flattery; nor does sin lurk in a gentle touch. Where is the sin in a laugh, in a whisper?—unless, of course, the hair shirts among Louis' companions observed and marked it down.

If I seem to toy with you, Aline, forgive me. I do not mean to. Truth or a lie may hide in a glance. Betrayal or loyalty may lurk in the slightest smile. Does a lie need words; does truth require a sermon? Posterity asks: what happened between those two proud Angevins and me? To tell truth—for I value the verdict of posterity—wishes may resolve to deeds without an uttering.

So it was in that hot summer. Fifteen years before, Louis the Fat had allianced France to me, not least to put the pincers on Anjou. Now these two proud Angevins remarked my dissatisfaction, and no doubt schemed to put the Franks between the anvil of Poitou-Aquitaine, and the hammer of Anjou.

For my part, I sought escape.

Even if the lies about me had been true—rumor shouted that I sought escape from Louis in the arms of Geoffrey—my supposed plan would soon have been undone. Geoffrey left us to ride to Angers. Approaching Le Mans, he plunged into the River Loir to quench the heat of day. Taking a chill, he quenched his life instead. Geoffrey Planta-genest, count of Anjou, was much the same age as my father when he died on his fatal pilgrimage. My father, too, had been the butt of Bernard's dire pronouncements from time to time.

To carry this mischief further, why would I seek escape from a king in the arms of a duke twelve years my junior? I speak of Geoffrey's son, Henry. The whisperers argued: he may become king of the English. But I was already queen of the Franks. Though the metal be tarnished, one does not lightly quit gold for lead.

If some matters are dark to history, that is because they should be so. Important events steal up on their protagonists. Thus it was with us.

What happened, happened. What happened, came about. The inevitable found the moment of its time.

Let me lay this down in ink: there was no betrayal on my part, no pact—unless it were with boredom, boredom to the quick, and gross dissatisfaction.

Nevertheless, the moment of the Angevins' departure marked a watershed in relations between Louis and me. What filth did his counselors spit in his ears? We could no longer endure. With as much discretion as remained to us, we set forth in the autumn of the year on a formal progress through Aquitaine. The administrative offices and garrisons of France and of my lands had mingled as long as our marriage. So it fell to us to divorce the details before we were put asunder.

Louis was accompanied on that mission by one whom I had little cause to love. I speak of the eunuch Thierry Galeran. For my part, the archbishop of Bordeaux had fluent knowledge of affairs in Aquitaine. I fear that the size of our train, its wealth of long-faced clerks and the silent hostility of our mien announced our purpose louder than a speech.

We lingered in the south through the harvest. Perhaps, while the weather held, movement itself and the pace of activities served to postpone the moment of parting.

I was not without sadness in the matter. Relief, yes; but sadness, too. In my own light I had not failed our marriage. Had Louis been able to throw off his burden of doctrine and guilt for just two days in every week we might have endured. A life-path interrupted is no small thing.

But at last we turned our faces to the north and parted in Poitou. Then came winter.

Louis loved me, you know. He loved me as if my body and soul were free of blemish. He loved me because he was a Christian, and because I was impossible.

The process of divorce itself fell just before Palm Sunday.[18] At Beaugency on the Loire. It was one of Louis' castles close to the border of Poitou. Our counselors decided on it so that I might come away from the proceeding and cross into my province without hindrance. Events put the lie to that.

The arbiters empanelled for the conclave formed a most impressive gathering. My first glance at these men hinted at the sunlit saints and apostles looking down from Suger's leaded lights in St. Denis: three archbishops, bishops by the dozen and a veritable tourney of nobles and knights.

See how I make light of it, Aline. I must. And yet I do not mean to.

Our counselors had established the evidence to our mutual satisfaction long before we came to Beaugency. Agreed grounds were put by Louis' side: our marriage was annulled by cause of consanguinity within the fourth degree. What else! Mercifully, even Bernard chose to shut his eyes to the fact that, before we married, our lines had not mingled for a hundred and sixty years. I had preached our sin of consanguinity from Antioch to Rome. In fact, not since Adelaide of Poitiers married Hugh, the first Capetian king, had Guilhems and Capets been linked

The Franks kept ward of my girls: Marie; and tiny Alix, one year old. They were soon packed off to Champagne and Blois, the households to which they were betrothed. As a practical matter, I would not have seen much more of them had I stayed in Paris. As it happened, in the years to come not only my daughters by Louis but all of my children lodged beneath my roof to further their education. Even after Henry and I were estranged. There, talk of two estrangements with one breath! It is time to bring this matter to a close.

So, Louis, here it ends between us. Divorce was done at Beaugency. Without hostility, I bid you fond farewell.

Where do we pick up the thread, Aline? Ah yes, divorce. The bitter matter of the thing was done, but my way home was pitted with troubles. I should have insisted on a royal escort to the border of Poitou.

Being once more the wealthiest unmarried heiress in Christendom, I was now fair game to fetch a ransom. Near Blois we had a narrow escape from men-at-arms in the pay of Thibault, son of the late count of Champagne. This was the family whose lands we had sacked in consequence of Pétronille's failed marriage. I was lucky to escape by night.

Nor was that all. At Tours my angel warned me from a certain ford across the Loire. Straightway I ordered my escort to take another, longer route into Poitou. My familiar spirit's warning proved correct. We discovered later that young Geoffrey of Anjou waited in ambush at the ford to seize me. And him a mere boy. Never had a razor touched his baby cheek, although his scrawny neck deserved an axe. This stripling hoped to ransom me or—God save me!—possess my person and my lands. He had neither asked nor received sanction for this doubtful enterprise from his brother Henry, duke of Normandy. Young Geoffrey was sixteen. Another mad Angevin.

I tell you, Aline, to be a woman *seule* is next to being carrion.

Thus it was that I, Aleänor, lately queen of France, came chased into Poitiers like a hind in mid-March.

Power of a Woman
✝✝✝

Part 2, Destined for England

12. Of marriage and love, estates far apart
1152-1153

Thanks be to Poitiers. I was grateful to come home to my city of gray stone. I always thought of it as home until the stream of my life bore me into the shallows and cast me up at Fontevrault. For which I am not ungrateful. However, wherever life took me, my mind returned to the thought of a still point, a center: Poitiers.

Thus I returned to the Maubergeon tower, which Grandfather built to house his prize, my grandmother. I went back to the Maubergeon, to the very chamber where Louis and I tasted one meaning of marriage. In that instant I felt suddenly alone. It was inevitable, and yet so keenly felt.

So long ago.

But not for long. I had intimations about the Angevins, father and son. Their parting from Paris had not been without backward glances and certain expressions of interest. The father was dead within days, but the son, Henry, very much alive.

It was after Lent when I received an emissary, come to pay respects on behalf of his master, Henry duke of Normandy. In essence the man's private message was: would I do his grace the honor of according him an audience? Well, of course. Why would I not?

I was assured that Duke Henry regretted the indignity plotted against my person by his younger brother, Geoffrey of Anjou. He, Henry, had chastised the cadet of his family—in so far as one could chasten a rebellious young bull. As for the other assailant, Thibault, it was—as I surely knew—Duke Henry's intention to upset that family's ambition at the first opportunity. Though he insisted on speaking through the subtle side of his mouth, Henry's messenger was confiding stale news: Thibault the younger was nephew to Stephen, King of England. Henry's mother, the dowager Matilda, had warred against Stephen for years to claim the English throne. Henry would renew the clash with fresh ardour.

Spring is for travelling, when roads are dry and hard, while flowers bloom beside the way. Spring is for mating, too. Hardly had Henry's man ridden north past the Abbey of Montierneuf on the outskirts of Poitiers before his master spurred south from Lisieux in his stead. Brash, arrogant, strong, set about by a mop of Norman curls and the muscles of a butcher. That was Henry. His head was too big for his body. He had the ruddy complexion which speaks a quick temper. A man of action. Not of action before thought, but never a man of contemplation.

I would be lying if I said that my thoughts about marriage to Henry were wholly dynastic. Of course that was the overriding aspect: he offered the only opportunity equal to the one I had for fifteen years enjoyed. But Henry lent an animal appeal to a young women's yearnings, an appeal which a garrison of men such as Louis could not match. Henry was a lion of a man. A lion in body, a lion in mind and, so far as I could tell, a man without fear at all.

Those qualities made Henry a trial to endure. He was another like Raymond of Antioch. And almost the age of Raymond when, twenty years before, the child in me fell in love with his flamboyant youth at Poitiers. Since then I had traveled and camped—the object of lust among needy men—from Paris to Palestine. Moreover, I had learned to bully vassals, Louis' as well as mine. In consequence, I thought I could manage Henry, within marriage or without. But no chain on earth could hold him. The man was dangerous. I soon discovered that. In Henry I met my equal, and eventually my master.

Nevertheless, barely had the ink dried on my severance from the Franks when, on the eighteenth day of May, Henry and I were wed at Poitiers. I would not lie with him in the same bed I had shared with Louis. Not that sentiment mattered. Where Louis approached carnal knowledge as if choirs of angels looked on, Henry was a stag in rut, and never out of season.

You seem less timid when I speak of men, Aline. Being in the company of your betrothed has given you more confidence. Remember what I said: men are born with worldly advantage on their side. We must be direct, or we must be subtle. But never capitulate. Never yield.

Henry was certainly not displeased with me. God's me! Coming after Louis, I never thought to know the like of him in bed. He was a heaving, wrestling battering-ram of an over-strong boy—eighteen years old to my thirty. I earned my new title, Aleänor, duchess of Normandy, through trial by battle in bed.

Aha, I see you catch up with the world, Aline. You are allowed to laugh.

Well, I should not have been surprised. His grandfather, Henry Beauclerc, had issue by thirteen women—and only one of them a legitimate heir! By the way, this may interest you: one of his daughters by Sibyl Corbet, they christened Aline. Alice Aline. Enough of history! I have made the leap from Louis to Henry, and bedded the bull. In consequence, I am with calf. That is sufficient for now. Let us contrive an interval, a time to discover softer things than state. We shall speak of art.

How is your young man, Aline? Improving his French? Ah, if he was born in England that explains his want of it. One plays with peasant children and quickly speaks their language better than one's own. A coarse tongue, English, but robust enough for peasants trading swine.

Do you have a sense of poetry, child? No? Normans are not renowned for poetry. Solid, heavy churches are more the Norman style. *Trobar* is properly a thing of the *langue d'oc*, a creature of the south, of the sun; of a land which holds women in respect. Unlike the Capets' Paris. Never mind. Try pricking this down:

> "Her body slender, fresh and fair,
> Her beauty, worth and subtle wit,
> Her virtues more than I can tell..."

You struggle with your pen, but surely I should find some softening in your eyes. Don't frown so; you'll crease your brow. Have you not heard those lines, Aline? Tsk, tsk, you *are* a country girl. Were I younger I should breed you up at court. Those words come from a living epitaph, locked in time, the way a poet saw a young and beautiful Queen Aleänor half a century ago.

It was Grandfather who shaped our language to high art but, as good as he was, it is no disloyalty to say that Bernart of Ventadorn crafted better verse.

A year or two before I went to London, Bernart entered my households in Poitiers and Angers. He was a perfect exponent of *l'amour courtois*. Too perfect! A man of words and a man of his word, especially when it came to *joi d'amor*. To put it bluntly, he wanted me. From him I sought diversion and compliments. The best *trobar* should be a mirror to one's own best thoughts of self.

Bernart had lost the patronage of his first master, Viscount Eble, by making too strong an impression on Eble's wife, Marguerite de Turenne.

Bernart's lyrics were not only excellent, but explicit: one gathers the lady rewarded the poet with more than her eyes and her smile. Bernart was born of a bowman and a scullion in Eble's castle. He should have known better than to stray across the line.

That was the year I wed Henry. Dismissed by Eble, Bernart came north and sought to set my twice-wed heart on fire. His history escorted him, of course: the stew-pot of a castle hall allows few secrets.

Whispers followed Bernart everywhere. His sword is not a man's only dangerous point, but a duchess twice over could hardly refuse patronage to the best poet in the western lands. After Louis was rid of me, he expelled every trace of poetry from Paris. *L'amour courtois* was not for him. Which was why troubadours approached my courts in search of a roof and a crust.

And why should I not indulge? *Trobar* is a celebration of nature and light, of earth and air; *trobar* suspends the circle of time, halting the press of affairs and the ills of world and body. In so doing *trobar* preserves precious moments, permits wonder at the fragile security of love. It whispers secret messages in praise of old beliefs which country people still respect; it speaks to the essence of being. *Trobar* still speaks, with a fainter voice, of gods in the earth and the air; not of God as a liege-lord in heaven above. *Trobar* rewards its listeners with a scaling-ladder into the sublime.

Enough of heresy. Suffice to say: from Henry I got bed; from Bernart I won compliments upon the miracle that was my being. What does any woman want?—pursuit by men's eyes, or a reassurance that is hard to find among the dirt-infested rushes of a hall.

Unfortunately, word of Bernart's verse reached Henry: his spies were as good as mine. He summoned Bernart to London, poor wretch, whence he sent back laments while he coughed in the fog:

"When the cool breeze blows hither
From the land where you dwell,
Methinks I do feel
A wind from Paradise..."

You smile at last, Aline. You caught an old woman sighing: for a po-et's passion; for the instant of it that is trapped like a fly in amber while time carries lives away. Yes, it is true. There is much *amor* in *l'amour courtois*. But it is the pining for an unrequited passion that imposes life-long love.

Henry was a cunning devil. Bernart had not long been on the scene before Henry imagined two hearts in one basket. He was, as the trouba-dours term it, *jaloux*. Thereafter, no matter how affairs of state pressed him, Henry kept Bernart on the opposite side of the Channel from the object of his homage.

"My spirit yonder flies,
My body here remains,
In France, far from my love..."

You can guess when he wrote that: I was in London or Oxford; he, in Angers. He abandoned my court before I could return. Henry assigned me to England, where I sat as regent for the first seven years of our reign; so Bernart turned his feet to the sun and served two patrons in the south for many years. We were much of an age, Bernart and I. Much of an age, much of a liking, much of a lust. But I was in love with a young, jealous king-in-waiting, pregnant and—above all, I was no fool.

Words in the air brought word that Bernart became a monk in old age. Better that a man of threescore years and ten should pray too much than starve for want of charity. Dead now, surely. My own troubles were such this past ten years he almost fled my head. Sometimes, in the still of the night, when nightingales sing… But the trapped moments I spoke of survive in his words; they thrust through time. The man may be dead, but his essence lives on.

The lady sighs. Yes, write that down, Aline. Why not? The old queen wipes a tear and sighs. I was mistress of kingdoms and duchies and counties and men. But Bernart's was a love that I dared not command.

13. An inter-regnum in Angers
1153-1154

I fear we must return to war and politics.

I was a single woman for just eight weeks. I cannot say why the Frankish council failed to consider that I might make the most favorable marriage open to me. Marriage to Henry showed every promise of restoring me to the rank I held with Louis. Perhaps Louis' overriding need to wed a wife who would give him a son was such a cloud as to block out other lights. His council could no longer call on the farsighted wisdom of Suger. Dead too were Louis' cousin, Raoul, and Thibault of Champagne. Those three were the first emissaries from Louis the Fat to cross the Garonne sixteen years before, when they asked for my hand.

Henry's first intention was to marry me and sail straightway to England in pursuit of his quest for the crown. But it was clear to me that the Franks would respond to our marriage as to a great affront.

If they had given any thought to the possibility of Henry's match with me they had surely banished it from their minds—in the way of legalists—because our marriage was illegal. As Louis' vassal in right of Normandy, Henry was bound to ask the king's permission to marry. He did not. Nor did I in right of Poitou. Permission would have been refused.

The Franks responded as I knew they must: with armed sorties. Now I had new enemies. Among them Louis and his brother, whom the barons had sought to crown while Louis and I tarried in Jerusalem. No bloodshed is as bloody as a family fight. The houses of Champagne and Blois sided with the Capets. So did King Stephen's vassals. These forces sought to reward our affront to the Franks by seizing Aquitaine and Poitou. But Henry was more than equal to their challenge.

The year before, Louis and I had spent the months of harvest on a tense royal progress through my lands, dismantling our joint administrations. Now I retraced parts of that route, this time with Henry, building again. For him it was a voyage of discovery; for me a wondrous easing of the mind, a time to loose the free spirit I kept in check through all those years with Louis.

I say "easing." If release of a mind can also spring its body from a trap, such was my reward. It was during those mellowing months in the distant south—in Gascony, perhaps—that I conceived our firstborn son.

Just after Epiphany Henry took leave of me and sailed to England in company with more than twenty ships. We agreed that during his absence I would govern his lands and mine. To that effect I moved my household to Angers.

Here was a graceful city, a place of high and cultured learning equal to Paris in every respect, except that distant Clairvaux had not managed to stamp Angers with a proper Christian sense of guilt and shame. It was in Angers that Héloïse, the love of Peter Abelard, received a schooling inferior to no man. Ah, how Héloïse could speak of love, preferring, as she put it, "love to matrimony, liberty to chains."

> "If Augustus, master of the world, offered me his hand in marriage and gave me command of the universe, I should still deem it more eligible and more honorable to be called the mistress of Abelard than the wife of Caesar."

In part that is true, Aline; and I speak as the widow of two caesars. Ah, for the freedom to go to the wall, to rest awhile at the edge of the chessboard of state! The mind of Héloïse owed much to Angers. Its liberty was not in those days confined by the shackles of Clairvaux. Gaiety was graven on the very landscape of green hills cut through by the Mayenne, the bucolic tempo of whose waters set the pace for lives lived on its banks. In the same way that Bordeaux preserves something of the flavor of Roman tolerance, so Angers practises a Christianity of an older, humane strain. At least, it did in my day.

It was to this hospitable city that I came while Henry was in England: and it was there that I found the liberty to place the arts upon a pedestal and proclaim the world of love and nature through the songs of troubadours.

In those days at Angers, and in later years, when I settled my court at Poitiers, I filled my halls with song through which women and men might realize their humors—by which I mean freely-felt emotions. The mind must needs a forum where a heart is freed to find release in the ideal love of another.

It was for daring to think freely that the Church silenced Abelard. His words took root in a soul-life of intense and honest feeling which the world saw fit to banish, unexpressed. Who could resist, during my first years in Paris, being moved by the murmured reports of his scandalous sermons? Peter's message spread like ripples on a pond. I confess he roused me no less than he roused my women. Héloïse could rightly boast her scorn for all who craved his glance or smile!

> "Married and unmarried women, when Abelard was absent, longed for his company; and when he was present, every bosom was on fire. There was no lady of distinction, no princess, who did not envy Héloïse possession of her Abelard."

Love, or faith? Which would conquer, which prevail? That was the real point of argument for which the Church broke down his door. Would that Abelard had chosen to preach to Anjou or Poitou instead of spilling his mind in the dust of Paris!

As a child, long before I learned of Abelard I listened to songs about the legends of an ancient British king called Arthur. Among my earliest memories is a wild-looking Welshman who, Nana said, regaled Grandfather's court in the olden days with poems about forbidden love twixt Tristan and Iseult. Well, that was what Nana said, and what did I, a mere child, know about trysts? While this fellow plucked his harp I perceived nothing but the dirt under his fingernails: Nana smacked my hands for dirty nails. His name was Bleheris. I gather he sang and recited wonderful tales. *Singan ond secgan*, to sing and to say, as the English express it.

Later, at our court in London, bards spoke his name with reverence. Bleheris was *famosus ille fabulator*, that renowned story-teller from Wales who breathed life into ancient tales of Tristan, Iseult and a knight called Gawain. In the next breath they would mention that his father entertained the Conqueror himself.[19] Ah, Bleheris. What does a child make of a living legend, Aline? He had a marvelous voice, but he attempted *langue d'oi* in an accent I would not hear again until I listened to Welshmen speak, in London. I remember his face, but his stories? They only come to mind because Father and, I think, Mother explained them to me. So long ago.

Aline, it may be hard for you to grasp, but those of us endowed with southern humors understand that subtle love demands to be expressed. How else will a woman, betrothed from childhood and living in her future husband's hall, experience the flowering of true desires? I myself knew a childhood of excitement and release followed by a marriage in a world of cool repression. Who better than I to extol *trobar*, employing it to find a point of balance in the games the human heart is bound to play?

For my patronage of courtly love, as for much else that I have done, I have been condemned. But why should she be branded "heretic" who endows a force of nature with its very heart?

Days pressed pleasantly at Angers. One could listen and debate with perfect respect for different opinions. No sullen voices. The mood was everywhere of openness.

Henry wished me to reside there to manage affairs in Anjou. In truth, Anjou's affairs had been rendered in good order since the days of his grandfather, Fulk of Jerusalem. Henry's seneschals had matters under constant oversight. I came to realize that Henry chose to place me in Angers the better to defend me from the Franks. Had I stopped at Poitiers I could have told him that my Poitevins were more than equal to that task.

In the event, I had much time in Angers for the counsels of scholars and troubadours, and for inward contemplation.

My pleasant interlude was rudely jolted when Henry returned from England the following April. More confident than ever that he would win the crown, Henry behaved like a bull in a flock of geese. He would no sooner come upon a group of retainers than he set them running on errands: now he was planning to take England; now surprising vassals with unannounced visits; now reinforcing castles on the borders to repel the Franks; now probing the Vexin; now trading news with market women as casually as if he were a country juggler. Henry had time to listen to everyone except fools. He had little time for hearing books, but he spilled their contents into his head by engaging wise advisors in discussion. He could answer points of trivia raised in a thousand books.

He was a man of boundless, restless energy. Often he would not sit at board, but must take a joint of meat and pace along the table asking the price of this, the quality of that and how the world fared, usually consulting those best placed to know—the people sitting below the salt.

Among his adventures great and small he found the time to conduct me on a royal progress through the fief to which I now claimed title: Normandy. Here I first set eyes upon the Channel coast. How different the cold, gray fury of these waters from the sunlit, sparkling ocean we observe along our western shores. I wondered if the land beyond was as rough and restless as the sea defending it. In time I would find out. How often I made that dreadful crossing in storm at every season of the year.

One does not marry a husband. One marries a husband's family, that family's history and, moreover, its aspirations.

My dealings with Louis' mother, Adela of Maurienne, had been polite, minimal and, for the most part, distant. It would be fair to say that Adela disapproved of me and of my courtiers. She had never seen fit to extend a woman's voice into government, and made no secret of her disdain for my attempts to do so. Adela removed from Paris soon after I arrived at the Merovingian palace. Which was as well for both of us. Thereafter I saw her seldom: the notable exception was her presence at Suger's re-dedication of St. Denis.

In contrast, Henry's mother nurtured a very different complement of humors. Matilda Empress, as she styled herself, was born of Matilda of Scotland and contracted in marriage to the holy Roman emperor, who also ruled Saxony. The court intrigues of Aachen had tempered Matilda to hard steel. There was not a man whose measure she could not assess. Matilda was articulate, educated, a patron to practical men and practical policies, and above all she was the counselor who held and commanded Henry's ear. Whatever Matilda suggested—or do I mean "commanded"?—had much to commend it.

This was the woman whose confidence I had to win. Despite initial trepidation on my part—the lady had a reputation to be feared—we became allies, even confidants. Although it must be said that I confided more than she. Friendship is too strong a word. But I came in a short time to command her respect.

Matilda's approach to command was closer to what I observed as a girl in Poitou than as a queen cloistered in Paris. There the similarity ended. Father was for ever fighting his vassals—how hot-headed he now seems—whereas the Angevins strove to command loyalty by holding inducements within sniff of men's noses, as if training dogs with meat. Better the meat than a beating! By which I mean it is better to train a man to loyalty by trailing promises than to drive him to fear and treachery through punishments.

Matilda was—did I say steel?—nay, harder than steel: she was as garnet. Less hot-headed than I in my thirty-one years to that time, but a lady of great merit. I think our outlook on power shared the same pod.

I recall our first meeting. She sat, enthroned in royal purple as befitted her rank, hoping to test me. Henry presented me. Matilda did not speak and would not take her eyes off me. She tried to stare me down. So I stared back, my eyes confronting hers: they were as dark as a Scottish winter. Clergy, notables and women stood arrayed on either side of her, for all the world as if I were a tattered juggler thrown a coin and told to entertain.

So I did. How many heartbeats passed before I spoke, I know not. Ten, eleven? Perhaps the span of a *Paternoster*. There we were, a spear-length apart, staring like cats across a mouse. Not a figure in the company moved. She had planned this odd greeting. That much was clear.

When it was obvious that I must speak first, I said: "Madam, protocol dictates that you should give the first word. However, since shyness ties your tongue, permit me to say that I am honored to be the vessel who will give you grandchildren."

She held her peace for the span of an *Ave Maria*. Then, laughing, she reached both hands to greet me. "Aleänor," she replied, "come here beside me."

I have mentioned this small point before, Aline. I have always linked the birth of Alix with the death of Abbé Suger. Both spelled the end of my marriage to Louis.

Likewise, my mind connects two events which took place in the heat of August in the year of our Lord one thousand one hundred and fifty-three. I performed my dynastic duty—as Pope Eugenius put it some years before—giving birth to my first child by Henry. Praise be to God, he was a boy whom I christened for his father's mighty line and mine: Guillaume. At last bells tolled to celebrate the birth of a child of mine. Lying abed in the melancholy that follows birth, the bells caused me to weep for the loss of Marie and little Alix. My midwives thought I wept for joy.

Some days later Abbé Bernard was called to meet his cherished maker. Within the short span of twenty years the Church pronounced him a saint. I say only that I have always felt indebted to Abbé Bernard and the prayers of Clairvaux for sending me Marie.

14. I, Aleänor, by the wrath of God, Queen of the English
1154–1155

Theobald, archbishop of Canterbury, was a saintly man cast in the mould of Suger, of blessed memory. May God keep both in grace and make them neighbors in heaven! Theobald was a divine who understood the weapons of diplomacy, having presided through fourteen years of strife in England. Rumor had it that Theobald's appointment to the see of Canterbury was inauspicious: he succeeded after a great darkness at noon seemed to mark the death of his predecessor in that office.[20] But that was a monkish tale, a malice born in the mud of foul and fearful times. Theobald knew how to blunt the edge of a quarrel, blur the borders between conflicting parts and show instead some speck of mutual advantage. It was Theobald who negotiated an end to hostilities in England between my mother-in-law and Henry against King Stephen. Anjou versus Blois! Here was a war between neighbors fought by proxies on the foreign fields of England. That country, in consequence, was much impoverished by the violence and duration of war, nineteen years, with its attendant cost in slighted castles, fired towns, death, attrition and pillage. But the ways of the Lord are strange indeed. While towns burned and castles fell, churches were building across the realm. The miseries of the flesh fired the English with a wakening of the spirit.

England was a prize, no doubt, but a much diminished one. It was as if two dogs shared the reward of licking their own blood because the bone they fought for was utterly destroyed.

During my inter-regnum at Angers we had the good fortune to learn that King Stephen's son Eustace choked to death on a dish of eels, a suitable end for one with gluttonous appetites for others' property. His army was wasting the town of Bury St. Edmunds at the time. (The English still hold that divine intervention killed Eustace. His forces ravaged the country without mercy. It was he, not his father, who most severely depleted our inheritance.)

Eustace's end-by-eels was cause for celebration. It deprived King Stephen of an heir. And it left Louis and the Franks, who favored Eustace's claim to the English throne, without the House of Blois to use as a stick against us.

With Eustace dead, Stephen ceded the succession to Henry, but not without long negotiations managed by Theobald.

Henry returned to Normandy in the spring of the year. The following months were for him a whirlwind of mending and strengthening alliances and borders, and punishing backsliders. Thus the spring and summer fled. We passed to autumn. I was lying at Rouen in the last week of October, when I heard wonderful news...

Alarums below, anxious women above and men-at-arms stirring from boredom. Urgent faces, all. "Come quickly, madam. Messengers from England." I hastened to the hall to find envoys from Theobald, rain-sodden after their post-haste from Barfleur. Premonition told me that this was such a moment as the one which visited me at Bordeaux seventeen years before. The envoys waited, dark silhouettes standing in puddles of their making, backlit against the gray light of the open door.

Henry was campaigning in the Vexin. In his absence I heard the message from Theobald's bedraggled men, three monks and the officers of their escort. They knelt, they said their say while I listened, staring down at the three pale moons of rain-damp tonsures. Their text was brief: King Stephen was dead. Theobald asked that Henry make a speedy passage to attach the crown ere anarchy and pillage spill the country into war again. "God save you, lady, soon to be the queen of England."

I bade them stand, and as they rose, so rose my heart and hopes. Here was indeed a vast, imperial image taking shape within my brains.

I sent to Henry straightaway. The Vexin, you will know, Aline, vexes Norman and Frank in equal measure. That strip of border country twixt Normandy and France, heavy with garrisons, pricks like a thorn and itches like a scab against whichever side does not possess it; and it drains the resources of him who does. Henry and his late father ceded the Vexin to Louis during their fateful visit to Paris. And they did so with good will, causing the Franks much wonder. In hindsight it became clear that, by ceding the Vexin, the Angevins hoped to mollify the Franks. Knowing that my marriage to Louis could not last, those canny devils were already plotting to steal me away.

You see how it was, Aline? As a piece on the chess board of strategy, I outweighed the Vexin. Well, why should that cause surprise? Together, Henry and I outweighed France.

Now I shall rest. Excitement tires me easily these days. When we meet again we shall voyage to England. It will interest you, if you are doomed to live your married life beyond the northern sea.

Within moments of Theobald's message our house was in a rush. Men-at-arms hasted to find Henry, while I bade others ride

like the wind to my people in Poitou. The courtyard was a moil of dart-
ing, dashing horsemen thrusting out on roads in all directions from
Rouen. Except for Paris! In no great time we had to raise a worthy company—a king's escort—and take ship to England.

By the first week in November we were lodged at Barfleur. Henry's
younger brother, Geoffrey, numbered in our company—the very
boy who sought to kidnap me two years before. We learned patience
at Barfleur; we learned to wait, and wait, pacing the storm-tossed shore
as weeks went by, praying for an end to adverse winds and waves.
But England is well guarded. She holds herself aloof behind a toss of
fierce gray seas and greyer skies. How we wished the scudding rain-
clouds driving up the Channel were our sails. But neither prayer nor
imprecation calmed the storm. Day by day we watched and waited,
mocked by gulls.

Did any land lurk past the rain-shrouds on the far horizon where the
sea and sky merged into one? Had I not known, I would have guessed that
Barfleur's sullen shore marked the world's end. The northern ocean has
always looked more final to my southern eyes than does the western sea.

We waited a month, one full cycle of the moon, but none of her
quarters gave us quarter from the weather. At last, on the seventh day of
December, Henry gave order despite the storm: we sail! Everyone in the
company knew that, thirty-four years before, the *White Ship* had been
lost here with three hundred souls, including William Atheling, Henry I's
only son and the heir to England. You may be sure that every member
of our company prayed that we would be spared the fate of wreck on
the Quilleboeuf rock.

But Henry had resolve enough to give the very devil spur-galls. It
was sufficient for him that the wind blew in the right direction. Never
mind that it wrested limbs from trees and carved the waters into louring
hills. His passion reasoned that, if we could not command the waves, at
least we rode the wind.

We embarked. I took charge of Guillaume myself. He was fourteen months old, and I was six months pregnant with Young Henry. Only I would be responsible if we stumbled on the heaving plank or he were dashed on tossing wooden walls. The wind was such that sailors could not loose the eyelets at the ropes' ends from the posts securing them. They had to cut us free. Those who stayed on deck and looked to the receding shore saw dockside handlers make the sign of the Cross. How I feared, not for myself but for my son. However, one day he would rule the northern barbary; better that he should master its defences in childhood.

Thus we tossed and pitched for a day and a night while many in our company spilled their tripes for wretchedness. Our fleet being broken, each ship made landfall where it might. Henchmen were await-ing our arrival at Southampton, but chance blew us far to the west. We came ashore in a forest, a veritable wilderness of storm-lashed trees which—this proved to be a great irony—was kept in a state of nature as a royal hunting ground. Thence, on foot and borrowed horses, Henry led our company out of the New Forest to Winchester, some twenty miles distant over woodland trails. From Winchester, which was the royal seat in Alfred's time, we made a progress to London, regaining a semblance of dignity *en route*. The late King Stephen's brother, Henry, bishop of Winchester, sent scourers ahead to beat the coun-try, hailing knights, nobles and not a few clergy to join our company. Thus we came to London, dripping, rain-besotted London, with a goodly host of Normans, Angevins, some Poitevins and English in our train.

I t was unfortunate that I first judged Paris after growing to age in Paradise. And it was unfortunate that I judged London after eigh-teen years of warfare, pillage and a month-long tempest. William Rufus, the son of Henry's great-grandfather, William the Conqueror, had rebuilt the old Saxon palace at Westminster in time of living memory. But Stephen's army sacked it, so we removed—even before we took possession—to Bermondsey across the river.

Nor war nor weather spoiled our mood. On Sunday, the nineteenth day of December, we took our coronation vows in Westminster Abbey. A noble gathering of Normans and English attended in good heart despite the leaking roof. The building had known neither mason nor carpenter since the time of Henry's grandfather, before the war. During the ceremony Henry placed a written promise on the altar, swearing to uphold the rights and privileges of the Church in England. That parchment would return to vex us.

We left the abbey to curious shouts of "Waes hael" from the crowd, taking a street they call the Strand. We did not go far: I was pregnant with Young Henry. I recalled the day, seventeen years before, when I walked in the heat of Bordeaux with the shy, embarrassed Louis, while women shouted coarse encouragement.

From several persons—everyone with a voice worth hearing speaks French—we gathered that the English admired us for breaching the island's bulwark of wind and weather to secure the throne.

Paris in summer heat; London in the muck of winter. I have met my royal cities at their worst, Aline.

London resembled nothing I had seen before. Paris is ancient and studious, besieged by abbeys; Constantinople is a wonder of wealthy buildings of the finest stone; but London is closer in its daily toil to Bordeaux and Antioch. I found it to be a city of traders who preserve a Christian faith, no doubt, but chiefly occupy themselves with business. Here were money-changers and lenders, wool merchants, dealers in ale, even wines from my lands, cattle and sheep markets, pie makers, lawyers' inns, pothecaries, stalls of all kinds. We saw many of these in the Strand.

So, London is a city of merchants, like Antioch, but also a trading port, like Bordeaux. In Paris, the Seine keeps the parts apart. But the Thames serves London as a great road by which merchants connect in commerce. There is such a gathering of boats, fishing vessels and coastal traders on the river as to cloak the water on all days but the sabbath.

Of all cities I have known, London looks the least permanent, as if the demands of commerce prevail over the wood and wattle of the place. Ancient walls surround it, to be sure, and prosperous merchants' houses stretch in a row from the city wall to the palace at Westminster, all set around by gardens and orchards. From afar I could see the ruined palace and the great tower built by Henry's ancestor. But much of London's fabric looks willing to slump into its mud.

Here and there churches rise above the trees. I include in their number the Templars' Preceptory in the parish of St. Andrew, near a stream called Holborn. In shape, the Templars' building is round, patterned after the Church of the Holy Sepulchre in Jerusalem. So careful are Templars to observe the dignity of worship that they built in a hard stone carried from Caen in Normandy.

Sad memories pricked me when I worshipped there. When Louis and I entered Jerusalem we went directly to the Holy Sepulchre, the very church which the Templars copied in London. We tried to give the appearance of entering the Holy City in harmony after the affair at Antioch. But on the day that Louis placed the oriflamme on the altar of the Holy Sepulchre in Jerusalem, I was all but in chains.

No doubt the drear appearance of London when I met it spoke to the trials of war. But its merchants still prospered: their ships traded with foreign ports where England's conflict was unknown. We learned that both armies had murdered peasants—whom John of Salisbury calls the "feet of the commonwealth"—burning towns and villages to deprive the other side of shelter and sustenance. Lord God, whole English counties resembled Vitry-en-Perthois after Louis put it to the torch. Manor lands lay waste, depriving liege-lords of rent and barons of treasure. The royal treasury could wring little from such wretchedness. And all to our cost. How could the head hold its station aloft without the labor of the "feet"?

We were crowned before Christmas. Winter followed. To view London from a rustic hall at Bermondsey across the river from the Tower was like contemplating Bordeaux from the far side of the wide Garonne. The focus of life and gaiety lay on the opposite bank.

The one benefit of those first months at Bermondsey was that I came to term in the cool of winter. At the end of February I gave birth to a second boy, whom we named Henry, for his father. His older brother Guillaume would inherit England—so we thought. Henry would attain Anjou.

Do you know, Aline, I am informed that men and women of lower ranks envy the highborn. Assuredly we are warm in winter, clothed in fine raiment, with shoes on our feet, scrip for our purse, and with servants to run at beck and call.

But we are not without cares. Nor are those cares ours alone; rather we carry the weighty burdens of all estates. Did not God consign us to noble birth to undertake high office in His name? At every stage of my life I have thought back to the naked waifs begging alms as Pétronille and I traveled on Father's formal journeys. What had those peasants to fear from alliances and strifes; from the burden of vows taken by their rulers in their names; from the sword's edge of war or the toils of government? Such folk have no care but to stuff their bellies with oats. Their condition is closer to their beasts than to their rulers' courts. How could such creatures contemplate authority? God in His mercy gives birth to each as He desires: the poor to shiver and scratch at the soil; the great to bear up straight beneath the heavy weight of state. It was for these, the "feet of the commonwealth," that Henry and I strove for years to mend England.

Anjou had been governed in peace and honesty for three generations; England lay in ruins. Stephen's war became the excuse for every vassal in the land to slip his leash. Here was a country without government; pillage without law; sack without repair; an empty treasury; and outlaws with neither hangman nor hearth to turn them from their misery.

In those first years I saw more of England than I chose to. Henry was never still. He could not bear to sit when he could stand, or stand when he could ride. I never understood why he developed a paunch. He was no glutton, and he was always on the move. Sometimes I accompanied his court in its perpetual wandering; at other times he went alone. There was not a high vassal in England whom Henry did not come on by surprise, no rebel whom he did not bring to heel. Thus we trailed the length and breadth of England in all weathers.

Here was Anatolia again. Storm, mud and rain assailed us. Roads were such that we traveled with extra draught horses to pull the women's carts and baggage wains from mud. I cannot count the times we waited while harbingers rode off to commandeer more horses—even mules and oxen—from some hapless vill or manor on our path.

Thus we traveled: Exeter, Clarendon, Winchester, Woodstock, Oxford—where schools were springing up in the manner of Paris—Nottingham, Lincoln, York. We ventured to the northern lands contested by the Scots, and west to Shrewsbury and Chester. Here I heard again the tales of Arthur of Britain, Merlin, Morgan, Tristan and Iseult. But their bards were difficult to understand. Just as our verse in *langue d'oc* is a rolled book to the Franks, so is the language of the Welsh—which they call *Kúmrig*—to the English.

I f a man have two estates, one in order and the other in disorder, he must look to mend the one in disorder. But let him spend too much time mending disorder, and the ordered estate soon slips to disarray.

So it was with us. To put England to rights was a labor of Hercules which Henry discharged to his fullest ability. But he could not be in two places at once; nor could he straddle the Channel.

In our first year Henry sent John of Salisbury to Pope Adrian IV to request the lordship of Ireland, but such were England's woes that I never ventured there.

The English are an obstinate race, little given to learning or enlightenment, and certainly not willing to hear counsel from women, although I did preside at several courts. At Clarendon and Woodstock I heard pleas presented through translators. That was almost fifty years ago. Common folk had been exposed to Norman civilization, Norman culture and Norman French for almost a century by then. But even now they scorn us, as if *we* were the barbarians: they think of us as something wretched washed ashore from overseas. Psha! They cling to a language of churls which scholars deride as a tongue debased to something less than peasant German. I knew I would never contrive such sounds as "th" and "gh" and "w" as long as I live. I have heard geese hiss and swine grunt with more aplomb than English speech. The English tongue is a fearsome thing.

15. Enter a Rival, Thomas Becket
1155

Even if I had spoken fluent English, we still needed competent administrators versed in the customs of the country and its laws. Henry had picked up a little English at his uncle Robert's court in Bristol—giving him an accent which caused Londoners to smirk behind their hands. But, language apart, we needed a chancellor to attend to England while Henry repaired to Anjou and Normandy.

The great Theobald, who did much to negotiate our succession to Stephen, stood ready to meet our need. The See of Canterbury instructed many young men of promise whose calling was to administer the Church in England. Theobald sent us one of these, an experienced scholar whose name very history shall not forget: Thomas Becket. How I wish this matter had ended otherwise. But that is a tale for another page.

Becket was a man of great ability, divine and secular. Together with John of Salisbury he had studied in Paris. They had both heard Abelard preach at Sainte-Genevieve. Becket had not taken priestly orders.

His father was in trade, as many English are, a state precluding true adherence to religion. But Becket had journeyed as far as Rome with his master, Theobald. He was well versed in the ways of court and curia. He would soon prove himself a competent administrator *in loco regis*.

Becket was three years older than I, fifteen years older than Henry. Just long enough in the tooth to personify Henry's father. He did so, for a time: as father to affairs in England, spiritual and temporal; and as Henry's advisor and bosom friend.

Now, Aline, I tire. The sun went in and so shall I. Just one more point: Becket never let Henry forget the document he placed upon the altar at our coronation, in which Henry swore to defend the rights and privileges of the Church in England. That text would become a great rub.

For a man who aspired to administer the Church, Becket's lust bent less toward spirit than to mammon.

No, no, I shouldn't say that. Strike it through, Aline. The man was remarkably moral. Therein lay his downfall and his end. I do not begrudge Becket his preferment. He was what Henry needed; I do not disesteem him.

However, one was struck by the contradictions of his inner man. More upstanding than many a bishop, and yet he invented a household in London so sumptuous that it put Byzantium to shame. Of course, it was Henry's exchequer whose purse Thomas pilled, but not a word would Henry say in those first years.

Yet, although his table seemed set to serve debauchery—such wines and viands I seldom saw in the richest courts—he permitted no gluttony or drunkenness; no pissing or carousing in dark corners of his hall. The meanest starveling pensioner might drink and eat his fill, but not beyond. Woe to the man who left the chancellor's hall less steadily than he entered it, for he might not come again.

There was much artifice in this stratagem. Thomas's house was an open door through which flowed the embassies of kings, the privy servants of dukes and other mighty lords, and the great and the glorious from many lands. It was as if the chancellor diverted the Thames to his door. You can imagine how I fretted, stranded at Bermondsey, constrained to watch elegant barges draw up the river on the tide.

At least in Paris I had access to Louis' ear while we lay abed. For what it was worth! My advice was too often thwarted by some pettifogging clerk in Bernard's employ. But I was alive to the traffic of minds and whisperings around the palace.

But in London—I should say Bermondsey—even when Henry lay there, the traffic of diplomacy diverted to Thomas. For the first time since Antioch I felt the weight of the term "a woman's place." Even Henry, though he stopped in London scarcely longer than it takes a bee to suck a flower, felt the press of affairs pass him by. I begged him for escape from Bermondsey. Accordingly, it was not long before every available artisan was toiling to restore our ruined palace at Westminster.

I am going to speak to you frankly, Aline. You may find this useful in the conduct of your life—especially as the future mistress in your hall.

There have been times since ancient days when Woman is deified. She attains a stature worthy of worship. Why our sex should be represented in this fashion used to mystify me. But it is a manifest failing in the minds of men which we can put to great advantage.

The Church has seen fit this past century—since the time of Grandfather's Crusade—to promote the persona of Mary to a station seemingly superior to God. The motive of the popes is plain; as plain as the voice of Eugenius when he bade me bide my time at Louis' court to give him heirs. They preach that women—the wombs of men—are to be meek, to swell with child and to obey.

But she is a fool who does not see this stratagem for what it is: an attempt to silence the persuasive sex by promoting her above decisions of the flesh. This cynical policy is designed to halve the Church's task in reducing men to blind obedience. I say "men" for it is they who are slaves to leaders; women (the Church would have it) are slaves to men. But priests cannot still a woman's mouth upon her husband's pillow or at the family board. So they would change our very nature, bending meekness to their ends. They laud the passive mask of Mary in order to silence women; thereby to rule men.

So, in spite of itself, the Church esteems the ancient Mother-goddess in a new and docile form. Louis and I—to his horror and my wonder—saw goddess idols venerated under many names during our year in Palestine: Aphrodite, Diana, Innana, Ishtar, Gaia. There was nothing meek about those deities. But our priestly masters would have the Mother hide her head behind a downcast mask. However, they cannot command both ends: if they would have her venerated for humility, she must be venerated no less for her sex. Because she is female; because she has power to withhold life or give—as I withheld from Louis and gave to Henry in oversupply.

If one lends the authority of Holy Church to contriving an image, there will soon be those who worship it. There will always be those who, imbued with the idol, seek to incarnate the ideal. To make it flesh.

You will scarcely credit it now, Aline, but, generations before you were born, this old carcass embodied the feminine ideal. It was not only Bernart of Ventadorn who sang my praises and pined for my touch. "I marvel not her love should fetter me / Unto such beauty none hath e'er attained." Fond fool! I hope God gave him a tranquil end. A queen embodies the virtues of her sex, yes, and one more besides. By virtue of her rank she is unattainable. As such she is worthy of worship.

As indeed I was worshipped in those days. Kings have lain me. But what man can claim me?

I have been watching you, Aline, wondering how you would react. You are shocked to hear an ancient lady spout such heresy. You think me mad in my dotage.

Listen to me, child. I do not speak as an old dame reclaiming her lost glory. I have wisdom enough to let the past pass by. No, I speak of facts. Many a harp has been plucked, many a song sung, many a poem composed in my name. Not at the court of Louis, but later at Poitiers, Angers and London. Even in my fifth decade, when I settled again at Poitiers: Aleänor, a gay young queen; Aleänor, the embodiment of beauty; Aleänor, the mother of sons—too many sons—and kings; Aleänor, a legend in her time.

There is a quality about a woman in her prime, transcendent of the flesh, for which men pine. Mark me, Aline, men's quest to possess us is a much greater thing than a stag sniffing hinds.

Thus was I worshipped, in song and in verse. I say this to you now, not from the folly of vanities past, but as the earthly embodiment, long ago, of that essence which is the power of a woman.

That is what draws, Aline. That is what draws men in. It is an essence of grace not captured or crafted in fine fabric and squirrel fur, though it may clothe itself in them. It does not depend upon beauty; it lives in a radiant hauteur, a comely and commanding presence. It finds life in the rustle of silk, but not the silk; in the lightest of footfalls, but not the foot; in the bearing, apart from the being.

It is this female essence that inspires lust in men, not to embrace, but to possess. And what they seek to possess, they are like to serve.

So it was in distant days. Men need their legends, and I supplied enough to keep crabbed scribes at work for many years. For decades this old body moved poets and bards, castles and kings.

I mention this in passing, for it was this power that I used to win back the influence I lost to Becket in my first years with Henry in England.

Thomas possessed the wit, the craft and—thanks to his high office—the substance to draw men of influence through his gate. He drew them from all ranks. Not the least of his conquests was Henry, for whom, at that time, Becket could do no wrong. To a degree their close liaison was appropriate. One did not wish to hide the light of Thomas's high office under a bushel.

But it was not fitting that his sumptuous court should usurp the customs of the king.

Henry and I entertained well, though our board was less ambitious than our chancellor's. Henry cared naught what he and our company ate and drank—one became accustomed to filtering wine through one's teeth—but he was as apt as any scholar to engage in discourse with learned men. He was as well-versed in the arts as Louis was with psalms.

During our first years in England we encouraged what we in the west call the *matière de Bretagne*: tales of Arthur and Guinevere, Tristram and Isolde. The old *lais* returned to favor, translated from tongue to tongue. Legends of Arthur became the vogue in London: they had long been fodder for bards in Anjou and Poitou.

Here were tales of noble feats by kings, the bloody toils of knights, the magics of wizards and fairies, the courtly loves of spell-binding ladies. Bards and troubadours infused the ancient tales of Arthur with the courtly manners of our times. And if it served us to be flattered by old reflected glories, so much the better. Certainly I made good use of it.

The matter of Arthur had one singular drawback. I have said that the English and Welsh are pagan peoples, much given to worshipping nature at holy wells and haunted groves. It chanced that the legend of Arthur predicts that the king will return in a time of dire need: *rex quondam, rex futurus,* they say. Thus, even in modern England we confronted the ancient Sibyll's prophecy about one whose death is hidden: "It will be said among the people, 'He lives,' when he is dead." This was awkward. People's belief in Arthur as a "Once and Future King" implied that Henry and I warmed our throne for a ghost, and that our line would last just till Arthur chose to come again. Henry and I wore double crowns in the minds of superstitious persons, as if we were flesh—and faerie, too. I was Aleänor, and I was Guinevere.

Aligning ourselves with legendary powers did us no harm in the eyes of the Welsh and the English. When Roland lay dying, God Himself sent His messenger to lift the sacred sword, Durendart, from Roland's failing hand. In Britain it is the Lady of the Lake who takes the sword, Excalibur, from Arthur's dying hand—a nice twist that serves to advertise our congruent feminine powers. Besides, whereas God's messenger reaches down from heaven for Roland's sword, the Lady of the Lake reaches up from the water, a medium which is better suited to the British, who hold sacred all manner of ponds and springs. Ah, Aline, such games we play.

Of course, the Church preferred to see me as Morgana le Fey, the witch. I have said that stories of Arthur found favor with all classes of men—except the Church.

Given Arthur's seeming longevity, we secretly hoped to discover his grave and lay his ancient bones—and the Sibylline adage—to rest. Henry did not live to see that day. It was not until later, in my son Richard's second year as king, that a tomb came to light at one of Britain's holiest shrines. I speak of Glastonbury Abbey, a day's ride from Bristol. Henry knew it well from his boyhood years at the court of his uncle, Robert, earl of Gloucester. How ironic that Glastonbury's monks should find Arthur's grave while rebuilding their fire-gutted abbey, a project endowed by Henry, and perforce by me, since Henry ordered his chamberlain, Fitzstephens, to provide from our family funds.

Well, perhaps I should not have used the word ironic! Let us write that Henry and I contributed to the new abbey; that the monks eventually returned the favor by electing the king's kinsman, Henry de Sully, as abbot; and that, under de Sully's guidance, the monks contrived to find an ancient sepulchre in their cemetery. What a treasure, to lay claim to the resting place of King Arthur and Queen Guinevere! The man's bones bespoke a giant; the woman's skull yielded blonde hair. The bones were found beneath a hollow oak, no less. How wonderfully British! I imagine pilgrims are stuffing the abbey's coffers still. Lest a shred of doubt remain, the good monks laid bare an inscription written—curiously—in Latin rather than the language of the Britons: "Here lies buried the great King Arthur with Guinevere, his second wife, in the Isle of Avalon." The great king has found eternity in death. He is not likely to return.

From our first years in London we strove to lay to rest the myth of Arthur's second coming. Would that we had unearthed the mortal remains of that legendary couple thirty-five years earlier! But our first efforts were thwarted. When we were crowned, the abbot of Glastonbury was the ancient Henry of Blois, who insisted on living until after Becket was slain.[21] By then, we faced bigger crises than laying King Arthur's ghost. In his other role, as bishop of Winchester, Henry of Blois served us loyally enough; but as King Stephen's brother he had no love for our Angevin line. Besides, in the first year of our reign, my Henry confiscated most of Bishop Henry's property.

If one is to build a good reputation by constructing an apotheosis for one's family it is best to do so early and enjoy the fruits thereafter. To that end we commissioned a poet from the Norman island of Jersey to write a book based on a popular treatise about British kings. Our book would pull in threads from Arthur to weave with our own reign and times.[22]

Our book—our poet's name was Wace—served several ends. Twenty years under Stephen had broken Henry's line and the Norman grip on England. We had to reassert the Conqueror's *droit* and his line. And we faced another challenge. From the day we were crowned we presided over as many peoples as Charlemagne: English, Normans, Poitevins, Angevins, Welshmen and Marchers, Gascons, Celts and a host of others, including my souls from Aquitaine. The Arthurian tales describe a golden age in which diverse peoples live at peace with each other, inspired by a single ruler. We had urgently to show a similar benefit. To that end, this Wace contrived a literary conceit which he called a "round table," where all might eat as one without respect to degree, where no one sat below the salt and where all might address their king across his board. This curiosity appealed greatly to Henry, who ate standing up: he chewed his meat while pacing up and down, engaging in chatter with all and sundry the length of his board.

For me, stranded in Bermondsey, these Arthurian sleights of mind bridged the physical and diplomatic divides posed by the Thames. By subtly promoting these legends in our first year I clawed back some of the influence I perforce had ceded to Becket, across the river. Wace's round table made our court seem less remote from the English; more like Becket's. New poems and songs about Arthur inspired other arts: comedies, dances, bards who mingled the stuff of Britain's mighty king with our old-fashioned *chansons de geste*. Profane arts found voice at our court; imagination took flight. We learned from the Welsh, who are expert at part-singing, although I swear they are in love with melancholy. They insist on tuning their strings to the dolorous scale of B flat. Nevertheless, we followed their example, and plainsong gave way to a fashion for choirs where people sang different parts.

This did not please my critics, chiefest among them Theobald's secretary and Becket's bosom friend, John of Salisbury. You will recall, Aline, that I first clapped eyes on John when he served Pope Eugenius at Tusculum. During our years in London Becket filled the role of Suger— without the old abbé's humility—while John of Salisbury stood in for

Bernard by deploring my sins. John had a brilliant mind: one wished that he had absorbed less of Bernard's sainted bile.

Men said that the arts and manners of my court debauched the morals of modest London. Pish! I but lit a flambeau in a northern gloom and woke the living death of dullness to a thrilling, modern life.

16. Splendor, the Subtle Servant of Diplomacy
1158

Do I mock Becket unjustly, Aline? Oh, I can ask that freely now, half a century later. I certainly felt that he challenged my authority and usurped my place in Henry's affections, though I do not mean to suggest they enjoyed a Greek passion. No. I had reason enough to know that Henry took his release in women, though for companionship he turned to men.

How hard we worked in those first years. The three of us. To rebuild England; to assert our power in Henry's lands and mine; and to establish marches on the frontiers. We had secured an empire the like to which the west had not seen since the reign of Charlemagne. But we were vulnerable. The Capets had no love for Angevins even before my break from Louis. And afterwards...

Well, Louis lost no time betrothing my little Marie—she would have been seven—to Henry the Liberal, count of Champagne. As for Alix, sweet Alix, they affianced her to Thibault of Blois. Dear little thing, shoved across the chess board to the enemy. I hadn't seen either of my daughters since my divorce, when Alix was barely two. But now she was firmly betrothed to the foe. Having lost England to the Angevins, Blois was firmly in the Capet camp. But I'm wandering again.

Henry and I commanded lands extending from the Scottish borders to the Pyrenees. There is surely no more fertile country under heaven. It was one month's travel from north to south, but at its slender waist it was less than a summer day's cavalry ride from French border forts to the western sea. We had to secure that waist. The appropriate move was to annex Berry—transforming a narrow waist to a pregnant belly to assure our own defence.

There was also the sensitive issue of the Vexin, that chain of ridgeway forts commanding the Seine and the route from Paris to our Norman seat at Rouen. Henry's father, Geoffrey, had yielded the Vexin, you recall, during their brief but portentous summer visit to Paris. That would have been some seven years before the time of which I speak.

Such a strange thing! To give a valuable gift—the Vexin—in anticipation of a prize for which he dared not ask. Within the walls of Louis' palace Geoffrey and Henry hardly dared whisper the notion between themselves. It was as if Geoffrey conceded the Vexin to the Franks as payment in advance for the wife he—in the event, his son—was soon to steal. They dared not discuss it in Paris. The very walls were Louis' spies. Or Bernard's. And that was worse.

Despite the latent hostility between them, Henry and Louis met in May one year to blunt the edge of mutual suspicion and attempt to negotiate affairs. In sum, the kings agreed to affiance Queen Constance's infant, Marguerite, to our three-year-old, Henry's namesake. I should mention that Constance of Castile was the intended brood-mare who replaced me in Louis' bed. She, too, gave him only daughters.

I feel scattered today, Aline, my mind astray. Too many thoughts. All racing, a-flutter. Hardly can I sit. Fetch the sister, what's her name?

Bid her come and bring valerian. Or is it the herb of St. John? No matter. She knows.

I should have mentioned this before: my firstborn by Henry, Guillaume, named for both paternal lines... He died not quite three. I'll never forget that first, ferocious Channel crossing from Barfleur, embarking with him as a swaddled baby heavy in my arms, with a second, Henry, heavy in my womb...both gone...so many gone. Only I, it seems, was destined to live beyond my years...although methinks the fate of living on to plough and replough ancient furrows from the past is but a death in life...it is as if my young-dead children passed their unlived lives to me...would it had been otherwise... Enough, Aline. Fetch Sister Hortensia. I can no more today.

How fresh this morning dawns. That thunder in the night cleansed all the evil humors from the air. Where were we? Don't tell me. Today I feel foolish for taking ancient memories to heart. An old woman should at least live beyond a sense of tragedy if she can't rise above it. God knows, too many have gone.

Yes, yes, you needn't prompt me, Aline. I know. I was talking about Henry and Louis, and our children affianced in order to restore to us the Vexin.

The two kings met in the spring and reached an arrangement in principle. But there was still—six years on—a fervid body of resentment against me in Paris. As Louis' queen I had long shared the Franks' distrust of Angevins. And now, though years had fled, the Franks still resented me: resented my past reluctance to give the Capets heirs; and resented my haste in doing so for Henry. So, we decided that negotiating the fine points of delicate matters involving land and marriage were best assigned to the negotiating skills of Thomas Becket.

We reasoned that it was not sufficient to move the affections of Louis and the Frankish court alone. The age of decision-making by sanctity which marked the rule of Suger and Bernard was passing. Indeed, it had passed. Our counselors felt—I was the main mover among them in this matter—that the schools, abbeys, merchants, even the lowliest of Franks must be swayed before our cause would prevail in the Capetian court.

To that end, Becket set out from Rouen between the haying and the harvest—a quiet time for country folk—to process along the road to Paris with such a train of wealth and display as was seldom seen before and, I fancy, never after. It put me in mind of our departure for Crusade.

Becket and his retinue took nine days to complete a journey which a speedy horseman might post between a summer's dawn and dusk. More than a dozen wains transported his personal effects, his suiting, bedding, chapel plate and sundry furnishings. Carts followed, heavily laden with English beer: when a peasant presented a cup, a drawer from Becket's company held it to a spigot and filled it to the brim. Other carts came on with meats and sweetmeats which, servers said, the Franks must eat before they rotted in the heat. Guards marched past, then squires in livery and knights with silken banners and their finest chain-mail sand-rubbed to a polish in the summer sun.

Sumpter horses by the score and by the dozen followed. Grooms in silken livery led chargers; falconers with jewel-spangled gauntlets bore their falcons which, in turn, were decked in bright, cockaded hoods. As if these trappings and display were not enough to drop the jaw and fix the eye of every onlooker, the leading horse of every wain bore—seated like a wagoner—a long-tailed Barbary ape.

Nor was that all. Following this ménage came better than two hundred singers, actors, jugglers, acrobats—such tavern-trash as stirs a laugh at every inn—roaring rustic songs in mysterious English, dancing, prancing, tumbling and swallowing swords and fire through every town and hamlet on the road from Rouen to Paris.

Long before this caravan reached its destination it attached a following of several thousand Frankish burghers and yokels, drunk with beer and affection for Becket, and fed to bursting with love for his cause, whatever that might be. What was it the Franks so famously said? "If this be the English chancellor, pray God we clap eyes on the English king."

I smile to imagine it still. I, of course, was *persona non grata*. Twenty-one years earlier, Becket had lived in Paris as a shivering student warming his hands over candle stubs. Now he rode in gilded state and glory, dispensing largesse to crowds. Echoes of that English largesse—a commodity we could ill afford, for England still lay in ruins—wafted through the walls of Louis' miserable palace.

It had been suggested earlier, when the kings met, that Henry's proposal to the Franks—a royal princess in exchange for land—would need careful cultivation among the populace. Hence Becket's ill-afforded venture. At great cost he succeeded. So our empire gained a princess who would, in time, bring the Vexin to us as her dowry.

Furthermore, if God so willed, she would bear a son who would unite the crowns of France and England on one head.

Some months later Henry himself came to Paris with the barest escort, to conclude the business. On this occasion we chose harvest-time, when folk had better things to do than gawp at kings.

I still have difficulty imagining Henry as a model of lamb-like moderation during that excursion. It was a restraint that ill-became him. But all reports agreed, giving those of us who knew him a hearty measure of mirth. He toured with interest; he ate placidly with Louis and Queen Constance; and he gave unsparingly to Parisian lepers and the poor. (Which meant that he withheld with the other hand, perforce sparing lepers and the poor of London and Rouen the burden of carrying coin.)

Then came the day, a Sunday, when Henry left Paris with the baby princess, Marguerite. And she just six months old. It was surely a wrench for Constance to part with her first-born at such a tender age. No matter that royal duty calls, a queen is no less a mother for being a queen.

I thank God that I was not put to wed until I reached fifteen. What grief to be reared in the misery of the Capets' palace! Had I been affianced at six months of age I would have grown to woman's estate without knowledge of comparison: without the sweet air, the better life or the fellow-feeling for women that mark our other, western world. I speak, of course, of Poitou and Aquitaine. Thank God, I say again, for fifteen years in Eden.

By the same token, the baby Marguerite was fortunate to escape that dungeon in the Seine. And yet, as a woman I have always felt it cruel to remove babies...

No matter. Let it pass.

They took the child to Normandy. Henry wryly told me that the Capetian counselors insisted on a clause stating that the princess Marguerite must never lodge or receive instruction "in any household of her majesty the queen of England."

You raise an eyebrow, Aline. And dare to smile! I shall make you an extrovert yet.

But I'm surprised you ask the reason for that clause. From Louis' point of view it was straightforward. I refer you to Genesis, Chapter 30, the tale of Jacob, Laban and the straked and spotted goats. Study the text, Aline. The Bible teaches that an infant absorbs its nature from features influencing its mother before, and perhaps after, its birth. A mother's impressions imprint themselves upon the being in her womb. Why else would we trouble to raise infant brides in the households of their betrothed? It is because the infants of those infants are truly of the place where they are bred.

Men care nothing for such things, of course. After they deposited the child and her household at Newburgh, Henry and Louis toured Normandy together. Then they parted, liking each other well enough.

17. Toulouse and other turmoils
1159-1160

Nor was the kings' mutual liking tarnished by the sorry affair at Toulouse the following year.

I had always counted Toulouse as mine, part of my patrimony from years gone by. But the link was loosened when Grandfather—the Troubadour—returned destitute from Crusade, and Toulouse became a pawn, a matter of surety for debts. No matter that Grandfather was born there. And Raymond of Antioch, of precious memory. In time Toulouse drifted away.

By the year of which I speak, Toulouse had passed to the Capets. That mattered little in itself: Louis was also my liege-lord for Poitou, and later for Normandy. But a quarrel between the counts of Toulouse and Barcelona threatened to remove the fief beyond my grasp.

In consequence, Becket taxed the English bishops—fat geese in a barren manor—raised an army with the spoils and shipped it in convoy to Gascony. Thence Henry led his force to the walls of Toulouse in support of my cause and Barcelona's. However, when Henry reached the town he found King Louis himself commanding its defence. Unwilling to risk their hard-won rapport of the previous year, Henry withdrew his soldiers from the walls. Foolish boy: it suited him to put the cause of his overlord before that of his queen. The sore that was Toulouse would have to wait.

And thus the year slipped by. That year, and many years. At thirty-seven I thought myself an old woman. Hah! What must you think, Aline? No, don't say. I know too well. Looking at life from fifteen years of age—the age at which I married Louis and came as queen to Paris—you must consider thirty-seven nigh upon the end of time.

You smile again. That's good. I shall bring you to a state of worldly wisdom ere we're done.

Look how the clouds move. One moment I find in them the traits of people I knew long ago: a seamstress, a cleric, a bard. Often Suger, bless him. Even Henry. And John—vexed and troubled John.

Three breaths later the same cloud rises in a billow like great sails. Have you ever crossed the sea, Aline? No? That is your fate, as it once was mine. No reason to fear, child. Persons of your standing all speak French, albeit those who were born in England honk like Flemings.

Look there! See how the sun pokes through the clouds to drive a spear of light into the ground. Whenever I see those shafts of light I think of mother—or whoever she was whom I imagined to be mother. I can't help myself: those sunbeams hint at the sheen of light on the folds of her skirt. From a child's point of view, of course. What was I? Three? Four? It was blue like the sky. The skirt, I mean. Did you know that peasant children live with their parents until they are old enough to wed? Incredible. How strange. And yet how wonderful. Even a churl enjoys riches which high-born folk might envy.

Where was I? Oh, yes. Clouds and sails. Do you know, they say Henry crossed the northern sea twenty-eight times. His *esnecca*[23] had a crew of fifty oarsmen. Barfleur to Southampton usually. They rigged a roof for the women. Sometimes when the shipmen had time to prepare I crossed in a vessel with a room below the deck.

Ralph Calf. Now there's a name. It just came back to me. He was a ship master of Southampton. The *Vitulus*. That was his ship. But look at me now. Becalmed. And riddled with the shipworm of old age.

How did I wander so far from the highroad, Aline? You must chide me when I stray. At my age byways have more appeal than the rutted track.

I was thinking of ships because, in that very season when storms rake the sea, Henry commanded me from England to join him in Normandy. Alarums and alarums. Louis' queen, Constance of Castile, had no more luck giving the Franks a male heir than I did. Presenting Louis with another daughter, poor Constance just had time to name her Adelaide before they died. Mercifully, the mother died before her child. At least I escaped from Louis with my life.

This turn of events put us in great turmoil, because Queen Constance's body was barely cold before Louis married Adela of Champagne. Beyond other precedents, this act cemented the three-way pact among the Capets and the houses of Blois and Champagne.

It also created great scandal. Barely two weeks passed twixt Louis' obsequies for one wife and his marriage to the next. In their haste, the Franks chose to overlook the fact that, long ago, a marriage between Adela's sister and Louis's late brother, Philip, had been annulled by cause of consanguinity. To our pleasure and the Franks' discomfort, Samson, archbishop of Reims, refused to anoint Adela as queen, which mightily displeased her father, Theobald of Blois.

Nevertheless the marriage took place and we were obliged to look to our defence.

So we hasted to Newburgh in early November and married Young Henry—he was five, I recall—to Marguerite, who was not quite three. Not a lot of time to prepare, but done nevertheless in impeccable legal form. Fortune sanctioned the match with the presence of two cardinals, Henry of Pisa and William of Pavia. Happily their mission co-incided with ours: they had come to solicit Henry's support for their papal candidate. Not that their man returned the favor after his election. Alexander III was nothing but a stumbling block in our soon-to-be troubles with Becket.

Had we known that, of course, we would have supported the holy Roman emperor's candidate for pope instead of backing the cardinals' choice—and Louis'.

We married the children on the fifth of November, giving our men-at-arms time to seize the castles in the Vexin—they were Marguerite's dowry—before winter. They had to evict the Templars who had occupied them as guarantors. Becket's and Henry's agreement with Louis had stipulated that, as neutral parties, the Templars would hold the forts until such time as little Marguerite was wed.

Louis made less trouble than we feared, being preoccupied with his own swift courtship and his contract of betrothal.

Eight years earlier I had predicted Louis' violent reaction to my second marriage, which he celebrated by attacking Normandy. The Capets were still predictable in that respect, but they continued to underestimate Henry, a man who was always several moves ahead of his foes. The count of Champagne had the effrontery to express the Capet alliance's anger by taking up arms against us. Which was as wonderfully opportune as it was foolish. Louis and Count Theobald expended much toil and more coin building up the walls at the strategic castle of Chaumont. This was no sooner done than Henry besieged and took it, obtaining not only Chaumont, but the ransom of fifty-five knights from the house of Blois.

First the Vexin; then the castle at Chaumont. With these two stratagems, rapidly enforced, we put a strategic girth of muscled belly around our narrow waist.

18. Theobald's death rings out the old
1161-1162

Until Archbishop Theobald's life began to ebb we took for granted his contribution to the good of England. He was a splendid man. I say that not least because he had negotiated Henry's passage to the throne. But I do not view Theobald's contribution from narrow self-regard. He did much to redress the slough that almost twenty years of civil war had wrought. In a time of chaos he trained a small army of disciplined and sober minds against the day when order would once more prevail.

During Henry's first years as king our better provinces commanded his attention. England bestowed on us the purple and the crown, to be sure, but our first allegiance was to the lands of our ancestors. In consequence Henry spent four years in six attending to affairs from Aquitaine to Normandy. In England, meanwhile, disputes between the crown and the Church festered through neglect. I sat as regent in England, but the Church was not eager to hazard its business on the judgment of a woman, especially one who had been a constant thorn in the side of

Abbé Bernard—and who had dared to point out the Church's folly in Palestine. Thus, by a tacit accord to let sleeping dogs lie, important issues were set aside until a later day.

Being busy elsewhere, Henry failed to name bishops to several English diocese. As a result, funds destined for the Church fell by default into royal coffers. This grievance was the subject of several petitions by the Church at a time when Henry was nursing his own sense of injustice: the king's law remained a mockery as long as better than two subjects in ten pleaded exemption from our royal courts by virtue of their claims to be in holy orders. Rascals of all stripes came under the protection of the Church. Better a dozen *Paternosters* than a whipping. Better six hundred Hail Marys than one noose. Before the king's law might be seen to be just, the mesh in the net had to be of one size.

This matter touched Henry to the quick, because his first sustained exertion on behalf of the English was to mend and install courts of law in every shire. He and Becket strove to appoint honest officers and judges and to ensure that punishments were neither too lenient nor too severe.

But Henry was youthful and vigorous—he was barely twenty. Theobald, meanwhile, was growing old.

In his final decade, Theobald smoothed strife, negotiated peace, strewed good will on Henry's path to the throne and raised his protégé, Becket, to be second in the land. Before that he had steadfastly guarded the Church while war and pillage wormed the world to ruin. But, in the end, it was one step too far for Theobald to salve the list of irritants between the Church and the crown. So, while arguments festered, the archbishop lay dying.

Henry and Becket, the men whose earthly prospects Theobald did so much to advance, made no move to offer solace in the dying months and moments of his life. I say "dying months" because, though the outcome was certain, the Almighty was in no haste to bear His servant hence. Report after report told us of Theobald's creeping approach to death's door. Report after report had him sliding across the threshold. Months passed before black sealing wax attested to his end.

Oh Henry, how did it come about that kingship made you more of what you were before, but stripped you of the wit to see as others saw? Does a king sit so much higher than a duke that policy obliterates the importance of a gentle gesture to a dying man?

We'll leave the matter there, Aline. It shall be a matter for my private contemplation.

In passing I should say that Theobald was another soul who waited for the coming of long days in spring before he loosed this life and died.

Speaking of which, Aline, you will find that the days are both longer and shorter in England than in Poitou. It is a quirk of England's nature: summer days seem eternal; but at midwinter they are but three finger-spans of candle serving just to punctuate the dark. I never understood why the inconstant sun flits between seasons like a drunkard stumbling from tavern to inn. He staggers about the English sky much more than in favored southern lands.

There I go, straying again. I had in mind to say: Theobald never saw the greening of the leaves. It was said that he turned his face to the wall the better to repudiate a world which in the end repudiated him.

What else befell us in that year? Ah yes, I had Aleänor. Born at Domfront.

You must think this disquisition on Theobald is an old woman's morbid fascination with death, Aline. Not so. I am well endowed with that quality, of course. What ancient is not? God knows death has touched me nearly and often. But I must give this very Christian prelate his due.

He was mourned greatly by the convent of Trinity—which is to say the monks of Canterbury. Indeed, Theobald was mourned by simple people everywhere. Those who study the history of the Church in England liken his contribution to that of the great reformer Lanfranc, who lived a century and more ago.

In spite of which, when Archbishop Theobald fled his flesh he left affairs twixt powers temporal and spiritual in a sullen state of disarray. Henry might ignore Theobald's dying, but he could not ignore his death. Urgent jousting between Church and crown could wait no longer. Curiously, although the archbishop had gone to great pains to train worthy young men in the arts of administration, no one candidate stood out above the others. Besides which, since the battle between Church and crown would be heated and long, Henry was in no mind to appoint a powerful adversary to pit against himself. Accordingly, it took no mental toil before his mind fixed on Becket.

Oh Henry, when your lot fell on Becket, was it because you held him in too much liking, or in too slight respect? As your chancellor he fought *beside* you. There he could safely play a man of many parts: your henchman, officer, confidante, tax gatherer and bosom friend. For your sake he could prick the Church and call it duty.

You who have unhorsed friends and drawn their blood in tourneys, did you think Becket would take to the lists *against* you with a broken lance? He was too noble a soul to bend, even for his life's love, and that is what you were. Until Falaise. Until one fateful day.

How wrong you were. And how awry things went thereafter.

Aline, have you had occasion to observe the fond attachments between men? I do not mean the unnatural kind. There you go, blushing again, although I think you can have little notion of my meaning.

I speak of friendship, the very special, boundless friendship that may join the souls and beings of two men. It is as if two creatures occupy the space that is one mind and permit no access by another. It is a friendship which can challenge even the sacred bond between spouses—not that noble spouses marry to be friends! The bonding between two men is a formidable force. It is not enough that they drive their horses headlong in the same direction; they also whip each other's steeds, each goading his fellow along.

I can speak like that after all this time because they are both long dead and time's advantage rests with the last to die. It is no disloyalty to offer explanation for a husband's folly, especially a husband who kept me little better than a prisoner for fifteen years when his rage overwhelmed his love. But that is a tale for another page, another day; perhaps, if God wills, another season.

Summer is upon us, child. Did you notice? Of course you did. Only the old feel cold in every season. How high the sun flies; how he warms the days. We started this endeavor at the end of winter. Around Ash Wednesday, was it not? The cycle of the year has fairly sped. We must be halfway through. Lord grant me life enough until this task be done!

But now I'll bid Him give me rest; I'll sleep the sunny hours away. Lay down that quill, Aline, and help me to my bed.

I s it not strange how one takes one's span of life for granted? Time and purpose, time and drift. Not until my dotage did I dream of starting on a work which needs the one commodity I cannot buy for its completion. But my time, precious time, is overspent. Some day, sooner than later, God will call me to redeem it.

Such a fatal "Good morning" I offer, Aline! Never mind. I am anxious, you see. So much to do. Had I dictated my book years ago I could die in this moment with an easy grace. The breath of uttering passes, but the uttered word endures. The world's affairs speed past me now. Let hap what will! This island of stone walls is all the world I need in all the world.

Anxious. Too anxious. Too anxious to start. More anxious to end. But how to think? Where to think? My heart races; thoughts skip like butterflies. I fear I must begin this morning with a posset. Bid Sister Hortensia hither.

Becket was a chancellor no king would wish to better. His duty to Henry, in office and in friendship, offered no scope for conflict or complaint. As chancellor he undertook a task for which, in a general way, Theobald had readied him. Even when he taxed the bishops—to Theobald's keen distress—he did so with a clear conscience. Duty was uncomfortable, but duty called.

I wonder if those taxes were the itch that turned the old man's face against the wall. Did my business at Toulouse hasten Theobald's demise?

But that is a side text. To continue: the very notion of appointing Becket to the see of Canterbury was folly. I told Henry so when he launched the thought at me. Folly! As chancellor, Becket's only master was the king. As archbishop, his sole master was God; and Becket, for all his worldliness, was not a man to shirk or shed his faith. If two forces hailed his name from opposite directions he could not but answer the higher call.

We hissed over the matter in bed, Henry and I. He sought a nominee to be *his* man, and his alone. Their first six years as twins in office seemed to prove to Henry that Becket wore the king's badge, and his only. But Henry, puffed in glory, failed to see the pride of righteousness that drove the other on. Yes, we had bitter words over Becket—but later we had worse.

What could I know, a woman and a bedmate? Nor was I alone. Henry's mother, Matilda, swore a thousand vows against Becket's appointment to Canterbury. As empress in Saxony she had seen the folly of vesting the affairs of Church and crown in one head. But Henry would not hear his mother, either.

Henry and Becket were soulmates in those days, as if joined at the hip. As chancellor, Thomas had done no wrong—could do no wrong! But Henry could not see that he who served one lord with zeal would serve a higher master with even greater diligence. The Becket affair evokes the adage: "One man can but one master serve."

It was around that time that I felt the first rift between Henry and me. I had challenged his judgment, and it was not long before events proved him wrong. Mark me, Aline, I sought no victory for myself, but only for the Angevins. That is how a dynasty must function: one body serves the higher purpose, not the other way around. But Henry was always one to sum his gains and losses as if they were tokens to be tallied on the cloth at the exchequer.

Urgent or not, the matter of nominating a new archbishop to the see of Canterbury took more than a year to resolve. Which, in hindsight, was just as well: it saved an additional year of strife.

I mentioned a certain day at Falaise. We had held our Easter court there. This was the sort of day which northern lands impose too often at that time of year. The fog at Falaise rolls down through the slot in the hills. Grey days and a damp cold cut like a dagger to the bone. The walls at Falaise are long and low, gray like the fog, and on that morning they were lost in it. I could barely see the far end of the wall from the gate where we waited to bid the company farewell.

Henry always felt confident when we lay at Falaise. It was said that the mother of William the Conqueror, Henry's great-great-grandmother, was born to a seamstress in Falaise. Or was she his great-grandmother? For reasons I have never understood, this knowledge seemed to buoy him up.

Henry had summoned Becket from England, ostensibly to escort Young Henry back to Winchester, there to receive the further homage of the barons. His father was punctilious in the matter of oaths. Including his own to Louis.

Becket's party stood ready to travel to Caen, thence to take ship at Barfleur. It was then—and this was typical of Henry—that he broached his mind to Becket. I see that scene clearly, forty-one years later, perhaps because it was a turning point. Horses chafed and men-at-arms dismounted, speaking in low voices while they shivered in their chain-mail, all eyes turning from time to time to watch Henry and Becket confer. They drew apart until they seemed wraiths in the fog: none dared disturb them. The fact that he did not broach the matter of Becket's preferment until the last minute was an indication that even Henry was of two minds.

Becket was far from blameless in the matter. He knew what the effect of such a preferment must be. He told Henry as much in that chilly, fateful hour. Afterwards, Henry lost no time telling me. And yet Becket did not refuse the king's bidding. Would that he had!

19. From love to hate: a bridge soon crossed
1162-1164

Perhaps if that year had taken a different track… But we were at swords-drawn against Louis and his allies, Blois and Champagne. Henry was in constant motion that summer: diplomacy and readiness for war commanded our attention. Diplomacy prevailed, fortunately. War is so costly. The kings met at Fréteval, and for a time the Angevins and Franks were reconciled.

After his fateful conversation with Henry at Falaise, Becket took ship for England with Young Henry (whom I had brought to Normandy from England to marry Marguerite). Becket stated his misgivings at Falaise, but then he kept his reservations to himself. Perhaps his commission preoccupied him: it would be his final major task as chancellor. Henry had instructed Becket to summon the bishops and barons to Winchester in May, instructing the company to take oaths of fealty to Young Henry. I often imagine the scene: our son appareled in finery and crowned with a coronet wrought in gold to fit his little head. Becket himself set the example, offering his personal homage to Young Henry before the other nobles, abbots and bishops of the realm.

As to the other matter, the clergy of the province of Canterbury were summoned to London where they elected Becket as their next archbishop: the king's judges and Young Henry witnessed the conclave. John of Salisbury carried their warrant to the pope, returning with the blessing of the curia and a pallium for the new archbishop. Becket was soon ordained priest, and then—the bishop of Winchester presiding—he was enthroned archbishop.

I say it again. Would that the deed had not been done.

You may imagine that Becket's appointment was not popular with the monks of Canterbury or the more ascetic members of the clergy. Here was a man who had practised neither humility nor austerity, but at the instant of his consecration he assumed pretensions to both. They say Becket exchanged silk and brocade for a hair shirt swarming with vermin. Even Louis did not toy with such foolishness. Had he done so, he would have slept alone. They say that for drink Becket took water that had been used for boiling hay.

As for his conduct, he changed utterly. He who had eaten with kings now took to washing the feet of beggars, thirteen of them each day. We know that God employs a mystery to turn grubs into butterflies. The greater mystery in those days was to witness Becket's butterfly become a grub.

It was not long before popular histories invented pious explanations for Becket's transformation. It was mooted that his mother had been blessed with a vision revealing the very church of Canterbury in her womb. Later, when Prior Robert at Merton supervised Thomas's education, it was said that Becket's father, visiting the priory, fell down to worship at his son's feet. Those wonders were current forty years ago: after this span of years I cannot say how much of Becket's apotheosis was rooted in people's surprise at his new beginning, and how much was fashioned from the outrage and grief which followed his death.

Aline, you will have to sort these notes so that they follow each other in the order of the happenings which I describe. With respect to other events in my life, I have no trouble placing one before the other as if they were my feet. But with Becket, the life is but the setting to the outcome. His death overshadows his life as a bailey looms over a motte, so one rides through his final years in anticipation of the end.

We returned to England towards the end of January. Henry had been absent four years, having wrought order in Normandy, Brittany, Maine, Touraine, Anjou and Aquitaine. I had not set foot in England since Louis' intention to marry Adela of Champagne forced me to bring Young Henry to Rouen.

We landed at Southampton—another mid-winter crossing—to be met by a panoply of nobles, including Young Henry. He ran forward to greet us from a hiding place under Becket's cloak.

There was not a person in the party who did not wonder how the king would greet his former chancellor. It was said that Becket met Henry "without true goodwill," but for my part I think they were both apprehensive. We managed to journey together to London with civil discourse, but heated argument began soon afterwards.

The reason for discord was clear enough. Becket no sooner took his pallium of office from Canterbury's high altar than he began to erase the inroads of the king's laws in Church affairs—the same laws, mark me, which he and Henry had fought to impose through a system of county courts eight years before.

Becket also took steps to reclaim lands and manors which had slipped from the Church into the clutches of barons during the chaos of Stephen's reign. Henry had good reason to hear of these actions. Long before we returned to England, scalded nobles and their messengers were ploughing the Channel and rutting the roads to Rouen with pleas for the king's intervention.

That was a year of public rage and private furies. Henry was never content to be quiet within his skin, but I was spared many of his outbursts because for much of our marriage we had lived apart, separated by the sea. Besides, when Henry had Becket to confide in, he had no cause to turn for confidant to me. Suddenly, after eleven years of marriage and nine as Henry's queen, I found myself promoted to the role of key advisor to my husband and king. As such, my burning ears became the butt of his rages.

To be sure, Becket's incursions were intolerable. In July that year he summoned the earl of Hertford to give homage in respect of Tonbridge castle. Homage! To Becket? Roger de Clare refused, of course, claiming he held that domain from the king.

There was also the matter of a vacant living at Eynesford. Becket installed a certain Lawrence in the living, causing William of Eynesford to claim that he alone had the right of gift. So William expelled Lawrence, whereon Becket excommunicated William. This took place without so much as a memorandum to the king.

I stood firmly with Henry in this matter: it was not for the Church to rule the crown. Nor did the Church grow in stature because it winked at crimes and extortion by those who took holy orders expressly to claim immunity from royal courts. If the Church in England were reduced to the corruption of pardoners, what must the realm as a whole become?

Not that I had to caution Henry, burned as he was by this affair. He had appointed Becket to cleanse the Church—at least, that was his intention—not to protect it in the worst of its corruptions.

Which brings us to Westminster in the autumn of that year. In October, Henry convened an assembly of abbots, bishops and barons. Fifty magnates, spiritual and temporal, sat in attendance.

Henry had been pondering a more reliable way of discovering mischief in the land. He proposed to swear twelve of the more law-abiding men in each district to report those known to be murderers and thieves. Why twelve, I asked? Why not ten? One for each finger was surely enough. But no. Henry showed populist leanings in curious ways. He had set his legalists striving to codify the *common* law, and twelve is the common measure in the market-place, where traders use their thumb tips to tally on the twelve bones in the other fingers. Twelve pies, twelve onions, twelve measures of peas, twelve law-abiding men. In the event, the matter was postponed until the business of ecclesiastical courts was settled to his satisfaction.

To that end Henry thundered at the bishops—Becket among them— listing tales of corruption and the venal shade cast by Church courts; of evil men seeking ordination in order to use the cloak of priesthood as a licence to commit murder and mayhem with impunity. Thomas, in his new role as shield and protector of the Church, gave Henry no response worthy of the hearing. Whereupon Henry washed his hands of them, leaving lords and prelates in confusion.

His next tirade took flight at me. He paced and shouted into the night, grinding the rushes to dust.

He was no better next day. He demanded that Becket surrender the manors of Berkhamstead and Eye—the mainstays of his income.

Then, to winnow his grain from Becket's chaff beyond all doubt, he removed Young Henry and the Princess Marguerite from the archbishop's household, ranting: "Is a fellow who shelters murderers and thieves fit to rear a future king of England?"

Young Henry was most upset; Marguerite, too. God knows, nothing is permanent in the lives of noble children. But they had become accustomed to living with Becket since returning with him from Normandy the previous year. They had lodged with their well-beloved "uncle" since that day at Falaise.

If that were not enough, Henry insisted on holding our Christmas court at Berkhamstead, in Becket's former hall. Indeed, the ashes in his kitchens were still warm when our household took possession. I recall moving to Berkhamstead in late November, and hearing mass there on Advent Sunday.

During the years that Henry and I cohabited, there were times when I wished he would gather his household and go. The five weeks we spent at Berkhamstead was such a time.

Advent should be joyful, but it offered little respite that year. Henry was set on facing Becket with a litany of grievances going back to his grandfather's reign. To that end the castle overflowed with lawyers and jurists in place of Christmas choirs.

Ah, but I gained one wondrous consolation. Young Henry and Marguerite lodged with us that Christmastide. All my life I have educated children; mine, my grandchildren, and the offspring from most of the noble houses in the western lands. But I cherish that month in spite of Henry's anxious business. Young Henry was two months short of his ninth birthday, which falls—which fell—in February.

You see how it is, Aline. Memory is deathless, until its bearer dies.

Barely had we passed Epiphany before Henry removed his person, his scrolls, his lawyers and his anger to Clarendon. Thither he hailed Becket and the bishops, to browbeat them again.

I recall Henry pacing, pacing, pacing the floor at Berkhamstead. It gave him special pleasure—how heady is righteous indignation!—to fashion a bridle for Becket in that miscreant's former hall.

The hall was like a market place, a jostling of folk at all hours: lawyers talking, contradicting; Henry smacking his hand on the board and punching his fists in the air; scribes grinding ink while others, black-lipped, tried to suck it faster than reluctant quills could feed it... What relief when they finally fashioned a preamble! The remainder was days in coming, too, but the preamble was finicked to a fault. I remember it as if it were a well-worn ballad:

> "In the twelfth year of Henry II, most illustrious king of the
> English, there was made, in the presence of the said king, the
> record and recognition of a certain portion of the customs
> and liberties and rights of his ancestors and of others—which
> ought to be observed and held in the kingdom..."

For the longest time the sticking point was the word "recognition."
But Henry insisted. It was the word which jurists had also proposed as
an instruction to the twelve men sworn to "recognize" a crime.

I will say this for Henry: the Constitutions of Clarendon acknowl-
edged the pope in the preamble. Two years later, Pope Alexander's aid
to Becket moved Henry to such apoplexy that he expunged the pope's
name utterly from the Clarendon Assize.

I see it still: the wagging finger, hectoring tone; the jurists John of
Balliol and Richard of Lucy attempting to speak; lawyers cowed like
baggage-mules beneath Henry's whip of words; scribes writing, striking through and sending urgently for ink and parchment; dust from the
floor and smoke from the fire shading the flames as Henry paced:

> "And on account of the dissension and disputes that had
> arisen between the clergy and the justices of the lord king and
> the barons of the realm concerning customs and rights, the
> recognition was made..."

And so on. Always "recognition," as if the justices were rooting out
the crimes of Holy Church.

Oh Henry, if the very stars had dared to cross you in those days you
would have hauled them into court. In later years it was better that you
sent me into exile than that we lived together! We would have made
each other mad.

It was Henry who stalked out of the conclave at Westminster. It was Becket who turned his back on the king and rode away from Clarendon. He would never agree, he said, to set his seal to a document which stole a march on the Church: he held that the Constitutions of Clarendon went far beyond restoring to the king those customs and revenues which prevailed before the civil war. Becket was persuaded that Henry meant to seize certain ancient privileges of the Church. As indeed we did, but not without a certain subtlety.

When he shook Clarendon's dust off his feet, Becket had the presence of mind to take his copy of the Constitutions with him. In his place, I should have tossed it on the fire in parting. I say that because, although I was very much of Henry's mind in the matter, I had counseled moderation. The document was too severe. I was party to its drafting; all through Advent my ears had burned with lawyers' legalisms, twists and turns. I argued in private that the Constitutions gave Becket no room for compromise. But Henry would not hear of it. Had he listened, I do believe we would have turned the ship of state away from rocks.[24]

Now I am tired. We must break off soon, Aline. But I make one more point before you draw the shutter across the window. I have been party to negotiations since I merged my fate with Louis' and my people's fates with his. Sixty-six years have borne off lives and times since I first set my duchy's seal upon a contract. Never have I known a treaty to establish lasting peace when *force majeure* attached the weaker party by the hand and set its seal upon defeat.

Well met, Aline. You look downcast, child. Where is the flagrant lock of hair today, the ready smile, the bright "Good morrow, madam"?

Ah, your betrothed returns to England. Too early for the harvest, surely? That comes later beyond the northern sea.

How fortunate that your dowry goes to the purchase of a wealthy manor. And bordering his parents', too. It is always better to live among family: his kin will soon be yours. Let him go with good grace, child. Your parting is for the best of reasons. He will furnish a hall worthy of a wife who has served a queen.

But your news puts me in fear that I must lose you before we write *explicitus* to end our chronicle. When do you marry? Ah, then we shall have until next spring. God grant me breath till then!

Can it be that in the month he has been here you have learned to love him? I am happy for you. A marriage cemented by love shall surely endure. How wonderful. Unusual, too.

Yes, yes, we must get to work. I fear I must treat of Becket again, today, and it may be, for ever. He is destined to be the most impertinent ghost of our age.

I have seen madmen in anguish hold their humors in check better than Henry in those strange days. He could in no way bridle his anger; he had to strike at him whom once he loved above all others. The matter of Becket consumed Henry. Indeed, it consumed us all at court for a full two years. And this was but the first pass at their tourney.

The following year, hard on the feast of Edward the Confessor—a holiday which the English hold much in respect—Henry summoned Becket to Northampton. He hailed him there to answer a trivial business which served as the mule to carry Henry's grievance to the market. This pretext was made to seem so great a matter that Archbishop Roger of York—who was firmly of the king's party—was also summoned to attend.

Henry was determined to stamp his contempt on Becket's face. When Thomas arrived for the appointed day, Henry and his entourage were miles away, coursing falcons. That gesture alone was not enough to ensure Becket's discomfiture. So Henry's harbingers, riding ahead, placed men of no great rank in lodgings marked for Becket and his party.

This gave the people of Northampton much to peer at through cracks in their shutters—the sight of the great archbishop, sans roof, and standing in the street. What a striking contrast between Becket's arrival at Northampton and the panoply of wealth and grace which had carried him as our chancellor to Paris.

How are the mighty fallen. No one, no, not even Becket, can voice that adage with more authority than I. And yet I can say in perfect truth that she who ruled a duchy and a kingdom and an empire is quite content in age to be ruled within these walls. Sweet Fontevrault!

But, to return to Becket. What began as a studied insult to Becket turned in time to his advantage and Henry's shame, for there was not a churl in England who did not understand the implication of the phrase "no room in the inn." It took no stroke of genius to liken Becket to the baby Christ, and Henry to Herod.

On the day following, as he walked to mass and breakfast, Henry chanced upon Becket but gave him no greeting. From which Thomas surely guessed what the proceeding held in store.

As to the case against him, it was argued according to the items in the Constitutions of Clarendon, to which the archbishop had refused to set his seal. Nevertheless, the king in his court set a fine of three hundred pounds. One curiosity in the matter was that, of those who sat in judgment, none of the judges consented to report the verdict to Becket, who waited in an anteroom. He learned of the fine from old Henry, bishop of Winchester, who had consecrated Becket to his spiritual throne just a year and a season before.

To my displeasure there was more. I say that not out of compassion, but from the practical lesson a long life has learned. The most enduring victory is not that which reduces an enemy to hating, but rather brings him to love.

Henry fined Becket a further three hundred pounds for monies owed from the manors he formerly held of the king. This charge did not sit squarely, for it seemed that, before Becket's consecration, Young Henry's counselors exempted him from the obligation to report his manors' accounts.

I blush to repeat what came next. Many of the bishops in attendance were in the king's camp, not Becket's. They owed their preferments to the king; they still wore the welts of the whip which Becket had cracked as chancellor. You will recall, Aline, that he raised funds at Henry's urging for my war to regain Toulouse, six years before: the costs of an army; the costs to ship horses and men to Gascony—a heavy expense. Becket raised those monies by taxing the bishops. Accordingly, Henry's court now worked its way into a fine rage, venturing a third fine on Becket to recover the money he had raised in taxes: the sum of a thousand marks.

20. Escape, pursuit, rebuke
1164

I noticed you put down your quill some time ago, Aline. No need to make excuses; it is I who should do that. I have been silent too long. For too many minutes; for too many years.

No, child, I am not tired. Only weary of the world, and in particular the one I cannot bear to hear myself describe. It stirs mud in a mind which would rather forget.

The event was ugly. Very ugly. I speak of Northampton and the pressure of cankered minds. Bishop Gilbert of London remarked that Becket "always was a fool." Perhaps. But this affair showed me that Henry was malign. The start of our end took root in this: I am sure of it. Not that I took Becket's part. He had soiled both the king's bed and his own. He was determined to be difficult. But those years brought the devil out in Henry.

Henry had seemed to get the better at Northampton. But he came away marked, distrustful. Northampton exposed a vindictive quality.

The headstrong youth of old became a man who discovered ways to fear the world.

He expressly denied Becket the right of appeal to the pope. But Becket replied boldly that he would do just that. That night the archbishop decamped from Northampton without Henry's safe-conduct, made his way via byways to Canterbury and thence took ship from Sandwich, a port no great distance away. Henry had sent orders to close the ports against him, but someone shipped Becket to Flanders, putting him ashore on the mud at Oye. Thence by hard travel he came with a few companions to the monks at St. Omer. From there, one monastic house escorted him to another. Becket put his new-found persecution and poverty to good use, being refreshed in body and spirit by sundry abbots and bishops all along his way. And so he entered France.

It chanced that Louis was holding court in Compiègne, which lay on Becket's route to the city of Sens, where Pope Alexander lodged—having been driven out of Rome, again. In Compiègne, Becket regaled Louis with his woes: Louis—I would stake my soul on this!—would scarcely conceal his glee. From Louis, Becket made his way to Sens.

That lamentable conclave at Northampton took place in the autumn of the year. I recall that Becket took ship into exile on All Saints Day, which seems appropriate: eight years later the very pope to whom he fled would make of his martyred ghost a saint.

Meanwhile, Henry lost no time sending his own ambassadors to Alexander. Having wished them Godspeed, a vile humor gripped him for the month they were away.

This latest tourney twixt king and prelate exhausted exactly one year. Preparations for the Constitutions of Clarendon had overwhelmed our previous Advent and Christmas, as Henry's lawyers jostled our household and children in Becket's former hall.

Advent was on us once again. And once again Becket was the motive under-propping every policy, the whisper under-propping every word.

We were holding our Christmas court at Marlborough when Henry's ambassadors returned from the pope.

They had taken ship not long after Becket slipped his leash at Northampton—that man married the grace of God with the luck of the devil in this affair! The ambassadors made speed to overtake Becket *en route* to Alexander, but turned aside at Compiègne to ask for Louis's passport along the roads of France. They took small comfort from Louis: he challenged the very premise of their mission. He always feigned incredulity well, especially when matters temporal challenged the role of the Church. Louis could never admit it, but his mind was that of an archbishop, never a king. He had, for example, learned nothing from our forces' debacle at Damascus. That lesson taught him not one useful jot about the folly of letting prelates command an army. No, the Church could do no wrong.

He welcomed Henry's envoys with the sarcastic opening: "A prelate subject to the judgment of his king?" Ah, Louis, you never did change! Your whole life through you were the boy-monk walking in the shadow of dead Philip.

Nevertheless, Louis granted Henry's envoys a passport towards Sens, to which they made such haste that they passed Becket's retinue waiting to cross the River Yonne. They were quick to notice that Becket, who scrambled out of England with barely a habit on his back, now commanded a retinue of clerks loaned by the sundry abbots and bishops who sheltered him from Flanders to Compiègne; and a significant escort of men-at-arms provided by Louis, who had reasons enough to respect Henry's tricks.

By happy chance, Henry's ambassadors claimed the pope's ear before Becket. But small good it did them.

It is no exaggeration to remark that Henry's ambassadors were mocked in the officious manner favored by priests: in the first place, as to the rightness of the king's cause; and second, Pope Alexander chose to forget Henry's support of his election to the throne of St. Peter, two years earlier. In short, Henry's cause and our envoys were dismissed with no success.

The telling of these events, you may guess, soured our Advent again.

When the envoys reported their news at Marlborough, a devil mixed Henry's humors to a fire of rage I had not known before. Some years later he directed a similar fit at me, to my extreme cost. He frothed as one smitten by the falling sickness, he shrieked as a man put to torture, he rent his clothes, threw fire logs, turned tables on their heads. For an hour and more no voice or reason could reach him, much less govern him.

We have inked many pages, Aline, since I mentioned the sainted Bernard's verdict on the infant Henry, the man destined to father my children and conceive their souls. Bernard, who was in every way contemptuous and distrusting of ambitious men, condemned Henry thus: "From the devil he came; to the devil he shall go." I had for years dismissed this as black bile. But, at Marlborough, a part of my being inched further away as I watched Henry rant.

One comment never reached the king's ear directly, for no one dared speak it, then, or after. I heard it later, and chose to lock it in my head. The pope, or some officer of the curia, remarked that what King Henry wanted seemed neither in accordance with the law nor reason.

The next thunderbolt fell on St. John's day. Henry gave order to expel every member of Becket's family, all kith and kin, from England. Infant or ancient, fit or frail, seigneur or server, man or woman—better than four hundred souls were marched to the coast with what they could carry, crammed into ships and cast ashore in the sodden cold of Flanders to find such mercy as monasteries and the Church might offer them.

21. BECKET: BLAST AND COUNTER-BLAST
1165-1166

Thus we entered the year of our Lord one thousand one hundred and sixty-five, rich beyond measure in a wealth of lands, trade, ports, castles, assets, treasure—and much out of temper! And, I may say, set about by foes.

Becket now became a sore to our cause and a salve to Louis', who rewarded him by taking the archbishop under his protection and rejoicing at our discomfiture. No one knew better than I how Louis could vacillate between too little action and too much. Now he discovered resolve. It was in this season that he set his seal upon the Capets' alliance with the houses of Blois and Champagne. To that end he put my daughters to marriage: Marie, who was twenty, to Henry of Champagne; and little Alix to Thibault of Blois. I always called her "little" Alix, for that is what she was to me: she was a baby when I had to abandon her to Louis as a prize of divorce. But in the year of which I speak she turned thirteen, became a woman.

Perhaps it was the birth of Louis' son which improved his outlook and increased his prospects and resolve. It needed more than good intentions by his third wife, Adela of Champagne, to reward his prayers for a male heir. Reports reached us of Louis' sundry pious pleadings. I myself had besought the prayers of Bernard—conceiving Marie in consequence—but Louis enlisted the prayers of all Clairvaux and much of his kingdom besides.

God or Adela obliged, giving birth to Philip Augustus in the full heat of summer on the twenty-second day of August. The year was without doubt a watershed for Louis, though not one which was kind to us.

I should observe that I carried Joanna that year, giving birth at Angers. She was our youngest daughter. I fear that my sweet infant did not give rise to the exuberance of bells with which the Franks greeted baby Philip as their heir.

One gains and one loses. Or, as the *chanson* has it, "One loses, the other wins." Joanna was no sooner born than we began negotiation with Emperor Frederick Barbarossa for the hand of our eldest daughter, Matilda. I had first encountered Barbarossa eighteen years before, when he escaped from the Turks and encountered the van of our army, weeping and shouting for aid while the Turkish cavalry destroyed his Germans in that hell of Anatolia.

Barbarossa was now emperor. Archbishop Reginald of Cologne represented him in talks with us. They were good friends, those two, as thick as Henry and Becket had been. They were ardent supporters of the anti-pope, and loathed Alexander, too. We considered affiancing two daughters to the Germans, but in the end we sent them only one. Matilda was already nine, but we kept her back a full two years before we let them take her. She was destined to marry Henry the Lion, duke of Saxony and Bavaria. And he was nearly forty. We were of course discreet in the matter of the nuptial contract. From that point of view the match was undesirable. But Henry the Lion was the most puissant baron in the German lands, excepting Barbarossa. And by happy chance Matilda's grandmother of that name had ruled Saxony for many years.

Try as I might, Aline, I cannot escape this business of Becket. He was a severe trial, in our dealings with the Franks, with the pope and with the Germans. The man was wont to change his coat more often than the vainest woman. Now he took upon himself the white habit of a Cistercian monk and retreated—I should say retired—to the austerities of their house at Pontigny. As a monk he could not venture forth, but he had time enough to publish his cause by writing letters. I speak in particular of his letters to Henry. You may imagine how they were received.

Late that year Pope Alexander was restored for a time to his palace at Rome. Here was a man who trimmed one policy with a second before annulling both with a third, always diligent to erase with one hand what he set forth with the other. Alexander lacked the courage to decide which foot to stand on. Unfortunately, he re-entered the Holy City encouraged by a tumultuous welcome. Thus emboldened, he suffered a brave moment and did a thing which enraged us.

No sooner was Alexander restored—briefly—than he appointed Becket papal legate for all England, saving only the diocese of York, which has been governed separately since ancient days. This deed served the papacy no good, for it reinforced our support for the German schismatics and the holy Roman empire.

We were holding Easter court at Angers when word of Alexander's edict carried to our ear. A week later Becket sent three emissaries. Over time he sent several letters as well, informing Henry of the limitations of his earthly power. I recall a scrap or two, a puff of holy wind, from these communications:

"These are the words of the archbishop of Canterbury to the king of the English…I have desired to see your face and to speak with you; greatly for my sake, but more for yours…For your sake, for three causes: because you are my lord; because you are my king; and because you are my spiritual son…"

In his better moods Henry joked that Thomas mistook his own will for that of Providence. Privately we knew that willfulness had made Becket an effective chancellor—and a mule of an opponent. What else did that meddler write? Oh yes…

"It is certain that kings receive their power from the Church, not she from them but from Christ. So, if I may speak with your pardon, you have not the power to give rules to bishops…or to draw clerks before secular tribunals, or to pass judgment concerning churches and tithes…and many other things of that sort which are written among your customs which you call ancient."

Henry took special umbrage at Becket's suggestion that the king had broken faith with his coronation vow…

"Remember the promise you placed in writing on the altar at Westminster when you were consecrated and anointed king by my predecessor, of preserving to the Church her liberty…Otherwise, know for certain that you shall feel the divine severity and vengeance."

Both to quiet these pinpricks and, as a principle of discipline, Henry wrote to the father superior of the Cistercians, threatening to confiscate certain properties in England if the monks continued to house Thomas and his coterie at Pontigny.

This threat was enough to bring Louis himself to Pontigny. The Cistercians might wash their hands of Becket, but not Louis. He escorted the archbishop to Sens, where he housed him at Ste. Colombe for the next four years. Louis staged this removal to convey to us his high regard for Becket: not only had the pope recently vacated Sens, but its diocese includes Paris. You will recall, Aline: years earlier, Bernard had chosen the exalted precinct of Sens cathedral from which to condemn Peter Abelard. Louis' gesture was wasted on Henry and me: we had both inherited healthy disdains for the gambits of priests.

Becket, in no way humbled, now strove to smite with spoken words what he failed to move with letters. He took himself to the church at Vezeley, the town where Abbé Bernard had sanctioned my Crusade. There, after giving the sermon at Pentecost,[25] Becket excommunicated Richard of Lucy and John of Balliol for drafting the Constitutions of Clarendon; and Richard of Ilchester and John of Oxford for conducting Henry's diplomacy with the schismatic Germans. There were others, as well. They were good men, all.

He was careful not to excommunicate Henry in person. By the same token, Henry tilted at Becket with a blunted lance. We had our reason: Young Henry—now in his twelfth year—had not yet been crowned king of the English, and ancient custom dictated that only the archbishop of Canterbury could perform that ceremony. So we were not eager to burn bridges. Nor was Becket, whose informants were telling him that the business of England moved forward without his aid.

Becket's best-informed spy was the bishop of Winchester, old Henry of Blois. Bishop Henry had no love for our Angevins to begin with; still less after King Henry confiscated his English manors. Bishop Henry served as Becket's eyes and ears beyond the sea, and we were powerless to stop him—although we were careful to feed him misinformation. Old Henry was both the bishop of Winchester *and* the abbot of Glastonbury—an unprecedented feat, and a measure of his influence on popes. His skein of influence was all-encompassing. In some respects he *was* the English Church. No, old Henry was too lofty to bring down.

Furthermore, he had never allowed himself to be used by kings, including his brother, Stephen.

We did not sit idle while Becket issued taunts and excommunicated our loyal servants. We put about that King Henry was sick, because even a pope cannot excommunicate a king when it is known that he is ill. The notion is unthinkable that divine right vests in a body which may die excommunicated. The thread of divine and royal authority would be broken.

So Henry lay at death's door for as long as it served our purpose. Then, by way of riposte, he rose from his sickbed, emerging from the walls of Chinon to announce to the world that Becket, the pope and sundry members of the curia were "in his purse." This was a wonderful invention, but not without some scattered grains of truth. By this time we had studied the swings of the pope to and fro—giving, taking, sanctioning, annulling and giving again. Alexander's contradictions were as timely as the tides.

And he obliged us. The pope waived Becket's appointment as legate in England; and he suspended the excommunications which the archbishop had so recently pronounced with flourish of bell, book and candle at Vezeley.

Of course it did not hurt our cause that the army of the holy Roman emperor was battering the gates of Rome—again—helped in no small part by English coin.

22. A brief digression on Fair Rosamond
1165-1176

I am tired beyond measure of Becket. The man still has some years to live in our account, but I cannot bring myself to speak of them. Not yet.

Furthermore, in those same years I drank my fill of Henry, too.

I hope, Aline, that your husband will cherish you, and you alone. Keep him by you in your bed, child; keep him gratified; keep him drained. If you keep his seed in you and not in him, you will discover that the feral humors of his sex won't reach for other women.

You wince. Tush, tush, I do not mean to shock you, but I hope that you can learn from what I have to say. Listen, and life may spare you from trial by the all-too-ready lance.

What I say is true. Too many men behave like rams in rut, but surely there were few as hot as Henry. He was insatiable. He sired eight—nine—living children on me as well as more bastards than I choose to count. He lured women to his bed-lust by the score.

Wives learn to turn their face the other way—as did I for fourteen years. But there came a season when I could no longer wear a tranquil mask in my husband's hall.

Does the name Rosamond Clifford mean anything to you, Aline? No? You are too young. But it will when you have been a wife in England for some years. Bards and jongleurs will beg meat and a night at your manor in exchange for a song and a poem or two. And you will then be surprised to learn how, out of spite and jealousy, your former mistress, the old Queen Aleänor, killed sweet Rosamond.

Hah! I thought that slander might stir you. It startled me the first time I heard it.

I speak of the summer after Becket fled to Louis, the year I governed our lands from Angers while Henry went warring—or should I say whoring?—in Wales. Over time I gleaned news of Henry and this woman.

Among the knights serving in Wales was Walter de Clifford, a Norman who held an estate in the border country, near Bredelais. Perhaps in his remote and rustic world this fool had not learned to lock up his women at Henry's approach, although, God knows, my husband's reputation galloped before him along every road. No wife or daughter, no female ward or hostage, was presented to Henry unless the lord of a place where he stopped had either malice or ambition in his heart.

It may be that de Clifford, seeking some advantage, steered his daughter in harm's way, but that I cannot say. Or Henry may have come on her near Oxford, for she was schooled there, at Godstow, by nuns.

This Rosamond Clifford smote Henry as no paramour had possessed him before. I'm sure he thought only to bed her, perhaps for a night, perhaps for a week; but she possessed him till she died. Here was an attachment without precedent in its intensity. I gather this naughtiness was all a-buzz for a season or two before word reached me. The fool confused the hurt in his loins for love! Love, mark me! Henry in his lust was so confused that he squandered his love—the quality by which men attach each other—on a woman! In the world of noble liaisons this affair was passing strange.

Until this Rosamond bewitched his senses, Henry summoned enough discretion to manage trysts and conquests in dark corners of a hall. But Rosamond! With her he must be seen. With her he must display affection. On her he must lavish gifts. Her he must install within a short ride of our palace at Woodstock! You may believe me when I say that Henry was quicker to give the kiss of peace to Rosamond than to Thomas Becket.

I spent my first decade with Henry believing that a bull in March must yield in time to November chills, becoming a sober, wiser soul. For the longest while I thought I might one day check his bridle. But it was not to be. Years spent apart, on opposite sides of the Channel, did not help me command him, although they eased the tensions between us. Then the first blasts of the Becket affair taught me what I should have learned, that Henry would not be ruled.

Not even in the matter of discretion. He had stabbed his blade in women by the score—I see I have inured you to the coarser world, Aline—while retaining the decency to greet them next morning as if they were nuns. But his whore Rosamond left him drunk to possess her, again and again. Would that she but sapped his seed. However, she also sapped his brains. I heard constant whispers of their dealings, of course. If a noble lady does not equip herself with ears she will be as innocent of news as any village idiot. But this infamous liaison was a fire; the closer one got to the source, the hotter the whispers became. Here was one woman whom the late Saint Bernard might hate with a blameless conscience *and* my blessing—for in truth she was a fallen angel.

But in the matter of her death the Almighty knows me innocent. When I had power to send her dead, I did not; and when God wisely chose to take her from this world I was under constant watch by Henry's spies.

Henry himself spent the winter wearing out horses on the frosty road between Rosamond at Woodstock, and Clarendon, where he rewrote the laws of England. For that I cannot mock him. We landed in a kingdom where it seemed that every manor and shire had its own ancient laws and punishments. So I grant the devil his due: Henry imposed on the backward English a common "law and custom of the land."[26] It was there, at Clarendon, that Henry's conclave of nobles and prelates approved his idea of swearing twelve just men to report malefactors. It was there, too, that Henry slipped his lance past Becket's shield: the Assize forbade religious communities inducting a person from the lower classes unless he could prove good repute.[27]

That done, Henry took ship to preside at our Easter court in Angers. No doubt he came hot from Rosamond's bed to mine, where he conceived John on me. That October I resumed my role as regent of England. I traveled in Oxfordshire—Woodstock was always a favorite palace—where it seemed the very birds clamored "Rosamond, sweet Rosamond." I spoke just now of approaching a fire. I knew soon enough that our seat at Woodstock was the burning hearth: Henry's hussy lodged mere miles away. In that season I experienced something that never befell me before or since. Whenever I moved through a crowd, people fell silent.

No matter. I lodged at Oxford castle, giving birth to John the day after Christmas. He is named for the saint on whose day he was born.[28]

Granted Rosamond was three-and-thirty. I was forty-four, old enough that I no longer roused passion in the husband whose children I bore. To Henry, my body was as well rehearsed as a hasty mass before breakfast.

But kill her? No, I would not dignify his harlot in that way. No plot of mine would stoop to canonize her beauty by sealing it in death. Unless perhaps my prayers condemned her.

23. A PARTING OF TWO WAYS
FROM 1167

Rosamond Clifford was one slight too many for me to bear. Henry's soiled succubus! She struck me as an insult to my very being. I did not seek divorce. I merely chose to live apart. Henry once chided Becket: "This island is not big enough to contain us both." After sixteen years of marriage I felt the same about Henry. Let him parade his whore! When he made it impossible for the world to be blind to her he shamed me beyond cure. He forfeited the dignity of my silence and earned my lasting vengeance and reproach. Henceforth we would travel separate paths to separate fates.

I decided to return to my lands and my people after an absence of thirty years. Once more I would rule as countess and as duchess in Poitou and Aquitaine. So my household took ship—I brought young Richard with me as my heir to those provinces—and our fleet left England, shifting from the edge of the world to the center. Most of my people would never see England again. They were grateful for that.

After that, the tiresome matter of Becket trudged forward with little counsel from me, except in moments of crisis. I was too much about my own affairs to give much thought to Henry's, although we merged our minds and resources when duty required.

Should I have heeded the whispers—nay, the tumult—that I was slighting the king's honor? Had he not diminished mine, and me?

Although I held Henry's person in contempt, we could not divorce our politics. My vassals in Auvergne and Poitou had smoldered with resentment for thirty years under the lash of "foreign" kings, my French and Angevin husbands. Now they would have their duchess back as overlord, with young Richard as her heir. But first my lands had to be restored to order. To that end, Henry stormed castle after castle for much of a year; the same year, I recall, that his mother died.

We lost two Matildas that year! Henry's mother, and our daughter. I mentioned that we negotiated her marriage contract to Henry the Lion of Saxony. They came to collect Matilda in September. I escorted her across the Channel, which was a dreadful mistake. Her grief at the prospect of parting was pitiful, and crossing together did nothing but extend it. To make matters worse, Matilda had been born in England. That crossing must have seemed so final. Poor child, destined to be borne off to Saxony the moment we reached port, never to see any of us again—as she thought. Such a parting. Such tears. My poor daughter! Dead now, like the others. She gave Henry the Lion three sons and a daughter and died at the age of thirty-three.

As for me, I stayed on the mainland, joining Henry for his Christmas court at Argentan. We managed to abide each other with a cool civility which was certainly a novelty, but not unpleasant.

Henry's solution to any problem was action, so it came as no surprise when we took to the roads in late winter for a royal progress through my lands in the south. Sixteen years earlier, before I annulled my match with Louis, he and I had traveled the same southern roads in the warm and fruitful days of autumn. But not Henry! He must whip us along on frozen ground, bruising horses' feet and enriching farriers in every hamlet. Then he rushed off to quell a disturbance in Anjou, abandoning me on the road before we came to Poitiers. What happened next was adventure indeed.

It has always seemed to me that some events strike chords which echo down the avenue of years. When I rode away from the proceedings which divorced me from Louis my escort was attacked twice *en route* to Poitiers.

Sixteen years later, when Henry abandoned me—again *en route* to Poitiers—he gave me into the capable charge of a strong escort commanded by Patrick, earl of Salisbury.

But Patrick's escort was not strong enough, as events soon proved.

The previous summer, Henry wreaked terrible vengeance on my most rebellious vassals, the Brothers Lusignan. He razed their castle to the ground, burned crops, destroyed orchards and in every way condemned the clan to brigandage and penury.

Now Guy de Lusignan returned the favor: he ambushed me. When his force fell on our company, Earl Patrick's first thought was for me, his charge. But ensuring my safety cost him precious time. In consequence he rode to confront the Lusignans' attack bareback, bareheaded, and barely armed. In this condition he was cowardly struck from behind.

Thanks to Patrick's courage I escaped. I abandoned the woman's saddle, hitched up my skirts, threw my right leg over my palfrey and rode like a man, naked from above the knees! I remember thanking Our Lady that I was not with child, for the high pommel bruised my ribs and punched my belly cruelly as I thrashed my steed along.

But Patrick lay dead, foully murdered by the Lusignans.

What happened on the road behind me seems, to this day, a miracle.

A young knight in the company, William Marshall, saw his uncle fall and rushed, bareheaded, to his aid. The Lusignans came on us so suddenly that barely a man in our company was fully armed. They say that William attacked a body of more than sixty horsemen. Aided no doubt by the very crush of the enemy he managed to kill six of their horses before taking a defensive stand against a hedge.

How could one man fight off sixty? One of their brigands worked his way along behind the hedge and stabbed William through the foliage, wounding him in the thigh. It is small wonder that Poitevins have such wretched reputations. North of the Loire they speak of us as being faithless, lawless and treacherous. That was true of the Lusignans. Guy and Geoffrey never kept faith with any master.

William fell, grievously wounded, and the devils made off with him, and with others of lesser degree, to hold for ransom.

With regard to that affair, I may say I took little comfort from my mother-in-law's similar experience during her war with King Stephen. Pressed by enemy forces near Marlborough, Matilda had fallen back, coming under the protection of John Marshall, William's father. Matilda's presence slowed the whole company. Stephen's cavalry was almost upon them when John, throwing courtesy to the wind, shouted at the empress-queen: "Lady, I swear to you by Jesus Christ, you cannot spur your horse in that posture. You must take one leg and put it over the saddle-bow!" Thus, with the rumps of their horses warmed by the hot breath of Stephen's steeds, they won to the walls of Marlborough castle.

Oh, the indignity of being a woman at war!

No, I am not weary, child. I pause. You mistook my silence for death, no doubt. My essence has not yet slipped hence. 'Twas but a pause.

More thoughts rush through my head in hushful moments than a body could gush in a lifetime of words. Would that William Marshall had been mine to command in every way. In the winter of life it is sweet to think on such things.

William tells a story—What is he now? Almost sixty!—of how his captors moved him from place to place to keep my men from finding him. In one such prison he woke in the light of evening to find a lady "liberal and debonair" gazing at him from afar. He says she appeared a woman of quality, a noble's wife. She never approached and never spoke to him directly, but asked his guards how he came by his wounds. Then a servant came to William on the lady's behalf to ask his needs. Later, as if to commend his courage, she sent him strips of linen concealed in a hollowed-out loaf of bread to bind his wounds.

He never knew her name, her rank, her place.

By stealth, Aline! She worshipped him by stealth. What is it about a woman's state that we are bound to hide desires behind a mask of purity? Pah! Within ourselves we are as free as men to lust; but to the world we must appear as saintly as the Virgin.

William Marshall was, and remains, brave beyond all men. He was a youth past twenty in those days, a young man already hardened in arms: he was Raymond's age when he took ship for Antioch; about the age of Henry when we wed. Had I been the unknown lady of that evening twilight I would have dressed his wound myself and lingered to support his head, holding a cup to his lips and moistening his fevered brow. And how I would have cherished the valiant blood which stained my skirts and sleeves. No reliquary could have been more precious.

So! I have said what I have always wished to say. I ransomed him, of course. Ransomed him, fed him, armed him, and took him into my service. And desired him. Were desire the deed, I should be an adulteress. Would that I had taken William to my bed.

24. Towards an End-Game: Bishop versus King 1169-1170

We have had a pleasant reprieve from Becket, but I fear we are bound to tell this wretch's story to his end.

We find our thread on the feast of Epiphany after our Christmas court at Argentan. Louis and Henry met that day at Montmirail: Henry to preen in the glory of our surviving sons, and to do homage; Louis to preside as philosopher-king.

Even now it seems strange to me that I was wife to both these men. What a careful accident! Or was it a careless plan? Looking down on life's experience from my tower of old age, I wonder which one I would favor if I had to choose again. Who knows! One can but judge the fitness of a boot when one has seen its sole. Perhaps neither. I might choose a third, a man not high-born, but high-become.

Oh folly, folly, folly, Aline! In days when I controlled the labyrinth of power I had no time to parse such foolish whims. I have another piece of business...

The problem of Becket so beset Henry that even now, over thirty years later, another matter almost slips my mind: that summer we betrothed little Aleänor to Alfonso, the heir to Castile. She was not quite eight.

That year blessed me in two ways: I was restored to Poitiers; and much of my family was restored to me. Young Henry and Marguerite attended at court. Geoffrey turned ten, and in May he received the homage of his subjects in Brittany before arriving with his betrothed, Constance of Brittany. And of course there was little Joanna.

I was re-establishing my seat at Poitiers when my husbands met at Montmirail, a town well housed behind thick walls. Henry presented Young Henry to Louis as heir to England, Maine and Anjou. When it was Richard's turn to give homage—as my heir to Poitou and Aquitaine— Louis presented him with a bride, Alice, his first daughter by Queen Constance. Alice came to us with the county of Berry as her dowry. Ah, that Louis was a cunning fox: one must give bait to catch fish. He knew how Henry lusted for Berry to widen the wasp's waist of our empire. By giving Berry now, the Capets might attach my lands a generation hence. Finally, Henry presented Geoffrey as our heir to Normandy.

Such was the smooth and practised scene which our magnates and prelates were summoned to witness at Montmirail. But Henry and I had spent more time arguing over the provisions for our sons than over the malady of Becket. That day's events at Montmirail were won by hard-fought diplomacy: between Henry and me; and only then between the Capet and the Angevin.

As to Louis, all through our married life he had pondered the scourge which our Lord visits on the pious. How it must have irked him to take in his hands the hands of those three sons whom I gave Henry.

You will recall, Aline, that Louis had married my eldest child, Marie, to Count Henry of Champagne. His second strand in this policy involved giving the count's brother the bishopric of Sens, the diocese which had spiritual responsibility for Paris. This arrangement endowed Capet and

Champagne with a mutual clasp on each other. Unfortunately for the bishop, he inherited the burden of Becket.

The bishop persuaded Becket to attend the kings' conference at Montmirail. How could he refuse? He himself and four hundred members of his exiled household were a continuing charge on the bishop of Sens, and on Louis.

All went well at first when Henry and Becket met at Montmirail. Becket threw himself at Henry's feet; Henry raised him graciously. Then Henry heard Becket's mind smoothly enough until it seemed that Thomas asked him to repeal the Constitutions of Clarendon. Whereupon Henry lost his Angevin temper in the midst of that great crowd of worthies. He was quite beside himself. But then he managed to check his humors, even reversing the bias in the minds of his hearers by appealing to Becket: "I ask the archbishop only for such concessions as the greatest and most holy of his predecessors extended to the least of mine."

This drew great approval, but Becket would not yield although a great flock of his exiled kinsmen and bishops begged him to bend his stiff neck and relent. Four hundred English had suffered four years of exile on his behalf; perhaps as many Franks paid heavily to support the dispossessed. But Becket was deaf to all pleas.

I n the end, the pope became the butt of appeals from all parties—and there were many, Henry's not the least among them—for Becket threatened to prevent Young Henry's coronation by calling down anathema on England. He had already excommunicated the bishops of London and Salisbury for taking Henry's part.

As to the next season of verbal battles, I tire to relate the sheer bulk of Henry's gaddings about, Becket's thunders, the weight of letters to and fro, and the pope's attempts to find his balance by hopping from foot to foot.

In sum it came to this: in January the pope required Henry to give Becket the kiss of peace before the first day of March. If this were done, the pope would repeal the excommunication of bishops supporting Henry, and lift the threat of anathema that Becket held over England.

Mercifully, I was removed from these tourneys, being busy with my court at Poitiers. However, I followed the news with interest when Henry contrived another attempt at reconciliation, this time at Montmartre. But that blossom withered when Henry declined to give Becket the kiss of peace, pleading a prior oath, despite promises of absolution from the mass of prelates present. By this time he would sooner have kissed a mule than a truculent archbishop. Henry escaped to England well before the first of March—the date of the pope's ultimatum—with a great company and, naturally, in the foulest weather. Four hundred souls died on that crossing when our newest ship was lost. Rumor attached great superstition, of course: the number lost was equal to the number of Becket's intimates whom Henry exiled from England; and the ship itself, being our newest and largest, raised the specter—as well as the omens—suggested by the loss of Henry I's flagship, *The White Ship*, fifty years before.

Walled in once more by the Channel, Henry set to bullying magnates and prelates alike, closing English ports lest Becket send letters to clerics barring Young Henry's coronation. Dire were Henry's penalties for any who dared admit a messenger or proclaim a message.

That year, we planned to fix our cornerstones on two fronts. In June, Young Henry would be crowned king of England. Meanwhile I arranged to have Richard proclaimed duke of Aquitaine in ceremonies at Poitiers and Limoges. Then I hasted to Normandy.

Henry and I agreed I would keep Young Henry with me at Caen, well beyond reach of Becket's spiritual strictures. For once in my life I blessed the accursed Channel, ordering Norman ports stopped. Both coasts were sealed to block English ears against their archbishop's rages. But the cursed Becket had wings.

On Ascension Day, a great press of Londoners came to hear mass at St. Paul's. Lords of the Church being absent for fear of Becket, a priest of no standing celebrated mass in their place. As this man, Vitalis, made ready the bread and wine, a stranger entered the chancel, fell on his knees, seized the priest by the hand and said: "I present to you this letter from the archbishop of Canterbury conveying the sentence he has pronounced on the bishop of London, enjoining him and his clergy to observe this sentence: I bid you, by God's authority, to celebrate mass no more in this church until you shall have delivered this letter to the bishop."

Well!

Then the stranger disappeared. Despite a hue and cry, no one laid hands on him although all London searched—and was searched. The very next day—how was this possible, except to messengers riding post?—a person of the same description delivered a message in York, prohibiting the archbishop of that see from celebrating Henry the Younger's coronation.

All England seethed to know what sleight of hand produced this double deed. Henry, of course, pressed forward with accustomed speed. When all was prepared in England I sent Young Henry to his father. It chanced that the bishop of Worcester sought passage from Normandy the very same day, armed with a letter from the pope blocking the coronation *and* a summons from Henry to attend it! Acting with the constable of Normandy, Richard du Hommet, I detained the bishop—who happened to be Henry's cousin—at Caen. Henry the Younger's coronation took place in Westminster Abbey on the fourteenth day of June, Archbishop Roger of York presiding. The deed was done.

Whereupon Henry crossed to rejoin me, at Falaise. We had excluded Princess Marguerite from Young Henry's coronation, intending her no slight, but judging this action the least of several evils in the light of Becket's thunders. Now we confronted the wrath of the Franks. Yet again.

25. Murder in the Cathedral
1170

Wars and alarums. Alarums and wars. Oh how I yearn for peace, and yet... How can an ancient body rest tranquil whose soul and spirit, heart and mind, have steeped so long in the vinegar of conflict? Let the tumults of the world pass me by. Perforce I am done with them; let them be done with me.

This matter troubles me, though God-He-knows I am not culpable. I shall go to confession, Aline, before we commit another line. I saw Brother Lord Roger not long since. Give me your hand, child. Help me rise.

So. Let us be done. Now we embark on the stormy path that raised the stubborn Becket to his sainthood. I pass lightly over our unintended slight to Marguerite, excluding her from Young Henry's coronation. Louis avenged the insult by warring into Normandy. But we appeased him with the promise that Marguerite would receive her full dignity as the Young King's queen when Becket was restored to England.

God willing, said Henry, that day would come soon. The promise was enough to reconcile the kings. For his part, Louis managed to prevail on Becket to meet Henry.

Their meeting was set for the feast of St. Mary Magdalene. By what stroke of irony, I wonder, was the feast day of a fallen woman chosen to restore a fallen prelate?

They met at Fréteval, doing so in a spirit of amity and forgiveness—to some degree. Becket, however, declined to lift the excommunication on the English bishops; whereon Henry refused to give the kiss of peace. Tears flowed, and passions, like a river. But still no end. Nevertheless, they had repaired a bridge which did not crack beneath their load though neither was willing to cross it.

Henry took to the roads, again, wearing out horses, wearing down men, flying from Becket, always one *journée* ahead of the prelate who followed the dust of the king's household, claiming that just one kiss would seal their pact with peace anew.

They met for the final time near Amboise. By then they were two twin torrents worn to summer streams, mere winterbournes, exhausted in effort and mind. Imperfect though their reconciliation was, they did agree that Becket should return to England.

They agreed, also, to meet at Rouen, there to assemble sufficient escort and travel to England in amity and peace—and with the dignity of wealth, for Henry undertook to equip Becket for his passage.

However, Becket found neither Henry nor funds when he reached Rouen; there was only a letter explaining that the king was called to douse flames which Louis had chosen that moment to light. Would to God that Henry had learned to discern a greater evil from a less! Had he done so, he might have quieted his six-year war against the Church and fought the Capet later. As it was, he assigned as Becket's escort to England the very foe whom the archbishop had excommunicated four years before, John of Oxford.

So Becket traveled to England with a small company, in a single ship paid for by Archbishop Rotrou of Rouen. He came into Sandwich on the first day of December, almost exactly six years since he fled that very port into the arms of Louis and the pope. That Henry should accord Becket the opportunity and advantage of returning to England in true Christian poverty was inexcusable! The poorest classes, even townsmen, greeted the archbishop as if he were the risen Christ. On the other hand, he appeared in England so suddenly that persons of rank had no knowledge of the terms of settlement. Prudently, lest they offend the king, lords and magnates stayed away. Young Henry, well advised, never budged from his court at Winchester. Or perhaps it was Woodstock.

In the end one can only say that both men were fools. Becket wasted the popular sentiment for his restoration by renewing his war: against the bishops of London and Salisbury, requiring them to swear an oath "in our presence that they would obey our order"; and against the archbishop of York for celebrating Young Henry's coronation. If forgiveness be a Christian virtue, it is one that Becket lacked.

These twice-offended bishops lost no time seeking passage to Normandy, where they chanced to fall in with Henry on the road to Bayeux. Many of our children—Geoffrey and Richard among them—as well as our vassals, were converging for Henry's Christmas court. After the bishops of London and Salisbury poured out their own griefs they went on to list clashes between Henry's lieges and those of the Church.

Henry arrived at what should have been a tranquil Christmas court in no small agitation. Becket had extracted concessions guaranteeing that property would be restored to those of his kindred sent into exile. To that end Henry had sent a missive to England as surety.

> "Henry king of England, to his son Henry king of England, greeting. May you know that Thomas archbishop of Canterbury has made peace with me in accordance with my wishes.

Therefore I order that he and his followers may have peace,
and that you see to it that he and his followers, who on
his behalf left England, should have their possessions
in peace and with honor...
Witness Archbishop Rotrou of Rouen, at Chinon."

Now, instead of Christmas revels, it was the text of Henry's letter that commanded the court's attention. Whatever Becket was doing seemed to exceed the terms of the letter framing his restoration. We also had to assist those clergy who had supported us against their archbishop throughout.

Venting mighty oaths, Henry shouted: "If all who shared the coronation of my son are to be excommunicated, I will be counted among their number."

It was unfortunate that men well warmed with meat, with mead, with a roaring fire and wine should descend to politics. One injudicious member of the company offered that the king would know no peace as long as Becket lived. Indeed, a voice from the bishop of Salisbury's retinue went so far as to suggest that Becket be hanged.

Henry himself suffered a fine Angevin fit as if the falling sickness wormed him.

At length one policy was firmly resolved: Becket would be arrested.

Later, someone noticed that four young men had slipped away. Given the tenor of the talk, no one doubted for a moment that their youthful minds might be fixed upon some purpose foreign from the king's intention.

Every effort was made to arrest them: riders posted to all ports. Even a posse of nobles set off in pursuit, led by the constable of Normandy in person. This was surely the highest ranking posse ever assembled. To no avail.

What else is there to say? All Christendom knows the outcome. On the fifth day of Christmas, those same young men slew Becket at the altar of St. Benedict in Canterbury cathedral.

Henry, ripe with prescience, dismissed the court and took himself to a self-inflicted jail in Argentan, where he heard the news on the last day of the month. Henry called for sackcloth and ashes even before the messenger finished speaking, throwing off his clothes. He wailed for days, dismissing all who loved him and suffering visions of Becket in every corner of the room. Bishop Arnulf of Lisieux failed to calm him; even the venerable Rotrou of Rouen—who did so much to bring the men to reconciliation—could not break through his despair.

I have said enough. Truly those were sad, unhappy days.

Power of a Woman

✝✝✝

Part 3, A Woman Alone

26. Poitiers and the Court of Ladies
1168-1173

Ah, Poitiers! How sweet the change you wrought in me. When I returned to you, how perfect was my transformation in the bosom of your orchards and your walls.

Three decades had passed since Louis and his five hundred swept me off to Paris. What an end to youth! By the time I returned to Poitiers as sovereign in my own right I had reached mid-life. Nay, I was nearly old in years. And I had thrown off two husbands to become a woman *seule*[29].

Henry made a modicum of restitution for his carnal sins by inflicting discipline on my vassals. His campaigns had the salutary effect of shaking loose rents which were long overdue. A well endowed treasury combined with a too-short span of peace allowed me to tear down much that was ancient and decrepit, building Poitiers into a city more wondrous than before.

We had started rebuilding the cathedral of St. Peter years earlier, when we still had Becket's support as tax collector. Fire consumed the building I knew as a girl.

You have seen the new cathedral, of course, Aline. A marvelous structure. But a work still in progress, forty years on. Will it ever be done? I was determined to commission the biggest church I had ever seen, and Henry—in those days he tried to please me—approved my plan. I insisted its windows should be pointed at the top to show the path to heaven, just as Suger designed them for St. Denis.

Did you see our likenesses in the colored glass, Aline? Oh yes, we are there. Under the crucifixion of Saint Peter. Henry and I are kneeling, in robes as blue as the sky, holding a plan of the cathedral for the approval of our Lord. If Suger could affix his image in church glass, then so could we. I hope the Almighty forgives our little vanity.

When I returned in my own right to Poitiers I restored the household apartments, improving them for women. Men might bed down between draughty casements if it suited them; I had had enough of hardship. Let Grandfather's tower stand in the centre of town, proud as a male member. Around it, lying low, I built chambers suited to women as well as men—and a hall where I could feast the world or hold court to deem sentence on sinners. May my *grande salle* stand for ever! It's a chamber worthy of Byzantium, with views to rival those we gazed upon from Antioch.

For five precious years I reigned as the one and only ruler of my life in my own realm. Let Henry strive and Louis pray. I had given them both their due. With Richard as my heir I held sway in the only lands my heart has never left—Poitou and Aquitaine. My sense of release was palpable. For a season my mind wept with joy. I felt myself to be the last worker hired in the parable of the vineyard: to him who came early, one penny; to him who came late, one penny also. I had come late to the vineyard that was my own place, but I had more than earned my pay.

Those years at Poitiers refreshed me when I was most at need. And, being at need, I sought advice. My uncle, Raoul de Faye, did much to guide my feet through the pitfalls of policy in a duchy from which I had been absent too long. When I sat as duchess and countess in my own right, Aquitaine and Poitou acquired the allure of a neutral state. My great hall became the market place of seasoned diplomats and lustful youth from many lands. The wars of their fathers were long ways away. I suddenly found myself the tutor and protector of offspring from every house allied with Capet *and* Plantagenet. What noble child did I *not* rear in those precious years?

Thus, in my fifth life, I came to be mother to children apart from my own.

It scarcely seemed possible, but a dozen years had fled since Louis presented Henry with baby Marguerite to betroth her as Young Henry's bride. You will recall, Aline: Louis stipulated that his daughter should never lodge in a household of mine. And yet Marguerite and Young Henry stayed with me at Poitiers. A sweet girl. At twelve, she was almost a woman. And of course we had her sister, Alice, whom Louis present-ed at Montmirail to become Richard's bride. There was young Aleänor, too, destined to become queen of Castile. (It was her daughter I fetched some years ago to marry the heir to France.) Geoffrey and his spouse, Constance of Brittany, lodged with me. How could I know the harridan that Constance would become? And Joanna, soon to be queen of Sicily, and afterwards… Life is such a train of tragedies! Young Matilda was gone, wed to Henry the Lion.

Thus I became nurse and chatelaine to wards from lands as far apart as northern England and the south of Aquitaine; from Bordeaux to Flanders, too. My great hall brimmed with youth, men and women both. We were such a crowd as to make me feel young and gay once more. In those years nothing seemed impossible; nothing lay beyond fortune's grasp.

It was there I discovered the south again—my south—whence min-strels hastened to regale me. Eager talents from our many lands turned their feet to Poitiers. Bernart of Ventadorn was long gone, but his songs found fresh life in new mouths. I confess I seldom noticed the faces of those who sang them, for none dared love me in song with his eyes as well as words, the way Bernart had done. Youthful and striving, these novices plucked new notes from old harps and tuned their voices and viols to the service of Arthur and Roland. And Aleänor, too.

At Poitiers I strove to create a more equitable ethos than the one my women and I had endured in the courts of two kings. I had escaped the brute world I served for too long. But I had yet to wash away the shame imposed by Henry's all too public lust—a failing in princes which the Church continues to censure with a blind eye, a deaf ear and a silent tongue.

Freed from serving as the instrument of kings, my angel fired me with a passion for reform. Let Henry draft his Constitutions, his Assize! Let him prefer his twelve just men! Let him judge England! I would decree my Code at Poitiers in the shadow of Grandfather's tower. The Troubadour knew the ways of the heart better than any man, and as well as many women.

Looking back, those days resonate as clearly as the deep-set memories of childhood. Would that you had been in my service then, Aline, to write my edicts down. In those short years at Poitiers I established an ethos by which women practised of their own free will what the Church enjoined on us as duty. I imagined for women a state above strife and far above men. Would that our human estates were ruled by twelve just women! But that has gone the way of flesh. All that survives of our ideal is a folly penned by Marie's chaplain—a shallow ripple stolen from the Roman lecher, Ovid; and twisted, as if a woman's being is but the mirror to a man's.

A line, we'll stop awhile. I want to speak of Marie, but I am tired and it all took place so long ago...

See where the birds fly south. That is the first chevron of geese to pass this way. A harbinger of winter coming on. Would that I could fly to the sun. But I shall never leave this place again: the affray with young Arthur last autumn nearly stopped my heart for ever.

This is the season when fowlers set their nets in the marshes downriver from London. In my first autumn at Westminster the sky to the east was black with birds. Look there! More geese.

Put that cloak around me, child. The chill comes earlier each afternoon.

It seems no more than a heartbeat since spring. But *next* spring... For me it may be a foolish hope, an eternity away.

I started to speak of Marie. I was seven years childless before I had her. That was the first and only time I sought spiritual intervention from Abbé Bernard: to conceive Marie. I still think of her as Clairvaux' child.

We had a special bond in that we both disappointed the Franks. Marie was seven when I divorced Louis, and I had no choice but to leave her to that fortress in the Seine. By the time Louis made up his mind to marry her to Count Henry of Champagne she was nineteen. By then she was one of several links binding the alliance between Capet and Champagne.

Marie came from Troyes for a season after I established myself at Poitiers. I count her visit among the best rewards of my neutral years. By then she was in her mid twenties; it had been nineteen years since we last touched hands in greeting.

Before Louis and I made our final journey together through my lands, I visited little Marie where she lived with her nurses. I knew of course I might never see my firstborn again. But I couldn't tell her that. Such a sweet child. Seven years old; an impressionable age. I left her so calmly that day, as if I had made a routine maternal visit. But when I was out of her sight I hitched up my skirts and fled. Even a queen must sometimes be a mother. I was that age when my own mother died.

Seldom in my life have I been as anxious as the day Marie arrived at Poitiers. Again and again I looked at the mirror, willing away the years and wondering what I would say by way of greeting. All I could think was: "When I was your age..." Well, when I was her age I was freezing through winter in Anatolia, seeking a ship at Adalia, or pressing Raymond's stillborn argument to Louis' deaf ears at Antioch.

On the day she arrived I wanted to fling myself through the crowd to greet her outside the walls—as Queen Melisende had met us at Jerusalem. Of course I did no such thing. I was not sure how I would react, so I chose to greet Marie in the great hall where the midday gloom might—in that first precious minute of meeting—conceal my years and my anxiety. The great hall is bright in the morning and bright again in the afternoon. But the ridge of the roof runs north-south, so the light is subdued at midday. And that—as luck had it—was when she arrived.

I have encountered emperors, kings, popes—even Greek pirates and Lusignans—with less trepidation than I felt when I met my firstborn after all those years apart.

I see it now. I'm sure Marie had rehearsed the moment, too. She was well into the hall before she pulled down the wrap protecting her face from the dust of the road. In that instant I saw myself in her, and she smiled at my reaction. Then she plucked off her riding gloves, handed them off to her woman and stepped forward, away from her household. God knows, but in that instant I felt fear. A silence of anticipation stilled both our companies, as if the two of us alone were flesh and all the others ghosts. Thus she approached, her footfalls and the rustle of her skirt the only sounds in that great hall. I remember her dress; rose-colored with small, fine pleats below the waist—it was all the fashion those days—and pleated sleeves extending past the hand. She came to me; I stood quite still; she pulled back her sleeves; our hands reached out. And they touched. She said quite simply "Mother," and I felt tears wash my face.

So much flew between us in the first heartbeats that followed. So much. So much time and heartbreak fell away.

Forgive an old woman, Aline. I have said all I will today.

The Capetians and Plantagenets have written much, muttered more and understand nothing of our Court of Ladies and my Code of Poitiers. What we conceived was a return to the birthright of women which I had known in the south from my earliest years, as persons equal to men—not in might—but in nature, in virtue, in soul.

We are different, I grant. But the only power I concede to the "better" sex is that of brute strength; in which respect an ox is a mightier thing than a man. It is women to whom God gave the germ of fertility and the mind to thread the maze of social politics.

Is it not enough that women are bartered as infants, bartered as children and traded away so that world-weary barons may ravish anew the beauty of youth? And in our dotage they would put us here, at Fontevrault, and a hundred abbeys like it!

What child of high estate is not torn with loss when she is exiled to her future husband's hall? If women are to be put to marriage without love, then let us claim love as *our* mystery. As such, love is as worthy of study as those mysteries which the Church claims for her own. That was the subject matter we conceived for my Court of Ladies. That, and nothing more.

Then, to lead us to love and into the ways of love, we let troubadours guide us. To serve that end they took the name "finders"[30] a century ago, in Grandfather's prime. From a man's point of view, such a love is the love of a *princesse lointaine,* a faraway love. As such, she is as unattainable as if she were a cloud—although the man and his lady tread the same floor. *L'amour courtois* was, and remains, love of the muse of love, in flesh exemplified.

What I brought to effect at Poitiers was not new. It had lain through violent times, a buried trove, long undiscovered. If you would discover the spirit of women and loving, Aline, read the book by Fortunatus on the life of Radegonde.[31] Not a month dies into the dark of the moon but I think of her example.

The woman-centered ethos I established had ancient origins. In the year of our Lord five hundred and twenty-nine, the most savage of the Merovingian kings, Clotaire, sacked the kingdom of Thuringia in the eastern, German lands. Among the many he slaughtered were the king and queen, but he spared their ten-year-old niece, Radegonde.

Clotaire, who had four wives and more concubines, sent Radegonde to Picardy until she was old enough to take to his bed: apparently he had scruples in such matters. Nine years would pass before he sent for her, and in that time she learned to read and write. She also acquired a fine, liberal education from the best of royal tutors.

Rather than obey the summons, Radegonde fled. To no avail, for she was captured and forced to marry Clotaire. She then took solace in a life of prayer until the king murdered her brother in order to extirpate her family's male line. Whereupon, with two women, Radegonde fled, again. Folk say they evaded the king's hue and cry by lying in a field of growing corn which sprang up in a heartbeat or two, hiding the women from view.

After sundry wanderings, during which Radegonde became a nun, she founded a monastery at Tours before settling at Poitiers. (Those cities were Clotaire's first conquests.) Poitevins considered it a second miracle when the king agreed to a separation and gave Radegonde treasure to build a convent, which later took the name Ste. Croix.

From that time on, Radegonde lived life on two levels: as a nun she wore a hair shirt, tended the sick, salved the stumps of lepers and scourged her flesh.

But between religious duties she encouraged a lively social, cultural life at Ste. Croix. A wandering scholar and poet, Fortunatus, begged Radegonde for a "marriage of the minds," whereon they also forged a "friendship of the heart." This platonic love—their kiss of minds—endured in words, letters and song for twenty years.

I propose a contrast here, and a comparison. When he was chancellor, Thomas Becket lived for mortal extravagance; when he became archbishop, he lived and died the very model of an austere soul. But Radegonde, our patron saint, taught that we can live both lives at once.

As a Norman, Aline, the life of Radegonde will be a new leaf in your book. But every Poitevin, highborn or low, learns of her example at a nurse's knee. We recite her qualities as if they were the verses of the *Paternoster*.

I do not tell this tale to titillate. I tell it to instruct. Love between minds became the essence of an ancient social pact. That love—the love of Fortunatus, Radegonde and Agnes, her companion—became the first bud on a great bush. For the next two hundred years amorous letters flew on busy wings between nuns and clerics all over Poitou. In the end, King Charlemagne forbade the practice. He was a great-hearted man with a thirst for learning, but he was first, and only, a man. In Charlemagne's day as in ours, love was a bond which men claimed as theirs, and theirs alone.

Do you see where I lead you, Aline? Courtly love refines that which is vulgar. It lifts that which is low. Should we emulate cankers which dwell in the mud, or spirits which fly in the face of the heaven? True courtly love brings fellowship, for men and women both.

Grandfather, and the troubadours who followed him, wrote and sang of *le joi d'amor*; it was never *la joie d'amor*. The ethos we established at Poitiers was not a quest for joyousness, though that was one result. We sought to build a lasting cult of love—love as a game, as a *jeu* or a *joi*, a game played in the realm of courtesy and *politesse*.

Grandfather's ideal in a man was one in whom cheer and charity co-mingled with wisdom and wit—and a slight taste for war. Knights, he knew, might assail each other with blows till their brains rang like bells in the name of chivalry. For men of our times, and Grandfather's, there is no higher calling. But it took more than valor to be a "gentle-man," a style which was still in its infancy when Grandfather was old.

The Troubadour was long gone by the time I re-established the ducal court in his tower, although he seemed present whenever I pondered and paced its floors. Long gone—he died when I was three—but not forgotten. I had inherited his titles, titles descended through ten generations of males. And with them came duties, one of which I set myself: to build a better ethos for our polity. And what better cement than love to join the parts in a civil society?

So, in the name of women, we claimed possession of *amor*. Who better than women to judge matters of the heart and thereby, stitch by stitch, to weave a tapestry of better things?

Since it appears that pure love cannot cohabit with marriage— Marie was a stronger advocate on this point than I—then love, a true platonic love, must grope its way around the mire that is the wedded state. Twixt man and woman, then, pure love is but a balance on a sword's edge between constant desire and timeless chastity, between eternal longing and eternal disappointment. *L'attente amoureuse*, love's longing, found in our court—as in Radegonde's convent, six hundred years before—the ears and tongues to give it peaceful voice.

Ah, Aline, the quest for *fin amor*! Just as nuns are wedded to the perfect man, our Saviour, so our Court of Ladies sought to lift all hearts by virtue of attachment to the perfect love.

How very simple it seemed to women of Marie's generation, and mine—women raised in a culture of warfare and abandoned for seasons on end. How can a soul's life thrive in a barracks, behind stone palisades, where every eye throws lust and every act prepares for violence? How simple it seemed to us in those shining days at Poitiers. And how our message was twisted, by courtiers, kings, and by the ever-damning Church.

27. Feeding the hungry falcons
1171-1173

Is that you, Aline? Pull the screen aside; let in the light, pale though it is in this season. You find me on my knees, but I am done with prayers. Other thoughts hold me to the stones. Sometimes it seems that I wake only to be weighed down by regrets. And at my age, why wake at all?

Have you noticed how old fruit trees strain to bear a good crop in their final year? Oh yes they do. They expend their life's limit, and die. Any peasant will tell you that. I wonder why God in His grace smiles on my crop of years? What design can they serve except to encourage confession?

Well, if that is His purpose, so be it! Help me up, Aline.

Ah, child, what can you know, in your simple country way, about the clash of minds and the wars of contrary opinions that fight for a hearing at nobles' courts?

Battles among courtiers remind me of a patch of sunny ground I had little reason to love. It lay in a bright angle of wall beneath the flinty height of Salisbury tower. Each spring a crop of tiny tansy plants turned that angle of ground into a feathery, verdant lawn. Some tansies grew taller than others as the season advanced, over-shading their brethren. At summer's end the little angle was still green, but only a few of the plants which emerged in the spring survived. They had crowded out the others, do you see? It was these that opened their daisy-like flowers and set their seed.

That is how it is at court, Aline. The boldest, most enduring voices claim their lord's or lady's ear. Often such persons, proud in their strength, impart angry counsel rather than wise and measured words. I learned that to my cost. Anger thrives in crowds; wisdom finds voice in the silence of reflection. The bustle and pretension of a ruler's court stifles wisdom in a hundred subtle ways.

What I am trying to say is that some of the mistakes I made in my years at Poitiers were not mine alone. I had help from louder, younger, more persistent voices.

I had cast off Henry as one sheds an undergarment seething with a season's vermin. When I led my household into seven ships and sailed for the last time—as I thought—from England, I felt hatred for Henry that no Christian soul should harbor in her bosom or her brains.

Then came my Court of Ladies. Through those five years of blessed peace we built an ethos which raised women in the real world as the popes raise Mary in the Church. For that very reason, clerics and barons were careful not to mock us too loudly: the feminine nature whom we sought to seat as our judge is not unlike that which the Church promotes for the Blessed Virgin.

But I fear those years at Poitiers also served me badly. They lulled me into a false sense of security. I was too willing to believe that the greater world would be tamed simply because I wished it so. Safe within my borders I began to advance the interests of our sons.

You are such a patient confessor, Aline. Hah, my little heresy still has the power to shock you. I call you "confessor" to assure you that I do not willingly lie to posterity. What I tell you is true, child, although I am careful to select which truths to tell.

Thirty years later I can speak without guile: I sought not only to advance our sons but to avenge myself on Henry. If that meant assisting our "eaglets" to strive for their inheritance, so be it! For my part, I wanted only to rule in my own place. Henry might rage from Northumbria to Normandy. I cared nothing for his statecraft in those days.

It has long been clear to me that Henry and I unwittingly impressed our sons with my mother-in-law's "hungry falcon" habit of state-craft. The Empress Matilda had a ruthless ambition for power. In her days of strength she ruled Normandy from Rouen as she had once ruled Saxony from Aachen. Compared to her I am a kitten to a kite.

She attained her ends by dangling promises in front of vassals to ensure their loyalty. Dangle the whole, then offer scraps; dangle to daze the eyes and maze the brains with greed; dangle and promise, promise and defer. That was how she sustained alliances through nineteen years of war against King Stephen. She wore him down as water wears rock. Thus, in the end, she delivered the throne of England to her son.

As for *our* sons, I fear they were reared in worlds without want. Gains and titles heaped upon them as leaves cover ground in autumn—but as entitlements, not as rewards. It is one thing to dangle a promise in front of a vassal. It is another matter to hold it before a son of royal blood. To give to one vassal deprives another. To give to one's son deprives a parent, or another son.

Oh Aline, I wonder how it came to pass that the word *droit* sloughed off its burden of responsibility to stuff its purse with rights? That was how our eaglets construed their destiny. Even Richard.

I blame Henry for turning the mind of Young Henry. How many times did the father make the barons of England swear allegiance to the son? Twice at Winchester, I recall. And one coronation was not enough: Young Henry must be crowned twice, at Westminster, and then at Winchester—although I do concede that pressure from Paris forced that matter beyond all sense.

During those years at Poitiers, when I presided, as I thought, over a new enlightened order, our sons were comparing envies and possessions. Would that Henry and I had patched our quarrel. The outcome would have been a different, better world.

You may recall, Aline, that neither Henry nor Becket saw fit to attend the deathbed of Theobald of Bec, archbishop of Canterbury. Perhaps it was in a spirit of contrition for this omission that, ten years later, Henry took himself to Wolvesey Palace, to the deathbed of Henry of Blois, bishop of Winchester. He was an ancient man, exactly as old as the century, accomplished in years and in duty. Old Winchester was the third son of Adela, you know, the Conqueror's daughter; and, of course, King Stephen's brother. In spite of which he served us well. It was he who enthroned Becket as archbishop. The very next year it was he who brought word to Becket of Henry's judgments at Northampton. Dying, the old man reproached Henry for Becket's murder. Word reached us that he predicted—correctly—much pain ere Henry's days were done. And then he closed his eyes upon this world and went to God.

Henry took ship for Ireland later that year. It was already the storm season, but he meant to win that troubled land for our youngest son, John. Indeed, he did reduce the country for a time. The natives had so wasted each other with wars that they welcomed the intervention of an overlord. It was a boon to our household's peace of mind that Henry wintered overseas through Christmas and the first anniversary of Becket's death. His business in Ireland also kept him a jump ahead of legates whom Pope Alexander sent to negotiate terms of penance in the matter of Becket. Those cardinals, Theodin and Albert, stuck to Henry like hounds to a scent.

Would that he had stayed in Ireland! But he returned to England the following spring, to escort Young Henry and Marguerite to Normandy. She was still uncrowned, to her father's displeasure.

The papal legates ran Henry to earth at Savigny. Briefly. But he found their price for remission too high, put heels to his horse and made to return to Ireland.

How churchmen cling! Like barbers' leeches. Becket had followed Henry from town to town, demanding the kiss of peace. Now several Norman bishops chased Henry as far west as Avranches, where they begged him to receive the legates and put the matter to rest. Which he did, waiting till the cardinals and Young Henry caught up. It was essential that the Young King should swear the same oaths as his father respecting the Church's rights in England.

What we heard of that encounter made me wonder greatly: Henry dealt fairly with the papal legates, dousing his Angevin fire with the milk of human reason. The firebrand became a penitent, admitting errors and making fulsome confessions—though he swore on the Gospels, and on every holy relic in Avranches, that he never intended by word nor deed to compass the murder of Becket. To my certain knowledge, that was true. Avranches, by the way, is awash in holy relics: the town is as old as Bordeaux. I'm sure Henry *intended* the legates to unhorse him at Avranches. The abbot was a friend, Robert de Torigny, whose election Henry confirmed in one of the first acts of our reign. Robert was Henry's privy councilor and a trusted historian, too. Were the king to do penance, Robert would set down the facts without malice. If the Almighty leavens His policy with irony, He could not have performed a more subtle feat than directing my Henry to Avranches: two of its bishops of old were elevated to the see of Canterbury.[32]

Still, I suspect the history of the town came last in Henry's thoughts that day. There and then he made the concessions the Church required in order to grant him absolution. He stripped off his garments and knelt in the porch of the cathedral, *la Belle Andrine*, where some monks beat him with a rod, each taking a turn.

At first I was shocked to hear such news. Monks flogging a king! But then my maid, Amaria, whispered that some of their strokes must atone for the shames which Henry dealt me! And of course she was right.

Aline, you know it has long been a custom among the nobility to send boys away from their fathers' households at an early age. They must be torn from their nurses and sisters and hardened to life as men-at-arms. So they grow up in the hall of an uncle or a cousin, as chance may provide. There, in a household far from their own, they learn the bruising profession of arms and the warlike skills that young men require.

Perhaps I owe my life to just such a young man's love for his guardian-uncle. I speak of William Marshall. Earl Patrick of Salisbury, whom the Lusignans slew in the road, was the uncle in whose household William completed his training in arms. If William had not tried to wreak revenge on the Lusignans' men, they would surely have overtaken me.

My point is, that young men usually come of age with more love and reverence for the uncle in whose house they were reared than for their father. I mention that aspect of love between men because I have thought for a long time that Young Henry's bond with Becket became the rub of his discord with his father.

Young Henry spent much of his childhood in Becket's household. What a wrench to the boy when his father removed him from his beloved "uncle" during that angry Advent when Henry was drafting his punitive Constitutions. From Advent to Epiphany Young Henry watched and listened while his father reviled his beloved mentor and plotted his fall—*and* did it in Becket's former hall at Berkhamstead, the very roof which had sheltered Young Henry as a member of the archbishop's family.

The following month his father made Young Henry share the king's bench at Clarendon as if he, too, sat in judgment on Becket. Then came Northampton, and the disgrace and exile of the man whom Young Henry dearly loved.

I recall a winter morning in happier times when Henry and I landed in England to be met by barons and prelates led by Becket. Young Henry dashed to greet us from the shelter of Thomas's cloak. Young Henry was as much an Angevin as his father, as tempestuous and as sudden in his moods. He had already been crowned king of England. Yet, while his father reigned, he had no kingdom. To rub salt in the wound, he would soon be crowned again, for in August of that year Marguerite was crowned queen of England to appease her father, Louis. So Young Henry received the diadem anew—all trappings, Aline, and no power! The boy found himself impotent.

Furthermore, he had observed his father's fury over Becket for too many years. What must he have thought when he watched his father whipped in reprisal by monks?—and he himself compelled to swear the oaths his father swore at Avranches: that he, as king, would observe the terms of his father's penance.

Henry did penance for his archbishop, but none for his queen. I wish I had flogged him myself! My hurt was so deep that nothing could assuage it. It was better for my peace of mind that we were far apart.

In those days at Poitiers I was close to my uncle, Raoul de Faye. It is true, as the whisperers have it, that we spoke of Young Henry's impatience, of his vain and violent companions, of Henry's all-consuming rages. Raoul advised me in the matter of my policy, certainly, but Henry made him out to be a veritable fount of treason.

Later, Henry accused me of turning the hearts of our sons against him. If Richard and Geoffrey lodged with me, so what? As their mother I took it upon myself to ensure their education. It was surely Henry's distempers and demeanors, not any act of mine, which turned his sons and set them on opposing paths.

Crowning Young Henry *twice* did not help balance his humors. You recall that Louis had taken offence when our boy was crowned at Westminster, without Marguerite. We had judged it best to keep her with us in Normandy, Becket's venom being then in full force.

So we had to crown Young Henry again, at Winchester, for the benefit of Marguerite—and her father. The archbishop of York and the bishops of London and Salisbury were excluded, at the Franks' request. From beyond the grave, Becket still reached down vengeance on those three. And with all the more authority, since the curia had canonized our erstwhile chancellor *Saint* Thomas six months before. Rome canonized Becket even faster than they sainted Bernard.

After their coronation, Henry met the young couple in Normandy. It was early winter and they were on their way to Paris for a family visit from the newly-crowned queen of England to her father, the king of France. No doubt Henry had time and occasion enough to explain his policies to Young Henry before the couple moved on to Paris. There, I am sure, Louis never ceased to undermine Young Henry's love for his father. And yet Henry held me responsible for estranging our son— our sons!

At the end of that year we gathered at Chinon for Henry's Christmas court. He had recalled Young Henry and Marguerite from Paris before the Franks could fill the boy's ear with too much bile. He invited me amiably enough; and I brought Richard and Geoffrey from Poitiers.

Young Henry needed no help from me to challenge his father. By the time he was seventeen he had attracted a rough and greedy following of young knights and squires bent on stirring trouble from Normandy to Flanders. This left me as worried about him as about his father. The jousting season, from Pentecost to the Feast of St. John, threw whole counties into fear. It set loose thousands of young men-at-arms to feast on danger, drink and a fearful populace.

We heard of William Marshall's exploits in those years. To my regret he had passed from my service to Henry's, who assigned him to Young Henry's headstrong company. Whether Henry imposed William on our offspring as a rein or a spur I was never sure. We both hoped William's presence would provide a sobering touch. Instead of which he won enough ransom, treasure and horses at those tourneys to meet Young Henry's debts and spare his father's treasury. But I digress.

The first hint of a serious rift between Henry and our sons came early the following year. The roads were still frozen—well suited for fast travel if one cared nothing for horses—when Henry summoned the Young King to Angers. They rode south to Limoges to negotiate betrothal between our youngest, John, and the infant daughter of Count Humbert of Maurienne. This was an excellent match. Maurienne's lands stretched east to the Alpine passes commanding Italy. He was well placed to control traffic to Rome.

John had just turned seven. He had been three when his father received Louis' blessing at Montmirail for our other sons' portions. But it was John's misfortune to be born when I was renouncing Henry, so the matter of our infant boy's inheritance was never a subject for reasoned discussion. Nevertheless, the fact that Henry made no provision for John at Montmirail angered me greatly. It meant lifelong shame for

John. As we write this, Aline, John has been king of the English for nearly four years, but they still call him "Lackland."

We had discussed John's inheritance by the time we all met at Limoges—I went with Richard and Geoffrey—but when we arrived it was clear that Henry and Young Henry would soon come to blows.

Count Humbert was not eager to settle a daughter and a dowry on a husband with no inheritance to call his own. So Henry proceeded—and this was no fault of mine!—to give John the three great castles of Chinon, Mirebeau and Loudun with all their wealth and lands. They lie in a crescent, in that wedge of Anjou south of the Loire which Henry ceded to his brother at their father's dying, and later took back by force. This swath of land touched all our domains. It would have made a fine provision for John. Unfortunately, it came from Young Henry's portion.

That did not sit well. Henry could not have alienated the boy more thoroughly had he tied him to a pyre and fired faggots at his feet.

Remind me later, Aline, I must speak of Mirebeau again. Just last year that ancient pile sheltered me until John rescued me. But I shan't be distracted. Time in good order, and all in good time.

It was Count Raymond of Toulouse who warned Henry that he courted rebellion. But Henry would not be warned. He took one minor precaution. He invited Young Henry and his followers to go hunting near Limoges. There he observed how they behaved together. Returning to Limoges he dismissed several troublemakers from Young Henry's service. He could banish troublemakers, but he could not banish trouble.

After we settled the terms of John's marriage contract, I returned towards Poitiers with Richard and Geoffrey. For his part, Henry, well aware of Young Henry's anger, would not let the Young King out of his sight. By threatening to stop paying his debts, Henry forced the Young King to accompany him to one of the very castles he had deeded to John: they spent one night at Chinon.

It was there—and I say this as wife to one and mother to the other—that the Furies entered the Henrys, father and son. Henry the elder commanded Henry the younger to sleep in the same chamber, lest he escape his father's guard.

Which he did. That very night Young Henry stole away, taking horse to Paris to lay his grievances before his overlord and father-in-law—namely Louis, who had no small interest in stirring our mud in this matter.

The next we knew, Geoffrey and Richard, who were lodging with me, took horse with their respective households and joined their brother in Paris. They feared, you see, that their father would use them as he was even then using Young Henry. And as, in the past, he used me.

In those days I feared for Henry's reason. He was so certain of his virtue, so peripatetic in his movement, so watchful of his enemies, that he was a man possessed. What devil's imp visited his head nobody could say.

In our normal, healthy state, barbers and midwives understand that fevers mark some illness or adverse possession. But much of the time I knew him fever appeared to be Henry's normal state. He must gallop with it through fair or foul, good times or bad.

So I was not unhappy when Richard and Geoffrey removed themselves from the reach of Henry's frenzy to visit their liege-lord in Paris. That was in March. By Easter, Louis had so taken advantage of our three sons' disaffection from their father that he knighted Richard and encouraged them all to rebel. I may say it was an uprising backed by many with cause to fear Henry; the dispossessed and the disaffected from Belin to Berwick and a score of baronies between. Word reached me in Poitiers that the barons of France and Flanders lost no time splitting England among them in their haste to join our sons' rebellion against Henry.

What cared I? I had no aspirations for England, except on Young Henry's behalf.

What a cry of oaths and ink and hot wax it must have been, bringing some life to Louis' dreary hall. And all for naught. Never, I swear, did a man live who could rise from misfortune faster than Henry. The harvest still stood in the fields when our three sons met their father at Gisors beneath the elm that had marked a place of diplomacy for generations. This was not the end of their rebellion; but it was the beginning of the end.

28. Mars conquers Venus. Banished to England
1173-1174

As winter closed in I found myself the object of an embassy from Henry. From Henry, yes. But to couch his message in soft and hard words he turned to the archbishop of Rouen. He, writing as Henry's instrument, informed me that Henry was prepared to forgive me for the wrongs I had done him and restore me to his grace. He would forgive *me*! There was not one word about his sins against his wedded wife.

Such impudence! This missal was penned third hand, of course. Not by Henry; not even by Archbishop Rotrou on Henry's behalf; but by Peter of Blois, who has served as many masters as any *routier*—including me. Peter waxed lyrical about marriage as an indissoluble union, "So the woman is at fault who leaves her husband and fails to keep the trust of this social bond." Pish, pish!

> "We deplore publicly and regretfully that, although you are a prudent woman, you have left your husband. The body tears at itself. The body did not sever itself from the head, but what is worse, you have opened the way for the lord king's, and

your own, children to rise up against the father. Heed how the prophet says, 'The sons I have nurtured and raised, they now have spurned me.'"[33]

The archbishop, or Henry, or Peter, went on: that I should cease to poison the minds of our sons against their father. If I did not, Henry would visit me with extreme penalties. I recall my first reaction: he thinks himself Claudius to destroy my Messalina.

I wish I had given Henry the comfort of some reply, no matter how slight. But I held my peace. I remember thinking: I'll keep my bolt in my bow against another day. Little did I know that, against Henry's wrath, I was unarmed.

Henry countered my silence with a scorched-earth campaign against my vassals and kinsmen north of Poitiers. Nor did he quit his ravages until he had wasted the lands, uprooted the orchards and vines and slighted the walls of Faye-la-Vineuse. Henry knew that, during my years of exile from his court, Raoul de Faye had been my consolation and my counselor.

I stayed in Poitiers until my city was overwhelmed with the dispossessed and their tales of woe. Then I fled. Raoul—I still thank God for his escape—had already gone.

As for me, dressed like a man, astride a man's saddle, I left Poitiers with a small escort and we rode like a Mistral towards Paris. We made a ragged company, few of whom were men-at-arms: in that way we hoped to avoid inspection. But such was Henry's unholy luck that one of his patrols waylaid us on the road. This was not to be a repeat of the gallant escape which William Marshall had made possible six years earlier. A man-at-arms pulled down my hood to reveal, not a squire, but a queen.

Thus began the most unpleasant epoch of my life. I had more freedom as a child. I even had more freedom as a queen! But now I was my husband's prisoner.

It was perhaps as well in those first months that I was kept at a distance from Poitiers, for I was spared the sight of Henry ravaging my hall. He left the *grande salle* standing, and for that I was grateful. But the feminine way to *courtoisie* which we had labored mightily to build on the foundation of *trobar*... That he ripped out, root and branch. Poets, envoys, scholars, women and the noble youth of many lands—gone! Henry was not content until he had reduced my court and capital to the barren cloister I had known in Paris. All we had striven for, he cast away.

Mars vanquished Venus. Of that there was no doubt. In a matter of days Henry destroyed the songs and traditions of troubadours that had flourished in Poitiers since the day Grandfather gave them birth and breath.

Henry, you see, had finally learned with a jolt a secret I never explained: it must have struck him as a belated epiphany. He discovered the powers of a woman's persona and mind as weapons of war and as the battlefield on which she fights to great advantage.

As a next humiliation I was made to feel the shame of an adulteress marched naked through her town, for in June Henry marshaled us like the hostages we were through his "loyal" Anjou and Normandy until we reached Barfleur. There, he consigned us to vessels and shipped us to England in the worst of weather—an English tempest in July! He dared not wait for better weather. Philip of Flanders and Young Henry were also waiting to cross with men-at-arms to seize England in support, as Henry put it, of *my* rebellion.

It seemed he would wreak his vengeance on us all. My exile would be shared: with me came John and his betrothed, the infant of Maurienne; Young Henry's Marguerite, Richard's Alice, and Constance of Brittany with young Geoffrey; and Henry's kinswoman *à main gauche*,[34] Marie de France—a wonderful *trobairitz* if you excuse her Vexin idioms. Marie's sin was her subversive verse: she dared to suggest that a man who invades a woman's chamber should knock. Well, we all knew what that implied.

Henry also seized young Joanna.

Oh, and Emma of Anjou, a half-sister whom Henry's father sired on a lady of Le Mans. Henry gave Emma to Prince David I of North Wales. He had expressed great lust for her. She was indeed very beautiful. Not that lust alone sealed Emma's fate. David, being at wars with his half-brother, Rhodri, thought a match with the king's sister might tip the balance in his favor. Small good it did him. He is exiled to England, I hear.

There seemed a special vengeance in Henry's design, to rid Poitou of noble women. I confess with pleasure that my court of feminine wiles caused Henry more apoplexy in six brief years than Becket did.

I must teach you about men, Aline. Don't think that I shall let you stray defenceless in their world. They fear women, you know. We mire them in confusion. But never let a man confuse *you*, child. He may manifest his fear as arrogance, anger, or even respect. Male fear takes many forms, and I have felt them all, including exile.

A man's gender is sculpted upon him. His body is explicit in its nakedness. He conceals nothing. And that includes his littlest member, raised like a lance by the lust-fired incubus of his desire. But a woman... A woman's power is concealed. Her gift, the gift of giving life, is hidden. Is she not God's marvel? Her mandate to go forth and multiply is a compact twixt her and powers divine.

The secret that is woman is a sacred canon which men cannot know. And what a man cannot know attracts him. It seduces him, draws him as a mouse to the smell of cheese, eager to explore. Let a woman only smile and she may stab him to the heart. Let her pass close by, and the breath of her passing stirs the pennant of his want. A man who desires a woman becomes another self, fired to a heat that seeks for one, and only one, release. That is the carnal act. How different they are before and after: as rampant lions transformed to limpid sleeves, their humors turned upside-down.

It is his inability to be indifferent to her presence that rouses a man to exalt the female form: it is that which he worshipped in his mother and his nurses. She and they were at once a present comfort and a sacred mystery. When a man comes to his ripe-grown years he cannot set aside the worship of the idol that informed his first decade. So he stands in awe of that which he cannot ignore. He stands in awe of her hold upon him; he stands in awe of the mystery of her being; he stands in awe of the pain, the urgency, with which he craves her and the power with which she chains him to that craving. As rubbed amber draws hairs from one's head, so women draw men to their will.

In my experience, men do not speak to women as they do to other men. Discourse between man and man or between woman and woman is, as it were, secular. It is not unlike the language of the marketplace. It treats of a commerce of concepts where much is known, and, being known, passes unsaid. But let a man speak to a woman, and he will plumb the depths of his brains to invest his words with inner meaning, and he will seek to find innuendo in her response. Nor is she innocent, for language is a woman's weapon. It is the siege engine that knocks down male walls. A woman's body and her language are twin powers, Aline. Use them to negotiate from strength.

Therein lies man's fear. That his very being lives in awe of women is a secret he dare not disclose, although females know it, deep in their bones. Men's awe makes them vulnerable. It is the hole in their chain-mail, the rip in their cassock. Priests are no less men for being priests. They are vulnerable, too. Hence the fear and loathing shown us by the Church. If you would negotiate with men, Aline, you have but to dazzle, reject, enchant, confuse, torment and allure. Men need their goddesses, child. They need their Virgin Mary in her very flesh and warmth.

A stiff west wind and sleeting rain. We shall stay in today, Aline. Leave the screen across the window; light the candle. God, how I feel the cold. But the chapel must be colder. The Almighty shall hear my prayers from here today.

I was speaking yesterday of Henry's special vengeance on the women of our family. Damn him. How I love and hate and praise and chide the memory of that man.

Think of the bleakest hilltop that you can, add a wind that seldom stops, and there you have it: Salisbury Tower. What is it about the benighted English that they love to suffer so?

Forgive me, Aline, I forget that fate is guiding you to live in England. But not until the spring, child. Let us make the best of our company together: yours, in my service; and mine, in this life. Together, what tales we shall write.

Where is your future husband's estate? Did you tell me? Ah, south of Shaftesbury. A summer day's ride west from Salisbury. A prettier country, spared from those upland gales. I pray you grow old in comfort and sufficiency.

As a matter of fact, when Henry's shipload of royal women landed in England, he packed off Marie de France to the abbey at Shaftesbury: she became in time the abbess, where she lives to this day. I, for my "sedition," was assigned to exile in Salisbury Tower, and Winchester, among other strong places.[35]

S cholars who know England say that long ago an ancient race of men dug deep ditches around the summits of the hills and piled the soil up in great banks, turning hilltops into earth-walled fortresses. They say the ancients must have been a race of giants, because to this day the ditches they dug are as deep as river gorges, and the earthen banks behind them rise up higher than a modern castle wall. You have seen the walls of Chinon, Aline. Now imagine a man-hewn earthen bank three times as high, piled up around the summit of a hill to enclose a plain the size of a jousting yard. There you have it: the fortress of Salisbury Tower.

Perhaps in other circumstances that dreary palace would have weighed less heavily upon me. William the Conqueror chose Salisbury to pay off his troops. That took place one hundred and four years before Henry sent me packing, and local folk still celebrate that tale of ancient glory. Heaven knows they have little else to praise. I gather William thought highly of the place. His barons swore fealty to him there. Stephen ordered it sacked, but before he could raze it, he died.

Was ever a garrison more drear? The town itself stands at a crossing linking half the major roads in southern England. Never a day passed but pack-trains came through and cavalry hurried around. To that extent, Salisbury was a frigid Antioch. But those signs of life took place in the market town, a bow-shot away; and the town was sensibly set in the lea of the hill. We lived in isolation behind the great ditches, stuck up like a baron's pennant in the wind. Mark you, I should have become accustomed to it: I was born at Belin, in a motte and bailey on just such a stub of a hill.

By the time I reached Salisbury they had rebuilt William's old palace in stone. Work without end! Excepting the sabbath, there was never a day without builders and their winches and their carts of facing stone, dust and flints.

I will say this: Jocelyn de Bohun was courteous and kind, although he was cursed with the usual bishop's obsession. He expended more attention and treasure on a new west front for his cathedral than on pastoral cure.

Why do I chatter on about that wretched place? I feel compelled. Joanna remarked it in me, and I could give no answer. I wore the first months of my exile on that hill as a thief wears the livid scar of a newly-burned brand: uneasily, in shame. Yes, I admit it, I had to force my head erect lest I cast down my eyes for shame. God help me, Henry made me feel like a felon in that place.

Always guarded, although from a distance. Always watched.

The palace housed two chapels, one above the other: St. Margaret's on the lower floor, for common folk; and St. Nicholas, where we celebrated mass. It was along a private passage from the royal chambers. One could feel one's way there safely after dark. Though I forget who endowed it, our chapel boasted a perpetual flame.

Never since my childhood in Bordeaux and Poitiers did I take such pleasure in hearing common folk speak. Just outside the chapel window was a well as deep and deeper than the hill was high. My pleasure, if I may so describe it, was to linger behind the casement and listen to the women bantering with soldiers. Among themselves the women were a rolled book: my ears never did drop their guard against the foreignness of English. Nevertheless I delighted in their laughter and the spirit of their voices. Coarse, ordinary folk who measure their lives from one bowl of oats to the next, and yet...

Some of them, the ladies' maids, had a smattering of Norman French. I understood them when they bartered lewdly with the soldiers—a kiss in exchange for helping with the bucket in the well. Such merriment! And winding that well was a labor indeed: they used two mules in the wheel. One day they hoisted the bucket to fix it and laid out the rope. It measured two bow-shots, end to end. No mortal man had dug that well. They must have been devils who delved so deep.

As to the Norman soldiers, I learned more than I cared to know about their officers' vices, including the names of their mistresses and the lovers of their wives.

You have gathered that I had to make friends with trivial joys, Aline. It is true. And yet, if one has never been diminished—as I was then—one cannot appreciate what it is to be great. Respect your servants, child. They have their place.

How one's circumstance changes the view.

And how in God's name that weather-spited little hilltop housed both a religious community and a garrison, I shall never know. They mixed like water in fat. The clergy looked down on the soldiers; the soldiers abused the clerks.

The older folk had fond memories of a Bishop Roger, who had served Henry's grandfather. They were bishop and king for thirty-three years together. Indeed, Bishop Roger had been Henry I's chancellor, sometimes even regent of England. It never ceases to amaze me how a prelate can set aside blessing souls to take up the lopping of limbs and the hanging of thieves, instead.

Oh, if only my Henry had kept his bishop in splendor as a chancellor, not made him change his coat and put on holy ways! How different, how much better, our outcome would have been.

Never mind. Strike that through, Aline! I stray from the path again. I intended to speak of Bishop Roger, who rebuilt the king's palace in stone and enlarged his cathedral on that dreadful hill. I often thought of his guiding hand: his works were all around us. I never knew Bishop Roger, but I think of him as Salisbury's Suger.

How early it gets dark these days. How long the nights. Time weighs so heavily in winter. So heavily.

I am tired, child. Even here, in the comfortable south, this season draws down the dark. Leave me now. I shall use the coming of the night to contemplate, alone.

Aline, come back!

Come back, child! Don't go. Please stay.

God, how these recent years of reckoning are tearing at the fabric of my being. Since Richard and Joanna died I've been so very much alone. Hold my hand. There. Ah, yours is so warm, so young. Do you know, Aline, you are perhaps the last of thousands who have served me through the years. From Nana to you, a course of fourscore years and more. She was wet-nurse to the infant I once was; you are the handmaid to my mind in my old age.

It is as well that it is dark. No one should see a queen laid low by fear and frailty.

Do you know, there were times when I stood on the parapet at Salisbury Tower and saw the smoke from Clarendon's chimneys rising from the woods. In the interval between holy offices one can ride from Salisbury Tower to Henry's lodge at Clarendon, with all its fateful implications for our times. Oh yes, they are that close.

Henry loved that place. I wish he had given me leave to lodge there more often. It is wrapped in the embrace of woods and a clover meadow, not stuck in the cold and the wind on Salisbury's frigid hill. Some nights I slept at Salisbury dreaming I lay beneath the bright metal stars adorning the sky-blue ceiling in Clarendon's hall. Wishful thinking, Aline. Just wishful thinking. Still, I never could tread the gold-brown tiles at Clarendon without thinking of Henry hurling invective at Thomas, and the archbishop turning his back on the king and walking away. It was in that very instant that Young Henry watched the love between his father and his mentor rend like the veil of the Temple. Poor boy. He never healed. What a sad breach, Aline. So signal. So complete. It was there that the Angevin future cankered and died.

Henry let me travel, of course; to Young Henry's court at Winchester along the old Clarendon Way which linked those palaces. Sometimes I lay at Ludgershall and, after that woman died, at Oxford and Woodstock.

But it was Salisbury that left its mark, proclaiming through its vast, en-circling ditch and wall: You are your husband's prisoner.

I t must be ten years since the bishop of Salisbury asked Richard's consent to build a new cathedral down in the valley far from that hill. And Richard—may God hold his memory fast in our hearts!—gave his consent. He knew how I felt about the other place.

One came to dread the holy days, when the chapel did not suffice. We had to follow a steep path off the bank to descend to the cathedral. They were building Bishop Jocelyn's new west front when I was there, so the wall at the weather-end stood open, breached by the worst of the elements and funneling wind and rain along the nave. I tell you truly, a perpetual tempest beat through that church so much that boys and clerks could hardly hear each other sing.

And in every place the builders stripped away the grass the chalk glared through as white as if it were the virgin light of heaven. It shone brighter than the cliffs of Greece or the roads in Palestine. Several of the builders and the monks went blind.

You can guess my response when Richard mentioned the bishop's request to build his cathedral nearer to Clarendon, down in the valley.

And now, let us leave Salisbury Tower behind.

29. Henry settles accounts.
Castle checks Queen, King prevails
1174

After so many decades of giving whip and spur to royal policies, it was difficult indeed to observe the giddy world from the prisoner's paddock. That was how exile attacked my mind, as if I were a bachelor knight bested in a tournament and escorted to the prisoners' circle, knowing he must soon be stripped of everything: horse, trappings, chain-mail, lance and tabard; left without a farthing and deserted by his squire; the very device on his shield scratched off and painted anew for another owner.

When, Oh when would Henry reap the troubles his affront to me deserved? Never, it seemed. With his accustomed luck and speed of action he always managed to prevail.

After Henry landed the women in England, he hied to Canterbury. Young Henry and Philip of Flanders were still waiting a favorable wind in a Flemish port to land their rebel force in England. Any other man in Henry's position would have looked straightway to his forces and materiel, but Henry plucked at the sleeve of a spiritual resource. He entered Canterbury as a penitent, with neither badges, arms nor shoes, and spent the night on his knees before Thomas Becket's shrine. The following morning the monks scourged him.

Oh Henry. Would that I had cracked a whip across the twice-harrowed field that was your back! How many ridges and furrows did Rosamond count when she traveled her fingers along your spine? No, no, Aline. Scratch that away!

He prayed, fasted and denied himself sleep for three nights and three days in Canterbury cathedral. That done, it became apparent that Thomas's ghost had come to love Henry more than Thomas the mortal man had done in his final six years of life. Perhaps his spirit was placated by Henry's gift of forty pounds a year for lamps to burn at the martyr's shrine. Forty pounds! That was enough to light a town through a year of new moons.

As for Thomas the Martyr. Pah! The man was a martyr to his own pig-headedness.

Be that as it may, Thomas's ghost worked its will to Henry's advantage. It happened thus: Henry, weary from penance and fasting, made his way to London where he went betimes to bed. In the middle of the night a man woke him with an urgent message. This was one Brian, servant to Henry's justiciar, Ranulf de Glanville, whom Henry often charged with guarding my dangerous self. This Brian rushed to wake Henry, shouting "William the Lion is taken!" William the Lion, king of the Scots, had conspired with certain English barons to ravage the north of England in support of the attack which Young Henry and Philip of Flanders planned for the south. The capture of William the Lion beheaded this stratagem straight away.

Well, you may guess that the southern assault withdrew immediately. When word reached Louis that the rebellion in the north of England had collapsed, he withdrew his support for invasion across the sea.

Ah, Louis, you were always fast to make a wrong decision, slow to make a right one. You were no ally in my troubles with Henry's Angevin moods. But at least you did the next best thing.

How much of the history from those years shall I relate, Aline? Neither those years nor their tales are truly mine. For the first time in my life I was a woman bound to work at woman's things. Embroidery! I put enough stitches in coarse-weave stuff to hang a chapel. Nay, to hang Salisbury Cathedral!

I could only wait and listen, listen and wait, while voices and letters from across the sea spoke of waste and ruin in my lands. First came galloping rumors by word of mouth and then, at a trot, followed news.

So, let us stop to consider how much of this tale we should tell.

I suppose we should follow at least a thread of history through my enforced exile. How strange that my sons and my husbands should war with each other through all those years while I perforce stood off, seemingly aloof, pricking my ears to learn about the fray.

I felt like one touched by St. Anthony's Fire, the madness that strikes peasants in the spring. It is then, wise barbers say, that evil voices and visions rule the head and heart, masquerading as one's own, whereas in truth they manifest the work of evil influences raised from hell.[36] By which I mean that what I heard during my exile was not of my own mind's making, although it touched me to the quick. It was as if the temple of my head became a reed or harp-string rather than its player. The world in which I was the central pillar—my world, the world to the south beyond the English sea—whirled and turned beyond my grasp. Ink and voices bade me heed a constant message: madness reigns! Lady, we would tell of madness in Anjou, in Normandy, in Aquitaine! Moreover, in Poitou.

All this news of worlds gone awry. And nothing I could do.

S o then, we are agreed, Aline. We must a little history...

Louis could not overwhelm Henry in England, so he thought to wrest Rouen away. That summer, Louis, with Young Henry and Philip of Flanders, encamped their force of French and Flemings before Rouen, a city well placed to defend itself, lying in a river bend and backed by the embrace of hills.

On the tenth day of August, the feast of St. Lawrence of Rome, Louis lifted his siege from dawn to dusk as a mark of respect. His ally, Philip, tried to use the occasion to take Rouen by perfidy when the citizens opened their gates. But that is another tale...

Suffice to say that Louis' delay threw to the winds any hope of humbling Henry. Well advised by spies—we had built an excellent skein of posting roads throughout the empire—Henry embarked at Porchester with a formidable force of Welsh and mercenaries, reaching Rouen just four days later. Louis, Young Henry and Philip of Flanders folded their tents, burned their engines and fled.

It took Henry another month to bring Richard, Geoffrey and Young Henry together for a parlay at Montlouis to settle a truce between father and sons. Once more he returned the prodigal sons to his favor. At ruinous cost, I might add. In his triumph, Henry was quick to forgive those who trespassed against him. Instead, he heaped the fault for *all* his trials on Louis, and on me.

Thereafter I readied my mind and my spirit as well as I could for a very long sojourn in England.

I t was summer when you and I walked beside the wall, Aline. Do you remember? I told you that Henry had tried to force me to come here, to Fontevrault, as abbess. Had he but waited a score and more of years, I had come of my own accord.

He attempted that gambit in my first year of exile. He sent a cardinal to entreat me. A cardinal, sent by one who belittled the pope's own nuncios! Henry had carefully rehearsed this fellow, Huguezon: I heard my husband's Angevin idioms recited in a stranger's voice. Via the mouth of his scarlet messenger, Henry proposed a divorce—by reason of consanguinity, of course. After which, I was to take the veil and hie myself to Fontevrault to reign as abbess. Hah! You notice he dared not divorce me unless I agreed to take holy orders. Otherwise I might convey my lands into another marriage. Nor could Henry leave me in my duchy as a woman *seule*, for then my liege-lord would again be Louis. By how much Henry feared to lose Poitou and Aquitaine, by so much Louis lusted to regain them. And all at the whim of a woman's caprice!

Oh Henry, how you must have longed to immure me for ever at Fontevrault. But it is you, my lord, who lies buried these thirteen years in our crypt. And Richard. Poor Richard. And Joanna, too. One day I shall join you.

But this is no time to be maudlin. His bones may be buried here, but Henry had no lust to be a monk. A rumor spread abroad around the time Henry dispatched his cardinal to me. You recall, Aline, that Louis gave his little daughter Alice to Richard at Montmirail. Well, in the year Henry proposed a divorce to me, Alice was sixteen and still a virgin. The couple had not been wed! Louis thought it shameful: he demanded the pope call down anathema on Henry's lands.

Henry's scheme was as clear as the moon in a cloudless sky. If he divorced me he would be free to take Alice himself. And if he divorced me on grounds of consanguinity, he could disinherit our issue and sire less troublesome sons on her. That was the buzz that jumped the northern sea in the autumn of that year. Perhaps Henry himself charged the wind with that whisper, knowing that Young Henry and Marguerite would carry the desperate message to Paris. Poor Louis. So many trials, and always borne in piety. A veritable Job.

Henry learned much from his mother. It suited him to keep each of our noble houses fearing the worst. In truth, he probably intended to defend the narrow waist of our empire by holding onto Alice's dowry, the county of Berry, rather than cede it to Richard and Poitou.

As for our sons, Richard took pains for three full years to quiet my vassals in Poitou and Aquitaine. He waged energetic warfare worthy of his father, who was all too aware of his son's prowess. When Richard saw fit to lay waste, he laid waste. He had a way of teaching loyalty by powerful example.

Geoffrey achieved a measure of peace in Brittany.

And Young Henry? Poor, troubled mite. He was at once our oldest and our youngest child. He counted counties and kingdoms as if they were playthings that he, in his womb-joy,[37] must own. Nothing would quiet Young Henry until he commanded the substance as well as the trappings of his title, king of England. His humors burned like a flame in a fitful draught, now reaching the rafters, now guttering low. Young Henry lived for the gaiety and pleasures of my court at Poitiers; for the reflected glories that William Marshall earned by victories on his behalf in tournaments; for the contents of his father's treasury, liberally spent; and for diversions with wastrels in Paris. He wanted no part of the chills and assizes of mumbling lawyers in the sea-sundered province whose crown he wore. English property rights might fascinate his father, but learned questions of *novel disseisin* were not for the father's son.

Some hounds are best kept on a short leash lest they bite their master. Thus, I fear, was Henry compelled to keep our eldest son.

30. Sundry Trials and Injuries
1177-1179

Wherever I lay in England, word reached me from Aquitaine of slighted castles, burning towns, orchards and vines destroyed. The troubles were such that Richard felt compelled to sack rebels' lands from end to end. I feared for my treasury. From what I heard, it seemed that Aquitaine must soon resemble the ruin we confronted in England after the civil war.

Meanwhile Young Henry's envy of Richard and his father grew apace. Richard was active in war in defence of his—and my—estates. Young Henry could only think of himself as the duke of Normandy in-waiting and the king of England in-waiting. Waiting. For his father to die. Hence his envy of Richard and to a less extent Geoffrey as masters of their own lands. Nor was Young Henry's humor helped when his agents exposed a spy whom his father had placed at his court. A certain Adam was taken with letters on his person warning Henry of his son's seditious designs. Only the fact that the man was in holy orders saved his life. Young Henry ordered this wretch—his father's servant—whipped naked in every town from Poitiers to the dungeon of Argentan.

One bright moment pierced my darkness in a troubled year. Despite the treasure Henry lavished on the curia, Rome denied his plea for a divorce. Furthermore—the Church knows no shame—at Louis' bidding, a papal legate clung to Henry, pressing him to marry Richard to Alice according to the terms of Montmirail. Henry, of course, was loathe to sanction a match that would break his grip on the county of Berry. Nevertheless, opinion outweighed him. His path of least resistance led to a meeting at Ivry in the autumn of the year, where Henry had to confront Louis, Louis' advisors, the papal legate, the ever ambitious Philip of Flanders and the barons of France.

At Ivry, Louis appealed to Henry on behalf of his daughter, Alice, and then retired, claiming himself a worn and heartsick man. I fell to prayers when I heard that. Louis was a gentle, if an often foolish, soul. There were times in our marriage when I loved him and he, fond fool, never ceased loving me.

Even at Ivry, with his foes aligned like hostile planets against him, Henry retained his devil's luck. Louis had purchased the legate's tongue to demand a speedy marriage for Alice. But the prelate choked on his brief, voicing an aside about the latest anguish in Jerusalem and the need for a Crusade. Offered this route to decamp, Henry embraced it. He set his seal to some vague articles and sprang to horse, thus winning the battle of wits at Ivry.

His opponents never grasped the point; uppermost in Henry's mind was Alice's dowry, the county of Berry, not Alice herself. Berry's leading baron, Raoul Déols, had recently died, leaving a three-year-old daughter, his heir. Fleeing Ivry and the legate, Henry made haste to seize Déols' castle, Châteauroux, and his infant girl.

I could speak for ever about the wrinkles etched on the face of that miserable year, but one will suffice. With all his foes put down again—and me still put away—Henry celebrated Christmas at Angers with our sons and his vassals. Word reached me that Henry's court was of a splendor unsurpassed even by our coronation.

Meanwhile, I spent my sixth Christmas in exile.

I recall that the year following brought strange omens from on high. I cannot speak for conditions at Angers, but in England we suffered through the deepest snow I ever knew. Then came such winds that roofs and sheep were lifted and hurled away. The English make much of Midsummer Day, but that year it was a source of worry. Three days before the longest day, people spoke of the fire that sparked from one horn of the bright new moon. Then, in September, the sun was eclipsed. I yearned to employ some wise-woman to tell me what these signs foretold, but I was closely watched. You can guess how carefully I listened through the casement to the Norman women drawing water from the well.

I should mention that in May Richard found it necessary to humble Geoffroi de Rançon by laying siege to the fortress of Taillebourg. The place always held special meaning for me. It was there that Louis and I first knew each other on our wedding-night. At Taillebourg I became a wife, in body as well as in troth.

Ten years later, de Rançon commanded my forces on Crusade, taking the blame for the Turks' ambush of Louis' army. I was just able to save him from being hanged: I always thought well of Geoffroi. But Taillebourg became an endless source of trouble. Furthermore, the house of Rançon married with the Lusignans. Bad blood. Legend holds that Lusignan descends from the fairy Melusine—and she was part snake! My experiences of her family bear that out.

Richard, undeterred, took Taillebourg, a feat never before tried, let alone done in a mere ten days. Its defences were formidable. He razed the Rançons' fortress to the ground. That, I am pleased to say, had a salutary effect on our vassals.

31. Philip and Louis, waxing and waning
1179-1180

News from the kings' conference at Ivry made me suspect that Louis was not long for this world. The fact that he spoke plainly to Henry's face exposed his measure of concern. But at least Adela had given him a son. When Philip turned fourteen, Louis arranged to crown him in the cathedral at Reims. They set the coronation at the height of summer, an appropriate season to vacate Paris.

En route to Reims, the royal party lodged at Compiègne. A vast tract of forest nearby had long been a royal chase. One day, young Philip went hunting with his companions. As befitted his rank, the master of the hunt assigned this fourteen-year-old boy a splendid horse. Unfortunately the beast was so mettlesome that in the heat of the chase Philip outpaced his party and lost himself in the woods.

You can imagine Louis' anguish when, towards evening, members of the entourage returned to the king without his only son.

As for Philip, he rode miles through thick forest. Reasoning that his horse might know its way home, Philip gave the animal its head. Hither and yon they went at the whim of the horse. Dark was falling when they burst by chance into a clearing where a blackened fellow in rags took fright at the sight of Philip—as Philip did of him. When the prince found voice to explain himself, the charcoal burner led horse and rider down a short path—a siege engine could have thrown a stone farther— to the royal hunting lodge. The prince had only to grope his way to the light of torches.

I never heard how Louis rewarded the churl: liberally, I assume. He was a generous man by nature.

Philip was out of the woods, but not out of danger. His adventure caused him to take fever. Next, he fell into that state of death-in-life when the heart still beats and breath still fogs an iron blade, but the soul in the body can neither speak, nor hear, nor see.

While his son hovered twixt life and death, a vision of Becket—*Saint Thomas*—hovered above Louis' bed for three nights on end. There was nothing for it but Louis must venture to England! His advisors stood aghast, for they had no time to arrange safe conduct. But Louis was adamant: he posted to the coast like a common messenger, took ship from Wissant and landed at Dover on the twenty-second day of August.

Sometimes, whether one wills it or not, reflections come to one's head in pairs, as if they were twins. For me, hearing word of Louis posting to the coast summoned the specter of the aged Suger riding on the spur forty-two years before to conjure mercy for Poitou. I see an ancient abbot rushing in haste to a young king, Louis, who had now become an old one. Those images visit in tandem. I suppose they always will.

Those were strange days. A pigeon must have brought word to Henry, for he rode all night from London to meet Louis at Dover, only pausing when some force of heaven eclipsed the moon. How fateful the dying of the light must have seemed to Louis, as it snuffed out the moon-bright cliffs at Dover.

Thence they rode to Canterbury, accompanied by the archbishop and a ragged escort of bishops and nobles, hastily chivvied together to dignify the person of the king of France.

Louis prayed at the martyr's shrine, presenting assorted treasures and a fine gemstone. After pious reflection the kings returned to Dover, Louis taking ship again just four days after he arrived.

Would that I had spent just four days in England!

It was a measure of Louis' fear for Philip that he ventured to cross the northern sea. He did so exactly thirty years after the sea tossed him ashore in Calabria: he swore to me then that he would never set foot in a vessel again.

His sacrifice was worth his pains. On his return, he found Philip restored to health.

Philip's coronation was postponed until All Saints Day. His uncle, Guillaume, archbishop of Reims, performed the rites of conse-cration. I wish I had been there. As seneschal of France, Young Henry carried the crown at the head of the procession. Richard and Geoffrey represented the homage of their provinces. Henry himself supported the crown of the Franks on the young king's head, a gesture implying that the Franks could rely on his kingdom's aid. A handsome thought, but a false one, before and after that special day. What lies we contrive for the sake of spectacle. I shall attempt an essay one day, Aline, on the distance twixt wishes and deeds.

Philip of Flanders had two roles that day, as chamberlain of the royal feast, and as bearer of the sword of Charlemagne. In spite of several campaigns, Flanders had failed to shake Henry. He would have had bet-ter luck had he plunged the great sword into Henry at the coronation!

Louis was a husband for twenty-eight years before Adela presented him with his only son. No wonder people styled Philip *Dieu-don-né*. Only Louis knew better than I what hurt and frustration he endured through those years: the prayers, the fasts, the mortifications for nearly three decades. Although I failed to give him a boy he never spoke a word on the subject to hurt me. Not even after Antioch.

I mention this because I know that Philip's coronation was more important to Louis than life itself. And yet he could not attend the ceremony. From Compiègne, he hasted to Paris to invoke the aid of St. Denis as a second assurance on Philip's young life.

The strain of it all taxed Louis' health: he fell gravely ill. It took him as long to die as it takes a child to come into this world. Indeed, there were those who said that Louis, in his lifelong naïveté, was but a child grown old. Near the end he caused his treasures to be brought to him and, when he had inspected the wondrous things among the royal goods, he told his servants to scatter the horde to the poor.

Mark this, Aline: Louis esteemed the deeds of St. Lawrence of Rome. St. Lawrence, you may recall, dispersed the wealth of the Church to the beggars of Rome, causing the enemies of Christ to martyr him over a fire. I have no doubt that St. Lawrence's act was upmost in Louis' brains.

Be that as it may, Louis lingered until harvest the following year. Then our Saviour gathered him. God rest his noble soul. For all his faults there were days when I felt for him a measure of the great, abiding love he often expressed for me.

32. THE PAST WAS NOBLER THAN TODAY
1182

Advent is almost upon us, Aline. How quickly these November days surrender to the dark. The mood suits the season; or is it that the somber season suits my mood? Nature itself would stop her ears against the story of the lost and futile years which we must contemplate. So much waste; so much brought low that had been rich in every way.

Word reached me wherever I lay in England: Henry was here, Henry was there; in the year after Louis' death, Henry was everywhere. In the matter of governance he came to understand—*we* came to understand—that my late mother-in-law's "hungry falcon" policy had become a recipe for war. During the decade of my exile times had changed.

I do not say that just because our sons had grown from boys to boisterous warriors, careless of each other and of their father's honor. No. Loyalty itself came under strain. Vows counted for less than the hot breath pushing them past lips. Too many rootless young men-at-arms stalked the land—younger sons, bastards, orphans, squires—all eager to pillage in a master's service, or their own.

Young Henry was no better and no worse than his fellows in those days. Looking back, I see that the passion of young men for tourneys and strife made new demands on a commodity we seldom spoke of when I was young: money. How the decade of the Eighties debased us! It was as if the very world turned, making nobles beholden to stall-holders and men in trade. Money-lenders' contracts forced bonds of fealty to the wall. Nor do I see any sign of the times returning to a decent respect for values we cherished of old.

These changes struck me as I pondered the news, brought to me letter by letter and mouth by mouth across the sea. During several terrible months of strife at Limoges I realized that the world had become a new creature, and a fearsome one. A strange egg was hatching, not into a cuckoo, but a cockatrice.

Years earlier I had been the first to celebrate the passing of Abbé Bernard's influence. How that man vexed my being! But, a generation after his death, we sorely needed a measure of his austerity and discipline.

Henry's actions suggested that he had reached the same conclusion. He left the highest barons in their castles and looked to men of intelligence for advice. In that respect he followed Archbishop Theobald's example. Thirty years before, Theobald had spread his net to draw competent clerks from all walks of life: Becket's father was a merchant. Henry adopted the same policy, selecting officers among base-born men who chanced to have brains. Henceforth fathers pressed their sons forward, not to serve the Church alone, but to seek advancement in the service of the king.

Can it be that, half a century after their death, Abelard is defeating Bernard? A generation ago I wished it so. Today, I am not so sure. It certainly looks as if reason is tearing down faith. If it be so, reason is an ugly thing. In recent years I have set my face towards faith.

I t is cold in here. Too cold. I shall not speak another word until my old frame thaws. I am sure my lips must be blue. There have been too many days of late when I would barter this room with a scullery drudge just to sweat by a kitchen fire.

Come, Aline, light a taper from that candle and give me your arm and my stick. To the hall! I am weary of mortifications. Surely in this weather God and the abbess will forgive us if we find some comfort near a fire.

W e come to the year one thousand one hundred and eighty-two. I can hardly bring myself to speak of it. We shall be brief.

Richard continued to beat out fires raised by rebels in Aquitaine. The troubles were so bloody that it seemed they might leave my provinces the way Stephen's war left England. It is true that visiting fire and the sword on a rebel's peasants does him more lasting harm than razing his castle. But allegiances these days are as fickle as weather. One is reluctant to kill a generation of toilers on land which may return to one's fold the next year.

Our vassals pulled at the rein in Father's time, God knows. But in those days no baron would accept another as leader. We had leisure to swat them one at a time, as one kills flies.

Unfortunately, while I wasted in England, our vassals invented enough grievances to seek the banner of a leader. In this they were encouraged by Bertran de Born. De Born was an upstart, a man of low birth. He had married well, to the sister of a viscount; and his brother was wed to the viscount's daughter. This gave the brothers joint tenure of an impressive fortress, Hautefort, in the Dordogne. The castle commands a fine view of the valley of the Auvézène. But Bertran expelled his brother, becoming the sole master of Hautefort.

Rumor had Bertran de Born vying with Richard and Geoffrey for the favor of Maheut de Montagnac. Maheut was the daughter of the viscount of Turenne, and wife to… Oh, what does it matter! Suffice to say that Richard and Geoffrey lost the lady's favor to Bertran. The older man was more skilled in the manners of courtly love.

> "She craves not Poitiers [Richard] nor Toulouse,
>
> Nor Brittany [Geoffrey] nor Aragon,
>
> But worthily bestows her love
>
> Upon a poor and valiant knight [Bertran]."

Try to write that in the *langue d'oc*, Aline. It sounds coarse as a jackdaw in the *langue d'oi*. Not that its meter is valiant in any tongue.

You look puzzled, child. Oh, I should have explained: this Bertran fancied himself a troubadour.

Given the lustful urges of men, the exquisite Maheut posed a powerful motive for strife. But she was neither the only motive, nor the greater. Bertran de Born's brother had appealed to his liege-lord, Richard, for support in winning back the castle of Hautefort. Richard responded, sacking Hautefort's estates, but the castle proved impregnable. Richard's excursion on the brother's behalf fired Bertran with a thirst for vengeance. However, he lacked the authority to lead nobles. For that he looked, in his malice, to Young Henry, whose furious incubus sat as firmly fixed as ever in his head.

Word of their pact reached Richard, who was always alert to his elder brother's mercurial ways. To defend Poitou against Young Henry and the rebels of Aquitaine, Richard rebuilt an old castle at Clairvaux, in the strategic land-of-three-forts—Chinon, Mirebeau and Loudun.

Aline, make it clear that this is not the Clairvaux of Bernard's abbey.

Meanwhile the rebellion in Aquitaine reached such fury that Henry himself came to Richard's aid, marching mercenaries south in the summer heat.

I am as sure as I have ever been of anything in life that our stars stood misaligned. And not only over us. The German emperor, Frederick Barbarossa, chose this season to exile Henry the Lion and our daughter, Matilda.

We should have let young Barbarossa perish with his uncle's army in Anatolia, thirty-five years before. To think that we sent them aid!

Henry the Lion had caused offence by sacking lands belonging to the archbishop of Cologne. Barbarossa and his nobles seized on this nuisance as the pretext to divide Henry's ducal fief. How deceitful, those people, like the Roman soldiers tearing Christ's robe!

Duke Henry and Matilda vacated their German towns and castles peaceably, bringing with them my grandsons, Henry and Otto, their daughter and an escort of several hundred knights. This caravan reached Rouen, where the duke's family threw itself on the mercy of Henry—at the height of his wars in Aquitaine.

Henry responded by summoning Young Henry to Rouen. Who better to comfort his sister in her exile than the young duke of Normandy? But Young Henry's incubus clouded his reason. The Capets and Bertran de Born—may God debase his seed!—continued to feed him a diet of envy and lies.

Verses from the quill of de Born made poor poems, but powerful weapons. He wrote in the *sirventès* style popular in the Dordogne and the Limousin. *Sirventès* is well suited for warlike themes. De Born used it to pen poems attacking Young Henry as a man of empty titles and no achievement whose brother, Richard, fought real wars. Bertran never preached his own slanders: the harp and voice of his Catalan jongleur, Papiols, broadcast his malice through castles and halls. By mocking Young Henry, Bertran sought to goad him into supporting the rebels against his brother, Richard, and, if need be, his father.

Damn him! Damn the very soul of Bertran de Born. In no great time he brought about Young Henry's end!

No. No. I spoke in haste. Blot out that line, Aline. I cannot let it stand.

To the chapel, child! Never in a long life have I cursed a man's soul so roundly—or seldom with such cause. But I must not burden my vital soul with malice. Not at my age. Take me to the chapel. Then fetch Brother Lord Roger. I must haste to shrive myself of evil words.

33. The nearer in blood the bloodier. Conflict from Caen to Limoges 1182-1183

Henry chose to convene his Christmas court that year at Caen. Meanwhile I was shivering on a paltry stipend at… I think it was Oxford.

This was the first year in which the newly anointed King Philip held a Christmas court in his own right. Lest our sons and vassals be tempted to find better song, stronger drink and a brighter fire in Paris, Henry's entertainments at Caen were exceptional. I recall he forbade our vassals to host their own Christmas courts. As compensation, he presided over a board which seated a thousand knights. Old wives who still had enough wits to remember his grandfather spoke of Henry's court at Caen as more glorious than anything Henry Beauclerc had convened.

Young Henry, Richard and Geoffrey attended with their households.

I shall not dwell on this troubled season. No doubt the chroniclers have spilled their careless rumors into careful ink, but I shall not. It still gives too much pain.

Young Henry would not be reconciled to the joyous mood of his father's court. Its gaiety passed him by; envy and jealousy ruled his head. As his mother it grieves me to say so, but his incubus ruled him fully by this time. Meanwhile de Born's jongleur, Papiols, was spewing his master's ordure to heighten the discord between Richard and Young Henry. The matter of Richard's castle at Clairvaux was one he noised abroad:

"Twixt Poitiers and Île Bouchard,
hard by Chinon, Loudun and Mirebeau,
someone has built a mighty fortress
at Clairvaux, and there it sits,
athwart the very middle of the plain.
The Young King should not know of it,
for it would scarcely please him..."[38]

De Born and his singing ape composed another verse for Richard:

"Papiols, go with speed
and tell Sir Yea-and-Nay
that peace has lasted far too long."

Sir Yea-and-Nay! Bertran clep'd Richard *Oc-e-No* when he withdrew support from de Born's brother after they failed to take Hautefort. Never mind. History will surely know Richard as *Coeur de Lion*.

Henry's Christmas court at Caen suffered another vexation— which was just as well, for it distracted attention from the ugly struggle among our sons.

William Marshall's prowess in arms had long since won him the coveted office of master of the Young King's household. This provoked jealousy among lesser knights, some of whom used the Christmas court to destroy William's prestige. To that end they spread word that William knew Queen Marguerite at least as well as her husband, Young Henry.

Marguerite was already a focus of attention at the Christmas court: she served as mistress of festivities during my continued absence. On this occasion, she shared those duties with her sister-in-law, Matilda, during our daughter's first Christmas in exile from her German lands.

Into this full, majestic assembly at Caen, William Marshall rode like a roll of thunder, demanding of Henry the right to prove his innocence—and Marguerite's—through trial by combat. He offered to fight three different champions on three successive days; and if he did not defeat them the king might hang him or burn him alive. Such was his challenge. But no man in that thousand-strong company was brave enough, or foolish enough, to take arms against William Marshall.

Unable to clear his name by battle, William turned his horse, left Henry's court and rode fast and far. He heard Christmas mass at the shrine of the three kings, in Cologne.

As to the Christmas court, Young Henry and Richard showed such loathing for each other that Henry withdrew with them from Caen. They rode to Le Mans, there to reconcile their differences—yet again.

More than that I will not say. Truly, Aline, until the denouement is done I shall have difficult days.

What madness fired my Angevins? My Poitevin father was fierce in his rages, but the constant warring among our sons—and twixt father and sons—was truly a feral thing. And yet, to the end of his days Henry blamed *me* for estranging his sons—*our* sons—from him. I raised my boys to be men who esteemed their own rights, not to disesteem their father's. If it chanced that I spoke harshly of Henry in their hearing, my tongue cut no deeper than the lash his public whoring earned him.

Sometimes I think of Abbé Bernard's dire prediction for the Angevins: "From the devil they came, to the devil they shall return." But my next thought reconciles me to the narrow man that Bernard was, and the narrower man that he became. He was not evil. It was not he who cursed Henry's line. But he did impose the certain past upon a more uncertain future and descry a devil in it.

No, no. I cannot leave it there, Aline. We should add that it is the lot of young nobles to fall out. And the greater the father's portion, the greater the falling out among the sons. One has only to mark the tale of Alexander's heirs. That which is built up with pain and care can be carelessly undone.

I have spoken enough in this vein. What must you think, Aline? You hear me pondering the men of my flesh as if I were a Grecian playwright, not a modern woman.

I come to the fatal events which ravaged the Limousin between late winter and the early summer of the year.

Frost was still in the ground when Henry sent Geoffrey to speak to the rebel barons of Aquitaine. Geoffrey was asked to convey the message that his brothers had settled their quarrel and sworn great oaths thereto. Henry's advisors expected that the rebels, hearing these news, would dismiss their forces. Late winter was too early for war: no man-at-arms cares to fall from a horse onto frost.

Instead of that happy outcome—I shall not trouble to explain the minutiae of fealties pledged, not pledged and unpledged among our three sons—it came to pass that Geoffrey joined the rebels. Oh, how I prayed that he would shun his brothers' quarrels!

Hearing this, and fearing for the borders of Poitou, Richard led a force against them. Had his forced march not tired his horses he might have captured the leaders near Mirebeau: they had gathered there under the banner of Viscount Aymar of Limoges. Pressed by Richard, they fell back to defend a stronghold in the city of Limoges.

God knows what evil spirit seized Young Henry in that fatal year. I forbear to guess at the mind of God, but whatever purpose He intended was unkind. Now came the four most tragic and troublous months of my life. Would that I had been allowed to mediate!

The town of Limoges is split by the river Vienne: on one bank stand the houses of merchants, markets and the cathedral; across the river are the castle of the counts of Limoges and the abbey dedicated to the patron saint, Martial.

It was into the castle that the rebels' leader, Viscount Aymar, took his forces including, incredibly, Geoffrey. Fourteen years before, Richard had sworn oaths on the relics of Martial when he was invested as the duke of Aquitaine. Now, he dared not cross the river or enter the abbey. Richard deemed this rebellion such a threat that Henry himself marched south to help stanch the wound. Henry encamped across the river from the chateau, a Welsh-arrow's flight beyond the town.

Young Henry, consumed by jealousy for Richard, interpreted his father's aid to his brother as a war against himself. Goaded by the poisons which Bertran de Born put into his head, Young Henry threw in his lot with Geoffrey and Aymar's rebels. Thus the cauldron simmered: two of my sons joined the rebels, confronting my husband and my third son on the opposite bank of the river.

I swear, Aline, that year gave fair force to the adage, "Madness reigns."

Henry, of course, forbore to wage war during Lent, but Young Henry, Geoffrey and Viscount Aymar's rebels were not so constrained. It grieves me to say so, but the rebels used the forty holy days to loot silver, gold and altar plate from churches, shrines and abbeys in the Limousin. Geoffrey led many of these forays.

There is also the sordid matter of two arrows. Henry himself approached the castle of the counts twice under terms of truce. The first time, an arrow fired from the walls pierced his tunic to lodge in his chain-mail. This caused him to withdraw, with Richard, to the castle of Aix. They were visited there by Young Henry, approaching under terms of truce to explain the error of the arrow.

Then the same thing happened again. Henry approached the wall at an hour fixed for parlay, and was met by a second arrow. On this occasion the Almighty saw fit to make his horse rear—quite unexpectedly—so that the animal took an arrow in the neck which had otherwise struck Henry full in the chest.

I recount what follows accurately, for a reliable messenger brought word within days of these events. Furthermore, five years after that fateful summer I met William Marshall at Winchester. He was posting to London to claim a bride bestowed on him by Henry and confirmed by Richard: but he tarried long enough to describe events that took place in that unholy June.

I knew a great deal about this matter before I encountered William. But he bridged a gap my mind ached to fill. Not for the first time he gave me comfort by replacing missing tiles in a passage my soul often treads.

On the eleventh day of June Young Henry, returning from one of the rebels' diabolical raids on churches and shrines, took sick in the heat of the afternoon. Turning aside, he found rest and shade in the house of one Etienne Fabri, at a place called Martel.[39] Priests were summoned and, it relieves me to know, Young Henry confessed his sins.

With his life failing fast, he desired to make peace with Henry. Messengers from the son found the father camped beside the Vienne within sight of Limoges.

I am sure Henry's first instinct was to leap to horse and ride to Martel, which is no slight journey: it lies as far south of Limoges as Poitiers is to the north and west. But Henry's advisors restrained him. They reminded him of the arrows aimed at him during hours of truce, arrows which struck his person and his horse. Furthermore, the Young King kept company with evil men—saving William Marshall, who served the son by order of the father. Young Henry's supposed sickness might be a trap contrived by his evil advisors. Only the life of the king himself stood between the son's ambition and his father's crown.

These cautions prevented Henry riding to Martel. I do not envy the decision he was forced to make that day.

One of the emissaries from Young Henry to his father was the bishop of Agen—indeed, it was he who heard our son's confession. Henry now entrusted this bishop with a ring which had once belonged to Young Henry's great-grandfather, Henry I, Beauclerc. With this ring, Henry sent a message conveying his forgiveness.

When the bishop reached the house in Martel, Young Henry lay near death. Fever bathed him but, as God would have it, he was lucid.

William Marshall told me in full what followed. First among Young Henry's dying requests was this: he begged his father to show mercy to me, his mother, and to restore me to favor. Then he asked that his father provide for his queen, Marguerite, whom—perhaps with foresight—he had already sent for safekeeping to her brother, King Philip, in Paris. Third, he begged Henry to meet the expenses of his household. This was an extraordinary request, although at vast cost Henry did discharge the debt. These were men, *routiers* of wicked disposition, who had warred against the father and stolen coin and precious plate from every church and abbey as far west as Angoulême, and far to the south, beyond Martel. Indeed, on the very day Young Henry fell sick, some in his party had climbed to the shrine at Rocamadour and stolen much that was precious. Some say they took Durendart, Roland's sacred sword—a mischievous notion, since we know Roland's sword was carried into heaven! They say great powers were bound in the hilt of that sword. Small good they did Young Henry.

A month earlier, for no other reason than to confound his father, Young Henry had sworn on the precious relics of St. Martial to take the

Cross and go to Palestine. This being now beyond his power, he had his men cover him with his crusader's cloak. Then he requested William Marshall, who stood at the bedside, to discharge his vow and carry his arms to the Holy Sepulcher.

This done, Young Henry required his men to lay him on a bed of ashes, where he renounced his worldly goods. He gave orders for the division of his possessions, which were frugal indeed, for he surrounded himself with wastrels. There he lay on his bed of ashes, naked but for his crusader's cloak and the ring by which Henry conveyed his forgiveness.

One of the attending monks remarked that Young Henry should put off the ring, the better to renounce the things of this world. But our son replied that he kept it on his finger not to possess it, but as a token and proof of his father's forgiveness and love.

I would that this would go away, Aline. Twenty years later it still stabs my heart to speak of it. Nevertheless, our Lord drank his cup. Who am I to spurn mine? A sip of water, child. Then I shall carry on.

I n time Young Henry agreed to put off the ring which his father sent him, but when the monk knelt to remove it, it would not budge. All who were present took this as a sign of God's forgiveness as well as Henry's.

Thus my eldest surviving son died, towards evening, having lived twenty-eight years, fourteen weeks and six days from the hour my womb gave him into this world at Bermondsey.

So died Henry's favorite son.

I knew of Young Henry's passing that same night. He came to me in a vision, in a state of grace, with all the troubles of the flesh stripped away. His countenance shone in all sanctity, and his head was adorned with two crowns. The lower crown was of dull, earthly stuff, perhaps gold; above it shone a celestial crown, dazzling with the brilliant light of heaven. No mortal being brought word to England that night. No horse could post so fast, so far. No ship could sail that sea. It was as if the veil twixt heaven and earth were rent to tell me, gently, and to let me glimpse my troubled son within the compass of eternal peace.

Lest people think me foolish in this matter, I shall struggle to explain my mind-sight in material terms. It is said that spirits of the newly dead are like fowls of the air. They communicate, like winds which touch and relay all manner of things in their passing, because the airy element commands their natures. That is why wise women study the movements of birds, to predict events, as soothsayers did in Greek and Etruscan times. Beyond that I offer no apologia for a vision which is sacred to my heart.

Perhaps I should have known Young Henry's life would be curtailed. The Almighty drew him forth of me on the final day of the shortest month and he lived just that number of years. I thought his birth-tide was peculiar. Oh dear. Now I sound like an Etruscan crone. No matter. I have said what I must.

Aline, light our taper from the embers and return me to my chamber. I shall be grateful for its gloom. If my body does not yield to the lure of sleep I shall spend this sorry night in prayer and contemplation.

Today we shall finish this woeful tale. And afterwards I shall speak no word on anything until tomorrow. If my Saviour calls me hence before my account is done, so be it: His servant awaits her end. But He shall not rush me in the matter of my recollections.

Those of Young Henry's household who remained with the corpse bore his bier northward, stopping at Grandmont. He had given instructions that certain of his organs should lie there, beside the grave which his father had prepared for himself—King Henry gave generously to rebuild the Grandmontine monastery near Limoges. This was the mother-house of an ascetic order which the rebels had utterly despoiled just days before. Indeed, they had done such damage to holy places in the Limousin that the bishop of Limoges had excommunicated Young Henry. But word reached Grandmont that King Henry would undertake—at enormous cost—to pay reparations for damage and theft. So the ravaged monks sang solemn requiem over Young Henry's corpse, watched by the men who had ravaged them.

I heard that those monks never got over the shock. In spite of Grandmont's ascetic extremes—"Here," they say, "you discover the cross alone, and poverty"—the monks and lay brothers took sides between Angevin and Frank. The prior, Guillaume de Trahinac, resigned some years later. Never forget, Aline, whether men play at the politics of poverty or riches, they play for the same stakes: power.

It was not one of Young Henry's companions-in-arms, but a monk, Bernard Rossot, from that very monastery, who broke the news to the king. Most of Young Henry's household dispersed after the requiem: they could milk no further profit from his corpse. And no one from his household dared come into the presence of the king! Except one: William Marshall.

Henry asked William to escort Young Henry's body to Rouen, the capital seat of Normandy. But William was not at that time his own man. His service was held in bond against a debt Young Henry owed to a mercenary. Furthermore, William himself was bound by the Young King's dying wish to carry his sword to Palestine. To that end Henry armed William and equipped him for the road.

I mentioned that Young Henry came to me in a vision. I was therefore prepared when an envoy from Henry delivered the fatal message.

How time rushes on. That was twenty years ago, but I still bear my vision as I once bore the child who became a troubled king.

Henry appointed the archdeacon of Wells to bring word to me of Young Henry's passing. This gentle man was taken aback by my prescience, but he covered his surprise. Henry, I am sure, chose Thomas of Earley to break the news because he came of a fine family with a most Christian disposition. Henry knew the Earleys from his boyhood years in Bristol. Thomas's kinsman, Bishop Reginald FitzJocelin, founded a hospital for the poor of Bath; and his brother Stephen was the abbot who rebuilt Sainte-Genevieve at Paris before Philip appointed him bishop of Tournai. I heard he died a month ago.[40]

Now I'm straying again, Aline. So many connections struggling for expression. In Thomas of Earley's mind I am sure that my vision explained the poise with which I heard his news. Besides, it is in the nature of churchmen to accept the unknowable ways of God. I think I gave the archdeacon as much consolation as he gave me, for I had wept a mother's tears before he set foot in the ship appointed to fetch him to England.

On that sorry tale I close this too short day. We shall meet after lauds tomorrow.

34. The survivors play the game, again
1186

Don't chivvy me, child. I know where to start. This is one epoch that needs no recalling. I was bred and fed on politics.

So. The world as we knew it renewed itself. All over again.

Young Henry's passing left the centre of the chess board as depleted as a charcoal burner's clearing. So many squares to fill; so much to mend. Imagine: Normandy without a duke; England without a crowned heir to the king.

Fifteen years earlier, at Montmirail, Henry had rushed to allocate our provinces, omitting our infant, John. He hurried the matter because I had recently abandoned his court to return to Poitou, where I named Richard my heir. Montmirail was Henry's response, a settlement with Louis to secure our borders and provide for our sons. Hence Louis' gift of Alice to Richard. The still-unwed bride of Berry! Poor creature. Such a beauty, too. In the year of which I speak she put a score of years behind her, still unmarried, still a poisoned pawn.

Suddenly, all was confusion again. The puzzle of power became a contest worthy of the *jeu de dames*. And the *dame* whose counsel they sought was me.

But not before Henry confounded us anew. It was clear to all that Young Henry's unbalance of mind had been born of the fact that he wore the highest titles but no shadow of royal authority. The contrast mocked him to the quick and served to feed his incubus in his final, tragic years. Now, to my anger and surprise, Henry convened a meeting of our sons in Angers, where he asked Richard to yield Poitou and Aquitaine and assume the same hollow titles which destroyed his elder brother.

To make matters worse, it was clear to Richard that Henry had settled the matter before they met, although his father had not discussed it with him. Moreover, Henry did not ask Richard to cede his lands to Geoffrey, but to John. Unknown to Richard, Henry had already summoned John from Britain, anticipating that he would do homage to Richard for Aquitaine and Poitou. What folly moved Henry I cannot conceive!

Richard rode out of Angers in fury. He had no intention of ceding lands he had fought to defend through three hard years. John was seventeen years old, not yet a warrior of Richard's mettle.

Besides, Richard cared not a fig for the crown of England, still less for its people. He was bred of the south, a creature of warmth, of reds and grays; not of greens and misty hills. I raised him as a Poitevin, to uphold and inherit the Guilhem line.

After Henry's *faux pas* at Angers, the eaglets returned to their mother's nest. To be precise, I welcomed them to a great stone nest built by their ancestor, William the Conqueror. I refer to the castle at Windsor.

It was at Windsor that I blocked Henry's aspirations for John. I bore no grudge against our youngest child. I loved him no less than my other sons. The matter was simple: Poitou and Aquitaine were not for him. I told Henry that if he chose to apply *force majeure* I would become an active, rather than a passive, foe. If he insisted on misplacing John in my seat I would appeal with all the power at my command to my liege-lord, Philip of France. (By this time it was clear that Philip was a rod of sterner stuff than Louis.) My proposed defence enjoyed both weight of law and precedent. Indeed, my argument won support from many who attended us at Windsor.

For the first time in a decade my influence became the hub which turned the wheel. Four years earlier Henry had forced me to cede Poitou and Aquitaine to Richard's rule. Now, with Richard both unruly and well versed in war, Henry sought to regain my lands. But he had no claim to them, except through me.

The upshot was that Richard returned to Poitiers as my heir, and Geoffrey added the protection of Normandy to his fief of Brittany. And John? Henry hoped to use him as one positions a knight on a chess-board, as a place-holder to deny an opponent's march. John might be Henry's new favorite, but he still lacked his proper place.

Thus we wrestled, warring against our loves no less than our foes.

The game we played at Windsor inched us forward, and then restored the *status quo*. By the time we adjourned, Henry and I had moved from check, to check, to check. But never to checkmate. My king was not defeated. But neither was his queen.

Vanity, vanity, all is vanity. Thus the Preacher. Much of what we debated at Windsor soon wasted in vain. The skins recording our deliberations still smelled of the goat when Geoffrey died on the eighteenth day of August. God keep his soul; in the fullness of time may it rest with mine. He was unhorsed in a tourney and trampled, then took a fever and died. In that respect he died a death not unlike that of his namesake, my father-in-law. What subtle ghosts these fevers are, utterly invisible until they manifest themselves as two heats burning in a single body.

In his lifetime, Constance gave Geoffrey two daughters. We soon learned that she was with child at the time of his death. The following March, Constance marked Geoffrey's memory by giving him a son. True to her Breton lineage, she christened the boy Arthur.

I hope Geoffrey's confessor examined him in every particular with respect to those assaults against the holy places in the Limousin. I have few fears in that regard: the Capets are scrupulous in sacred matters of that sort.

Geoffrey was lodging with Philip in Paris when it happened. They were the greatest friends. Philip was inconsolable. I heard—and this reached me with the weight of some authority—that Philip tried to throw himself into Geoffrey's grave. Hearing that, I recalled a verse of Abelard's: "Low in thy grave with thee / Happy to lie / Since there's no greater thing left for Love to do / And to live after thee / Is but to die..."[41] Some likened their friendship to that of David and Jonathan. My dear Marie attended the requiem and gave funds for an annual mass. Poor Geoffrey. He lies beyond our care in God's good keeping beneath the choir at Notre Dame. I wish I could comprehend our Lord's indictments.

35. A well-timed diversion: Crusade
1183-1188

Our changing fortunes raised two problems with respect to the late King Louis' daughters. With Marguerite a widow, Philip sought to reclaim that portion which had long since been ceded as her dowry. I refer to the Norman Vexin.

As for Marguerite's sister, Alice, the Franks continued to press for her marriage to the heir apparent of England, Richard. It was to him that she had been betrothed in infancy, at Montmirail.

Henry held the Vexin, through Marguerite, and Berry, through Alice, but he was far from willing to part with either. We were poorer by one death, but still two dowries richer.

Would Henry ever consent to marry Richard to Alice? The passage of time made it unlikely. The precedent of Young Henry's example was all he needed to warn him away from that match. The Young King had spent more time lodging with his father-in-law in Paris than with his father. Would Richard look to Paris if he married Alice? Furthermore, such a marriage strengthened the Franks' claim to Poitou and Aquitaine.

The two kings met to debate these thorny issues. The Franks had a more inspired leader in Philip than in his father, but some of the old clericism remained. Henry turned it to good advantage. They met under the ancient elm tree at Gisors: the tree stood for centuries on the border between Normandy and France, and for almost that long it marked the site of royal conferences.

The Franks came well prepared to debate precise points of argument. Henry, as ever, confounded his foes in discussion as well as in war by fighting on different ground. At Gisors, he went so far as to suggest that he might give Alice to John. Hah! This threw the fox in the dovecote—and not just among the Franks. Did this signify that John, not Richard, would be named Henry's heir to England? To compound the mystery, Henry suddenly knelt before Philip at Gisors and did homage for all the Plantagenet lands south of the sea, including Poitou and Aquitaine. With this single gesture he voided Richard's claim to my lands.

Not only that. At Gisors, Henry undid the division of lands he had made so long ago at Montmirail. He would be king—and duke and count—of all! John and Richard, no less than Philip, felt the sting of Henry's maneuver and returned—for the moment—to their father's fold.

Into these, our incestuous adventures, marched an external threat. The infidel was making advances against Christian kingdoms in Palestine. The plight of those states was so dire that the patriarch of Jerusalem, Heraclius, came in person to England to solicit Henry's leadership in a general Crusade. Heraclius came all the way from Jerusalem, but not to the pope in Rome, though he passed him by. He came not to the king in Paris, though he passed him by. He came directly to Henry, as the most puissant monarch in the western lands.

Henry had no illusions about the success of a Crusade. Through our years together we often chatted about Louis' disasters. In the first years of my marriage to Henry I was especially scathing: Louis had come close to losing his kingdom as well as his army. Furthermore, Henry had imbibed the flavor of our foreign woes in countless halls. For thirty years he had listened to too many disastrous tales from the wine-rinsed lips of knights and counts to entertain the prospect of Crusade lightly. Moreover, he was hearing the same stories from his guest in exile, Henry of Saxony, who had marched with Conrad and survived the ambush by Seljuk Turks.

Despite the patriarch's emotional pleadings, Henry was in no mood to waste a fortune in treasure and lives to endure the same Church-directed folly we suffered at Damascus. When John offered to go in his father's place, he was firmly rebuffed. The news from Palestine might be bad, but Henry was in no humor to make our own condition worse.

Two years later the stream of affairs turned the tide. Franks, Angevins, Flemings… All manner of men seemed more amenable to a convenient diversion offered by the prospect of Crusade.

Aline, you may notice in your journey through life that the affairs of men sometimes reach a ferment of impatience with the ways things are. It is then that the mass of people swarms forth, like bees in the spring, to clamor for change. You are too young to have tasted what I mean. You were swelling your mother's womb the last time the buzz of Crusade displaced reason. But at last we are treating of events which took place in your lifetime. Your waxing, my waning, Aline.

How long now? I am impatient to bring this account to a close and yet, when I do, I shall have no more excuse to hide in this fading flesh. Lord, grant that I may reach *the* end before *my* end. We are too close to deny me that!

Where was I? Ah, the urge for change in restless times. A change comes over the air, a restlessness, the tide of the times flows, slows, stops, turns. To put it bluntly, the impact on the collective mind is not unlike the rising and the lancing of a painful boil. Perhaps the animus that wills this change is like an angel of disease, a fever, not of the body but in the soul.

Whatever agency was responsible, Philip again took Henry to task beneath the elm tree at Gisors. During their conference, the archbishop of Tyre preached dire news from the holy places. The archbishop was a better spokesman for the Church's cause than the patriarch, who won nothing from Henry and died, they say, a broken man.

The archbishop was more fortunate. I am sure he himself believed that he arrived on the scene of an opportunity given by God. After exhausting travel across the Alps he found before him a ready congregation: two kings and all the mighty men of Flanders, France and the Angevin empire assembled in conclave. All heard him speak. I should say "preach." Forty years earlier, Abbé Bernard took to the roads for a year to fire the faithful with the will of the Holy Spirit for Crusade. At Gisors, the archbishop of Tyre managed the same feat in one week.

To general amazement, Philip and Henry set aside their quarrels, gave each other the kiss of peace, and adopted the cause of the Cross.

Mark me, I have never been convinced of Henry's sincerity. It struck me that he acquiesced because it bought delay. He was old, and he was tired. Crusade would serve to rein our rebel vassals to his banner, employ Richard in a war on the same side as his father, and even win reputation for John. Let Crusade commence, consigning to history the arguments voiced beneath the Gisors' elm.

Henry departed Gisors with a large following of clerics to set up a court at Le Mans. There, he presided over detailed and minute arrangement for Crusade. That was Henry. Whether he dictated laws for England or an order of march he was meticulous. Meticulous to a point. Beyond that point he discarded his hard-wrought plans and improvised.

After he settled affairs in Anjou, Henry took ship to England around the first day of February and summoned a council at Geddington, near Northampton. Archbishop Baldwin preached, and many magnates of England took the Cross. Then Henry sent Baldwin into Wales with my sometime jailer, Ranulph de Glanville, to enlist the Welsh to Crusade.

Henry would have stayed longer in Britain except that trouble beckoned overseas. It appeared that Philip had broken the Truce of God agreed by the two kings and was even then sacking our county of Berry. Indeed, the Franks had already captured Chateauroux.

The sequence of cause and consequence went like this: Philip attacked Berry in reprisal for a foray by Richard against Count Raymond of Toulouse. Raymond had offended Richard by failing to root out bandits who were killing Poitevin merchants passing through his lands. In consequence, Richard captured seventeen castles around Toulouse. Raymond then sought his liege-lord's protection. Hence Philip's punitive raid into Berry.

Mark me, I suspected more than a sniff of collusion between Philip and Richard in this chain of events. Still, I remember thinking at the time: under Richard, perhaps the Guilhem line might once more claim our lost Toulouse.

I mention this petty strife on the eve of Crusade because it took Henry from England—for the last time, as God saw fit. He visited me before he embarked, in late July. We argued. We cried. We both expressed our loathing and our love in roughly equal measures. Then we parted like lovers. Grey-haired lovers. Even Henry's red head was streaked with gray. After that he took ship, leaving England and me for ever.

Small sparks light large fires. The year began with general acclaim for Crusade, but the sacred pretext for war soon slipped to an afterthought. While Saladin lay siege to the holy places, Richard was toppling Raymond's towers, and Henry was pressing for truce with Philip. Before long, a tooth-for-a-tooth engulfed our lands from Toulouse to Normandy.

This sort of thing brings out a common condition in men. Perceptive persons know it for what it is: self-righteousness. There is not a ruler in our time who has not succumbed to this temptation. I recall my own war against Champagne when I was young and certainly less wise. Who can forget the enduring name Vitry-le-Brûlé?

Unfortunately, this latest spark struck fire at the very moment when Henry, Philip and a score of counts and barons were wealthy with taxes extracted for Crusade. These had not been extracted easily: the Saladin tithe made the English howl; and Philip had resorted to razing the lands and properties of at least one monastery to instill Christian charity in others. Besides this new supply of treasure, some thousands of men-at-arms were following their leaders, war-ready, for Palestine. These were not the shoeless yokels who trailed at the rear in Louis' Crusade. Henry and Philip took their pick of the warrior crop. In consequence, the year saw some thousands of crusaders abrogating the Truce of God to fight each other the length of the land.

The tinder was dry indeed. Especially in mid-summer, when the kings met again at Gisors. Henry's English, Welsh, Bretons and Normans, arriving first, rested in the shade beneath the giant elm. This left the Franks to wait in full sun. A fight ensued, during which the French turned their swords and axes against the tree and cut down the elm. Never mind that this massive tree had served as the site of royal parlays from time out of mind. The incident distressed Henry, who was always careful of property rights: he had spent years enshrining them in English law. Now he took one look at the fallen elm, renounced his fealty to Philip and challenged the French to war.

In the middle of this, a messenger from the master of the Templars thrust a letter into Henry's hand. Jerusalem had fallen to the infidel!

All this in the space of an hour on a hot afternoon. Forgive me, Aline. I cannot help smiling: it is better to laugh than to cry. The unfolding situation became so very Greek!

I pass over a failed conference two months later. By November, matters had gone from bad to worse, for now Philip arrived at the place arranged for conference attended by Richard. To put it bluntly, our son saw better opportunity to advance himself under Philip of France, rather than his father, the king of England.

Henry, I am sure, was shocked. More so when Richard threw himself down before the king of the Franks and paid Philip the homage that his father had renounced at Gisors. Thereby, in the law of the Franks, Richard became master of Henry's continental lands.

And he knelt before Philip in plain view of his father!

I have often had occasion to curse Henry, alas, but never since I rode away from Louis as a free woman have I sought to profit the Franks. Not in that fashion!

After the conference, Henry sent William Marshall in pursuit of Richard, to no avail. At Amboise, William discovered that Richard had sent letters to more than a hundred of Henry's vassals, summoning them to join his cause.

Henry's Christmas that year, at Saumur, was no better than mine had been the previous eleven years. Few attended him, and most of them were priests. Meanwhile Philip and Richard disported themselves with lavish entertainments in Paris. Gone for all time was the austere Merovingian citadel overseen by the ghost of Bernard.

36. Knight takes King
1189

My mind is uneasy, Aline. Be patient with my wanderings today. I said at the outset that time is a thief in the storehouse of memory. On the other hand, a ruler's decisions are bound to hurt innocent lives: one cannot prevent one's shoe crushing ants. In consequence, the need to forget is a salve to one's conscience, a balm to one's being. My habit is to use recall as a valued tool for guidance but never as a lash with which to beat myself. I have managed the life of my mind in this way since the earliest days of my marriage to Louis and our disasters in Poitou and Champagne. Those calamities stamped themselves as a seal in the wax of my youthful brain. Much later I discovered the work of a scholar whose counsel supports my opinion: "Deliver moral wrongs to oblivion, for forgetfulness is the one remedy of unanswerable evils. He who thinks again of what he hates, suffers to a degree from what he does not love." I could express his notion better, but Henry's old tutor speaks truth in his musty way.[42]

For that reason I shall not dwell on Henry's passing or on Richard's role in it. Thirty-seven years of love and war between Henry and me continue to constrain my tongue. Besides, I dictate this account at Fontevrault in the very presence of my husband's mortal remains. Richard lies entombed here as well—Richard, whose precipitate actions, taken of lust and anxiety, undoubtedly hastened Henry's end.

I prefer to remember Henry as the strong young man of principle and purpose who ruled me with a compassion which frustration stole from him in later years.

B riefly then, following his inauspicious Christmas court at Saumur, Henry lay in poor health in his native city, Le Mans, until the end of Lent.

Meanwhile, in Paris, Philip and Richard spent an exalted Nativity rejoicing in each other's company, using the quiet season to gather forces for war against Henry in his weakened age.

In the spring of the year, Henry appealed to Philip for conference: he met Philip and Richard at La Ferté-Bernard in Normandy. But Henry was by this time so weakened in body and drained of resources and allies that he could do little but listen to terms.

Even intercession by the Church to heal the rift among the leaders of a holy cause had no effect. Philip and Richard, both, abused the cardinal legate whom Pope Clement sent to hold them united in support of Crusade. In that respect, of course, Richard was no more careful of threats by prelates than his father and mine had been.

H enry was born at Le Mans. Many of his forebears lie there. Indeed, his line rose from obscurity there. So it was to the church of St. Julian in that town that Henry carried his father's corpse for burial during the fateful summer in which we first met.

Now, thirty-eight summers later, it was to Le Mans that Henry took himself with such companions as remained: his eldest bastard, Geoffrey the Chancellor; and William Marshall, whose loyalty and sense of duty have attached him to his liege-lords like a cockle-burr through right and wrong.

Even as Henry's party fell back to Le Mans, Philip's and Richard's forces occupied towns and castles behind them.

During the quiet days of Lent, Henry had ordered the castle at Le Mans reinforced, but those repairs were not enough. On the eleventh day of June—the very day Young Henry took ill six years before—Richard and Philip attacked Le Mans.

Chroniclers have written much about what happened in the next four weeks. For reasons I have stated, I shall not.

Suffice to say, Richard knew the intricacies of Le Mans as well as Henry. So it was no surprise when the Franks and Poitevin rebels attacked the south gate, only to suffer a bloody rebuff at the hands of William Marshall. Meanwhile Stephen of Tours, Henry's seneschal for Anjou, ordered the eastern suburbs set on fire, denying the French access from that quarter. But the wind turned, bringing the fire to the town.

William now rallied the king's household. Driven by the flames and, at the same time, protected by them from immediate pursuit, Henry fled Le Mans with those who remained to him, some seventy knights, and John. The account I heard had him cursing Christ.

The day was hot, the roads dusty. The king and his escort retreated at full gallop towards Fresnay, while William Marshall brought up the rear. At one point William turned in his saddle to see, fogged by the dust kicked up by the king's horses, a number of knights in hot pursuit, led by Richard.

I met William at Winchester a month later, and Richard six weeks after that. Both told the same tale. William had the advantage of surprise, for Richard and his escort were riding into the dust and into the sun. William turned his horse about, blocking the road. Richard came within a lance-thrust before he stopped.

"God's legs, Marshall," he called, "don't kill me. I am unarmed." Whether he had off his hauberk or his helmet, I cannot recall.

William, by his own account, replied, "I shall let the devil kill you, for I will not." So saying, he ran his lance through Richard's horse.

I thank God that, in the heat of war, William took an action which was prudent, rather than hot-blooded. Otherwise I should have lost a son as well as a husband inside a month.

By the time Henry came safely to Fresnay, he was too exhausted to undress. He passed the night covered by Geoffrey the Chancellor's cloak.

Meanwhile, in the confusion of the day, John had disappeared.

When he was rested, Henry continued to our castle of Chinon, while William and Geoffrey did their best to rally forces and bring them to his aid.

Henry, I am sure, was sick unto death even then. Over the years he had sustained a number of sores and injuries, some of which no barber or surgeon had managed to heal. One saddle-sore had become an ulcer: even comfrey failed to drain the humors from it. Furthermore, his legs were bowed from riding and thickened in the ankles. I never knew a man to stay his horse like Henry. Methinks too many decisions of his later years were made while he fought against pain.

However, he agreed to meet Philip at Colombières [Villandry] near Tours, a town dear to Henry which had lately fallen to the French.

I shall not recite the terms which Philip and Richard dictated while Henry listened, supported, on his horse. What he heard were no better than terms for surrender. Henry, his very life draining from him, had no alternative but to accede to the allies' demands. However, something of the old lion endured. As the meeting concluded, Henry was forced to give Richard the kiss of peace. There and then he spoke the last words that he ever spoke to any member of his blood except his natural son. "God grant that I may not die until I have my revenge upon you."

That said, his companions—he attended Colombières with only a small bodyguard—returned Henry to Chinon in a litter. When they were getting near he cursed himself and his sons by me. I hope he was delirious by then, for surely God forgives great oaths hurled from the snake-pit of delirium.

Even fourteen years later I am relieved to report that this oath was soon undone, for the clerics in Henry's escort included the new Archbishop Richard of Canterbury and the bishop of Hereford. Arriving at Chinon they carried Henry to the chapel in the castle, where he confessed his sins, received absolution and then Communion.

Henry had made only one request of Philip and Richard: to receive a list of the barons who gave their allegiance to his opponents. To that end a member of his company, Roger Malchael, tarried in the enemy camp while the list was drawn. When Roger returned to Chinon and read the first name on the list, "Count John, your son," Henry turned his face to the wall.

I am moved to remark that his eldest bastard, Geoffrey the Chancellor, ministered to his father tirelessly at the end. Many loving words were exchanged. I give thanks that one member of Henry's blood attended his departure; I regret that that member was not out of me.

And thus my Henry died at Chinon, on the sixth day of July. As one scribe put it: he died "within the Octave of the Apostles Peter and Paul, in the nineteenth lunation." His last years on earth were not happy. May his suffering weigh against his durance in Purgatory, and may our Father hasten his soul to Paradise.

How came Henry to lie among us at Fontevrault? Some years before I arrived here to live among the quick, Henry's remains arrived, to rest among the dead. We make a fine complement, he and I:

together we command two kingdoms, the quick and the dead.

Henry had chosen to be buried at Grandmont. But Young Henry lay there. Henry's father and many of his ancestors lay in his native city, Le Mans. But the ruins of Le Mans still smoked. A decision was made as a practical matter in the heat of summer. Fontevrault lies just ten miles west of Chinon. Thus, he who tried to consign me to this place as its living abbess rests with our community as its departed king.

Richard attended Henry's lying-in. Some say that when he knelt beside his father's corpse, its nose began to bleed. Court officers use this superstition to determine innocence or guilt: if a murderer is made to stand beside his victim, the body bleeds. Thus the expression, well known in our time: "This crime will bleed!"

The incident at Henry's bier gave rise to many hissing tongues. But it does not dignify us to believe such malice.

On that sad note, Aline, I end our interview today.

37. A new yoke and new burdens for England
1189-1190

I said earlier that William Marshall reached England within days of Henry's passing, riding hard to the Tower of London to claim his bride. He naturally had the itch of a penniless man who hungers to claim his new wife's estate in law and her body in lust. Despite these urges, William did me the courtesy of attending me first.

No, that's not right. I run ahead of myself, Aline. In my haste to remark on my new-found freedom I goad my steed forward too fast. I shall start again...

Richard rode hard to Fontevrault to pay respects at his father's bier. There, he accused William Marshall of trying to kill him during Henry's retreat, not quite one month before.

William, as disciplined in peace as in battle, replied that, had he intended to kill the count, Richard would now be dead. Whereupon Richard pardoned him.

I have observed men in peace and in war for eight decades, Aline. I am a better judge of character than most. Richard and William were exceptionally hard men in an iron world who lived by the rules of fealty. Indeed, Richard owed no small part of his character to William, who had once been his tutor in arms.

Richard told me later that he leveled the charge to test William's mettle, and found his resolve unbending.

For William, his encounter with Richard at Henry's bier was no slight moment. His future hung on that exchange. Shortly before he died, Henry awarded William a rich prize in return for his many years of service to us and to our sons. The prize was a lady whose wardship and marriage the king held in his gift. She was no less than the countess of Pembroke and Striguil. This latter is a mighty fortress a half-day's sail on the incoming rush of the tide from the wealthy port city of Bristol.[43] This young virgin was perhaps the wealthiest heiress on the British island, and Henry gave her as bride to William Marshall.

But Henry was dead.

Richard had promised her, too. He had awarded her to Baldwin of Bethune, who fought with him through the flame and fury at Le Mans.

There they stood, Richard and William, side by side at the late king's bier. Imagine: in the hour of Henry's death this poor *bachelier* knight had neither coin not prospect in the world. William was but a boy when he saved me from the Lusignans; as a young man he earned fortunes for Young Henry at tournaments; as Young Henry's master of the household he obeyed our son's every whim and discharged his dead lord's vow to take the Cross to Palestine. Returning to Henry's service he fought at his side until, before Fresnay, he stayed his hand from killing Richard.

In that moment, standing beside Henry's bier, Richard revoked his promise to Bethune and confirmed his father's gift to William. The Bride of Striguil was his to have and to hold. In the span of a breath the poor *bachelier* attained the prospects of a count with wealth and estates beyond measure.

William supposed that he would be the first to bring me word of Henry's death. After all, he rode with another from Fontevrault to the coast and reached England within days. Indeed, he was so eager to claim his bride that he crashed through rotting boards on the quay and broke an arm. When I saw him his arm was bound in rough splints.

However, by the time William brought me the news, Ranulph de Glanville had sniffed the change in the wind and set me at liberty.

It was clear that Richard would be occupied in our lands for some time and that I alone would have to bend England to the new regime. Accordingly I formed a rough and ready escort rather larger than a queen mother might warrant, rode to London and took on myself the office of regent.

You may guess that the Bride of Striguil was not the only noble ward whom I gave to strong men in order to bind their loyalty to the new King Richard. In his later years, Henry had left much undone: among other business he had accumulated a hoard of noble wards and valuable brides. Three years before he died he had ordered an inventory—of any and all wards who might be subject to royal claims.[44] I made good use of that list.

I should mention that Richard, although I gave birth to him at Oxford, was unknown to the English: those who did know him disliked him. Persons of wealth and those who owed military service had, for some years, either paid heavy tithes or risked their lives in Henry's service to war against Richard and his recent ally, Philip of France. To that end we needed to take popular measures quickly. What better way than to release others who had wasted in jail while their lords made war across the sea? Accordingly, I emptied the prisons.

The Church, too, had ached under Henry since the death of Becket, nineteen years before. I immediately relieved abbeys of their obligation to stable and feed royal horses to serve the king's post roads.

Richard and John crossed to England in different ships. I met them at Winchester in the middle of August. How sweet was that hour; how joyful the day. In the five weeks between Henry's death and Richard's landing we had so transformed the mood that those who groaned under Henry rejoiced for Richard; those who labored under levies and tithes straightened their backs a little; those who feared under Henry, under Richard rejoiced.

The joy of the English did not last long. England would soon groan more loudly than before. We had to tax the country to the very stones to send Richard to Palestine; and then I redoubled the load to free him from a German tower. But that chapter must wait another day. Meanwhile, a fair start made England somewhat more pliant to our exactions later.

Thence to coronation. My fellow Poitevins had long understood that royalty must be seen to be royal, that royal events demand a more than ordinary display of pomp and care. To that end we imposed a show of sumptuary on the long-established tradition of the English coronation such as the country had not seen before. Our coronation for Richard, held on Sunday, the third day of September, was fit for several kings. As for me, my standing had improved so much in two months that the magnates of England considered it judicious to invite me, a woman, to the coronation.

The feast that followed Richard's coronation was somewhat spoiled— as my first wedding-breakfast had been spoiled threescore and two years before. On this occasion the bother concerned certain Jews. Several leaders of these people presented themselves at the coronation feast, contrary to Richard's express decree. Our officers beat them roundly and threw them back into the street, some of them grievously injured and others dead.

Several sores led up to this fury. We were greatly in need of money to advance our readiness for Crusade. In consequence we made demands on the Jews. They in turn called in loans made to lesser borrowers, including many merchants who had taken money on interest to meet our commands for provisions and ships. This imposed hardship, such that angry people rose up in London and other towns, venting their fury on the Jews. This strife lasted almost half a year until about the Ides of March when more than a hundred of these people gathered in our royal castle at York. Beaten severely by the crowd, they elected to kill themselves rather than suffer death at the hands of Christians. On that occasion one hundred and fifty persons died, doing our property not a little damage.

I had learned of old that there comes a point in rising troubles when a thing must be speedily brought to check if it is not to get worse. This trouble at York rang such an alarm. After that we moved quickly to prevent Christians murdering Jews.

We could not permit the English to bathe in a generous stream for long. Richard was sworn to take the Cross to Jerusalem. Where previous Crusades had marched overland at the mercy of the Turks, Richard wisely chose not to recruit the vagabond-crusaders so beloved of Abbé Bernard. He would take seasoned men-at-arms; they would travel by ship.

Here our venture confronted the mercy of winds and tides. Sailing-ships from Britain and the continent's ocean coasts can pass between the Pillars of Hercules into the Mediterranean Sea, but they cannot escape again. Galleys can row through the straits against the current and thereby escape to the western ocean, but ships with sails cannot. So, sailing-vessels chartered from English or Norman ports entering the Mediterranean Sea are lost into that world for ever.

This increased the cost of Richard's Crusade. Although men-at-arms from Britain and the Angevin lands would march south to take ship at Marseilles, their transport and cargo vessels would sail from Norman and English ports. There were other costs, too.

To this end, the English and Marchers had to pay. Thirty-five years earlier, when Henry and I assumed the throne, England lay broken by war. We spent treasure from our continental lands on its repair. Now our continental estates lay broken, while England, left to itself, grew in prosperity.

No, that won't do. Strike out "left to itself," Aline.

We had to resort to selling offices to their office-holders. Many a wealthy bishop enriched his see by investing in the royal lands and rents we sold to equip the mission. In the general zeal for Crusade the Holy Spirit inspired many men to take the Cross who later repented their vow. We let these persons revoke their oaths, at substantial cost. Voices began to whisper that we were returning England to the yoke of moral decay it had known in Stephen's time. People said that our tithe but served "as a mask for rapacity." That was not true, of course. We had a sacred mission to fulfill.

In the matter of taxing the English we found my late mother-in-law's "hungry falcon" practice of governance to be fruitful. To this end William Longchamp, the bishop first of London and then Ely, served us as chancellor. Longchamp had less learning than Becket's shoe, but his personal ambition more than compensated for the meager content of his mind. Ambition, linked with the commensurate fear of failing to advance, made Longchamp as loyal to his masters as a dog. His strivings also made him contemptuous of others and, did he but know it, of himself. These qualities made him a zealous tax collector and a scrupulous stick with which to beat backsliders. Thus, for a little dangled meat, we reaped enormous profit.

Leaving such as this to manage England, Richard returned to the continent before Advent. I followed two months later, bringing Alice.

Alice! Alice! What would become of Alice?

Richard would never marry her, although another year would pass before he divulged as much to Philip, stating his reason. Nor would he return her to her brother, and her dowry with her. So, to guard her the more securely, we established a household for Alice within the fortress of Rouen. When the two kings met later that year Alice was once more the nub of their argument. But this was no time for skirmishes over an ageing female pawn.

From Rouen I proceeded to Tours, the marshalling point whence our army would march to Crusade. What a splendid sight. Our soldiers were gathered rank upon rank as far as the eye could see. Thence, with many kisses and embraces, cheering and tears, our valiant men marched off to Vezeley.

I t was at Vezeley that Richard's army camped for a time with Philip's. Forty-four years had passed since Abbé Bernard preached Crusade and read the papal bull to a host beyond number gathered on a slope outside the town. On that occasion the large, new pilgrim church of St. Mary Magdalene was too small to hold the crowd.

Twenty years later, Becket preached in that church at Pentecost, then excommunicated Henry's loyal officers.

It seemed to me that several lifetimes had passed since my own Crusade. Every leader from that earlier time was dead. The defence of the holy places had passed to our sons who, in those olden days, were still unborn. No matter. This Crusade belonged to Richard: I supported and provisioned him against this sacred day.

He was the object of every eye at Vezeley, to the discomfort of Philip, for whom jealousy added to his frustration at the eternal problem of Alice. These matters simmered, never quite absent as the French and Angevin armies marched south from Vezeley to Lyons, where they parted company: Philip to lead his men-at-arms through Italy; Richard to embark his at Marseilles.

38. Curious Diversions in Sicily
September 1190 to April 1191

I have good reason to know that wars do not proceed as one would wish. So it was with Richard's preparations for Crusade. Contrary winds prevented his fleets from England and Normandy passing through the Pillars of Hercules. In consequence, his army reached Marseilles before its transport. Richard decided to take ship ahead of the fleet. He engaged several galleys flying the colors of Pisa and set course for Sicily with a small, select force. Around the middle of September his ships dropped anchor at Messina, on Sicily's eastern coast. King Philip arrived with his forces two days later, having marched overland as far as he could. Just like his father. Terrified of ships—doubly so when news reached the west that Barbarossa was dead, drowned in a Syrian river.[45]

Richard had every reason to expect a joyous reception in Sicily, but it was not to be.

Look back to find this point, Aline. One benefit of my exile was that fourteen years earlier our youngest daughter, Joanna, spent a season with me at Winchester. We were very close, even in her childhood. I was homesick and she was waiting to be assigned in marriage. We were both in search of—how shall I put it?—an assured way forward.

The fates were kind in her first marriage, to William of Sicily. A fortunate choice as long as it lasted.

Richard had not seen his sister Joanna since she was eleven; not since she left England and traveled to Sicily through our continental lands to marry King William. Richard escorted her south through Poitou.

Landing in Sicily fourteen years later, Richard was dismayed to find his sister a virtual prisoner in her palace. After King William died, his bastard nephew, Tancred, seized the kingdom, confined Joanna in Palermo and appropriated her treasure and furnishings, including her marriage portion.

You may be sure that Richard demanded liberty for Joanna and her dowry. Whereupon Tancred released Joanna to her brother's keeping, but by no means her full dowry. Richard had to make threats in order to shake loose her goods as well as a bequest which the late King William had made to Richard's father. When Tancred learned of Richard's mood he finally sent a fleet of galleys rowing along the north coast, ferrying Joanna's possessions from his palace to Richard's camp. It was fortunate that Richard landed on Sicily with the van of his army. Tancred had no stomach to resist my *Coeur de Lion*.

Joanna was then twenty-five years of age. A wonderful woman. So warm. People remarked how lively Richard's court became when she arrived. She learned her deportment and grace as a child with me, in Poitiers. In time she made her own place in the sun. Sicily suited her.

King Philip—foolish boy—fawned on Joanna at Messina. From the accounts I heard, he behaved as his father had done towards me in our better years. Really, men are as hot-loined as youths. To put a stop to it, Richard moved Joanna and her household to a religious house across the channel, in Calabria.

Water-clocks drip faster than the speed at which Tancred restored Joanna's goods and furnishings. Galleys arrived at Messina half empty, handed out their cargoes and made small haste to return for more. This business gave King Philip much amusement and an opportunity to make mischief between Richard and Tancred. He took the bastard-king's part in this dispute, writing a number of letters to Tancred describing Richard in the darkest terms. Fortunately, sensing that Richard was the stronger of the allies, Tancred showed him Philip's letters.

Normans had ruled Sicily for as long as they had worn the crown of England. Tancred's confidence in Richard, no matter how fickle, offered an opportunity to strengthen our alliance. To that end Richard affianced his nephew, Arthur of Brittany, to Tancred's infant daughter. To bind Sicily the more tightly, he also presented Tancred with Excalibur, the legendary sword of the great British king, Arthur.

Aline, we must be circumspect in describing the provenance of that sword. For years, Henry and I had encouraged men to search out the remains of Arthur and Queen Guinevere, the better to bury the myth that he and his line would return. This dubious relic probably came from the monks of Glastonbury. Under the resourceful leadership of their new abbot, Henry de Sully, they were busily contriving to unearth the profitable graves of Arthur and Guinevere within the precinct of their abbey.

The upshot was that Tancred received much more from Richard than he merited. No matter. The alliance was worthy. Our roots were as deep in the soil of Sicily as an ancient olive tree.

However, this display of amity soured relations with the jealous Philip who, in the heat of argument, once again blamed Richard for the plight of Alice. The Capetians' fury had been rising like a deep-set carbuncle for years. Richard decided to lance it on the spot. He told Philip that he would never marry Alice; that his father had seduced her; that she had joined the ranks of Henry's mistresses; and that she had given birth to his bastard child.

Well! Everyone with ears and a tongue in the Capetian and Angevin courts had whispered this buzz for years, but no one had ventured to open the lid of the box at a formal conference. Richard's challenge stifled the matter in an instant. It was as if a wind turned full aback and blew the ship the other way. Witnesses were appointed; Philip agreed to take Alice back; Richard agreed to return her dowry and pay the lady compensation for her wasted years.

And there the matter rested.

Well, not quite. The previous spring we had met as a family at Nonancourt, Richard presiding. I attended with John and his betrothed, Hadwiga of Gloucester. At that meeting Richard barred his brothers, John and the bastard Geoffrey, from entering England during his absence in Palestine—lest lust for the crown distend their ambitions as a full meal swells a gut.

I came to that meeting after settling Alice in the stronghold of Rouen. The matter of finding Richard a suitable wife commanded our talks at Nonancourt. I subsequently busied myself discovering an appropriate candidate. After some time I settled on Berengaria, the daughter of King Sancho the Wise of Navarre. Having concluded negotiations for the lady, I escorted her south to Messina to meet her future husband.

Berengaria and I had a lot of time to discover each other as we threaded the Alps in winter, hasting to bring her to Messina before Richard set sail for Acre. It was a trying journey, and not through the agencies of snow and avalanche alone. The land between the Alps and Brindisi is broken into as many tiny fiefs as a honeycomb has cells. Every hill sprouts bandits and soldiers, borders and bribes.

We were fortunate to enjoy the company and protection of Count Philip of Flanders during our journey from the foothills to Naples, whence he took ship to Messina. Berengaria and I continued by land as far as Brindisi. My ancient experience of these waters was such that

I preferred to risk bandits rather than pirates, and to die dry-shod, if need be, than to drown in the deep.

I had scant regard for Philip of Flanders until that journey. I refrain from harking back to old glories, Aline, but we should mention an unfortunate event that followed Henry's sack of my court at Poitiers. A vassal of Philip's, returning to his hall from mine, made the mistake of addressing flatteries to Philip's countess, Isabel, in the fashion of *l'amour courtois*. Whereupon Philip ordered him beaten by butchers and hung upside-down to die with his head in a drain. Walter de Fontaines: that was the poor fellow's name. He lacks restraint who treats his people so.

Nevertheless, the vilest among us may have an epiphany. Some years later, this same Philip of Flanders took into his service the very Chrétien de Troyes whom my own Marie commissioned to write treatises on the joys of courtly love and the glories of King Arthur. I must say, Count Philip was never less than charming on our journey; and of great service to Richard. At Messina, he smoothed the heated debate on the fate of Alice.

Perhaps it is true what they say: that all roads lead to Rome. We also fell in with Henry Hohenstaufen, whose splendid caravan was taking him to be crowned holy Roman emperor. He was perforce restrained on the subject of Richard's dealings with Tancred, the usurper of Sicily. Before Tancred seized the throne, Joanna's late husband, King William, had named as his heir an aunt who was Hohenstaufen's wife. Thus, the-about-to-be holy Roman emperor claimed Sicily as his. He would no doubt attach it when he had the force to press his case. Meanwhile, we found other topics for conversation.

Of course, we Angevins had our own grievances with the holy Roman empire. I alluded subtly to these. In the first place, my mother-in-law had enjoyed the rank of empress to that misnamed accretion of mismatched states which is neither holy nor Roman. I was therefore in no whit bowed by Hohenstaufen's pretensions. Furthermore, I reminded him gently that my army had been of service to two generations of emperors before him, namely Conrad and his nephew Barbarossa. There was also the matter of Barbarossa's expulsion of Henry the Lion and my own Matilda.

In light of what befell Richard on his return from Crusade, it was as well that I responded to Hohenstaufen's dudgeon with courtesy and good grace. Not, in the end, that it reduced Richard's ransom by one English farthing. Royal greed is none the less greed for being royal. Enough of Hohenstaufen.

South of Naples, the roads to the east being less troubled by bandits than the direct route to Reggio, Berengaria and I continued by stages to Brindisi. Thence we took a ship supplied by Richard. The weather was better than it had been during my previous adventure on this sea. To my pleasant surprise and peace of mind, our master mariner showed us a new, rare instrument; one peculiar to south Italian ports. It is no more than an iron pin which, placed on a floating leaf in a bowl of water, turns its point to the north. Thus, our captain exulted, gray days and dark nights no longer condemn mariners to take in their sails or steer blind. Would that Louis and I had enjoyed this invention forty years before!

I had heard of this device in—Oh, I think it was Henry's last year of life—from one of our family. It happened that Richard's wet-nurse gave birth to a son on the night I had Richard. We assisted her boy, Alexander—indeed, he accompanied Richard's Crusade, and is now an accomplished scholar. When I stood on that ship I recalled Alexander regaling the court with talk of north-seeking needles. But he also told us that hairy worms sprout silk, and that mirrors can be made of glass. The very idea! But there I was, sailing from Brindisi, fascinated by this frail little pin tilting its lance at the North Star.

Thus we came to Reggio, to be met with such a joyous welcome that I wish more such milestones marked the path of my life. Dear Joanna, how my heart leapt to embrace her again. I thought I had become inured to watching my daughters' backs departing for ever to parlous or comfortable fates dictated by chance, or by God. But what a meeting we had: she, no longer a child, but a woman in her prime; me, slower than I was of yore. But love is ageless.

And, of course, I had the pleasure of introducing Richard to his bride. They made a fine couple. She was so shy with him. As what young woman would not be, knowing she would soon bed the most accomplished warrior in Christian Europe—barring William Marshall.

I did not meet King Philip. The keel of our ship arriving cut the wakes of his ships departing, so close were we. The king and his captains took advantage of a fair wind. That was the excuse offered for Philip's leaving in the very hour of our coming.

It was for the best. Philip's departure afforded us four days in which to discuss the memories and hopes of family, past and future, without distractions of diplomacy. It was unfortunate that our Alpine crossing and the perils of the road slowed our passage, for it brought us to Messina during Lent. Richard and Berengaria could not marry while I was with them. But I had to leave. I had pressing business in Rome.

You will recall, Aline, that we had appointed Bishop Longchamp chancellor on the eve of Crusade the better to extract tithes from bishops and magnates alike. Longchamp's ambition, however, knew no limit. The man had gathered more power to himself than a sheep summons ticks. He had done so by obtaining a commission as a papal legate, which gave him extreme power over the bishops, and put barons at risk from their people's unrest in the event that Longchamp called down anathema upon them.

To that end, I returned from Messina by way of Rome, arriving on the very day of Easter. It happened also to be the day on which an acquaintance of long standing was consecrated as Pope Celestine III. I knew this new pope when he was a humble archdeacon in the years of

Becket's thunders. The Angevins had pulled this fellow out of ditches in those distant days; now, as pope, he would do the same for us. Mark me, the man was fourscore years of age: I had small hope that I could bend his influence to my policies for many years, but as long as his holy carcass breathed out and in...

No, no, Aline, put a line through that! Celestine was one year younger when we met than I am now, and I dare to speak of him among the nearly dead!

Acting in my capacity as regent of England I made, and was granted, two requests. The first was this: Richard's bastard half-brother, Geoffrey the Chancellor, appeared to lust for the throne. To divert Geoffrey's ambition we had nominated him to be archbishop of York: if he took holy orders he could not claim the throne—modern England is not the Frankish court of Louis' day. But the suffragans of York set their face against him, wishing to select another by means of an election. An election! The very notion. We were not about to indulge York with a repetition of Louis' trials at Bourges; or Father's in Poitiers, for that matter. Celestine obliged, appointing Geoffrey to the see.

Our second problem had to do with the acquisitive powers of our chancellor, Bishop Longchamp, who wielded his office as papal legate with neither check nor charity, save to himself. To put a rein on his authority I required Pope Celestine to confer on Archbishop Walter of Rouen the office of super-legate. In that way, Walter might undo such over-arching grasps as Longchamp made. We decided this policy in Messina: to that end Walter of Coutances had been discharged from his crusader's vows and he returned, by way of Rome, with me.

Richard could not tarry till the end of Lent to marry Berengaria in Messina, so he equipped a ship to carry his bride, with Joanna and their ladies. Joanna and Berengaria developed a warm affection for each other, which gave me pleasure. The lot of a noble wife can be lonely.

Richard's army left Messina on the tenth day of April in a fleet of more than two hundred ships, some of them mighty galleys, a gift from Tancred. However, Richard did not sail directly to Acre. On the twelfth day of May he married Berengaria in St. George's chapel, at Limassol in Cyprus, where she was crowned queen of a land she had never seen. What other queen of England has been crowned so far away?

39. Strife transposed to Palestine
1191-1192

How blown-about you look, Aline, and no wonder. The wind kept me awake all night. Hear it howl! That constant soughing conjures up too many ghosts of people gone: Nana, nurses, Father, Mother, vassals, grooms...

Support my elbow. Help me up!

...dukes, kings, ostlers, popes...

Steady, child! Lend me your strength.

...the women at my court in Poitiers, their laughter, poets, bards...

That's better. Ah, to be young.

...my sweet Marie; Bernart of Ventadorn; clerks in inky smocks; knaves and nobles, villains and a brace of saints...

I'll cling to your arm a heartbeat or two.

...The rotting bodies of so many simple, shoeless men who followed us to Palestine. Death undeserved. Oh Aline, how I struggle to pluck faces from the dying past and stitch them to a living now...

...Barbarossa, drowned in water that rejected me so many years before.

Faces bustle through my head. Restless lives in the past tense, stilled but for the ghosts of ancient voices crying down the wind. I find features in cobwebs, faces in clouds. Have you noticed how earnestly old women stare at specters taking shape in flames? Don't think me mad, child. We ancients are coffers overflowing with the treasures of subtle pasts. Not that anyone cares to know.

See how last night's wind has left me: restless and fitful. Or maybe I am at last discovering my own humanity, in loneliness and age. A humbling experience for a woman of my station.

Stay, Aline! Let me hold your arm a heartbeat more.

Just before dawn I thought of the ostler whose hand I used to take when I climbed Father's mounting-block. He smiles up at me: I always see him from above. What was that old man's name? I never thought of him as having one: he was what he was, as much a part of that place and time as worn stone. Oh to put a name beside that face and fix a lapse of history. He had a great scar from his left ear to his chin, won in a raid on Father's behalf, perhaps even Grandfather's. The blow that opened his face stole much of his tongue. He would hold his nose and breathe in and out through the hole in his cheek, to entertain me. How horrible, and how divine! As a child, I was one of the few who fully understood him. Such talks we had, he in his tongueless tongue and I in mine.

So many lives, a score of ages and a thousand faces promenade along the arches in the cloister of my mind. Each arch portrays a different being, moving, re-forming, moving on. It is as if each pair of pillars frames an illuminated page, or its initial letter, gilded in a distant time.

And my children! God Almighty, let me die before You gather in another child, or the child of a child, of mine! I would prefer to relinquish this old body quietly, but be warned! If I must be borne hence cursing Christ, as Henry was, I shall.

Tush, Aline, don't be afraid. The Almighty makes allowances for those who reach my age. One endures too many of His torments to absorb them all without complaint. Had I the disposition of Job I should have been trampled into the dust of strewn rushes long ago. Sit down, child. Forgive an old woman in a moment of trial. She who perforce lived her life with a sword running the length of her back in place of a spine is at last permitted to bend. After such a life as mine, how comfortable it is to yield, to stoop, to answer to a rule imposed by bells rung by persons of no consequence.

How strange this seems: that one who for so many years thrust policy on kings and popes should now set down—by your dear hand—a document which carries no weight, makes no demands and offers no threats. So. At last I am content to be simply a woman, and a frail one at that. Who am I to stand aside from the march to eternity? Where Charlemagne, Louis, Henry and Richard have gone before, why should I not follow? Oblivion cries with a black, open maw, and I am toothless to restrain it.

I want to talk about you, Aline. Soon, but not today. I have to rid myself of pressing thoughts. Where was I? Of course. Setting sail.

Richard's ship left Messina to make the three week crossing to Acre. He traveled in a fleet of better than two hundred ships ordered in squadrons shaped like arrow-heads, each led by mighty three-tiered galleys: the vessels wore close enough that a man might hail from one to the next. But the strong winds which usher in spring in that part of the world threw some of his ships onto weather shores. Among those Richard thought lost was the vessel carrying the royal women, including his fiancée, Berengaria of Navarre, and Joanna. You may imagine with what private fears he ordered his galleys to search.

In fact the women were safe: their ship had stranded on Cyprus. However, the ruler of Cyprus, one Isaac Comnenus, a relation of the emperor of Constantinople, scorned to treat our castaways with courtesy. Isaac's troops killed or plundered several of our shipwrecked men. Richard was therefore compelled to reward this impertinence by making himself the master of Cyprus: he shackled this Isaac Comnenus in silver chains, as befitted his station, and gave the man's daughter into the charge of Joanna and Berengaria.

As I said earlier, given this forced delay, Richard married Berengaria at Limassol, where she was also crowned queen. I heard them described as a couple set about by gilt and gold and rose and other fine stuffs, with Richard resplendent on a stallion seized from the former ruler. Such a vision, Aline! Imagine, a wedding beside an azure sea speckled with white and red, where the great fleet hastened to mend its broken masts and stays.

Enough of Cyprus: we must press on. Suffice to say that the island's treasures recompensed Richard's coffers for his delay at Messina. And its harvests fed our men-at-arms and steeds through two summers of war.

I should add that the king of Jerusalem himself waited on Richard at Limassol. This was the same Guy de Lusignan who had ambushed me on the road to Poitiers, killing Earl Patrick of Salisbury and wounding William Marshall. Henry had sent Guy into exile after that affray. Like Raymond of Antioch before him, Guy de Lusignan found new fortune in the kingdoms of the east.

I t is not in my mind to write Richard's apotheosis with respect to his glorious deeds overseas. I received some accounts, read copies of others and conversed through the past ten years with Richard and many of his comrades in arms. Although they spoke with some exaggeration to me, his mother, the tenor of their speech was plain: Richard's name and reputation will withstand attacks by history. Therefore I mention but few deeds from this trying and heroic time, incidents which bore directly upon the difficulty we had when Richard tried to return to our lands.

The city of Acre fell to us in the space of one hard-fought, bloody month after Richard's force arrived. Count Philip of Flanders was among the first killed during the attack on Acre's walls. He died without leaving an heir, so the land of Flanders reverted to King Philip and the court of France. King Philip was so jealous of Richard that an evil notion took root in his head which no amount of reason could shake. He imagined that we—to whit Richard—would move to seize Flanders, which borders Gisors and the Norman Vexin. I am sure he was not thinking clearly. Plague was carrying off hundreds, perhaps thousands of men in the trenches before Acre. Forty counts and better than five hundred nobles died of disease, and a multitude of common men as well. Plague left Philip himself without hair on his head or nails on his fingers and toes, which quickly persuaded him to abandon Crusade and return to Paris. His mind was surely touched.

His decision to turn his face toward home stirred a great and heated debate between the kings: Richard himself was laid low by the tertian ague [malaria] and had to be carried about in a litter to command his army. Before he left, Philip cited the terms agreed at Vézelay to demand half the spoils from Cyprus. By way of riposte, Richard laid claim to half the land of Flanders. This counter-claim persuaded Philip of Richard's greed.

I t would have been better for us if King Philip had died of the plague in Palestine. But by October he had reached Rome, where he spent a week with Pope Celestine, spilling I know not what mischief in the old man's ear. Certainly Philip stressed that Richard coveted Flanders. Then, no doubt, he repeated the dreary matter of Alice, which I had explained to Celestine the previous Easter.

Meanwhile the holy Roman emperor, Henry Hohenstaufen, had stayed on the Italian peninsula after his coronation. He spent that summer warring to win back the lands which Tancred of Sicily had seized from Hohenstaufen's wife, their lawful inheritrix.

No doubt Hohenstaufen was well pleased to listen to King Philip's jealous tales. From his point of view, Richard had given Tancred aid and comfort in Sicily, going so far as betrothing a nephew to seal an alliance. Furthermore, gossips whispered that Richard had ordered Duke Leopold of Austria's banner pulled down at Acre—and Leopold was Hohenstaufen's kinsman. Then there was the affair of Cyprus, where Richard shackled the ruler, Isaac Comnenus, seized his daughter and sacked the island. It later proved unfortunate for us that Isaac was Austria's kinsman.

Hohenstaufen heard all this through the green of envy in Philip's voice. Taken together, these odors made it all the more difficult—and expensive—to extricate Richard from the jaws of the Germans the following year.

After King Philip gathered up his coward's heart and fled, the terms of the treaty of Vézelay placed his French and Burgundian troops under Richard's command. Having taken Acre the Christian army marched on Jerusalem, time after time breaching sturdy defences across their path. But it would not be Richard's fate to enter the Holy City as Louis and I had done more than forty years before. The van of the army came within sight of Jerusalem. Then, in an act of pure spite, the duke of Burgundy took his force aside. The duke begrudged Richard his victory at Jerusalem.

So much wasted. So much lost. To travel from the western edge of the world to the very hills overlooking the Holy City and there to be thwarted by an ally's pride! Burgundy shall never remit his shame. Richard's Crusade had beggared us all, bishops and barons alike. We had mortgaged the very chaff in our fields to advance this adventure. Why? And for what? Strong men in the army wept.

I cannot leave Palestine, Aline, without recounting the mighty deeds Richard wrought at Jaffa. I do so because those deeds speak directly to the willingness with which the English again surrendered their very shirts to ransom their king and fetch him home.

Richard was already embarked at Acre when word came that the small garrison holding Jaffa was being attacked by the mass of the Mussulman horde. So Richard ordered his galleys to row south at best speed until they stood off the beach at Jaffa. There, he ordered all who could still wield a weapon to follow him ashore. Toehold by toehold they pressed the Turks back from the beach, and so relieved the garrison.

When all was secured, Richard's exhausted company fell asleep on the beach. But the Turks, reinforced, attacked again, after dark. That was how Richard came to win the battle for Jaffa, twice, in a day and a night.

As if we had not enemies enough overseas, we had too many at home. To my lasting sadness I had to send to Richard asking him to abandon his holy task and hurry to relieve *me*. King Philip, despite the Truce of God, was harassing Normandy. I took steps to strengthen the walls at Rouen, against which Philip had obvious intentions. I also took measures to move Alice to the coast, away from the Frankish border. It was clear that the French hoped to seize her and repossess her dowries.

Furthermore, John was fomenting trouble in England.

Why, Oh Lord, did you cast me to be the begetter of sibling wars and jealousies? God aid me! From the moment my eaglets came of age I was plagued by martial rivalries and angry sons. My boys cost me sorely; not least because Henry blamed *me* for engendering them with *his* Angevin blood! During Richard's absence in Palestine, John began to demand allegiance from the English barons: he set himself aloft as if he were king. He seemed to sustain a total eclipse of the heart.

Too often it has been my fate, Aline, to witness warfare twixt my husbands and my sons. For fifty years the men in my life have turned their pride and industry against each other.

I said that I had to ask Peter of Blois to craft his most skilful letters to bring Richard home. My news could not have reached the king at a worse time. The sweating-fever struck again, dragging him to the very lip of the grave. Nevertheless, negotiations with the heathen reached a tenuous, if unsound, truce. They set it for a term of three years, three months, three weeks, three days and three hours. Hah! Whoever suggested that span played a jape on the Turks. As any Angevin peasant knows, three months, three weeks and three days is the term of a sow! No matter. Both armies were wasted, leaning on each other for very exhaustion, hoping for respite.

You can infer the state of affairs when I tell you that, at one point, Richard offered the hand of Joanna to Saladin's brother to seal a lasting truce. My precious daughter married to a Moslem! Surely the tertian ague had fired Richard's brains. But we were spared that fate: Joanna staged a fit of fury worthy of her father and her brothers.

In the end Saladin permitted groups of pilgrims safe passage to Jerusalem for worship at the places sacred to our Lord. He invited Richard to enter the city under terms of truce. It was a civil gesture between worthy foes. But Richard declined to tread on holy ground which he could not by God's grace win. Thus my son parted from the Holy Land, never to see it again.

Not long until the solstice now. It puts a check to the nights drawing in. The halcyon days are on us again, with the hawks far out on the sea, but you, Aline... Is this little bird going home to Normandy for Christmas?

No? It is just as well. The roads are perilous. Although, if you change your mind, I shall order a handsome escort to lead you home to Parfura

Eskelling. You see, I recall your father's manor. What an entrance you would make, a fair maiden riding home from royal service in a picket of a dozen men-at-arms.

Is your answer still No? Then I am grateful, child. More relieved and grateful than I can say. We shall hold our court of ladies here, if you can overlook a surfeit of old women. Mulled ale, wine without the modesty of water to dilute it, and fine, rare meats. We shall spoil ourselves until the ghost of Bernard looks down with a frown. That hoary old kill-joy! Can it really be fifty years since he died?

Tell me, Aline, when will you next see your family, if not at Christmas? Ah, not until Easter. By then your year's service with me will be numbered. I remember: you told me your betrothed comes from England after Lent, that you marry in your manor church and then it's off to Barfleur and to England.

Would that I might see you wed! Oh tush, no, I cannot come. My traveling days are done. Besides, this old body would need a Cleopatra's escort of 'pothecaries and leeches in her train.

No, Aline, you will have your memories of old Queen Aleänor, as I will have mine of you. Though yours, by the very measure of nature, are bound to last longer than mine. I would call you daughter, child, except that it might doom you to my children's too-short lives.

40. Queen Aleänor, the Bastion of Empire
1191-1194

I have a wonderfully clear memory of a hectic and unnerving time. Why should that be, when much more cherished memories escape my head? I should know better than to tax myself with such conundrums. The question I ask myself is: how much of these last, desperate years shall I set down? And I answer myself: not much. There is little point rehearsing the moves as long as the end is clear. To those who shall live beyond us, minutiae can only distract.

She who would lead others must employ bold strokes. To that end I exercised the royal power as queen of England during Richard's absence. And I did so without challenge, although those were fractious years indeed. While Richard carried Christ's Cross in Palestine, Philip Capet broke the Truce of God to invade our Normandy, and John—my precious John—schemed against me and his brother to attach the throne of England. To that end he strove to win the favor of the barons.

As if that were not enough, our chancellor, William Longchamp, made too many enemies gathering taxes for us and power for himself. This was unfortunate. Longchamp was scrupulously loyal to Richard: indeed, he lacked that special genius required to be crooked. Nor was he corrupt; merely ambitious beyond all decent respect for restraint. Unfortunately, that handicap made him obtuse to rising resentments against him. Longchamp, I fear, made himself so unpopular that he became more a liability than an asset. John, who is no end crafty, turned England's loathing to his advantage, taking the people's part against our chancellor. Longchamp had to flee across the Channel disguised as a woman.

Would that he had stayed a woman! As such he could not have issued a stream of excommunications and anathemas. As it was, he fell in with a pair of papal legates who extended to him the curia's pious sanction for his mischief.

Have you noticed, Aline, how often those villains travel in pairs lest one cheat the other?

Thus that fickle year rolled on, bringing us to Advent.

I had barely returned from delivering Berengaria to Richard at Messina when I took on the role of regent. In Rouen, I had a favorite high place where I could stand and gaze across the town to the arc of the river. I climbed to my aerie one day to find an orb spider weaving her web between the mullions of the window. I stood awhile, watching her move this way and that in response to unseen motives borne along her silken strands. She always withdrew to the hub of her web before venturing forth. I saw myself in that spider. I, too, gauged each scrap of news borne home by messengers from every quarter. Not that it made a crumb of difference to my conduct of affairs: I practised diplomacy with my accustomed acumen, rushing or tarrying as it suited; setting aside or picking up as events dictated; assuaging, making, breaking—and always winning better than mere compromise. One aims for true collaboration. That last is the skill of a woman.

Two especial strands demanded my attention: Henry's bastard son Geoffrey—the only one of his brood who stayed loyal to his father at the end—continued to make mischief even after we appointed him archbishop of York. Meanwhile, my all-too-present John was trying to woo the English barons' support from my all-too-absent Richard. As if this were not enough, our puffed-up chancellor, William Longchamp, was taking comfortable refuge with King Philip and seeking papal protection for a safe return to England. As for me, never distant from the centre of my web, I held my Christmas court that year hard by Rouen.

Enough! This past decade has drubbed me with too many tragedies and checks and disappointments. I need to walk, to breathe fresh air. Reach me that damnable stick, Aline. Let us to the abbey church. I would refresh my soul.

How calm it is in here. I was a girl when they built this church. A girl-queen to be sure, but still a girl. You and I have knelt here many times, Aline, but I never thought the Holy Spirit would compel me to confide in you. How parched is the thirst of my soul for God's embrace. Here, beneath the dome, circled by these columns straight as lances raised to serve the one true God, the Holy Grace reveals...

Hello child. Here, take my hand. The sisters kept you from me because Prioress Aliza said it was for the best. She meant well.

What hour does the sun mark? Such worry in your eyes, Aline. Set care aside. Christmas comes hard upon us and the turning of this dark end of the year lies but a breath of God beyond. Soon He will send us spring...

How long since you inked my words? Two days? Three? No! Tell me not so. A full two weeks?

That explains... I dreamt the nuns sang Christmas offices. So! It was no dream. Never in my years did the feast of our Lord's Nativity discover me in such a dire circumstance.

It is true, then: Christmas is spent. It was also at this rag-end of the year when Becket... No matter.

That day we walked to the church I felt unwell. A cumbrous dropsy in the ankles, a clutching for breath. All too normal in these latter days, but worse than usual. After that I remember nothing but a flash of the brightest light of heaven in my head. Then limbo all this while. Ah well, better *lux coelis* than *lux aeterna;* better *Christus natus est* than *requiem aeternam,* though my turn must come soon enough.

Two weeks! Two weeks of death in life; in life two weeks in death.

Yes, I am better today. Much better. Look at all this, stoppered vials, bowls enough to fill that bench, and the smell of I-know-not-what from that mortar. Sister Hortensia is better stocked than the cart of an army surgeon. She feeds me a mash of mistletoe berries, and I take the juice in weak wine. My timing was fortunate, she says: the berries are just now in season. She has men running hither and yon to gather them before the thrushes eat them. My heart, that skipped and fluttered feckless as a colt, now paces like an ox at plow, slow but steady. Bless her. Bless you all.

Dare I waste another day when I should divulge my urgent past and end this thing? Too tired, Aline. I must delay. If the good Lord intends this work to be *explicitus*[46], he will preserve me till its end.

I pass over the disquieting follies of King Philip and my son John during Richard's absence in Palestine. From Philip I expected no worse; from John I hoped for much better. Briefly, Philip's contempt for the Truce of God was such that, while Richard fought Christ's enemies, the Capet invaded Normandy, demanding I release to him his sister

Alice with her dowry castle of Gisors, as well as Eu and Aumale. The Vexin vexed us all, again.

Such arrogance from a truce-breaker, a coward and an apostate! A dangerous man in his falling from Christ. In the last day, King Philip's apostasy shall be judged. In the here-and-now it is clear to me that his leeches failed to bleed the fevers of Palestine out of his brains: word reached us how he walked the streets of very Paris armed, as if even the hands of his subjects rose against him. Would that some true Christian would find the courage to strike him with a cobblestone!

That's another thing. Small wonder he fled Acre. He can't stand a stink. He has had Paris paved!

Then there was John. I have known unhappy hours in recent years, surmising that our family's fortune would have been better had I strangled my last-born boy-child with his birthing cord. At other times I love him as my prodigal whose very survival awards him the fatted calf of all our hopes and trials. I spoil him, then I scold; and then I spoil and scold again, hoping the while that my infant's wits will one day grow to man's estate to match his beard.

There! I have said what I must. What care I? Posterity shall judge me and my progeny.

I mentioned that John used Richard's absence to turn the barons of England against his brother. They, not knowing whether their king lived or died in Palestine, found it politic to bend the knee to John.

Yes, child, I know I repeat myself. My brains must needs pick up the thread.

When I lay at Rouen, word reached me that John was raising an army among the English barons. He meant to join forces with Philip to seize first Rouen, then Normandy, a city and a duchy defended by me. My older boys respected their father's crown little enough: I had small faith that John would do honor to his brother's throne, let alone his mother's care and loyalty.

Philip and John intended that Philip would claim Normandy for France, and then John would do him homage for the duchy.

You may be sure I moved swiftly to thwart them, taking ship to England and summoning the barons to my councils: Oxford, Windsor, Winchester. I held four in all. Such threats, such tears, such insults and imprecations. I could not prove to the English magnates that Richard lived, although no vision informed me of his death. I fetched up skills from better than fifty years of statecraft in order to reverse the tide of belief stuffed into the barons' minds by John.

Finally I swayed them to my side. They in turn threatened to seize John's English estates if he took up arms with Philip.

Another tourney won. That was ten years ago. Even so, the effort sapped more of my strength than such struggles had done before.

I should have been a man, Aline. As a man I would have matched the best—even William Marshall.

To add to our woes in that God-forsaken year, the pernicious William Longchamp, our sometime chancellor, won support from Rome. A pair of papal nuncios now descended on our shores, presenting themselves to me, and then to John.

One has always suspected members of the curia as being thieves who best employ their subtleties of mind in stealing personal advancement. In that respect the dagger of a common thief rips its way through a purse with more integrity. But I never saw a bribe so plainly put as it was on this occasion. The nuncios offered John seven hundred pounds in silver if he, John, would support Longchamp's return to England. John promptly sent to me, asking the like sum to keep Longchamp out of England. We paid, of course. The treasure was little enough in return for excluding our too-ambitious villain.

Thus we ensured Longchamp's absence and, for a while, peace with John, the English bishops and the English barons. The interval won me precious months of relative calm.

Aline, I have not touched on the manner in which my gallant Richard *Coeur-de-Lion* came to fall into the hands of our foes. The matter is well known: I do not intend to waste such days of life as remain extolling our enemies' triumph.

Suffice to say that Richard, the only Christian commander apart from Flanders to acquit himself honorably in the war for the holy places, set his face for home in the autumn of the year. Unfortunately, uncertain winds and the uncertain politics of Raymond of Toulouse forced Richard to land on foreign shores where he was taken and miserably handled by Leopold of Austria.

This transpired a full year after the oath-breaker, Philip of France, abandoned Richard in Palestine and returned to piss on the Truce of God and to plot with John.

I recall it was just after Christmas when Philip of France received word from his confederate, the holy Roman emperor. Hohenstaufen wrote, crowing that he held Richard as his prisoner. Fortunately, the late Henry and I had invested heavily in building our network of spies. These now earned their salt. I received a fair copy of the emperor's letter to Philip through the agency of that best of allies, Walter, archbishop of Rouen.

How this news crushed me! At first I was struck by a heartsick gloom, a wish to abandon my more than threescore years and ten—and die. But no Pandora's Box of ills has ever kept me from my duty. Through very force of will I worked to liberate my son.

I must take a moment to recount a detail I still find wonderful. The English—those stiff-necked, mud-shanked, German-speaking churls—even as they fought against the blessing of Norman civilization they came together in common cause to liberate their king. For Richard's sake it was as well that I gave birth to him at Oxford. He never cared for England, except for its wealthy purse; but neither did he mock the province of his birth.

No sooner did word of Richard's capture spread than the bishop of Bath, a kinsman of the German emperor, left his affairs and took horse to lay our case before Hohenstaufen. And Longchamp abandoned his treacherous exile with Philip in Paris and made haste to the German lands: I fear I suspected his motives. Hubert Walter, bishop of Salisbury, heard the news near Rome on his return journey from Crusade: he followed prayer and rumor across the Alps until they led him to his king. I myself dispatched a brace of abbots to Hohenstaufen to ask his terms and bring me news.

Now, I suppose, I must treat of that spawn of the devil, Henry Hohenstaufen. I should say at the outset that his so-called Roman empire is far from holy: the emperor holds a blade to the pope's throat more often than he kisses his ring.

It did not help our cause that nothing but enmity passed between Emperor Henry and my late daughter's husband, Henry the Lion, of Saxony. Nor did it help that Richard fell first into the hands of Duke Leopold of Austria. You may recall, Aline, that a wicked whisper had Richard pulling down Leopold's flag when it flew from a high place at Acre. To make matters worse, Leopold was kin to the upstart whom Richard had punished on Cyprus, Isaac, ruler of that island. Here was a severe alliance of our foes.

The ways of the Lord are strange indeed. Richard, who had fought and won great battles for Christ in the holy places was now held by a compact of half-men who placed their own comforts ahead of our Savior's.

Ach, I should leave this alone! This gist will get me nowhere. I told you I dispatched the abbots of… I forget who they were. Oh dear, how I wander these days.

I sent abbots. They happened on Richard and Longchamp and Salisbury, the whole company escorted westward by the Germans.

Hohenstaufen was taking his prisoner from his forts on the Danube to castles commanding the Rhine. They spent Easter at Hohenstaufen's court above Speyer.

It was there that they hauled Richard before the emperor to answer a list of charges, namely: that Richard's support for Tancred in Sicily had deprived Hohenstaufen's wife, the Empress Constance, of her lands, causing the emperor expense and war to regain them; that Richard had occasioned grievous insult to Duke Leopold at Acre—the invented matter of the flag; that Richard had unseated and shackled the lawful ruler of Cyprus and seized his daughter; and, that he had put Philip of France in jeopardy. Hohenstaufen's jurists had invented a litany of lesser charges, too, all terrible in words but void of substance.

Methinks the only jeopardies to fall on Philip were the self-inflicted taints of cowardice, followed by his oath-breaking and betrayals. As for Isaac of Cyprus, he was well paid in his own coin. His daughter traveled to Acre with my Joanna and Berengaria. While Richard was defending himself before Hohenstaufen, the girl was safely lodged with my daughter and daughter-in-law at Rome.

Once I knew that Richard was in the emperor's custody I no longer feared for his life: Hohenstaufen could scarcely condemn the boldest leader in Christendom. Richard had sent very Saladin fleeing the field. Would Hohenstaufen do the fatal work the Mussulman had failed to do? Hardly. Besides, Emperor Henry lusted for coin to mount wars against his bishops and the pope; and he was ever mindful of the threat posed by Henry the Lion, my son-in-law.

However, for our part, we faced a second peril. We had good reason to believe that Philip of France was bidding against us, to purchase Richard for his dungeon. In return, it was rumored, Philip had entered some unholy pact with Hohenstaufen against the latter's rebellious vassals. Richard's person might be the price of that pact. How truth and rumors flew.

Ah, Richard, of all my sons you were the finest student of the *courtoisie* I taught at Poitiers. For which I thank our Lord. Your life stream of patience and politesse served you well in the prisons and courts of those brutish Germans.

I do not exaggerate, Aline. Those of our people who were present when Richard defended himself at the emperor's Easter court reported the calm with which he countered Hohenstaufen's invented charges. Where his judges forged words into blades, Richard deflected barbed sentences as a valiant knight turns the lance of a foe. My ambassadors, the abbots of Boxley and Pontrobert, reported that Richard politely, patiently turned the emperor's case back upon him, as if showing Medusa her face on a shield.

As I said, thank God it was so, or Hohenstaufen would have set the sum for ransom even higher. His demand—two hundred hostages to be held against delivery of one hundred thousand marks in the money of Cologne—was carried to us in England by William the Chaplain of St. Mary. I recall the poor man's face as he drew near: it hung like a bloodhound's, as loose as his robe.

Hostages, and treasure. Ah well. We shall come to that.

In the course of an active life, Richard had never had leisure to write as he wrote in those German forts: letters to all and sundry, in prose and poesy. Appeals, instructions, more appeals. He takes—he took—after me. Life's battle might carry him where it would, but he returned its compliment by venturing courteously. Some Greek said that a good man is worn down by his service to the world. So it was with Richard.

And so it was with me. Hohenstaufen's demand for ransom came just two years after we had seized every precious thing in our lands to send Richard to fight for Christ. Now I faced the same challenge all over again, thanks to those devils in Speyer and Paris who preferred to hoard our lucre in their treasure-chests, rather than salvation in their souls.

Such epithets we used to describe those Germans! I cannot count the times bishops and chaplains preached on a text from the Book of Joel about worms consuming the fruits of the field; and on the folly of storing up treasures on earth. Our complaint lay in Joel, to be sure; but for remedy we had to abide the torments of Job.

Aline, I crave a rest. I cannot concentrate for as long as I did a month or so ago.

So. A pause is as good as a rest in a long day's march. Would that I could push this bed across to look out at the brightness of the day. No, no, never mind. My essence has glided through countless such days and thought little of them before. Heaven shall be bright. Brighter even than the light that streams through Suger's painted windows.

And now I'm tired. There is a place below the Capets' palace in the Seine where two channels come together after flowing around the island. The waters flow smoothly, silently past the palace to the point where they converge. There they form an eddy, spinning and gurgling in confusion. That is a point I reach too soon these days. A wave of mental weariness confounds the tide of history.

I'll doze awhile. Perhaps it will dispel my inward noises of confusion.

Is someone here? Aline?

I can't see you for the dark, child. Strike fire for a rush-light. Ah, there you are. How short the days. Yes, I know they're drawing out. Even so, it gets dark early. How these evenings seel their days. How soft your hand is. My bedside keeps you from your own. And from the holy offices.

Were I not a queen I had thought myself an ant, a slave to duty. The sand ran past my allotted span while Richard fought the heathen for the holy places. I had hoped for a tranquil year or two on borrowed time to celebrate King Richard's peace, but it was not to be. God has granted me an extra ten years and more of time, but not ten *days* of peace.

Yes, yes, don't prompt me, Aline. I was speaking of raising the ransom for Richard.

My first task was to appoint lieutenants to extract money and treasure from the English. From our other lands, too. Just two years had passed since we cut the muscle to the bone to send Richard on Crusade. Now we had to cut the bone—from Belin to Berwick—what was left of it.

William Longchamp coveted the archbishopric of Canterbury. Richard and I had been equally careful to withhold it, wary of his over-weening lust for power. The gift of Canterbury now came in useful. As a mark of favor I gave it to Hubert Walter, the bishop of Salisbury—he who had spurred across the Alps to seek out Richard. However, I made sure that Hubert would earn his preferment: our new archbishop of Canterbury, together with my most faithful agent and spy, Archbishop Walter of Rouen, did sterling duty as tax collectors. Together they fleeced abbots, bishops and churches from Aquitaine to the Scottish border. Meanwhile the earls of Arundel and Warenne pried one fourth part of a year's income from the nobles. Nor was London spared our general levy. Her merchants and citizens went about very much lighter of purse. There was not a hamlet in our lands which did not yield a chalice or a goblet, the final jewel from a vestment or the carving of a saint. As for me, I took to horse, to ship, and to cart, now begging, now wheedling or threatening, now bartering future favors for present treasure or coin. It was fortunate that Henry's widow and his heir enjoyed the favor of his people.

There was also the matter of hostages. I put Longchamp to that task: he had no popularity to lose in England. Naturally, of the two cours-es, we pressed the collecting of treasure harder: the larger the sum we could deliver to Hohenstaufen, the fewer the hostages we had to leave with him in mortgage.

I pressed others no less than I pressed my own people. Throughout this adventure, the pope lifted not one finger on our behalf: whether through indifference, senescence or fear, I know not. Had we not empowered his enemy's enemy, Tancred, in Sicily? Tancred's alliance with us diminished the force of Hohenstaufen's threats against the papal lands. Furthermore, hadn't we supported Tancred's seizure of lands claimed by Hohenstaufen's wife, thereby bolstering the pope's strategic stance? Had we not expended blood and treasure beyond other Christian powers to win Christ's return to the holy places? Was not Richard Lionheart—alone among monarchs—the very Lion and Sword of Judah set against the infidel?

Whenever the pope demanded some trivial thing the roads from Rome packed hard beneath the steeds of cardinals and nuncios with their trains of varlets, cooks, harbingers, chaplains, doctors of canon law, men-at-arms and scribes.

But now, when Richard, the Lion of Christ, needed papal intervention and threats, we heard not so much as a fart from Rome. I reminded the pope in no behind-the-hand manner that my husband Henry had supported his predecessor, Alexander, to the throne of Saint Peter against the German-backed anti-pope, Octavian. It had not been the wish of England, nor of Normandy, Anjou, Poitou or Aquitaine to set aside the elect of Christ to enthrone the toy of a German war lord.

We deserved better than we received from Rome. In this matter we heard only silence.

Philip of France was not silent, however. Richard himself caught the whispers we heard, that Philip was willing to bid against us to buy Richard from the emperor. We confronted the prospect of watching, helpless, while Hohenstaufen sold Richard into the Capet's dungeon. Philip, of malice, might immure him for ever, or barter him against

Alice and her dowry—demanding a dozen counties besides. I was no more modest in bringing this point to the pope's attention. I ordered Peter of Blois to pen letters to Rome...

> "The kings and princes of the earth conspire against my son, the anointed of the Lord. One keeps him in chains while another ravages his lands...While this goes on the sword of Saint Peter rests in its scabbard..."

So much for the pope. Be constant in little, be constant in much. In truth, Aline, one may detect the inmost mettle of a man by his smallest actions. They are a fair guide to the conduct of his mind in large affairs.

To support my contention I judge it appropriate to mention the one-night marriage of King Philip of France.

Philip had been a widower since the precise day he rode off to Crusade, when Queen Margaret died in childbirth. Now he proposed an alliance with Ingeborg, the sister of King Knut, of Denmark. The Danes had harried England's coasts for centuries: Philip assumed his marriage to a Danish princess would unleash King Knut's formidable fleet against the island's coasts again.

In consequence, Princess Ingeborg was escorted to Amiens with a household and furnishings worthy of her station. Philip and Ingeborg were married in that city. Then Philip's uncle, the archbishop of Reims, crowned her queen of the Franks. This took place on the very Ides of August. Hah! The crown of France still bruised fair Ingeborg's brow when Philip decided that he had made a strategic mistake; that he should have offered marriage to the holy Roman emperor's cousin, Constance of Hohenstaufen. That match would have cemented a far more puissant alliance—and perhaps bought him Richard at a lower price. So, the very day after their wedding, Philip set Queen Ingeborg aside. How like a male fiend, a very incubus! Their wedding-night was the only one they spent together. One assumes that Philip was not slow to deflower the lady before he cast away her body with her person. Afterwards, he hoped she would take herself home to her brother's court. But Ingeborg, being of sterner stuff than Philip, declined to move from her husband's lands. The better to shame him, she moved in with nuns at the convent of Beaurepaire, in Soissons.

Evil minds conduce evil thoughts. Thus much the honor and the constancy of Philip.

Meanwhile Richard, although a prisoner, was not idle in matters of diplomacy. I like to think that our king, even while he stood in check, captured the enemy's queen. By the time Philip made known his desire for Constance of Hohenstaufen, she was married in a much, much better *alliance*, from our point of view. I'll come to that.

Indeed, Richard's imprisonment gave his mind and pen the enforced leisure to effect brilliant diplomatic strokes. Knowing that our enemies read his letters, he managed to convey to the archbishop of Rouen a means by which Walter should believe some things he wrote while ignoring misinformation. Thus Richard's friends gleaned wheat where his foes read chaff. Before his release was half resolved, Richard's letters allowed us to pull no small victory from the jaws of our predicament. It happened thus:

Emperor Henry enjoyed the same relations with his vassals as my father had done with his: at each others' throats, warring like Turks and Christians all the time.

Richard earned the respect of Emperor Henry's vassals when he defended himself at Speyer. Now he earned the emperor's respect as well, arbitrating matters between Hohenstaufen and his noisome vassals, confirming all parties in a bond of peace.

Nor was that all. One triumph followed another. Richard was able to quiet the feud between Henry the Lion of Saxony—husband to my late daughter, Matilda—and Emperor Henry. It was Richard who arranged the marriage between Henry the Lion's elder son—also named Henry—and the emperor's cousin, Constance. She was the wealthiest heiress in the emperor's gift, and now she married my grandson.

One last word before I tire, Aline. This was the very Constance for whom the foolish Philip discarded his unhappy Danish bride. *Honi soit qui mal y pense*! God does occasionally smile upon the just.

Now I have some business to attend to. Send Guy Diva to me; and Joscelin with his ink and quill. Guy lacks the craft of Peter's subtle Latin—how I miss Peter for that—but he has a subtler mind.

I t was ten years ago, Aline. Almost ten to the day since I journeyed from London to Hohenstaufen's court at the head of a monstrous train. We numbered my retinue, noble hostages with their retainers, wagons of ransom, a garrison of tally clerks and an army to protect our treasure. What an exhausting, terrifying—and yet exhilarating—time.

But before that could come about I had to take to the roads in all weathers, cajoling, threatening, borrowing and taking what I could to swell the hoard. Coin and treasure made its reluctant way to London from every parish in the realm. There, clerks noted it, attached my seal, and lodged it in St. Paul's. But the more our ransom waxed, the more my body waned. Lord God, in those days I frightened those who knew me: I resembled a peasant in a famine year or a woman dying of consumption. A foal could have carried my weight through the mists and the rain.

Thus we assembled the ransom, bit by hard-striving bit. Hohenstaufen sent agents to London to assess the growing hoard of wealth—and no doubt to gloat on his behalf. The English, especially Londoners, had learned in the five years of Richard's reign to hide their wealth against our tithe and tax collectors. When they discovered Hohenstaufen's agents eyeing the ransom hoarded at St. Paul's, their trait of feigning poverty became a precious asset: their very demeanor lived the lie. Burghers walked forth like beggars, merchants aspired to look like mendicants. Wretchedness, a quality as ever-present as its mud, mired London ever deeper. It served us well when Hohenstaufen's spies reported to their lord that England was bled dry.

Even so, it took a full year to meet the emperor's usurious demands. We heard news of Richard's capture in December; fifty-one weeks later we took ship to the German lands with ransom and hostages swelling our hulls. By then I had become inured to December roads and winter crossings. The timing was not of our choosing. We were summoned— yes, summoned—to deliver the ransom to Hohenstaufen. It was to be in the fourth week after Christmas, I recall. Richard himself required me to lead the expedition. As wasted and worn as I was, it was as well that I accompanied the treasure train.

Not content to pillage our purse in exchange for my son, Henry Hohenstaufen chose to toy with us. He devised certain ceremonies, the only one of profit to us being Richard's coronation as king of Provence. (Richard had contrived subtle whisperings, persuading the emperor to concede that country rather than try to hold it, remote as it was from his lands.)

We reached the valley of the Rhine in good time for the appointed day. Early February. As cold as an English winter. We were destined for Mainz, a more hospitable town for our people than the closeted court at Speyer. But a wicked stroke interposed on the very eve of our meeting with Hohenstaufen. He postponed it.

We waited from day to day for two full weeks while it seemed he would break an oath he had sworn to us on the Trinity and sealed with his very soul. His reason for delay was this: Philip and John had sent him a letter, formally proposing to raise one hundred thousand marks to purchase Richard's person. Meanwhile, they asked Hohenstaufen to hold Richard prisoner until Michaelmas to give them time to raise the funds.

The emperor toyed with their mischievous proposition for a fort-night. He himself had already paid fifty thousand marks to Duke Leopold for Richard's person. If he sold Richard to us he was contracted to pay Leopold a share of the ransom. But he was under no such obligation if he accepted the same monies from Philip and John. You may imagine how my body wasted during the fortnight we waited, riven by warring humors of anxiety and anger. Meanwhile, while conflicting emotions fought to command me, many in my train were forced to find shelter where they could.

My mind was far from still, of course. The archbishop of Rouen—dear Walter, he had offered himself as a hostage—helped me address the factors in our favor. Philip and John had given the emperor nothing more than a parchment inked with a far-fetched *promise* of wealth, whereas we lay within bowshot with a train of wagons whose axles creaked beneath the weight of our hoard. Furthermore, Hohenstaufen's vassals, never easy men to keep in check, were loath to see their liege-lord betray Richard. They served us well by threatening to break the peace which the emperor's prisoner had brokered twixt them and their master.

We came before Hohenstaufen on the third day of February, I recall. A devil in me made me wish to plunge a dagger in the rascal's heart. But the temperance and hard-won wisdoms of my life prevailed. Even as we faced him he dangled the letter from Philip and John. All seemed at an impasse until I suggested that Richard should renounce the ancient allegiance which our house owed the Capets, assigning it there and then to the holy Roman emperor. And that is what we did.

What price a man's vanity? In a trice I drove a wedge between the emperor and Philip. Then the archbishops of Mainz and Cologne spoke on our behalf. The deal was done. But what a wearisome day. Not until the ninth hour did Hohenstaufen order Richard's bonds struck off. On our return to England, the dean of London showed me the letter Walter wrote him, describing that happy hour: "The queen, ourselves, and the bishops of Bath, Ely and Saintes, and many other nobles, approached the king in person, briefly telling him the happy news."[47] Indeed we did. Need I say that the whole company dissolved in weeping, the emperor and I no less than others. Even as I wept, I thought it a miracle that my shrunken frame found tears to wet Richard's chest. For a year and more, worry and care had riddled my body and spirit with woe.

This momentous meeting took place at Mainz, in the bishop's great hall. It was not until our urgent affair was concluded that my mind found the freedom to think back forty-seven years. It was at Mainz that Louis' army and mine crossed the Rhine, destined for Jerusalem, our hearts still bound as one in happiness, and hope.

And so home, once again. As poor as peasants, but lighter of heart, we descended the Rhine at a livelier pace than we came. We lodged at Cologne with its gracious bishop, who had the goodness to refer, during mass, to Richard's deliverance from the hand of Herod. We did not linger. Spies brought word that Hohenstaufen, goaded by Philip, pondered sending a force to overtake us. Meanwhile, it was said, Philip was putting ships to sea to intercept us. Nevertheless, we came safely to Antwerp, into the protection of the duke of Louvain.

Thence we went home. It had been forty years since I first crossed the sea to England to become its queen, and never in all those years had I thought of that island as home. But now, after forty years and half as many crossings I may fairly say I was never so relieved to see the cliffs of England. It was a Sunday, the twentieth day of March. I took our return as an auspicious omen. The cliffs ahead and the moat of the sea behind eased my heart as they had never done before.

41. A settling of scores
1194-1195

Four and a half years had passed since Richard's coronation. It felt almost that long since we met as a family at Nonancourt. Remember, Aline, Richard anticipated trouble when he went to Palestine. He used our meeting at Nonancourt to ban John and Geoffrey from setting foot in England during his absence. But why do we waste our breath and brains upon negotiation! Despite that injunction, within months of Richard's departure, both were contriving mischief.

I managed to muzzle the dogs of ambition during Richard's absence. On his return, I alone was best placed to explain the balance of tensions by which I had kept a measure of peace in the province. England was in a surly state.

We landed, I remember, at Sandwich. Seldom has a king come ashore with less commotion. Some of those who should have greeted us were themselves held hostage against the unpaid balance of the ransom; others were caught up in skirmishes between Richard's allies and John's. This was the smoldering fire which John set in train. His response to

Richard's return was to find safety with Philip in Paris.

From Sandwich, the road to London threads through Canterbury, where we invoked the blessings of St. Thomas. He had been dead twenty-three years by then; and I had become less cynical about the saint's redemptive powers. God rest him. The man he became in his final years was a maze to me.

Thence to London, where the citizens greeted Richard with a joy reserved for a deliverer.

It came as a shock to those who had thrown in their lot with John to learn of Richard's return. John's allies had let it be known that Richard was dead. Now the corpse came to life with a vengeance, seizing rebels' castles and towns from Cornwall to Nottingham in under a month. Richard himself took Nottingham, a fortified town and the principal hub of sedition. Such was his reputation that it opened its gates without a blow.

Then he went hunting. Sherwood Forest seems less wild but more foreboding than the New Forest, where I first set foot in England. I recall Sherwood as a ghostly, boundless green-wood of mossy rides roofed by beeches and oaks, a haunt of outlaws and owls as well as of boar and deer. King William of Scotland joined us there, leaving his northern fastness when he heard of Richard's landing. A pleasant man—on this occasion—quick to disown his past dealings with John.

By now the season was leaning towards Easter. Richard therefore set his face to the south, to hold court at Northampton, a place convenient to all. The town which had been the engine of Thomas's exile thirty years earlier now welcomed Richard—from exile.

That Easter court had urgent business. We had to find money again. We had not paid Richard's ransom in full: our hostages lingered in Speyer. Beyond that, we needed monies to effect our policies. Accordingly, our officers had once more to buy their offices—including our chancellor.

You will recall, Aline, that Richard had repudiated his fealty to the Capets and sworn it to the holy Roman emperor. Now that we were safely removed from Hohenstaufen's grasp our legalists suggested clarification. It was therefore decided to rededicate the king to England, and to rededicate the barons to their king. To that end, all great persons converged on the town which had in times past been the ancient Saxon capital, Winchester. There, I watched with pride while Richard dedicated himself again to his people, and the vassals of England swore their allegiances, each in his turn.

The matter of raising monies was not effected without unpleasantness. One incident disturbed our equanimity for several anxious hours.

Henry of Cornhill, the sheriff of London, had been scrupulous in the matter of accounts prior to Richard's Crusade. But now, with the king returned, leading citizens shied at the prospect of paying more tallage to our exchequer.

The aldermen of London sought to avoid the tax by passing the burden to merchants and artisans. This sparked a great uproar, led by one William Fitz-Robert, a member of a notable family. People called him William with a Beard because males in his line went unshaved to protest Norman rule in England. Yes, Aline, I fear you will find a few of that ilk in England, even after a hundred and forty years. The English look ever backward to some imagined golden age.

This William the Bearded inspired others to rise in protest. But, being but a rabble, our people quelled their disturbance with some small force. William then took himself and his beard to seek sanctuary in the church of St. Mary of the Arches. To the surprise—and I may say, the shock—of many, the archbishop of Canterbury gave permission to pull the man out of the church. However, before officers could do so, he climbed the tower. Hoping to smoke him down, the officers set a fire which burned much of the church. Finally, William was taken, stripped and brought to the Tower for trial. They had him out again soon enough, dragged him at a horse's tail and hanged him slowly. And nine of his party with him.[48] The low-born still consider this fellow a martyr defending the cares of the poor. The poor, indeed! As if those whom God places above them are appointed to a fate as free from care as they! I seldom agree with Becket's companion of old, John of Salisbury. However, his maxim is apposite: "Inferiors owe it to their superiors to provide them with service, just as superiors owe it to their inferiors to provide them with all things needful for their protection and succor." Thus our Lord disposes the stations of men.

We had Canterbury to thank for the good outcome of this affray. He had risked his own life on Crusade and was among the first to fly to Richard's aid. He had seen too much of sacrifice at Acre to tolerate this fellow's folly. Canterbury had no qualms about doing this William to death—*and* his Norman-hating beard.

Did I mention that we gathered the nobility at Winchester? I did? Forgive me, child, I'm slow today. It was to dedicate Richard again to his throne. Sometimes I can't help myself: the voice speaks ere the brains command. And it was for the most pragmatic of reasons: to force the barons to renew their allegiance and sever their ties with John. I may add that the affair was conducted with much honor accorded to me. For years I had longed to play the role I played that day: simply that of *grande dame*; that of a woman! I was perfumed and garbed as a *woman* without the clinging stench of politics. How tired I am of being strong! Would that my life had given me time to embroider, to pine over Ovid and Marie's Chrétien, and to chatter. In my span of fourscore years, I have surely stored up the right to the honor they showed me there, at Winchester.

That respite was not to last, of course. We rode to Portsmouth, to discover our Welsh and Brabançon mercenaries fighting each other while waiting to board our ships. Richard himself restored the peace. The month of May found us tossing in a hundred hulls as we bade *adieu* to Portsmouth to be flung thence to Normandy. I was not to know it then, but I never saw England since, nor ever shall. I have said *adieu*.

It is strange how advancing years squeeze time, while youthful ones extend it. Or so it seems, looking back. Sometimes that final crossing seems more remote than my first, half a century ago. On that occasion I had my first boy in my arms and the second in my womb. Both dead so long ago. Had he lived, my Guillaume would be a greybeard of fifty. You'll see as you age, Aline: each day recedes at a gallop, eager to vanish into the void. Perhaps it is God's balm to vanquish pain. In my darkest moods my life seems detached from my being, as if I were my succubus, sitting in my forehead, looking on.

Come, come, this won't do! I stray into daydreams and what-might-have-beens. *Story* threads my brains more readily than *history* in this sad decade. But I have advanced too far with our tale to stop now. The track of our life—Richard's and mine—ventured farther together than I have yet come. Tomorrow, Aline. By your leave, child. I cannot manage more today.

We landed in Normandy to be met by crowds weeping and fainting for joy. Philip and John had broadcast rumors of Richard's death so thoroughly that people fought through the crush to touch their king, making sure he was flesh, not phantom.

We journeyed—slowly, by dint of the perpetual crowd cresting like a bow wave across our path—to Caen, thence to Bayeux and back to Lisieux. There, we lodged with Jean d'Alençon, in whose house we were reconciled with John.

John came at dusk, like a night creature shamed by light. He begged admission to see me, his mother, rather than his brother. My poor child-man! At his wits' end, and looking as no son of mine should: defeated by a reverse of fortune.

We have written how John fled to Philip's court the moment Richard landed in England. Philip, the fool, might have attached our Angevin lands to France by now had he treated John well. But Philip was ever steeped in his own vainglory. He used John so evilly that our prodigal returned to us, dragging himself to our board at Lisieux.

His return was inevitable: we had impounded his estates. Richard and I had even discussed how we would receive him. Left to himself, Richard would have been more severe. I hate to think how much more severe. But I had been counseling compassion since before we set foot in England. I had also pressed this point to Richard's chaplain, on whom I had some little influence. Abbé Milo had attended Richard at Acre: he knew my son's minds, in fever and in health.

Perhaps I had been too—how to put it?—*accommodating* with John. He was my infant, yes; but he was also my last male heir and a heartbeat away from the throne. For more than twenty years I had lived with the impacts of two grievous wounds to our house: the loss of Becket's amity, and then his disastrous death. So, regarding John, I counseled caution. We welcomed him as our prodigal, heard his woes, mingled our tears and wiped our eyes together. Then Richard and I made such assurances as we could to one who could never listen.

Oh John, how many hurts and harms you cost us all these years! To bid against the freedom of your very brother! The letter on which you and Philip set your seals surely cost us untold thousand marks. Then there was the sheer anxiety and grief to me, your mother. To think of you recalls the psalm: "I was shapen in iniquity. In sin did my mother conceive me." But it was your father's sin with Rosamond that shaped you in iniquity, my son. Would that you had been a girl to put to marriage and forget!

No, no. Strike that through, Aline! Disappointment makes me wander.

I recall our table on that occasion as it were yesterday. Someone presented our host with a large salmon as a gift to the resurrected king. We were set to eat when John appeared. He was so famished that Richard pushed the fish on its trencher in front of him. I think of that salmon as our prodigal's fatted calf. I still see its staring, gasping head: how eloquently that exhausted face expresses my recent years.

Enough of John's character. As we write, Aline, I do not forget that my youngest son is the king of England. Long may he reign! History's muse shall write his rights and wrongs at her own pleasure.

That evening, sitting at Jean d'Alençon's board, John was naturally eager to expunge his treasons, protesting devotion and fervent loyalty. Not for the first time! So, Richard assigned him some men-at-arms and sent him to break Philip's siege of Evreux. In that he did not fail.

Some days ago I mentioned that, having fled Acre with his tail between his legs, Philip took advantage of Richard's Crusade to harry our lands. He attacked us on every front. As far as the Truce of God was concerned he observed not so much as the dot upon an "i." Accordingly, Richard was as ruthless with Philip as he was compassionate with John.

We landed in Normandy on the eleventh day of May. Barely two weeks later, Richard relieved the Franks' siege at Verneuil and captured their engines. Again, Philip fled.

From Verneuil, Richard moved like the wind, relieving castle after castle, town after town: Vaudreuil, Beaulieu, Loches, Châteaudun. At Fréteval he winnowed Philip's forces as if they were chaff. Then to Tours, where the people's relief was such that they presented Richard with two thousand marks, in thanks. Hah! Here I can be happy. Here I can recite a list of triumphs as fluently as if they spelled the *Paternoster*.

Philip fled Verneuil on the feast of Whitsun. Five weeks later, Richard routed him again, near Vendome. We had in our service a splendid master of mercenaries, Mercadier. At Vendome, Richard and Mercadier chased Philip from the field while William Marshall seized his wagons of treasure, his engines, several cartloads of crossbows and all his chapel plate.

Richard and Mercadier overtook Philip, but he hid with his horse in a church while my son rode by. Why, Oh Lord? My long life long I have asked that question many times. Why does evil eat the sweet fruit of its foul designs?

Of all the goods captured from Philip, his secretariat was of special interest. There we discovered a list of traitors. I shall not recount that list, which ran to a depressing length. Nor shall I list the tally of Richard's victories in that brilliant summer when hope for our dynasty flickered with life again. It is enough to add that Richard purged the rats from Normandy to Aquitaine. His several years of absence upon God's work had given rebellion and evil much time to play. For example, King Philip's cousin, Raymond of Toulouse, rose in rebellion with the count of Angoulême and Geoffroi de Rançon.

Here we benefited from the marriage I had arranged between Richard and Berengaria, the princess of Navarre. During Richard's long absence her brother, Sancho the Bold, rode out of his aerie in the Pyrenees to keep the peace in Aquitaine. Now, Richard and Sancho broke rebels' walls to rubble, including Rançon and the count of Angoulême.

De Rançon, a rebel! Louis and I spent the first night of our marriage at his family's fortress, Taillebourg. And ten years later I preserved their very line: my voice alone prevented the Franks from hanging Geoffroi in Anatolia.

After Richard razed Taillebourg, no man dared lift his hand against us. That autumn we enjoyed an illusion of King Richard's peace from Normandy to the pass of Roncevaux in the Pyrenees. In truth, though, we were ready for war. Like fire in dry woods, it was a season when the tiniest ember might kindle and burn through the woods.

I t was then that I set up my offices here, at Fontevrault. The establishment was more considerable than it is now, Aline. You came to me after I had exchanged splendor for tranquility, power for a measure of solitude. You would have found more honor for yourself had you served me in times of old. But that was not to be. I hope I may still assure your future.

The spider at the hub of her web. Always listening, acting, reacting. There is not a road but passes near Fontevrault, not a buzz but stirs the air within these walls. And that is strange. Robert d'Arbrissel founded his abbey here precisely because this was a wilderness, a no-man's-land. But that was a hundred years ago. Look at it now! How modern times have worked their way with us.

I should like to think that my presence at Fontevrault, surrounded by so many cast-off women, softened my heart in the matter of Alice. God knows, I have suffered more than my own fair share of slights at the hands of men. The poor child had done us no wrong: on the contrary, she brought us the stronghold of the Vexin for a generation. No, Alice's fault was not intrinsic to her person. Looking back, it is clear that her status among us was fouled in the knots of too many straining powers. Our constant quarrels with the Capets on Alice's account had become a running sore. She served as the pretext for more Frankish incursions and insults than I care to recall. So, the summer after Richard pacified our lands, we decided to rethink our situation—and that of Alice. By then she was thirty-three. Lord, at her age I was twice delivered by my second husband. So, after twenty-something years in our keeping we returned Alice to the Capets. Members of her household had grown old and died in Normandy.

King Philip lost no time employing his sister to seal a breach in his frontier. Ever since Count Philip of Flanders fell at Acre, King Philip of France had been obsessed by the thought that Richard might seize Flanders. So, within a week of returning to her brother, King Philip dispatched Alice to marry a vassal, Guillaume de Ponthieu. Ponthieu's lands lie between Normandy and Flanders, straddling the lower reaches of the Somme. A strategic match, I must say. Philip is no fool.

They were married on the twentieth day of August. At Meudon. Ha, Aline, the old queen's fund of knowledge surprises you! I follow the fate of Alice with interest because I knew her husband's grandfather, Count Guy II of Ponthieu. He marched with Louis' Franks on our Crusade. He never made it out of Anatolia. Poor man. He died near Ephesus on Christmas Day. Such miserable months. Death reaped a surfeit from the highborn and the low. I will say this: Count Guy set his grandson a better example as a crusader than the craven king who assigned him his wife.

Alice had a little girl, Marie, four years ago. And now she styles herself the countess of the Vexin. She earned that title, God knows, after all those years in waiting, choking on her claim. May our good Lord preserve her in health.

While we assert the feminine side of diplomacy, I should touch on how my Joanna, poor child, came to marry a second husband, Count Raymond VI of Toulouse. She had been so happy as wife to William of Sicily: she grew in Palermo. That city is a treasure-store of peoples from around the landlocked sea. I found it very cosmopolitan, and that was half a century ago. It reminded me of Bordeaux.

But then poor Joanna's King William died, and it was some years before Richard rescued her from virtual arrest in Palermo. Richard was doing his best to extract her wealth from that thief, Tancred, as I was approaching Messina with Berengaria.

I'm straying again. Sew these scraps together as best you can, Aline. We shall make a fine dress yet.

Later, Richard rescued the women again, from Isaac of Cyprus. When they sailed from Limassol, Joanna and Berengaria had a companion, Isaac's daughter. By the time they sailed home from Acre, they were four royal ladies in company, having been joined by Bourguigne de Lusignan, a niece of my old adversary, King Guy.

Their ship reached the safety of papal lands in Calabria shortly before Leopold of Austria seized Richard. The following spring they took ship by stages to Marseilles—bringing them under the capricious care of Raymond of Toulouse.

One reason I always coveted the return of Toulouse was to ensure the probity of its ruler. An odd observation, Aline, but it's true. Counts of Toulouse hold their loyalties as lightly as they hold their women.

The only reason Leopold of Austria was able to lay his hands on Richard was because, at the time of his return, my son dared not risk landing at Marseilles: Count Raymond was then flirting with the Capets. His wife Constance was the daughter of Louis the Fat—my sister-in-law while I was allianced to Paris.

Raymond vacillated in his old age—he was sixty when Richard was taken—because his lands had become a haven for Cathar heretics. The curia would rather they were dead but many of Raymond's vassals protect these people from the Church. So, Raymond writhed with indecision. To our discomfiture, he made and unmade alliances with the speed of passing days.

By the time our royal women reached his lands the political wind from Toulouse had shifted to let them land safely at Marseilles. Raymond-the-Father sent his heir, Raymond-the-Son, to greet them. He should have known better. Raymond-the-Son took one look at the virgin Bourguigne de Lusignan and dismissed his wife to a convent. He promptly married Bourguigne. This did not please me at all, linking as it did the French king's cousin with one of our most troublesome vassals. I shall never forget Guy de Lusignan's murder of Patrick of Salisbury and my flight from that ambush, so bravely covered by William Marshall.

Fortunately, Raymond-the-Son's lust for women outdid even my Henry's. Raymond the Younger had already bedded more wives than a sultan. With such a man—one whose lust fed his affinities—it took no great effort to shift Raymond to our private ends. A few whispers, some saltpeter in his wine...

Louis, Henry and Becket all strove in their times to restore Toulouse to my control. Where heavy taxes levied to send two armies had failed, lust and appetite now won the day. It took some subtlety, but our agents managed to convince Raymond to repudiate the fair Bourguigne and marry my Joanna. The ceremony took place in Rouen. Joanna's dear friend, Richard's Berengaria, attended.

Thus the widowed queen of Sicily became the countess of Toulouse; and Toulouse returned to satisfy my lifelong-held ambition.

42. Is there justice in heaven?
1196-1199

What should I say about these recent, poisoned years? The task of remembering makes me fearful. Then I grieve anew. Truthfully, the closer I draw to these past few years, the less stomach I have for this tale.

Oh Aline, what do we win by employing my voice and your pen to kill Joanna and Richard again? And baby Alix, too. So many souls departed. In the end we are all dust and history. History! How we struggle to command that muse. We struggle to win what we hope is the future in order to write down our past.

I was never one to brood, but today you find me dark, child. My mind floats from its tether, too worried, too anxious to march. Then I think of the men in my life. Neither Louis nor Henry nor any of our sons has failed a martial challenge. Nor must I.

I mentioned that we returned Alice to her brother, and the Vexin with her. This strained our border with France, exposing even Rouen to the vow-breaker in Paris. Philip had tried to seize our city once before. No doubt he would do so again.

Richard responded by building a fortification such as we in the western lands had never seen. They say it looms bigger than Taillebourg. Siege engines have advanced beyond measure in my lifetime. When I was a girl, Father had no use for them against the precipice-bestriding piles our vassals built. But now engineers can build a trebuchet to hurl a rock the weight of three men. And they throw it as far as a Welsh archer lobs an arrow. So, fortifications advance.

Richard built his new city-in-the-air—one can hardly dismiss it as a mere fortress—on a crag called the Rock of Andelys. Andelys is a promontory sitting but a short trot down the Seine from our border with the French. Chateau Gaillard, Richard called it. A rude gesture of a name, and no mere finger in the air. The very notion of our "Saucy Castle" on his border must make Philip choke. Chateau Gaillard denies him the valley of the Seine, cutting Paris and its river from the sea.

Do you see where we've come to, Aline? This is no longer old history. It rolls off my tongue in your lifetime and in the present tense.

Oh God, I tire of war, the living for it and the dwelling on it. The expense, vexation, deaths—of loves, of sons…

I t is an old woman's privilege—and pain—to flit from thought to thought, evading the patches of mist that these drear years impose. This morning my head covers ground like a riderless horse. No forward motion. All dither and dash.

Give me valerian, child. There, reach me a spoon of that mash. My brains buzz like a bee above a bank of flowers. Which thought to light upon? Which ones to void aside? All's a-muddle. When will the buzzing stop and the sweetness of some wholesome memory prevail? Too much fretting; but I have too much to fret about. How can this ancient head select a single stitch from the scattered, vivid tapestry that weaves my tale?

Do you know, child, ever since someone translated it for me I have taken to heart a story beloved by the Welsh. I heard it first in London, nearly fifty years ago. What mystics those Welsh are. Quite unlike the English.

I forget the name of the bard: he recited the tale of a maiden, Rhiannon, and Pwyll the prince of Dyved. It seems that the maiden was wont to ride past a mound on which Pwyll sat. Day after day she trotted by. And day after day the prince mounted his fastest horse, but he never overtook her palfrey. Time after time she trotted past while Pwyll taxed his steeds to the frogs of their feet. But he never caught up.

There is more, but that will suffice. I use their tale to suggest the parable of my own progress along this mortal way.

Life is like the Lady Rhiannon. She moves along one's earthly course at a steady pace, never stopping, never at a gallop. As a child, you outrun her. Nor do you stop to turn and look her in the face, for a child takes Life's beauty for granted and races ahead: the mind of a child outwits and outpaces mortality. But in one's middle years, Life catches up. In mid-life you walk beside the lady, step for step. When your years start to weigh, she trots ahead. You hasten to keep pace but, try as you might, you falter while Life moves away. In old age it is all you can do to keep sight of her back. Never lose sight of Life's specter, Aline. The moment she slips out of sight, you are dead.

I weary you, child. You are used to my silly talk by now. Sometimes I cannot help myself. Dreams properly belong to youth: they treat of romance and riches; of years with two seasons, summer and spring; of lives that yearn for a future of harvests as perfect as life itself can never be. The dreams of youth consist of hope. In the world of an overtaxed aged mind, the rising smoke of wasted hopes fuels nightmares.

Years ago, at a time of great tribulation, I received a letter from the Abbess Hildegard of Bingen. A remarkable woman. Dead these twenty years, God rest her soul. She was corresponding with Abbé Bernard and Pope Eugenius at about the time I was falling from love with Louis and seeking diversion and remedy via Crusade. Bernard and his friend Eugenius lost no time holding this "German Prophetess" before me as a shining example of a saintly, righteous woman. Married to her duty to the Church, they said, and content withal. For that, I think I hated her. I also loathed her seeming arrogance: she advertised her oracles as emanating from a dove, the very bird in Christ's vision after John the Baptist baptized him.

But one matures. In later years she wrote to me: "Your mind stands like a tower while fickle clouds swirl all around. You search hither and yon, but still you lack peace." How did she know? "Haste to stand fast on the side of God and of man," she wrote, "and God will stand beside you in your troubles. God bless you and help you in all your works."[49]

I gather Hildegard suffered migraines as a child; so did Abbé Bernard. I am sure their nurses dosed them with feverfew, but evidently to no avail. Their sicknesses tell us how painful it is to harbor the Godhead in one's brains. Hildegard was a tenth child. For that matter, so was Abbé Suger. They were both given as tithes to the Church.

Moreover, Hildegard was subject to ecstatic visions. Where I had one great vision in my life, she had many. She wished me God's blessing in all my works. Including this book, I hope. But I hesitate to contemplate these recent years. Not today. I faint, Aline. And not from age. I feint from the wrath and hurt of recollection.

Write *Incipit*, child! Yes, *Incipit*! Here beginneth... I am resolved to dictate my book today and speak till I am spent. Last night, Hortensia put marsh myrtle in my herbal gruel. By whatever agency, it lifts my humors from despair and hoists them to God's sky. So, *sic statim inveterata regina incipit.* On second thoughts, the old queen will not stand; she will just begin to speak.

Where was I?

Ah yes, we touched on the Treaty at Louviers, by which we gave Alice and her Vexin to the Franks. We then set about reclaiming the lands King Philip had stolen by voiding his bowels on the Truce of God. Never has a ruler so impeached his own soul.

Now I recall: I said this already. You must tug on my rein when I stray, Aline. You are too passive, child.

Of course, having ceded the Vexin, Richard felt constrained to build Chateau Gaillard on the Rock of Andelys. They say it is a miracle of building. It stands on a height, and with such walls, that the most up-to-date engine cannot breach them with stones. Methinks God gave us that proud promontory for just this reason. Gaillard is perfectly poised to defend Rouen, and yet it sets its face against the Vexin and the road from Paris.

But I have had enough of Philip and of wars. When I lie awake a Latin couplet threads my head: "Why do the nations rage, and why do the people think upon worthless things?" I heard that often at Salisbury Tower. It is the *Introitus* to their *missa in gallicantu*, their mass at cock-crow. Oh, those frigid, wind-washed mornings! I suppose the time I endured on that height was catharsis of a sort. Surely, Oh surely, it will ease my soul's durance in Purgatory.

L et me speak of our dear Berengaria. In the rejoicing after Richard's return, we quite forgot his poor young queen. That persisted even after Richard left England for Normandy. In the twelve months after his release, Richard bedded women beyond number. I do not exaggerate. It was, I suppose, a second form of release. Those of us who loved him eventually prevailed: Bishop Hugh of Lincoln, a most compassionate and saintly cleric, tried to bridle Richard's lustful humors; and, on one occasion, Richard was hunting—during Lent!—when a hermit rebuked him for his sins. That may have been the preacher Foulques de Neuilly, or it may have been another. Several men rose above their stations to chide the king to his face.

Then Richard fell sick. The fever almost killed him, but it may have saved his soul. Lying stricken at Easter with sweats that first gripped him in Palestine, he began to reflect on the conduct of his recent life. He duly sought confession.

It was then that Richard finally brought Berengaria to court. She had a steadying influence on him. Beyond doubt it was her intervention that opened our granaries to the starving during that terrible famine in Normandy. Of course, she knew nothing of statecraft, poor child. It was to me that Richard sent for help.

I fear she is barren. She must be. It was apparent soon enough. Poor Richard. He has sired enough bastards on other women, but no heir on her. Perhaps their connubial humors mismatch. After all, I had but two daughters by Louis before giving nine living children to Henry. So I do not fault the girl. Richard and I made other arrangements to pass on our properties. Richard named Arthur of Brittany his heir—only to discover that the boy's tutor had whisked him to Paris, to be teat-fed on lies by Philip. As for me, I named my dear Matilda's son, Otto, my heir in Poitou and Aquitaine.

How patient you are, Aline. I must stray from the high road again, but this is a story will interest you.

I mentioned that excellent man, Bishop Hugh of Lincoln. Just over twenty years ago—around the time my Louis died—Henry appointed Hugh to be prior of the Carthusian order in England. At that time they were a shoeless band of monks at Witham, in Somerset. They were living in huts of stakes and turf when Hugh arrived and bargained with Henry over their grievous conditions—to great advantage. Before long,

Hugh had buildings for the monks, and a sumptuous bible, complete in both parts. Henry bought it for them from the monks of Winchester. The latter had copied it in their own renowned scriptorium, intending to read it themselves.

Then an earthquake razed Lincoln Cathedral and Henry appointed Hugh to the see. Hugh, whose energy matched Henry's, set about building his new cathedral on the ruins. Hugh once confided to me that an Englishman conceived its lines. That should cheer you, Aline: under our guidance, the English progress! Of course, this Geoffrey de Noyers got his inspiration from Suger's design for St. Denis and our own St. Peter in Poitiers.

I never raised this with Hugh, but I'm sure that his building-work drained his purse and led him to refuse to finance knights for Richard's service overseas. They were still jousting with sharpened words when Richard died.

But the story I mean to tell concerns a swan—Hugh's swan—a bird that appointed himself the bishop's guardian. People tell how this large male swan adopted the bishop: it was not the other way around. The bird—this is true, Aline—somehow knew when his master was coming home to his manor at Stow, near Lincoln. Two or three days before the bishop's return, the swan would announce his impending arrival with a fanfare of flapping and hissing and honks. Then, when Hugh arrived, the swan walked before him, hissing to part a path so the bishop could pass through the crowd. Strangest of all, Hugh visited Stow for the last time at Easter, a full six months before he died. On that visit the swan would not approach him. Throughout Hugh's short visit the bird predicted the bishop's death, hanging its head in grief.

Dear Hugh, a saintly man—though he had scant love for me. Dead these three years past. He died in London after John was crowned. In fact he died just as John was making a progress to Lincoln to visit Hugh's rising cathedral and confer with the king of the Scots. Although affairs pressed him, John stayed in Lincoln for the bishop's obsequies. As a mark of respect he helped many great men of both kingdoms to carry Hugh's bier.

He has a noble soul at times, my youngest boy. Would that he were endowed with judgment to match. Ah, well...

At last report I heard that Hugh's swan still lives on his pond at Stow. How passing strange.

I cannot help thinking that Hugh's inner spirit possessed a quality of openness that sprang not wholly from Christ. Before he was Hugh of Lincoln he was Hugh of Grenoble. Then people knew him as Hugh of Avalon, from his time with the monks at Witham. Avalon! You will hear much talk in England about that mystic place, Aline. The very mention of it lays an otherworldly veil on English eyes. It smacks of their old religion of sacred waters and holy groves; and of King Arthur's ghost, whom Henry and I never laid.

I wander again. I meant to speak of Hugh's influence on Richard. Indeed, the bishop had many grievances with which to upbraid his king. Hugh was as bold with Richard as he had been in dealings with Henry; chiding Richard for his lust—and in the king's own chapel at Chateau Gaillard. They met in private, in so far as that was possible, near the altar. But I heard about it. Richard might be king, Hugh told him, but he, Hugh, was his spiritual father. "It is I who, on the terrible Day of Judgment, must answer for your soul. Tell the state of your conscience, Lord King! Then I can give you help and counsel as the Holy Spirit shall direct."

Richard came away more amused than chastened. It took a full year after his captivity before he settled down. Just like grandfather. Aline, I remember mentioning that the same need to lust after women afflicted Guilhem the Troubadour when he returned from his Crusade. For men, it seems, the shock of battle looses their bolt into lust.

I should broach one other matter before I bring Richard's too short span of splendor to an end. The pope and his vassals never did comprehend the depth of disgust and distrust they instilled in us. I refer to the curia's indifference to Richard's fate, and mine, at the hands of Philip and the German emperor.

And yet I can hardly blame old Celestine for the mess, rest his foolish soul. He was older than me, nearly thrice-thirty in years. But he was the woman! Too aged, too timid, too ill-bred to politics. While Richard was wasting in Henry Hohenstaufen's towers, the emperor's troops were plundering the old pope's lands and cutting his envoys' throats.

Celestine's mind had been too firmly impressed by the seal of a world long gone: the world inhering to Church fathers, to Abbé Bernard, to faith and faithful certainties. That was the world of my first marriage. Even as a youthful cleric in his twenties, Celestine was ancient of mind. He was Hyacinthus Bobo then, one of the acolytes sitting with Bernard at Sens, one among the many drones who judged poor Abelard.

I had been queen of the Franks for less than three years at that time. Hardly older than you, Aline. But I could smell new vigor in the air.

I was speaking of the curia just now, of how Rome misjudged our anger in the matter of Richard. They misjudged us to the degree that Pope Innocent, who succeeded Celestine four years ago, sent a legate to Richard's court to inveigh against us on behalf of the Franks. This was one Cardinal Peter, of Capua. This princeling made his first tactical error before he came into Richard's presence at Gaillard. He arrived by way of Paris—the logical route, I grant—but the fanfare of wagging tongues held that he came fortified for his mission with the sort of courage that gold procures: carts and panniers stuffed with Frankish coin from Philip's treasury.

What a devil-brewed mixture of humors prompted that embassy! Consider this: the pope sent Peter via the French court—and on Philip's behalf—ostensibly to make peace in the interest of renewing the

Crusade. The reality was plain to see. Richard, flushed with the anger of revenge, had taken but a season to reclaim what Philip's betrayal had ravaged or stolen. Beyond that, he had laid waste to several estates in the Île. Richard had captured sergeants and knights by the hundred. Philip himself almost drowned in a panic, fleeing Gisors. Now, hiding beneath the papal skirts, the Franks were suing for peace in the name of another Crusade.

Such impudence. Did they think us fools to be so daft? Richard had all but forfeited his life, then lost his liberty, in the cause of Crusade, while a legion of devils no better than Moslems ravaged our lands with the tacit consent of the pope. Yes, consent! For he who is silent is seen to consent. Then came this embassy from Philip and the curia. What arrogance. These are men who would steal the flat earth beneath our feet while claiming to serve the Carpenter of Nazareth.

Would that you had known me as the Aleänor of old, Aline. It is only here, in my secluded lair, that I permit myself the luxury of lingering resentment. The active exercise of politics forbids it. Hatred drives out reason; and loss of reason breeds defeat. Though you treat with the devil himself, anger has no place in politics.

Cardinal Peter's next mistake was to demand, in lawyerly fashion, the release of King Philip's cousin, the bishop of Beauvais. This man was captured fully armed in the heat of battle, and yet he claimed the privilege of holy orders and the protection of the Church. Richard had him in a dungeon at Gaillard with other knights awaiting ransom.

Beauvais! What a vill! They celebrate a Feast of the Ass at Beauvais. *"Hez, Sire Asnes, car chantez / Belle bouche rechignez / Vous aurez du foin assez / Et de l'avoine a plantez."* Not quite your dialect, Aline. Write: "Get up, Sir Ass, and sing. Open that fine mouth. You'll have hay in abundance and plenty of oats." A fit fate for a fat bishop. A verse meet for Philip's cousin, at any rate. I doubt Richard fed Beauvais much of anything, let alone oats.

When Cardinal Peter made his request for Beauvais' release, Richard was moved to a rage worthy of his father. Though I will say this for Richard: I never saw him shred the bedding with his teeth or tear down tapestries, as Henry was wont to do.

Briefly, Richard called Cardinal Peter a liar and a swindler—and a host of epithets he was pleased to report to me. Then he sent Peter packing with his ears ringing—although still attached to his head—back along the road to Paris.

You can imagine, Aline! That news gave me a day of purest joy.

And yet I sensed danger. This new pope, Lothario—he styles himself Innocent III—was not an old slug like Bobo. Innocent is a new man, cut from new wool. He was young, as I was not. And it seemed to me, as I continued my watch on the distant world, that he might prove a match for my resolve. We would have been fools to drive Pope Innocent into Philip's arms in the first year of his youthful papacy.

So I took the initiative to arrange Beauvais' escape from Chateau Gaillard. You should write "arranged his deliverance," Aline. Even before the villain was free I set my people to whisper that Richard had relented and, in Christian charity, released this son of Holy Church. I managed this business in haste. It was imperative that Innocent should hear of Beauvais' release before the conflicting message from Peter of Capua sealed the papal prejudice. First impressions seat deeper in fresh wax than old.

It didn't take long for Richard to see the wisdom of my policy.

I n the matter of Richard's death, I shall be brief.

Some hapless peasant unearthed a pot of ancient coins near the vill of Chalûs, a poor place near the seat of the troublesome Aymar, viscount of Limoges. The finder surrendered the trove to his master, the lord Achard; Achard, in turn, relinquished the treasure to his overlord, Aymar.

Had our own coffers been replete at that time it is likely we would have let the matter rest. But several contrary factors dictated otherwise.

In the first place, as news of this trove spread, its purported size grew, until it seemed that the poor *campagnard* had discovered the Holy Grail wrapped in the Golden Fleece. One version had the coins boxed in a golden container bearing the device of a king and his court at table. Another had the fellow finding twelve statues of gold.

The second consideration was this: our treasury was empty, our lands having supplied the wealth to raise and support Crusade; having been taxed again to the extremity of three years revenue to free Richard from his foes; and, we were supporting a great army of Mercadier's *routiers* and others. These continued to fight Richard's campaign to win back our stolen lands from Philip. Then, of course, Richard had workers to pay for Gaillard, his vast fortress on the Rock of Andelys.

So, in March of that year, in advance of the warring season, Richard lay at our treasure-castle of Chinon, discussing affairs with his exchequer. Chinon is but a trot from Fontevrault, and it was with a dole face that Richard visited this news on me. You may imagine the state of affairs when I say he reported hearing his echo in the empty vaults.

Yet another factor in Richard's decision to march on Chalûs was Aymar's intransigence. Aymar alone, of all our vassals, had contributed nothing towards Richard's release. We also had reason to believe that Aymar was in treasonous negotiations with King Philip.[50] Furthermore, though its fort is antiquated, Chalûs is well placed to command the valley of Tardoire, where the Limousin converges with Poitou and Aquitaine. The fortress straddles the roads in all directions, including the one to the gold mines at Saint Yriex le Perche.

Thus the adventure on which Richard embarked, nominally to claim the "treasure" of Chalûs, had several motives. Not the least among these was to restore Aymar to allegiance to his lord.

Richard marched on Chalûs with a force of a hundred *routiers* led by Mercadier. On an evening in late March, the king was examining the perimeter of the place when an arrow shot from the walls struck him in the shoulder—just above the shield he carried for protection. Mercadier himself withdrew the shaft, but the wound refused to heal.

How this affair might have been different! When Richard fought in Palestine he offered the post of personal physician to a Jew, one Musa ibn Maimun. This Musa, whom Christians call Maimonides, served the ruler of Cairo, among other wealthy clients. Here was a doctor of great repute: he, in turn, had been trained by a Muslim heretic, one Averroes, whose fame burns even brighter than the Jew's.

But it was not to be. Though Richard offered every sort of inducement, Maimun still serves his master in Cairo, as far as I know. Had he been present to cut out the arrow, Richard would surely have lived.

What a perplexity: that crafts and wisdom persist, in the absence of Christ.

So, for the want of a barber's skill, Richard lay dying, his flesh rotting to become the putrid earth it must soon meet.

God in Heaven, what manner of injustice stalks the earth? Whom God protected from a thousand spears and arrows in His Holy Land, now lay dying by the hand of a farm boy who protected himself with a cook's iron skillet while digging our arrows from crevices between the stones and wooden palisades.

When it became apparent that the angel of death hovered by, Richard sent for me. I, in turn, sent our aged abbess, Matilda, to carry word to Berengaria, and thence to John.

Sometimes, Aline, I think the ways of men wend backwards. We had better surgeons during my Crusade than we have enjoyed these past forty years, a calumny for which I squarely blame the Church. Pope Alexander—whom Henry and Louis were fools to support!—proclaimed a great folly at the Council of Tours: *Ecclesia abhorret a sanguine.* "The Church abhors the shedding of blood." Overnight, physicians stopped practising surgery, because the best of our surgeons were priests. So, these past forty years we have had to put up with pig-gelders, barbers and lumpen hangmen styling themselves surgeons. Even the craft of surgery has disappeared. Richard might be living now if the Church had not winnowed surgeons out of Christendom. Small wonder Jews and Muslims make the best cutters and stitchers of wounds.

Joanna felt the same way. Her first husband, Roger of Sicily, took pains to bring medicine within the ambit of his laws. In part, I believe that was why Richard's death troubled Joanna so: had the Church not marched us back to barbary, it was unnecessary.

Would that Count Otto's battle-axe had cut down Alexander in his pride![51] But I must not be bitter or I shall set you a bad example, Aline. Let us move on.

It was the sixth day of April when I came to Richard's side, being consoled and supported in my passage by Abbé Luc of Turpenay. A kind man, and equipped with the wisest words but, under the dark angel's wing, I found slight succor on that journey.

Never, I think, have I traveled so far, so hard. A young squire would have been pressed to make that passage in two summer days.

It was, as I said, the sixth day of April when I came to Chalûs, the very day on which Richard's chaplain, Milo, heard his last confession and gave him absolution and communion. Thank God I came in time. Milo, the Abbé de Le Pin, had attended Richard on his every venture in the Holy Land. He must surely have expected to administer the extreme unction to Richard years before he did. Nevertheless, to watch that young life drain away in such a place, sucked from the flesh by the agency of a chance arrow shot by a boy...

It is of small consequence to record that Mercadier's men took Chalûs on the day Richard died, to whit, the sixth of April. My grief was in no way assuaged by the hanging of the garrison, some thirty men in all, and the subsequent torture of the youth who loosed the fatal bolt. On Mercadier's order he was, I believe, flayed alive and then hanged with the others—contrary to Richard's dying wish. I had neither the strength nor the stomach to intervene. The name of the youth is variously given as this and that. We never saw fit to publish it, lest our enemies sanctify the name, entwining it with that of the giant he slew.

Richard died that evening, ten days to the very hour after the shaft stabbed into his flesh. It was a Tuesday. Much later, I heard how persons of a superstitious nature thought it fitting that the Lionheart should die on the *dies Martis*. How odd that in French and in English that day of the week is named for gods of war. *Martis* or *mortis*: his end was the same.

God aid me, how I fought to preserve an outward show of sanity! On my advice, Richard at the last named John to be his heir. John was—Heaven guide him!—no less feckless at the time than my grandson, Arthur of Brittany, whom Richard had earlier named to inherit our provinces south of the sea. However, it was common knowledge that Arthur was a poor horse ridden by his mother, Constance, and she heeded every beck and call by Philip.

Abbess Matilda bore the sad news to Berengaria where she lodged near Saumur. She lay at Beaufort Castle, anticipating Richard's return to Chinon. Beaufort is but a sparrow's flight from Fontevrault, but you may guess that Matilda approached with rising foreboding: Berengaria is such a tender girl. She proved inconsolable, poor child.

Notwithstanding, Matilda could not stay to comfort her, but hastened on. I had warned her that she must reach John at all costs before news of Richard's death became public. John was even then conferring with Arthur, in Brittany. Had he remained in his nephew's court, I think he would not have lived another night. At least half of our empire would pass to one of these two. So, in the greatest secrecy, Matilda bade John spur south, to quickly possess what remained of Richard's treasure at Chinon.

By good fortune, the abbess crossed the path of Bishop Hugh of Lincoln, who was hasting to Angers to celebrate Palm Sunday services. Hearing Matilda's news, he sought to confirm the truth of what she said. This was not long coming. Approaching along the same road came a scholar of divinity, one Gilbert de Lacy, who confirmed Richard's death beyond all doubt. At some personal risk, Hugh turned his horse's head to Beaufort Castle. I heard later that he turned without hesitation onto a forest track infamous for cut-throats and thieves—and this, despite the fact that robbers had waylaid his own people not long since, relieving them of forty marks. Nevertheless, our Lord protected Hugh, bringing him to Beaufort, where he celebrated a requiem mass and brought some measure of comfort to Berengaria. When she was fit to travel he escorted her to Fontevrault. He spoke, she told me later, on the need for fortitude in misfortune. Ah, how many sermons I could preach on that!

It happened to be Palm Sunday when our sad cortège arrived to inter Richard's corpse at Fontevrault. I continue to commend Luc of Turpenay in my prayers for his compassion and kindness to me on my *via dolorosa*. Leaving Chalûs, we went part of the way by boat on the river Vienne. I cannot think of that pretty stream now but as a gloomy Styx. There were times when my mind stepped aside—to use a phrase, I stood beside myself—willing myself to see our cortège as something other than the truth. My mind tried to imagine us as if we bore King Arthur across a shrouded lake to Avalon. What role was mine in that sad fairy play? Was I Queen Guinevere, or the ever-scheming Morgana la Fée? I thank the Lord for the sober presence of Luc of Turpenay.

How one's thoughts clamor at such awful times. Grief and sorrow compete with the exigencies and cares of policy in a new world shaken by loss and our enemies' undeserved advantage.

Palm Sunday! Surely an irony as well as a comfort that that should be the day on which Richard entered his own New Jerusalem. We interred his major portions at his father's feet: thus he intends to atone through eternity for rebelling against Henry eleven years before. Dying, Richard consigned his heart to Rouen, his brains to Charroux in Poitou, and his bowels—a matter of expediency as well as contempt—remained at Chalûs. Berengaria and I were well assisted at the funeral: Abbé Milo had traveled with Richard since his distant days in England and in Palestine; Abbé Luc, whose words perhaps preserved my sanity; and the bishops of Angers, Agen and Poitiers. Of course we were attended by a cloud of lesser clerics as well as my family of Fontevrault and my grand-daughter, Matilda of Perche, daughter of my own Matilda. The unfortunate Peter of Capua, whom Richard had so recently upbraided, represented the pope.

Bishop Hugh officiated. The Abbess Matilda had told him of Richard's death soon after envoys from Richard treated the bishop most evilly. King and bishop had quarreled for most of a year over the degree of support the English bishops should render the king in his need. Hugh, for all his compassion, led the faction in opposition. But no hint of rancor stained the obsequies.

I prefer to remember the ceremonies I ordered thirty years before. I installed Richard as the duke of Aquitaine on the Feast of Epiphany. I installed him at Poitiers, and then in Limoges, at the cathedral of St. Etienne. Such a ceremony. He walked up the nave of St. Etienne with me—imagine, Aline, a woman in a clerical procession. How proud I was when he put on St. Valerie's ring. A diadem for his head, the spurs and sword of a new knight, and we left St. Etienne to the adulation of the crowd. It was like the day I walked in another crowd, after my marriage to Louis.

You can imagine why I prefer to remember that.

Thus departed my fair son, the very model of a chivalrous king, out of the tears and buffets of this sinful world.

Such doleful years, Aline. Made lighter only by the election of my own Matilda's son, Otto, to the throne of the holy Roman empire. Otto was the German barons' compromise. No matter. An emperor enthroned is an emperor no less. He experienced three wonderful days in succession: Aachen, the old capital of Charlemagne, opened its gates to Otto's troops on the tenth day of July; on the eleventh he wed the seven-year-old daughter and heir to the duke of Brabant; and on the twelfth, Archbishop Adolf crowned him to the throne of the caesars, in Cologne.

There was, of course, a *quid pro quo*. Otto had to relinquish the right to succeed me as the duke of Aquitaine. But that was but a pin-prick. The advantage his ascendancy gave us in the German and Italian lands outweighed the disadvantage.

Alas, in those same years I lost Marie and Alix, both of my daughters by Louis. And then Joanna.

Dearest Marie, and sweet Alix, conceived in Jerusalem. People called Marie the "light of Champagne": she was every bit as cultured as Richard. How could it be that she who brought such joy to her world would die of sadness? And yet they say she did. They ventured to bring me word that she pined away on hearing the fate of her eldest boy, Henry, king of Jerusalem. He fell to his death from his palace at Acre. So they say. Another dead child of a child of mine. How those eastern lands devour us.

So it must be with us all, in God's time. In the end we all fall from our place; to rise to a higher station, one hopes, in a less fleeting world.

Louis put my girls to marriage with two brothers in the same year: baby Alix to the count of Blois; Marie, to the count of Champagne. How little I knew them thereafter. And then there was Joanna and her infant son. She outlived Richard by five months. Ten children. Eleven, including little Philip.[52] Dead. All dead, saving John and Aleänor. Well, we shall soon be united again.

In retrospect, I think the shock of Richard's death and the slow strangulation of our dynastic hopes forced me to look more kindly on my former alliance with the Franks. One must be pragmatic. It is four years since Richard and my daughters died, and four years since I endowed a chapel at Fontevrault to St. Lawrence. Why St. Lawrence? My choice for a patron saint, inchoate at the time, is clear as spring-water now. Lawrence was Louis' favorite saint, the last Christian martyr when the heathen sacked Rome. Burned to death on a griddle. Methinks even that end was kinder than mine, lingering into a void of probable oblivion.

43. Birth, marriages and deaths
1199

I lose my appetite for this testament, Aline. And with it my appetite for life. But I do not bear the cuts and scars of nearly fourscore years to throw myself upon a midden of despair. We shall carry on. Still, I shall be brief. You have a life to live elsewhere; and I confront eternity.

It was William Marshall who swayed the English barons to elevate John to the throne, rather than my grandson, Arthur of Brittany. I have many reasons to bless William and his service to our house: none greater than this.

At one time or another all my sons had trafficked with the Frankish court, to our lasting damage and shame. I had hoped my grandsons might be immune to Philip's seduction. But Arthur of Brittany, raised at the skirts of his leprous mother, chose to gamble like a moth around a flame. One had hopes for Arthur, but never as king. Few outside Brittany supported his claim to our throne. Except, of course, Philip, intent on his mischief. But Richard was hardly laid to rest—on Palm Sunday—when war burst upon us seven days later, at Easter.

Arthur and his mother, Countess Constance, chose the very Feast of Easter to march their army into Anjou—a sure sign that the leprosy had blunted her wits as well as her limbs. Together, their force took Angers. Not content with rendering treason by halves, they then seized Le Mans. I confess, this double affront raised my lust for war as anger has seldom stirred it. I appointed Mercadier commander of troops and we fell on Angers, executing such damage on the town and its people that they'll pass a long year in torment before Anjou rises against us again. It piqued me that the Angevins opened their gates to Arthur and his mother without one token of resistance.

John gives me cause for many misgivings, but in this affray he proved himself a fine commander, moving to effect the same revenge on Le Mans that I exacted on Angers. How history repeats itself, like that beast that devours its tail. Just a dozen years before, Henry and William Marshall fled Le Mans under cover of fires and smoke. The town razed then now burned again, put to the torch by John.

Le Mans, the birthplace of my Henry and our firstborn, destroyed yet again by fire. And why not? Cowardice and treason are best expunged by flame.

I must be hardening in ancient age, like fired clay. Sixty-and-more years ago my eyes flowed like brooks for the fate of Vitry. I hate to recall how often I thrust that supposed sin at the wearied ears of my confessors.

I have no time for regret these days. No time; less patience. I was seventy years and seven when I slipped in the blood and choked on the smoke of Angers: too old for a queen to lead armies in war. And too late for remorse at the stench of burnt flesh. After so many trials, her final years should bring an old woman the solace of accomplishment, not the bitterness of still more loss and pain. I watched Mercadier's *routiers* make a pyre of a town that I loved, and I summoned not one tear. I had too much lust for revenge—as if the flames of Angers might expiate

Richard's death. I found no tears then; I find none now. I am done for ever with the burden of regret.

After our respective forays into Angers and Le Mans an uneasy silence fell on the land. This calm was as loud in its implications as it was disturbing. I refer to the false peace that settled on us after John and I—with the able assistance of Mercadier—restored our vassals to a semblance of obedience. We knew too well that the outward calm concealed the private reckonings of barons, great and small. Whose part would they take: ours, or that of France?

Whoever sits on his hands waiting for trouble is lost. No matter how dire the times, it is better to act. To that end I raised an escort and rode south on a formal progress through my own ancestral lands, Poitou and Aquitaine. We were, I recall, some eleven weeks on the road in those blessed worlds while I dispensed such favors as I could upon the newly wealthy towns. Forty-eight years, nine children and as many sets of troubles had come and gone since Henry and I wended our bridal way through these same lands. Forty-eight years! Long enough to see two husbands and all but two of my children perish on this mortal way. There have been times on my recent travels when I thought of myself as a woman of thirty again, unattached and free of a fated future, be it sullen or blesséd. Oh what a wondrous prospect! My lives have borne me along such bitter-sweet roads.

I will say this: the Almighty has been generous with His gift of years. I tried to reciprocate during my formal visits, dispensing freedoms on towns and charters on abbeys as if I made free to posterity in my will.

At the end of that tour I crossed the Vienne, passed our empty treasure castle at Chinon and threw myself on my knees at Tours. I refer to the politic need to swear my allegiance to that swine Philip. Poitou and Aquitaine are worth living a lie for a moment or two. Besides, persons of my station are habituated to doing the unspeakable in the interests of state. Nevertheless, kneeling before that apostate and traitor must count among the most unsavory tasks I ever performed. At least his people were considerate enough to provide a high hassock, assuaging my knees if not my conscience. Ah well... *Fecit, fecit, fecit!* The curséd thing is done. We shall set it behind and move on.

And then... Still no rest. From Tours I traveled to Rouen, for meetings with John. We hoped surviving members of our court would settle new policy in the wake of Richard's demise. But even here tragedy stalked us. I speak of my Joanna.

God help us all; this world is woe! Early that year, Joanna's lord, Raymond of Toulouse, had been called to some blighted castle to suppress a rebellion. With her lord absent, Joanna herself was then called upon to raise a second force to quell some other disturbance. However, as her campaign progressed, some among Raymond's trusted officers betrayed her. Among other acts of *lèse majesté* against their lady, they set her pavilion on fire.

Joanna thus joined a tradition begun by her grandmother, the Empress Matilda (chased to the gate of Marlborough Castle; later escaping Oxford over the frozen Thames), and her mother (fleeing the Lusignans on the road to Poitou). Escaping her betrayers, Joanna's small party rode north, intent on reaching Richard to seek redress. By then it was too late. Hearing of his death, she diverted to me at Niort. How we wept in the few private moments allowed us. Joanna was always closest to Richard, and he to her—notwithstanding that he spent her wealth on Crusade, and offered her hand to a Muslim!

After our several woes had drained our tears I consigned Joanna to the care of the blessed nuns at Fontevrault. But, hardly had they put her to bed before she insisted on attending our conference at Rouen. She came all that way, against my advice; indeed, against all counsel from her nurses. Such a fiery spirit! Despite being some months pregnant she had raised troops, laid a siege, fled the flames of treason and escaped to me through the heat of summer. Now she came into Rouen, after a halt, but hardly a refreshing one, at Fontevrault.

In the face of her obvious plight, our council took on aspects of Greek tragedy, complete with a chorus of dissonant views. Joanna reached us exhausted, took to her bed, and never rose. That was unlike her, for she was possessed of Richard's fiery spirit. They loved each other dearly.

It was soon clear to all, even to me, that Joanna would die. Her dying wish was to be allowed to take the habit of a nun in the community of Fontevrault. She had loved our abbey since she was a little girl. I brought her into this world at our court in Angers, so she had found Fontevrault early in her life, and at a relatively tranquil time in mine.

I have seldom demanded anything with the vehemence I employed to bring about Joanna's dying wish. However, her desire lay outside the bounds of matters temporal that lay within my power to grant. The archbishop of Canterbury was in Rouen to take part in our conclave, but Hubert demurred: he said that only the Abbess Matilda could acquiesce to Joanna's request. So of course we sent to Fontevrault.

How I hate to fetch back these sad years, Aline. They are but yesterdays, and yet they cut short and despoil the wonderful lives and events that came before. But of course I must go on, before this ancient well of memories also runs dry.

It soon became evident that Joanna might not live to answer Matilda's examination of her faith. So Hubert Walter presided over an *ad hoc* meeting of nuns and clerics. They agreed that Joanna's conviction was inspired by God: whereupon Archbishop Hubert laid his hands upon Joanna in the presence of all, commending her life to the order of Fontevrault and her soul to our Lord. Never, in my fourscore years, have I been so relieved.

Whereupon my beloved daughter died. But God had not in that instant finished with her earthly purpose. Some minutes later, Joanna's dead body was delivered of a son. A little boy, perfect in his form. Never had I attended so closely the birth of a grandchild.

He lived just long enough to be baptized. And then he died. Dear little life. His purpose in this flesh known but to God.

Necessity makes strange friends, Aline. Heaven has seen fit to chop the boughs off my once-fruitful tree. Therefore I moved to ensure the posterity of our line by making another graft. I mentioned some days ago that Richard's death forced me to examine my former alliance with the Franks. Indeed, even before Richard died, we had started negotiating marriage between King Philip's heir, Louis of France, and one of the several daughters of my own daughter, Aleänor.

One forgets about the girls. Until the men are dead.

I had given birth to Aleänor in October of 1162 at Domfront Castle. So she is a Norman, Aline, like you; although in Castile they know her as Doña Leonor of England.

Domfront defends a pass running north into the Normandy Hills. The castle is therefore blessed with a southerly aspect—which explains why Destiny placed Aleänor's fate in the south. Perhaps if I had delivered her on the other side of those hills, at Falaise, we would have married her to an Englishman. One must be so careful how one births a child.[53] Our first intention was to ally Aleänor with the Germans, but Fate saw fit to send her to Castile.

It was during my exile in England that Henry betrothed Aleänor to young Alphonso VIII, the king of Castile. Aleänor was not quite sixteen. How distant that seems. I was also fifteen when Louis fetched me from Bordeaux.

Aleänor and Alphonso wasted no time starting their family. God has seen fit to bless them with plentiful issue. They had nine children at the time of my visit, and she has had another since, a girl, whom they christened Leonor, for me. I hear she is expecting again.

Hence our opportunity to arrange a royal alliance between the heir to France and one of Aleänor's daughters. John and Philip met to seal the fine points of the contract in the dark days of the year. I believe it was at Christmas.

But then came an urgent consideration: which of Alphonso's and Aleänor's daughters would make the most suitable match? This is not a question one raises in most royal alliances. Diplomacy seldom extends to choice in such niceties. But, like Louis, Alphonso and Aleänor were blessed with a surfeit of daughters. And I was determined that the consort selected from among my granddaughters must graft well on Frankish stock.

This was not a mission I could entrust to another, notwithstanding that Christmas was not long behind us: the roads were frozen, the traveling season two months ahead.

Nevertheless, the thing had to be done, so I reconciled myself to a bone-jarring ride. Well cushioned, I ordered our captains and teamsters to make best speed, mindful that I might feel the full weight of my years before coming to the comforts of Fontevrault or Poitiers again.

We made good time until we reached La Marche. Lacking safe-conduct from the Lusignans, I should have known better than to try the journey without greater force. But the press of affairs had driven that cursèd clan out of my head. They stopped us; although less violently than in their ambush thirty years before, when Patrick of Salisbury was killed on my account and William Marshall almost lost his life. This time we were ill-equipped for fight or flight. Meanwhile, time pressed sore. So I yielded to the *force majeure* held over my head by descendants of the very brigands who slew Patrick. They were led now by Hughes le Brun, an ape of a man, but cunning, as is all that tribe. In my predicament, I took the only course of action open to me: I yielded to pressure.

Such gratitude! Hughes is the grandson of my former commander, Geoffroi de Rançon, whose neck I had saved. Had I let the Franks hang him, he would not have sired Burgone de Taillebourg, sparing the world her issue, the Lusignans, Guy and Hughes.

I will say this for Hughes le Brun. He wasted no time on niceties. He agreed to permit my passage to and from Castile if I would cede the county of La Marche, which Henry had seized after my first encounter with Guy de Lusignan. So, with no more ado, I ceded La Marche. Of course, since I conceded this transfer under duress it had no standing in law; and we would have no compunction in taking the county back, with vengeance to boot. Meanwhile, I acquired the right to proceed and return, and to do so under the safe-conduct of an escort.

After that, we fairly sped: past the place of my birth, across Gascony on roads I vaguely recalled from rumbling along with Pétronille on Father's ducal journeys in our childish, painted cart.

By the feast of Epiphany my company was ascending the Pyrenees, having followed the pilgrim road young Aleänor took—and my father forty years before her, on his fatal passage to Compostela. Be that as it may. My recent journey owed its excellent speed to that shrine. South of the Pyrenees, abbeys, churches and princes have improved the roads and built bridges for the passage and comfort of pilgrims. We came into Aleänor's court at Burgos before the end of January.

Oh Aleänor, of all my sons and daughters, God gave you the fairest fate.

She was thirteen when Henry ravaged my court at Poitiers and dragged me to England. Part girl, part woman, a wonderfully impressionable age. Now she stood before me in middle age, still pretty—if a little plump, the mother of nine and the consort to a king. What a bitter-sweet moment, that meeting. I missed the whole passage of Aleänor's youth to fruitful motherhood and middle age. Nevertheless, her bearing still recalled those youthful faces gracing my several courts. I recalled how, as a child, she had taken her baby sister, Joanna, under her wing. In Aleänor I saw time fled; and with it the years that Henry razed and threw aside.

But that was not all I saw in the face of Castile. Nor in the face of Burgos. Aleänor seems to have transposed the very temper of my courts into her own. Her halls still resound to the music and tales of troubadours. Their talents are as scarce in this new century as the last moths of autumn.

Do you know, Aline, I believe Aleänor and Alphonso are in love! How remarkable in marriage. In the usual course of worldly affairs one accepts what one gets. But that couple is an exception: they have nine children, perhaps another on the way, and their eyes caress each other like lovers!

Aleänor was pleased to show me a nunnery in Burgos which Alphonso commissioned for her a year before my Henry died. I must say, my daughter embodies an odd mix of traits. On one hand, she revealed a degree of religious zeal I confess to finding excessive, even oppressive. I never challenged her on this point: her happiness in life remains my sole concern. If she acquired this humor from her youthful exposure at Fontevrault, I am surprised. Neither Joanna nor John were imbued to the same degree. John, I must think, has faith in nothing.

On the other hand, it is undoubtedly due to Aleänor's authority that the nuns of the Monasterio de Santa María la Real de las Huelgas enjoy the same liberal governance as our community at Fontevrault. They appear to have taken to themselves several powers that the Church denies women elsewhere: the nuns hear each others' confessions, say mass, nominate priests to the many villages Alphonso granted them, and they preach! To my pleasure, I found that they educate girls. Our own founder, Robert d'Arbrissel, would have been proud. Alphonso wants Las Huelgas to become a necropolis for the bones of kings. My daughter wants it to be a liberal and lively community for *living* women. As young as she was when my court was thriving, she learned her lessons well at Poitiers. She is an excellent embroiderer, too. Even as a child she embroidered the bands for her sleeves. They showed me a cope that she made, full of gold threads and rich stuff. The thing shines with a radiance worthy of Suger's windows.

I fear that we who live north of the Pyrenees have been so taken with our own affairs that we scarcely consider the wars and alliances binding Castile—though, make no mistake, I have been kept informed. King Alphonso has placed his monks and nuns adroitly on his sunlit chessboard. As ivy seals a wall, so Alphonso positions new monasteries, giving them stakes in lands he has recaptured from the Moors. One admires his politics. The man is as bold as he is wise. He makes an admirable son-in-law.

There was much talk during our stay of an impending move to adopt Las Huelgas into the Cistercian order. Indeed, delegates from Clairvaux were present during my embassy at the court of Castile. So I suppose we must hazard my poor daughter's bones and her soul to the austere care of my old adversary, the sainted Bernard. He would approve the monastic zeal, although not our infamous Poitevin licence to women.

How garrulous I am today, Aline! I said this before: an old peach tree, moribund for years, puts forth a fine crop in its final summer. It summons all its sap. As for me, all of a sudden I see my past worlds with exquisite clarity. Like the tree, I am putting forth stored riches from my past.

To rein myself back to the matter in hand… My self-appointed mission was to return with a granddaughter whose strength of character would help her prevail upon the poisons of the Capets' court. Such a woman would have to inure herself to whispers while ensuring that she heard them. She would have to combine the endurance of a war-horse with disdain for braying barons and sniff-nosed priests. In short, she would have to develop a measure of my own contempt for noisy and noisome counsels.

I examined three of Aleänor's daughters, although only two were candidates for France. Urraca was fourteen at the time; Blanche [Blanca] was eleven; and little Mafalda, not above seven. For her, sweet child, our interview was but a rehearsal.

Urraca and Blanche were both striking young women, outstanding in deportment and accomplishment. They were skilled in languages, fluent in conversation and ventured lengthy oral histories of their mother's house and line. In the pride of young maturity, both would prove lovely in the eyes of men. And both had a well-imbued sense of their station and the destinies expected of them in the maelstroms of our world.

It is a hard thing to disappoint a child, especially when she has been primed for months to a point of expectation. There was not an eye in Alphonso's court that did not expect me to satisfy the monarchs' aspirations for Urraca, the elder daughter. However, some foreboding warned me that, although Urraca was perfect in every other regard, she was too accepting, too placid to oppose the gathered malice of the Capets. I found her diffident, reluctant to intrude. Urraca might master her future king and husband—the boy Louis is two years younger than she—but Louis was the smallest shard among many sharp edges in the Capets' broken pot. I recalled too well my own life-draining sojourn in their ancient tower. Cliques and whispers seem the more intense for being confined by the passing waters of the Seine. The very fabric of the place invites despair.

No, despite Urraca's fiery ancestor—she was named for a warring queen of Castile from Grandfather's day—Paris was not for her.

Accordingly, I chose Blanche. In Blanche I found the fire that forged the iron line of my fathers, the counts of Poitou and the dukes of Aquitaine. Her assertive Poitevin spark would serve the girl well in a life-long war with the follies of prelates and kings. I contrived to let the family down gently, the parents as well as their daughter. But I had to have Blanche.

You may guess that parting was difficult, more so for Aleänor and me than for Blanche. My daughter and I would never see each other again: of that there was no doubt. As for young Blanche, her childish mind had not yet assimilated the life-wrenching step to which she was committed. For a girl of eleven, our journey together began as a great adventure.

Easter Week was approaching when we took our leave. Our journey across the plains was slower now, for we were driving against the tide of pilgrims bound for Compostela. We had to shoulder our way against a wave of humanity as diverse as ever I saw outside the Holy Land.

We had much to talk about. We were so rapt in conversation that my bones, which stabbed with pain at each lurch on the way south, now ignored the wretched state of the roads. We spoke about men, about their lusts, their strengths and weaknesses; about the nature of the Capets' court; about the strifes that Blanche would encounter, and how she must counter them with her force of personality and the strength of her resolve. During our first hours and days together she stared at me in wonder, as if the miracle that placed us together was not her destiny in Paris, but her grandmother's very existence—with all my age written upon me, encasing a still-quick brain. To Blanche I am sure that history came alive as it flowed from my lips. As we rode I marched her back along the path of time to speak of persons and places she knew of only from tutors, nuns and books.

Although Blanche's life had been sheltered, she had never been sheltered from witnessing the miseries of life. As we watched the poorest pilgrims flow past, I spoke of charity. As we watched mothers carry children with bleeding feet, and girls with infants slung on their backs, I spoke of women's need to learn. I explained how it was that the Church in our time demands meekness from women. "Be not a virgin with children," I told her. "First and foremost, be yourself. Speak your mind, look men in the eye, and they will follow."[54]

This was difficult matter for a child, more especially since it concerned a court whose manners she had never known. But Blanche had been well tutored. She was adept at learning and absorbing my biases as well as facts. We had so little time together and so much to transfer regarding her future life in Paris.

Coming south I had felt quite ill as we climbed the mountains to cross through the pass at Roncesvalles: my heart pounded; I struggled for breath. But on our return I was so preoccupied with my charge that I felt no discomfort. Indeed, as we passed through the heights it was Blanche's turn to talk. What a quick mind the child has: she recited Priest Konrad's Song of Roland with never a pause.

Our households fairly raced from the heights to Bordeaux, pausing on Palm Sunday to celebrate the anniversary of Richard's death. When we crossed my lands, I was thankful that our fields and orchards resembled the plains of Blanche's native country. The grass was still green when we left Castile, not parched by summer.

We were destined to celebrate Easter at Bordeaux, a town not wanting in the sunlit warmth and graces of Burgos. To my mind, Bordeaux remains as it was when the Latin poet Ausonius praised it as his birthplace. Even now its skies are "soft and clement." I compare myself to Ausonius from time to time. He was another ancient fellow, well-traveled and bruised by the tides of his very being. Emperor Gratian made him the first prefect of Gaul, whence he had the sense to retire to Bordeaux. Would that I had done so!

Blanche took comfort from the city's appointments and its ambience. I know she found solace in the familiar rites of the Easter offices. How proudly I retailed the lives and histories of our ancestors as we walked the ancient chambers of the palace of the Ombrière.

When we stopped at our palace I got a severe jolt. A few years before, Richard had given Mercadier the estates at Beynac. Its strategic castle commands the baronies of Périgord from a cliff above a loop in the Dordogne. On our arrival, Mercadier came down from his aerie to pay his respects and escort us north to Poitiers.

But it was not to be. A rival's agent stabbed him, and death soon claimed our loyal servant. Of all men, I judged Mercadier least likely to die a Caesar's death in the market place. Like Richard, he had fought a hard life; and, like Richard, one imagined he would end his days cut down by lance or sword. Fate's ambush is surprise, Aline.

One heard that Mercadier was loathed by his peasants—but not his *routiers*, who would follow him to hell. They had done so on occasion, on our account. Mercadier was a hard man, cruel to those who incurred his displeasure. But he was first and last a soldier, with no thought of pleasantries; and with neither the leaven of mercy nor the sacred in his soul. We relied on Mercadier to inflict the harsh demands that enmities and alliances impose on kings. For that I mourned him. Not for the man himself—he would have found that unseemly—but for the loss of his loyal and effective service.

I concealed my concern from the child. But Mercadier's murder struck me to the core. I may fairly say, of all my warrior family, only John survives.

I t was with misgiving that I led our household from Bordeaux. A small, much too insistent voice in my head told me to abandon statecraft and content myself with a tranquil old age in a place I held dear. But the call of comfort has never commanded my character. Having crossed the Garonne and mounted our carts, I never looked back. Never instruct a child, by look or by sigh, to succumb to the past, Aline. We move only on! Thus we pressed forward, well guarded, though not—God rest his soul—by the loyal Mercadier.

Time had been my foe since the very outset of my mission. The kings had sealed an agreement stipulating that the betrothal of the boy

Louis and a princess of Castile would take place as soon as possible. After Easter certainly; but for obvious reasons we desired that the nuptials should be celebrated before the warring season. This alliance had to buy us at least a year of respite from Philip's attacks. So we drove our beasts and people hard to convey us with all speed via Poitiers to Normandy, and thence to Chateau Gaillard, where John held court. Notwithstanding the urgency, I had half a mind to slow our passage: I treasured every hour I spent with Blanche. We had much to do to build resolve upon her slight but firm foundation.

In the end, I fear I could no longer endure the roads. Exhaustion and the strain of the journey combined in no small measure with the shock of Mercadier's death. I was forced to abandon my escort of Blanche. We parted at Fontevrault. Had my very being depended on it, I could not have carried the sweet child farther. So we spent some hours together. Then I consigned her life and soul to the love of God and her care on the road to that fine Gascon, Archbishop Elie of Bordeaux. Beyond that, perforce her care must fall upon John, upon Philip, and upon her future lord and husband, Louis. Thus I bade Blanche adieu and sent her to her life in France.

King Philip's well-earned troubles with the Church made it necessary for the betrothal of young Louis and Blanche to take place in Normandy, on our side of the border. For a while, the alliance and the amity engendered by the event brought us closer to the Franks. The senior prelate of Aquitaine, Archbishop Elie, conducted the ceremony, which emphasized our role.

One wishes the marriage of one's grandchild to a future king of France had taken place in a grander locale than the Norman border town of Pont Audemer. No matter. The thing was done.

I heard that Blanche was soon afflicted with a malaise of the mind not unlike my own reaction to the Capets' barrack on the Île de la Cité:

she became greatly depressed. So much so that her young husband requested Bishop Hugh, who was then in Paris, to counsel her. I gather Hugh succeeded in lifting the gloom that befell the young bride.

One hears things imperfectly from a distance, of course. Blanche's misery might well have been caused by the appalling amenities of the palace, her natural homesickness, or the onset of womanhood. Naturally, given her age, this factor had been delicately embraced in the nuptial contract—just as my own daughters' betrothals had stipulated. But the sudden onset of so many novelties in life can strike the strongest of young minds. During our journey I had discussed the matter with several capable nurses and ladies of Blanche's house.

I was less disturbed by that news—faith and my prayers told me the child would mend—than by a second item of intelligence reaching Fontevrault as companion to the first.

During his pastoral visit to Paris—the last before he returned to England, where the swan at Stowe foretold his death—Bishop Hugh attempted to counsel Count Arthur of Brittany. The reward for his pains was to leave the young man no better than he found him, large in anger over perceived slights, full of resentment and jealous beyond measure. Given the defects in his personality it was clear that Arthur resented John and me for reclaiming our own at Angers and Le Mans the year before. Arthur did homage to John for Brittany at the tourney following Blanche's wedding, and seemed to do so in good humor. But, hearing of Bishop Hugh's experience, it became clear that too many cankers lay in the muddle and mud of Arthur's brain.

Arthur's reaction to Hugh reminded me all too much of Geoffrey, his father. Geoffrey, Young Henry—indeed, all my boys—toyed with treasons amid the flatteries of Louis' court and the taverns of Paris. But Arthur...

With Henry, Richard and Mercadier dead, we were not well prepared to deflect his boyish treasons. Not content with Brittany, Arthur wanted to rule all my lands. The Franks fired this incubus into his head. The boy had no firm ground on which to stand.

I t was John's lust for a woman that gave me the final—one hopes— and the most violent adventure of my later years.

Late in his life, Henry arranged a match between our son John and Hadwiga of Gloucester, whom we knew as Isabelle.[55] In his youth, Henry spent four years in the household of her forebears, Earl Robert, and his countess, Mabel Fitzhamon. Here I go, gossiping again! So many people; so many words, Aline. Interrupt me when I stray.

The marriage seemed propitious in so far as it brought John an income from large estates he otherwise lacked. They have six children— Fitzroys all—though John and Hadwiga have drifted apart. In the end, John crowned himself, without his spouse.

The upshot was that John used the peace secured by Blanche's marriage to seek a happier choice for his wife. He consulted me at Fontevrault. I recommended he seek a spouse among the issue of the royal house of Portugal. Accordingly, we dispatched an embassy in the summer of the year 1200.

Having put this affair in train, John turned to mending relations with our vassals, principal among whom were the brigand Lusignans. Eighteen months had passed since Hughes le Brun stopped me on the road, extorting the county of La Marche in return for my passage to Castile. Hughes was eager to ratify our so-called pact. He sported the title of "Count" as freely as my late father-in-law wore gorse in his hat. Hughes now besought John for the formal deed of our "gift."

Diplomacy is seldom simple. By way of *quid pro quo*, Hughes le Brun offered to arbitrate our quarrels with the counts Aymar of Limoges and Adémar of Angoulême. You will recall, Aline, that Aymar, alone of our vassals, gave nothing to Richard's ransom. This was a not-insignificant motive for Richard's fatal attack on Chalûs.

Hughes le Brun was well placed to arbitrate our quarrel against Limoges and Angoulême: he was betrothed to Count Adémar's daughter, the exceptionally beautiful Isabella de Taillefer.

This, then, was the situation: Hughes sponsored a great entertainment to celebrate the transfer of La Marche and the prospect of arbitrating our quarrels with Limoges and Angoulême. This event, at Lusignan, was attended by John, as well as the nobility of Limoges, Angoulême and Poitou. I was still too weary to attend. Nor, to tell truth, did I wish to break bread in the Lusignans' hall.

Would that John's next step had been to consult me before he poisoned our well! But a man of thirty-three does not confide matters of lust to his mother. In short, John was fired at first sight with an instant desire to possess Isabella de Taillefer—and she barely twelve. Nothing would satisfy him but that he should possess her. In what I say next, I speak only half in jest: would that the old Roman *lex prime noctis* still prevailed.[56] John might have bedded the virgin and quenched the heated humors of his lust. But no, not he. No sooner did he seek to satisfy his flesh than he determined to marry the girl. To that end he contrived a political motive that mired us all in war. He persuaded himself that if he permitted Lusignan an alliance by marriage with Angoulême, he would be encouraging our most rebellious vassals at a time when we were weak.

I must confess: John did mention his proposed match, although our interview took place when I was far from well. My return from Burgos robbed me of all energy, even that required to think! Besides, I harbored my own lust for revenge against Hughes. Hughes the Ninth, count of La Marche and Angoulême, indeed! So, John's proposed match with Isabella went forward in the utmost secrecy.

John's first tactic was to dispatch the Brothers Lusignan to distant parts on minor businesses.

The lady herself was never consulted: members of her household would surely have spilled the tale. From her betrothal celebration at

Lusignan, Isabella traveled south to Angoulême to prepare for her wedding—as she thought—to Hughes le Brun.

Her father, however, quickly succumbed to John's blandishments, agreeing to affiance his daughter to our house, rather than to Hughes. Better to install one's daughter as the queen of England than attach her to a title with a spurious provenance and a dubious future, as the so-called countess of Lusignan.

John had an excellent pretext to travel to the south. He had to settle issues concerning estates transferred to my grandson, the four-year-old boy whom my Joanna bore to Raymond of Toulouse. Aline, I should have mentioned that the little boy born of his mother's corpse in Rouen was Joanna's second child.

One assumes that the bride's father prepared Isabella for a change of spouse when she came to the altar in Bordeaux. Suffice to say that in the very place and hour appointed for her wedding to Hughes le Brun, Archbishop Elie married Isabella to John.

Oh Aline, we anoint ourselves with such troubles. The Lusignans' anger reverberates still.

I met the girl soon afterwards. John hied her off to spend their first weeks of married life behind the ramparts at Chinon, a sparrow's-flight away. A pretty child: one who might heat a man's poker, though not, I fancy, a Helen of Troy to set fire to a town. Still, men have their lusts and sate them, too. To stiffen her father's affection for us in the face of the brewing storm, I endowed her with Saintes and Niort, two of the richest towns in my gift.

Now I'm angry with myself again. I was too soft with John. I shall take valerian before I start to fret. Then I shall lie down.

44. Isabella plays Helen, the Angevins play Troy
1200-1202

Never was a man so besotted of a woman. Of that I am convinced. These past three years have given me too much time to repent at leisure for my tacit complicity in our disasters. I should have risen from my sick-bed to fight John's prick-fired lust. I should at least have fought for strength to think his actions through. But, how sweet it was to strike a blow against the Lusignans. Vengeance for me. Vengeance for Patrick of Salisbury. Vengeance for William Marshall and all the others robbed and maimed and murdered on those roads.

I confess, Aline, John's marriage was the first such test in my life that I failed. I let my thirst for vengeance bewitch my grip on reason. It is a curse of old age to let a soft mind impose upon critical thought.

The whole unfolding saga of these past three years resembles exactly a story told by bards in ancient Greece. Its resemblance to our present coil has harped on my night-thoughts through these past few months and years.

I speak of the *Iliad*, a great poem that tells the story of a beautiful woman whom many suitors hoped to marry. The woman, Helen, chose to marry Menelaus, king of Sparta. (In this tale, Aline, you must accept the curiosity that in olden days a woman of noble birth was free to choose her spouse.) But the matter didn't end there. A prince from the city of Troy, whose name was Paris, desired Helen, too. Paris came to Sparta, where Menelaus, knowing nothing of his lust, greeted him well and entertained him.

Paris had the support of the goddess Aphrodite, who contrived to send Menelaus away on a false pretext. Whereupon Paris seized Helen and carried her off to an island, Kranai. The following day they sailed for Troy.

The resulting warfare lasted ten years and led to the downfall of Troy.

Foolish, foolish, foolish thoughts. In past years I would not have let them lodging in my brain. But an idle body breeds anxiety. Never be old, Aline, and you'll never be anxious.

I see it all so clearly. Helen is Isabella of Taillefer; Menelaus is Hughes le Brun; Sparta with its warrior clan is Lusignan; and Paris, prince of Troy, is my foolish John. Paris! What a nemesis hangs upon that name.

Nor is that all. Hughes le Brun fed and entertained his betrayer, as did Menelaus. Hughes was sent on distant business, as was Menelaus. Chinon, where John harbored his stolen bride, is the island of Kranai. Timeless Aphrodite, who aided and abetted Paris, conceals herself in my ancient being. And Troy—God help me—Troy is everything my life's work built to be possessed and ruled by men now dead.

Leaving their love-nest at Chinon, John and Isabella set out on a formal tour through the garrison towns of Normandy before embarking, in October, for Portsmouth. Within days of landing, Isabella was crowned at Westminster. Then they traveled north, stopping at

Lincoln for the funeral of Bishop Hugh. I gather they spent much of that winter and spring on the roads—frost permitting or rain denying—holding their Christmas court at Guildford. I heard reports in those months that John showed signs of the promise his father displayed during our first years in England.

So, from October to Pentecost, government south of the sea reverted to Fontevrault. As for me, I watched and listened while the rising furies of the Lusignans did all they could to turn our vassals from us.

I count it as a coup of some magnitude that I managed to restore the affections of Count Amaury of Thouars to our cause. Within days of Joanna's death, John had made one of his more capricious decisions: he dismissed our cousin Amaury from the stewardship of our treasure-castle at Chinon. The matter turned on the fact that the Brothers Thouars, suspecting John of wishing harm to young Arthur of Brittany, whisked the boy off to Paris. In light of what followed, how right they were. John responded to the Thouars' precaution by branding our long-standing allies as traitors.

Without Amaury's support, the very valley of the Loire was set to rise against us. John has never understood the principle that constancy wins friends; inconstancy makes foes. His mind grasps tactics needed to sate appetites; not, I fear, to plan long-term strategy. He is a fox that looks no farther then hunting its next meal.

Not until early summer did John and Isabella return, through Barfleur. The two kings then made what I believe were honest attempts to let their peoples live side by side in peace. John and Isabella entertained Philip richly near Rouen, being careful not to embarrass the king by bringing him to Chateau Gaillard—where he would also learn first hand of its defences.

Then it was Philip's turn to entertain John and Isabella. Philip, we observed, removed his household from Paris, giving his guests the run of the palace. My own biased opinion holds that Philip got the more comfortable lodging, at Fontainebleau, through the heat of July.

Sundry ladies of young Blanche's household reported that she found it a great pleasure and comfort to keep company with Isabella. They are just the same age. How pretty they must have looked together—both of them beautiful girls. I hear they conspire to promote the latest fashion, wearing that new style of hair-net woven of rich threads with jewels.

The month of July passed in peace for all of us, except for Philip's bigamous wife, Agnes of Méranie. I shall come to that. John and Isabella spent the month on the Île de la Cité at amicable close-quarters with our once and future foe. However, Philip's good conduct towards us had nothing to do with a sudden change of character. It had everything to do with his troubles with the pope. I mentioned earlier that my first impression of Innocent III was correct: in office he proved to be a hard man and nobody's fool, least of all Philip's.

You will recall, Aline, that Philip repudiated his Danish bride, Ingeborg, on the morning after their wedding night. But Ingeborg was a woman of my mettle. For nearly eight years she browbeat the curia, the pope and the king for satisfaction. From her lair in the convent at Soissons she clung by tooth and nail to the title of queen and the crown of France. Spies told us that Pope Innocent found no room for compromise. The crux of one papal letter to Paris read: "The royal dignity does not lift you above Christian responsibilities. The Holy See will not abandon the defence of persecuted women." Hah, this fellow Innocent can play a chess game worthy of an Arab: Bishop covers Queen while Queen moves to checkmate King. For once, Aline, I found myself allied with the Church.

Philip had compounded his sins by going through a form of marriage with his mistress, Agnes of Méranie. Agnes gave him a daughter almost at once. Then she bore him a son whom they christened Philip Hurapel.

This ruction was finally settled just before John and Isabella returned from England. Philip, pressed hard by the pope and the Danes, agreed to take back Ingeborg and repudiate Agnes. Whereupon Agnes died of shock.

As a matter of fact, she died while John and Isabella lay in Philip's old palace.

The Church used Philip's marital troubles to quash him for nearly eight years: from his shameful Crusade through his shameful marriage. We were the chiefest beneficiaries, most especially during the comma of false calm after Richard died.

I cannot remember such a tranquil autumn—not since the interval between my years as queen of France, then England, fifty years ago. I received visitors: John and Isabella from Chinon; and Berengaria. How little we hear of her now.

Sundry sources hinted at Philip's frustrated ambition to push out his frontiers again—to retake the lands he stole while Richard was on Crusade. But nothing happened. It was late in the season for war.

Besides, I had taken a precaution against dynastic catastrophe, marrying one of my own to the Capet line.

Philip responded, taking another precaution. He asked that the Church recognize the legitimacy of his son by Agnes, Philip Hurapel. Young Louis was his heir; the infant Philip would be his spare. Pope Innocent must have been inclined to grant Philip a concession. The Church declared little Philip Hurapel to be a legitimate heir.

There is an ancient adage in English: "The knife beneath the smiler's cloak sometime is bared." That "sometime" struck in late April the following year, when Philip summoned John to Paris to atone for stealing the bride of Lusignan. In doing so he offered safe-passage to Paris, but neglected to mention safe-passage back to Rouen.

John naturally declined, offering instead to meet Philip in the customary way, mounted, at the border between Normandy and France. We recalled how Richard had distrusted Philip sufficiently that even that precaution did not suffice: Richard shouted to Philip from a barge. Nevertheless, in the new spirit of apparent harmony, they agreed a traditional meeting. Philip came to the appointed place with an army at his back, only to find that he talked to the air. John, for want of troops, stayed away.

Unfortunately this gave Philip the pretext a deceiver longs for. He launched his army into eastern Normandy, bypassing the largest garrisons, burning and razing his way from the Seine to the Somme. I heard with the utmost dejection that he knighted young Arthur near Gournay. To add affront to affray, he then presented the inconstant boy with Maine, Anjou and Touraine, as well as Brittany. As if this were not enough, he promised him Poitou, after his army had left me dispossessed. Me! Dispossessed!

Then, as if to effect that very object, young Arthur left the wasteland he had created in Normandy and galloped west to Philip's stronghold at Tours, where he merged his force with that of the Brothers Lusignan.

I did not wish my grandson ill, but I would willingly have drawn him a mile or so behind my cart. He was a mere stripling, a boy born in the same year as Blanche and Isabella.

Speaking of my cart, I had expected my mission to Castile to be the last excursion of my life. But it was not to be. From Tours to Fontevrault is but a day's trot for cavalry. It seemed best to put myself behind strong walls, safe from ransom by young Arthur and the French. Thus we left my beloved monastery for the greater security of Poitiers.

This is difficult country. I mentioned long ago that the Breton Robert d'Arbrissel founded Fontevrault here precisely because, one hundred years ago, it stood in no-man's land. It is still a hard country. These roads are not passable without a stiff escort, which I lacked. Nevertheless, I deemed it best to leave.

We took the most secure route, one that angled away from the border, passing beneath the ancient walls of Mirebeau.

My travels now became the keen-eyed concern of spies on both sides. As a hostage, the Franks would value me as they once valued Richard. My ancient person still had worth. Were I to fall into the hands of the Franks or the Lusignans, their demands on John would break us for all time. Accordingly, the Lusignans mapped my path towards Mirebeau while urging the French to launch a joint attack.

I have never believed in delay. Nor did I do so now. That is what saved me from falling into the hands of these creatures, because Arthur hesitated, waiting for additional men-at-arms from Brittany to join his Franks and Lusignans. That delay was enough: my company made the dash from Fontevrault to Mirebeau. Hah! Once again I thought of Matilda, winning the safety of Marlborough's walls a horse-tail ahead of Stephen. So long ago. History seems to circle and plunge and rise, like a kestrel, over and over again.

Mirebeau is not a modern fortress. It cannot compare with Chateau Gaillard. An outer wall or bailey surrounds the town, which in turn is built around a tall, central keep. To this we repaired, secure for a time behind heavy walls and a portcullis. Until Arthur and his allies could make engines, I was safe from capture. Before we entered this ancient stone and timber place, I had taken the precaution of sending messengers to John who was two days march away, beating the bushes for allies and troops near Le Mans.

Foolish Arthur! The boy launched at once into what he believed to be negotiation with me, his grandmother. In the way of naïfs, he understood nothing of my strategy as I heaped item upon item for discussion. King Philip had promised him Maine, Anjou and Touraine, as well as his own native Brittany. I said I must handle these as separate issues. As indeed they were. If that were not enough, I reminded Arthur that Richard's treaty at Messina had hinted at making him the heir to England. Then there was the matter of Poitou. Arthur was to have my province, by gift from Philip. Over my dead body! No matter. All these items had to be discussed, and all settled, before I would budge.

If I would concede to all his demands—which amounted to the list of Philip's promises—Arthur would give me safe-conduct to Poitiers. Safe-conduct! With Hughes le Brun and his Lusignan cutthroats in his train! Nevertheless, every item was grist for the mill of delay.

So there we were, absurd as we must have appeared to a dispassionate mind: below, the boy in the forecourt; above, his grandmother condescending to glance past an embrasure from time to time. Then, of course, I took advantage of my years to "rest" more often than is my wont. Old heads nod off, especially when occasion demands. That includes siege by foolish grandsons.

I had no trouble extending the parlay until nightfall, whereupon Arthur and the Lusignans broke off negotiation and took their ease in the town. As for us, we found what comfort we could in our ancient tower and prepared to talk away another day.

It was a bright, moonlit night, not unlike many I spent as a child gazing over the wide Garonne, or scanning the rooftops of Poitiers from Grandfather's tower. Excepting the curious circumstance of my durance in Mirebeau's keep, the night was wonderfully calm.

Staring out on that silvery scene brought to mind an event that befell the Empress Matilda ten years before I married her son. During the civil war, King Stephen had besieged Matilda for a full two months in Oxford Castle. Then, one night after Advent, she dressed in white to match the snow and had herself lowered over the wall with three knights as guides. They led her six miles through deep snow, never far from the shouts and horns of Stephen's pickets. At last, dry-shod, they crossed the Thames. Even the river had frozen to ice. Such a woman, Aline! And a suitable dam for Henry. But, as I was saying...

At Mirebeau we were disturbed around cock-crow by shouts and alarums; men's cries, crashing, and the unmistakable clunk of steel on wood, followed by the clang of steel on steel. At first we thought one faction of Arthur's force had started to war another: his *routiers* had spent the evening drinking. Arthur's French and Lusignans had broached every keg they could find.

But the noise of battle was too widespread and sustained for a drunken riot. If we could believe the clamor and sudden appearance of torches, the first assault came from a single gate. Before long the warfare below us was all-encompassing. For our part, my people stood to arms and waited for whatever Fate might bring.

It is a strange sight to view dawn from the top of a keep at the centre of a town such as Mirebeau. Beyond the city wall, first light tinges the land with rosy hues, its effect enhanced by shimmering dew. But the city wall had the effect of blocking the light so that, while dawn bathed the surrounding country, the sun touched only the tips of roofs in the town. From our point of view, the battle in the streets below took place in darkness.

You may imagine my joy and surprise when at last John appeared in the forecourt, not a little disheveled. Then, in a crowd of shouting, cheering men, Guillaume de Braose[57] and Guillaume des Roches, John's new warden of Chinon.

I had sent word of my plight to John, but none of us expected release at the break of the following day. John and his forces had ridden like furies from Le Mans, reaching Mirebeau in the space of a waning day and a moonlit night.

So complete was the force of surprise, so complete was John's triumph, that the number of prisoners was more than we could handle. The defenders, having blocked all but one of the gates, had nowhere to run. Not a man escaped. At a blow, we became masters of an army in chains—including Arthur.

I must add something of a codicil. I learned that John's allies held him to strict conditions before agreeing to launch their onslaught on Mirebeau. Guillaume des Roches had recently come over from Philip's camp; Guillaume de Braose lived in fear of our collapse. These, and others, were exposed to Philip's malice should the tide of fortune turn. They had therefore demanded, as condition of their support, that Arthur should come to no harm and that the many noble prisoners should be treated with strict regard for the code of chivalry.

Accordingly, Guillaume de Braose, to whom Arthur surrendered, took custody of the boy. Dungeons in Caen swallowed Hugues le Brun and his brother, Raoul d'Eu. No dungeon could be strong enough for my liking. Above two hundred knights and nobles, many of whom were my own fallen lieges, spent the next few days tied and sitting backwards in ox-wains, as John's people carted them to the strongest dungeons and keeps in Normandy and beyond. England's white cliffs became the jail for many. Its moated shore served as well as stone and iron walls.

Arthur's sister, Alëanor—the "pearl of Brittany," people call her—was among those shipped to England. I think she has yet to return. As for Arthur—feckless boy; so much like Young Henry—the compass of his dreamed-for realm was a dungeon in Falaise.

At a stroke, the seizure of Mirebeau blocked Philip's plan to install Arthur as his puppet in our western lands. He must have wondered how an army of experienced men could wallow into such a trap.

45. Faltering, fading light
1203-1204

I fear that my son is destined for disaster. John has in his being no grasp on dispassionate reason. Not so much as a spark. Cruelty has no place in affairs of state. I speak thus because John's subsequent conduct, more than any other factor, lost us our treasured allies. He continues to lose us much that we have owned.

I heard that Guillaume des Roches accompanied the carts of prisoners through Normandy, pleading for a measure of compassion for those whom John held in ropes and chains. When compassion was not forthcoming, Guillaume resigned his command of Chinon. Within months he led a growing rebellion of barons against us. They included Count Amaury of Thouars, whom I had summoned to Fontevrault and wooed to return to our cause. In the wake of Mirebeau, Amaury spied his brother Raoul tied like a pig on a spit in an ox cart destined for a Norman dungeon.

Would that I could take back years and mend the damage by dint of constancy and powers of persuasion.

John, of his anxiety, alienated our allies to pluck defeat from the jaws of victory. In the autumn of that year our rebel barons seized Angers again; and Guillaume des Roches, having joined their cause, besieged Queen Isabella at Chinon. She might lodge there still had not one of John's most trustworthy knights, Jean de Prealx, arranged her escape and spirited her off to join John at Le Mans.

Perhaps you know the Prealx family, Aline. Their seat is Darnatel, near Rouen. Jean's forebear of the same name fought with Duke William at Hastings. Guillaume de Prealx fought with Richard on Crusade—and saved him from disaster. During Richard's captivity, John used this same Jean de Prealx as an emissary to Philip. I forgive Jean for that. They make a trustworthy family. Pious, too. Two years ago Jean founded the Procuré of Beaulieu near Rouen...

I wander, child. My mind is awash with faces and voices chattering at my brains. A full life of voices and faces. Hear them press in, clamoring for attention, for solution, for redress. No, I am not mad: I know them for distractions in this sparse, winter landscape of old age. Guide me! I cannot but stray from my path, with no strength to master the rein. What care I for these lost and losing glories, for these ghosts with urgencies from other days? I ride along, I fall behind. Too far behind. I spoke too long today.

This is no pleasure. But I shall proceed a while. Perhaps an hour or two will see us done.

The barons' attack on Isabella led to reprisals. In the early winter of that year the warfare degenerated to a mêlée in which both sides took the other's wives and sons as hostages. Never—and I say this from long experience—never, not since Louis' campaign in Champagne, have I heard reports of such brutality and chaos. Anxiety is everywhere; people live their lives in fear.

That autumn, John engaged the services of a new captain of *routiers*, one Louvrecaire—or is it Lupescar? If he names himself for a wolf, the description fits. This man is ruled by sharper teeth and fewer constraints than a staghound. Methinks he sucked blood from his nurse's teat. Oh God, the smoke of loss and waste engulfs us all.

Worse, to fill our wasted treasury, John ransomed the Brothers Lusignan; whereon they joined the barons.

These points draw attention to the error of buying mercenaries. I was never able to convince John of this: his mien is too shallow to build trust; therefore he must buy it.

Theobald and Henry employed scholars to exercise the secular power; John promotes mercenaries, even above his barons. He demands that his Norman barons defend and supply this much-loathed Lupescar. William Marshall conveyed to me the message that John loses his people's love because he lets this and other devils pillage them as though they were razing an enemy's vines and vills.

Old loyalties have broken down, Aline. Honest vassals know their duty, but these *routiers* hear nothing of it. Their loyalty is bought with coin.

But this is a matter for future lives to resolve… I care not, because I cannot care, for there is nothing I can do about it.

And now to reach a point and bring the shade down on this day...

Many were concerned about the plight of Arthur, whom John held in chains for above six months. Great nobles on both sides pleaded for his safety, trusting not at all that John would keep him in this world.

Why must disasters strike at Easter? Father died on Good Friday. I divorced Louis just before Palm Sunday. We interred Richard on Palm Sunday. And Arthur, by whatever agency of John's, was done to death on the eve of Good Friday. God have mercy on his soul. And on my son's.

The Church would have us know that Christ died for our sins. Thank God he dies at Easter every year. From year to year our family's sins pile up.

Now, child, let me rest.

Good morning, Aline. Yes, you find me abed long past prime. Don't look so worried, child. I feel a touch delirious, but no matter. My mind is the better for it. We float—my mind and I—as free as a twig on a crystal-clear stream.

Last night I decided: we treat too much in a solemn vein. We are close enough to its end to say that my story is done. *Liber explicitus est.* One does not pour sour milk onto fresh. So I shall not dwell on the corruption of my works and of my world.

Whatever shall be, will be. Therefore I account catastrophes as necessary losses from which I shall move on. I choose instead to celebrate my pasts, for they were legion and lively, and many still live.

How fortunate to be born and bred in the south, among peoples rich in the diversity of many lands. A child observes. Heaven's gift of birth gave me so many chances to observe.

How fortunate to be born to a world destined to slough away its past and take upon itself new lives and times, as if our southern sun released the pulses of a northern spring.

How fortunate to be raised far from captious doctrine in a Church leavened by the mercy of fair humors and dissent. Wherever I have lived, I have lived my faith in the bright light that God pours on hovels and castles, on orchards and stones.

How fortunate to be my grandsire's granddaughter, riding through life on a palfrey of passage expressed by troubadours in words and song. So much is new since Grandsire taught his world and ours to speak its heart. He knew that laying bare the fullness of love's mind helps tame the sullen envies of our mortal beings. Rising, smoke spreads. So does understanding when the arts are loosed to lift her up.

In a subtle sense the civil arts I strove to build at Poitiers live on. Tides retreat and the world rebels, but that which I started I still impose. We claw our way forward, we women. In Poitiers we never tire of Radegonde. God grant that the seeds I sowed will grow, too. A land won by swords is not held by swords. Vassals must be led to loyalty by subtler qualities. Well handled, love will pull the dragon's teeth of steel.

How fortunate I was for a few years in my husbands: the monk, and the young bull in spring. Whether they would or no, they placed me on a promontory against which tides of time have crashed and fallen back. They left me worn, these men and their tides, but they did not level me. Only the throb and pulse of time and events have done that.

How fortunate I have been in my children. Too many have died, but they people the earth with counts and queens and kings, and heirs to queens and kings.

Winter has passed. Have you noticed, Aline? See how the sun moves his court into spring. *O viriditas digiti dei.*[58]

How wonderful I feel today. Elated. Buoyed in my mind above this earthly bourne. We must speak about you. Tomorrow, perhaps, but not today. I am tired. Leave me, dear child. I must sleep. Prepare a new quill and imagine your own fond thoughts of the family you will raise in England. Go, now. Until we meet again.

✝✝✝

Of weariness and age my lady spoke no more save slightly, to her officers, the abbess, sisters of this order and to her confessor. The pen being set aside this ink will dry upon the twenty-second day of March. This is the book of Queen Aleänor. All things that she can say are said.

Liber explicitus est.

✝✝✝

In this year of our Lord one thousand, two hundred and four
in the month of March being the thirty-first day of the month
Queen Aleänor came to her rest.
God grant her great soul Grace.
Her body lies at Fontevrault.

Bibliography

Other Eleanor of Aquitaine titles in chronological order:

Eleanor of Aquitaine and the Four Kings, Amy Kelly (1950)

Eleanor of Aquitaine: A Biography, Marion Meade (1977)

Eleanor of Aquitaine: The Mother Queen, Desmond Seward (1978)

Queen Eleanor: Independent Spirit of the Medieval World,
Polly Schover Brooks (1983) for young readers

Eleanor of Aquitaine, Zoë Coralnik Kaplan (1987)

Eleanor of Aquitaine: A Life, Alison Weir (1999)

Eleanor of Aquitaine: Lord and Lady,
John Carmi Parsons & Bonnie Wheeler (2002)

*Women of the Twelfth Century, Volume 1: Eleanor of Aquitaine
and Six Others*, Georges Duby, translated from the French

Other titles:

Pilgrims, Heretics, and Lovers, Claude Marks (Macmillan, 1975)

Plantagenet Chronicles, The, Elizabeth Hallam, General Editor
(Viking, 1987)

Devil's Crown: a history of Henry II and his sons, The,
Barber, Richard W. (1997)

ABOUT THE AUTHOR,
& SOME BACKGROUND

Born in Portsmouth, England, Robert Fripp grew up in Shillingstone, Dorset. A choral scholarship to Salisbury Cathedral School put him to work singing eight services a week in a choir immortalized by William Golding's book, *Lord of the Flies*. (Golding taught at a school next door.) Five years of choir-school, Latin and plainsong gave Robert a feel for a lost gothic world—the world of Eleanor of Aquitaine.

The first known graduate of Salisbury Cathedral School (founded in 1091) was John of Salisbury, who disapproved of Eleanor, as she of him, although she quotes John in *Power of a Woman* when it suits her. John served Archbishop Thomas Becket until the latter's murder in 1170. Salisbury Cathedral stands near the ruins of Old Sarum (open to the public), and Clarendon Palace (on private land), two places important in Eleanor's life. Both feature in *Power of a Woman*. During her years in exile Eleanor probably spent time at Old Sarum, which she describes in Chapter 28. Around 1190 her son, King Richard I (Lionheart), approved moving the cathedral and its clergy out of the military garrison in the fort of Old Sarum. A generation later the present Salisbury Cathedral began to rise in meadows destined to become modern Salisbury.

Leaving medieval and modern Salisbury behind, Robert studied natural sciences at Canford School and earth sciences at the University of Bristol. He married Carol Burtin in New York and they settled in Toronto, where Robert produced television for the Canadian Broadcasting Corporation. In the 1990s he created and wrote a continuing magazine about high performance computing, *IBM Visions*, and set up a company that made English-language TV documentaries from foreign-language originals.

Robert's writing includes: books about our cosmic and organic origins (published as *The Becoming* in the U.K., and as *Let There Be Life* by the Paulist Press in Canada and the U.S.); over thirty short stories; a four-part screenplay, *Edith Cavell*; and a play in the English of Shakespeare's day. Lund Humphries (London) will publish Robert's illustrated, co-authored book, *Design+Science*, about designer Will Burtin, in 2008. Readers can discover more, and find an Eleanor timeline, at www.RobertFripp.ca.

Robert and Carol have two sons, Eric and Will.

Endnotes

[1] Duke Guilhem X of Aquitaine was also Count Guilhem VIII of Poitou. The combined title had endured for three centuries, since Duke Guilhem III of Aquitaine was Count Guilhem I of Poitou.

[2] Duke Guilhem IX of Aquitaine, Count Guilhem VII of Poitou. Usually known as Guilhem VII.

[3] As well as the sense imported to English, the French *alliance* has a now archaic meaning, wedding ring, the symbol supporting the political alliance.

[4] A female troubadour.

[5] Written by Beatrix, Countess of Die, around 1190.

[6] Freely translated from Bernard's *Apology*, 1125.

[7] A crusader army entered the city of Mainz (Mayence) at the end of May, 1096, and slaughtered the Jews, who sought refuge in the archbishop's palace. The Jews armed themselves, but being weakened by fasting and prayer in hope of averting this fate, were unable to fight. They were killed *en masse*. The same befell Jews in several German cities as crusaders marched east toward the Holy Land.

[8] Revelations 3, 14-22, a text written about 95 AD.

[9] Queen Aleänor was a role model for women's fashions, some of which outlived her. She is attributed with introducing the barbette, a broad band of fine material worn under the chin, its ends clasped on top of the head. Seen in profile, a barbette passing under the chin extends back as far as the throat, covering the wearer's ears and much of the cheeks and lower jaw. A veil placed on top of the barbette hangs down the wearer's back, leaving the face exposed. The whole is anchored by a thin filet or coronet around the head. The barbette was worn into the thirteenth century.

[10] Antalya, in Turkey. Louis' chronicler, Odo of Deuil, calls it Adalia: Amy Kelly, Satalia.

[11] The Council of Antioch adjourned at Easter, 325. Emperor Constantine himself preached on Good Friday. The more famous Council of Nicaea took place just months later, in the summer.

[12] Psalm 79.

[13] Claude Marks places this among "the most frequently quoted phrases in all Provençal poetry".

[14] Cast out that which is bad from among you.

[15] Modern Frascati. Louis and Aleänor stayed with Pope Eugenius III on October 9 and 10, 1149.

[16] *The White Ship* was thrown onto the Quilleboeuf Rock off Barfleur on November 25th, 1120. Among those lost at sea was Maud, William Atheling's half-sister by Henry I, and Henry's mistress, Edith. Maud, princess of England and countess of Perche, was born in England about 1090. She had been married in England to Rotrou II, the count of Perche. It is said of Henry that, after this disaster, he never smiled again. Reporting the mishap, the usually reliable source, Orderic Vitalis, stated that the *White Ship* (*La Blanche Nef*) carried 300 people, all but one of whom were lost. Apart from members of Henry's immediate family, the cream of Norman and English nobility drowned.

[17] Suger died in January, 1151.

[18] Friday, 21 March, 1152.

[19] Some Welsh historians regard Cadifor, father of Bleheris (Bledri ap Cadifor) as the ancestor of several important families in ancient Dyfed. It is said that Cadifor entertained William the Conqueror during the latter's visit to St. David's in 1080.

[20] The *Anglo-Saxon Chronicle* reports this eclipse during Lent on "the thirteenth day before the kalends of April" (March 19th) in the year 1140.

[21] Born in 1100, Henry of Blois was a grandson of William the Conqueror on his mother's side. Henry served as abbot of Glastonbury from 1126. He was named bishop of Winchester in 1129. Securing an extraordinary papal dispensation, he held both offices until his death in Winchester in August, 1171.

[22] Wace: Born in the Norman island of Jersey, he presented *Geste des Bretons* to Eleanor in 1155. Henry and Eleanor commissioned Wace to write *Geste des Normanz*, dedicated to King Henry.

[23] *esnecca*: ships not unlike Viking longships, whose Norse name *snekkjar* means 'snakes.'

[24] The Catholic Encyclopedia observes of Henry's campaign against Church courts in England: "In his attack on the jurisdiction of the spiritual courts Henry may have desired sincerely to remedy an abuse, but the extent of that abuse has been very much exaggerated by the anti-papal sympathies of Anglican historians, more especially of so influential a writer as Bishop Stubbs."

[25] Pentecost falls on the seventh Sunday after Easter, itself a moveable feast.

[26] A phrase coined by Henry's justiciar, Ranulph de Glanville (d. 1190), Aleänor's sometime gaoler. De Glanville may have written *Tractatus de legibus*, Treatise on Laws. If one excludes regional Anglo-Saxon legal codes, this may be the oldest textbook on English law.

[27] This twenty-two clause code of laws is still known as the Assize of Clarendon (1166).

[28] John was born in either 1166 or 1167. The actual day of his birth is not in doubt.

[29] A woman *seule*, later corrupted in English to a woman sole: a woman alone. This medieval English legal term referred to a woman who lacked the "protection" of a male, be he father, spouse, son or guardian. The term had major implications for property rights.

[30] From *trobar* (langue d'oc), *trouver* (French).

[31] The Poitiers Municipal Library houses an eleventh century manuscript on the life of Radegonde, copied from a sixth century account by her contemporary, Fortunatus.

[32] Lanfranc of Pavia, an eleventh century reformer, and Anselm, who succeeded him as archbishop. It was probably Lanfranc who obtained the pope's blessing for William the Conqueror's invasion of England.

[33] Peter of Blois, Letter 154, to Queen Aleänor, 1173. Quoted on the Internet "Medieval Sourcebook," with an introduction by Michael Markowski, of Salt Lake City's Westminster College. "The specific electronic form of the document is copyright" by Paul Halsall May 1997, <halsall@murray.fordham.edu>.

[34] The nearest English equivalent might be "conceived on the wrong side of the sheet." The phrase alludes to one's illegitimate descent.

[35] The site of Salisbury Tower (the foundations of the fort and the old cathedral) is known as Old Sarum.

[36] St. Anthony's Fire: the common name for various afflictions marked by hallucinations and aberrant behavior. This typically struck in spring, when grain from the previous harvest was depleted and people scoured their bins for seeds which were moist and moldy after a winter in storage. In these conditions a fungus, ergot of rye, induced visions, psychotropic behavior and sometimes death. Ergot is a powerful vasoconstrictor: it can cause victims' fingers and toes to turn black and drop off. Less commonly, rust of wheat (*puccinia* sp.) produced similar effects.

[37] Womb-joy: the medieval English term for narcissism.

[38] Freely adapted from Kelly, p. 206, who cites as her source Thomas, Antoine, *Bertran de Born, Poésies complètes* (Toulouse, 1888).

[39] *La Maison Fabri* is now a tourist attraction in Martel.

[40] I am grateful to Miss S. Berry, Senior Archivist of the Somerset Archive and Record Service, who identified the "archdeacon of Wells" mentioned in many sources as

Thomas of Earley. Miss Berry provided a photostat of page 32 from *Bath & Wells Fasti Ecclesiæ Anglicanæ 1066-1300*, showing Thomas's relationship to Bishop Reginald of Bath and Stephen of Tournai (who died in September, 1203). Thomas's nephew, William of Earley, founded Buckland Priory, in Somerset. Thomas himself, "Magister Thomas Agnellus," was known as a writer of sermons. His audience with Queen Aleänor probably gave him grist for several.

[41] Translation by Helen Waddell, Mediaeval Latin Lyrics, Holt, New York, 1938.

[42] Sometimes described as the first English scientist, Adelard of Bath (c.1080-c.1160) may have tutored the future Henry II between 1142 and 1146. Henry and his mother, Matilda, were then living in Bristol with the household of Robert of Gloucester, a bastard son of King Henry I. (Matilda was no doubt using Robert's hall as a command-post in her war against King Stephen.) The widely-travelled Adelard introduced astrolabes to England. His treatise, *De opere astrolapsus*, is dedicated to a certain Henry, perhaps Adelard's former pupil and future king. Legend persists that, early in their marriage, Aleänor gave Henry a ring which, when dangled on a string, accurately told the relative time of day. If such a ring existed it was, in effect, a miniature astrolabe.

[43] Striguil is modern Chepstow. In Welsh, y straigyl means bend, describing the fort's location on the river Wye, close to its confluence with the Severn. Striguil may be the earliest stone castle in the British Isles. In the twelfth century only the central rectangular keep had been built. William Marshall added to it.

[44] Henry II commissioned an inventory of widows and heirs in 1185, to assess whether any were "king's wards" and therefore subject to royal claims.

[45] Barbarossa drowned on June 10, 1190. "The desire of comparing two great men has tempted many writers to drown Frederick [Barbarossa] in the river Cydnus, in which Alexander so imprudently bathed…but, from the march of the Emperor, I rather judge that [Barbarossa's river] Saleph is the Calycadnus, a stream of less fame, but of a longer course." Edward Gibbon.

[46] Literally, unrolled; to reach the end of a rolled parchment or book.

[47] The dean of London to whom the queen refers is Ralph of Diceto, a notable chronicler of the time. Archbishop Walter's letter to Ralph is taken from *The Plantagenet Chronicles*, p. 232.

[48] This episode accords with that given by Roger of Wendover. Another account gives William's family name as FitzOsbert. St. Mary of the Arches is now known as St. Mary le Bow.

[49] Walburga Storch OSB translated Hildegard's letters into modern German under the title *Hildegard von Bingen, Im Feuer der Taube, die Briefe* (Hildegard von Bingen, In the Fire of the Dove, the Letters). This excerpt is taken from Letter 318. Pattloch Verlag, Augsburg 1997.

[50] There was indeed a secret treaty. It still exists, in the French Record Office.

[51] In 1157, at the Diet of Beçanson, the future Pope Alexander III had the temerity to tell Frederick Barbarossa that he held office as holy Roman emperor at the favor of the pope, rather than by right of feudal fief. This insult incensed Count Otto of Wittelsbach, who drew his axe to kill the future pope: Barbarossa stayed his hand. After this incident the Germans set out to place a more compliant candidate on the papal throne. This pit the Germans and their candidate against Alexander, who requested and received the eager support of King Louis VII and a grudging nod from King Henry II. Henry thought, wrongly, that his support for Alexander would win him papal favors against Becket.

[52] Philip, born in England around 1160, was Aleänor's sixth child by Henry. He died in infancy.

[53] A point enlarged by Aleänor in Chapter 16. It was widely accepted that the surroundings in which a mother gave birth influenced her child. Genesis 30: 37-43 provides the doctrinal source, influencing opinion into the early modern period. For example, a passage in The Merchant of Venice I.iii.78 is one among many exemplars giving credence to this notion in sixteenth century drama.

[54] Later in life, Blanche of Castile lent her authority to fund-raising for the new cathedral at Chartres. It has been suggested that Blanche used her influence to ensure that Mary is depicted in the cathedral's stained glass not as a virgin, but as a power-figure, a queen.

[55] Also known as Hawise FitzWarin or de Warenne. Her mother's name was Hawise de Dinan.

[56] The law of the first night, le droit de seigneur, by which a master who gave a female vassal in marriage could, if he chose, take the bride to his own bed before she slept with her husband.

[57] An enduring belief in Falaise holds that William de Braose III's wife, Maud de Saint Valery, (1155-1210) once served as a lady's maid to Eleanor. If so, Maud's subsequent life shows that Eleanor taught her survival skills. Maud, "the Lady of LaHaie" (Hay-on-Wye) survived the bloody wars of Wales.

[58] Oh Life-green(ing) finger of God / in you God has placed a garden... These lines open one of Hildegard of Bingen's healing chants.

898756

Made in the USA